WHILE YOU WERE

Dreaming

ALISHA RAI

WHILE YOU WERE Dreaming

Quill Tree Books
An Imprint of HarperCollinsPublishers

Quill Tree Books is an imprint of HarperCollins Publishers.

While You Were Dreaming
Copyright © 2023 by Alisha Rai

Library of Congress Cataloging-in-Publication Data
Names: Rai, Alisha, author.
Title: While you were dreaming / Alisha Rai.
Description: First edition. | New York : Quill Tree Books, [2023] |
    Audience: Ages 13 up. | Audience: Grades 10-12. | Summary:
    Sixteen-year-old Indian American Sonia, who has undocumented
    family members, goes viral after saving her crush James's life.
Identifiers: LCCN 2022029563 | ISBN 9780063083967 (hardcover)
Subjects: CYAC: Interpersonal relations—Fiction. | Social media—Fiction. |
    Family life—Fiction. | Noncitizens—Fiction. | Illegal immigration—Fiction.
    | East Indian Americans—Fiction. | LCGFT: Romance fiction. | Novels.
Classification: LCC PZ7.1.R343 Wh 2023 | DDC [Fic]—dc23
LC record available at https://lccn.loc.gov/2022029563

Typography by Laura Mock
23 24 25 26 27 LBC 5 4 3 2 1

First Edition

For the ones who spend their days
with their heads in the clouds:
I hope you get to stitch all your dreams into reality

CHAPTER
One

The main character? Not me, not in real life. That's what my daydreams were for.

At some point, the disappointment of crashing back to earth might teach me to stop engaging in said daydreams. But—

"Sonia!"

That day wasn't today.

I jerked my mind away from my current preoccupation and glanced over my shoulder to find my boss's daughter scowling at me, frown lines disrupting her otherwise smooth face. Paris wasn't really good at anything except immediately noticing when one of us wasn't on task. "Hi, sorry. Yes?"

"Is that sandwich done yet?" She enunciated the words slowly, which meant she'd probably asked the question a couple of times already.

The bagel dropped out of the bottom of the toaster right then, saving me. I grabbed it. "Yup. One minute."

1

She gave an annoyed shake of her head but placed the customer's drink on the bar. "Hurry, please."

We had no backlog of orders at the moment, but I was quick. I assembled the BLT, wrapped it in the café's signature paper, dotted with little Eiffel Towers—Café Paris, of course—stripped my gloves off, and brought it to the pickup counter, snagging the drink along the way. "Harry?" I called.

A woman standing there glanced up from her phone. "Um, Marie?"

It wasn't unusual for Paris to screw up a name. "Large strawberry shortcake tea with a bagel BLT?"

"Yup."

I handed it over and eyed the customer as she walked away. Her purple-and-yellow spandex leotard and tights fit her like a glove, the cape spilling off her shoulders in a cascade of silk.

The entire block was filled with flammable fabrics today, since the bookstore next door was holding its annual comic book day. Costumes were encouraged.

I loved cosplay, both creating it and seeing it. I may actually love cosplay more than the comics that inspired it, though that was something I'd never admit to a *real* comic book nerd. I'd be crushed under the weight of their ridicule for being able to list the inseams of Superman's tights but not his parents' names.

"Veggie sub on everything bagel, toasted," Paris called out.

"On it," I replied, scurrying back to my station. I didn't mind working on food. The view from in front of the toaster couldn't be beat.

Through the massive window on the side of our small

building, I could see right into the bookstore. And the register. And the guy who was working it.

James Cooper, my oblivious soul mate. He was too far away for me to make out the details of his costume, except that it was black, and he wore no mask. It didn't matter; I was sure it looked good on him, because everything looked amazing on him.

He was a fellow junior at my school, he ordered a large drip coffee at 4:30 p.m. on his way to work, and he smiled a lot. My crush had bloomed when we'd wound up in the same AP Calculus class at the beginning of the semester. Twelve nonconsecutive hours of his sweet smile and kind eyes was all it had taken for my heart to get hopelessly entangled with his.

When he'd turned around in class last week and told me he hoped to see me at the event, I'd spun a fantasy. I floated invisibly through high school, not a main part of any social strata, so I wasn't in his circle of friends. But that circle had changed since he'd broken up with his popular/terrible girlfriend. Why couldn't I swoop in while he was on the outs of his clique?

On my mom's old sewing machine, I'd create the most magnificent costume and wear it during my shift. He'd see me through the window, abandon his job, and rush over to tell me how talented and amazing I was. Our capes would float behind us as we spun around in a tornado of passion and coffee cups and muffins—

Okay, so like most of my imaginary musings, this dream was a bit far-fetched, but I'd taken confidence in my neatly placed stitches.

If only my costume wasn't packed away in my backpack. Though the neighboring businesses had all gotten in on the fun, Paris had declared costumes cringey when I'd shown up for work this morning and banned them for the employees. So here I was in the baggy jeans and long-sleeved shirt I'd thrown on right after I'd hopped out of bed. Garb that was unlikely to get me into any kind of tornado of passion.

Perhaps I could change and go over to the bookstore after work, though. Casually peruse the shelves. Bring the tornado of passion to his workplace.

"Hey, Sonia. Can you come over here for a second?"

I handed the sandwich to the waiting customer and walked over to Paris. "I'm about to put a fresh batch of muffins into the oven."

"Don't worry about that. We're all out of mix anyway." Paris gave me a sweet smile, and it was such a contrast to her previous testiness, I put my mental guard up.

Hana, my newest coworker, rounded the counter. I waved at her, and she responded with a nod, then turned to the register to clock in. I had no idea what her full name was. She was Hana, one word in my head, like Gaga or Beyoncé. She was new this year, had moved from somewhere in California. Though I'd seen her around school, we were usually on different shifts.

"I'm so glad Hana's here. I need to head out soon, and I'm sure the two of you could cover the place until closing, right?"

I'd opened; I didn't want to close as well. Plus, I wouldn't get to go over to the bookstore at all, then! It closed an hour before we did.

Hana didn't look up from the computer. "Saturday afternoons are busy. There's usually three of us on."

"And the bookstore event will make us busier," I added.

Paris waved a hand. "Oh, now, I'm sure you'll both be fine."

Token protest lodged, Hana walked away, leaving me alone with our boss's daughter. I drifted closer. "Um, I actually, um, I have plans." The plan was simply changing my outfit, but Paris didn't need to know that.

A customer walked up and opened his mouth. "Excuse me—"

Without looking at him, Paris held up a hand, and the man subsided, which wasn't a huge surprise. Paris's fragile-girl-next-door vibe tended to get most men twisted around her tiny fingers.

Her wide blue eyes turned pleading. They were usually pleading when she asked me to cover for her, which happened a lot. "Please? I have a party to go to tonight, and I need to get my hair and nails done."

I bit my tongue to keep from asking if it was another high school party. Paris had an odd affinity for showing up at those, though she'd graduated a few years ago.

She clasped her hands in front of her. "You have to help me, girl. It's going to be *the* party of the year, I can't not be there."

I held my joke about double negatives. "I can't."

Paris spoke rapidly over me. "I'll make sure you get paid for my full shift as well as your own."

I stopped, and my conscience piped up. *Your sister would do*

5

it, why can't you? Funnily enough, my conscience often sounded like my mom.

I thought of Kareena at home. When I'd left for work, she'd been busy ignoring me, stretched out on the tired floral sleeper sofa in our living room in her garish pink work uniform, playing a video game on the console she'd gotten for her eighteenth birthday. Lately most of her spare time and cash seemed to go into video games, the more violent the better. One of the self-help books I'd gotten from the library said that grief often took the form of aggression. I was fine with that, so long as she took her aggression out on animated characters and not me.

Since she'd graduated last May, she'd taken every odd job she could find. In addition to the diner, she also worked at a movie theater. And at a gas station.

For you. There was only so much I could earn when I had to go to school, too. It was Kareena's jobs that paid our rent.

Damn it. Mentally, I kissed my latest fantasy goodbye. "Okay," I said quietly, interrupting Paris's hard sell.

Paris whooped and undid her apron. "Perfect. Hana, Sonia's in charge."

Hana, the personified embodiment of a shrug, didn't respond, as uncaring about my temporary promotion as she was about everything else.

"Oh, you're leaving now . . . cool," I said to Paris's back as she sashayed away.

"Can someone help me?"

I mentally sighed and stepped up to the register. "About time," the waiting customer groused.

"Sorry." I picked up a paper cup and the pen. "What can I get for you?"

"A large iced chai latte with oat milk. And don't put dairy in it by accident. I swear last time, one of you tried to kill me."

"Yes, sir." I kept my strained smile on my face as I rang him up, and he retreated.

"If I wanted to kill him, he'd be dead."

I jumped at the low, flat murmur right behind me, then checked to make sure the customer had shuffled out of earshot. I handed Hana his empty cup. "Here you go," I said cheerfully, choosing to ignore her vaguely sinister words.

Hana placed the cup on the counter. Her sleeveless red top was in defiance of the season, but I couldn't blame her. If I had that cool brightly colored floral tattoo on one arm, I'd ban sleeves forever too.

If you had tattoos at sixteen, you'd be dead by the hands of your ancestors.

Hana cocked her head. Her hair was almost blue-black and ruthlessly straight, the blunt cut just brushing her shoulders. "How long have you worked here?"

I straightened, oddly proud of my tenure at this, my first real job. "Almost six months."

"I've worked here for less than a month, and I can tell you that Paris will forget to make sure you get paid for taking her shift."

That was an accurate assessment of Paris's priorities. "I'll remind her."

"Hmm. Seems like it would be better to not be a mouse and let her walk all over you." Hana's tone did not modulate at all. "If you have plans next time, might want to keep them. I like money too, but the minimum wage they pay us isn't worth bowing down to the princess."

I tried to hide my flinch. "Thanks for the advice," I said, instead of what I really wanted to say, which was, *You don't know me, fuck off.*

Or more specifically, *my sister works three jobs so I can stay in school, and that minimum wage helps me feel less guilty. Fuck off.*

But I kept my lips zipped, because some things were better muttered in my own head.

"Nice perfume, by the way."

That was a kind thing to say, and usually I'd be happy that someone had complimented my mother's perfume, but I could only give her a tight smile. Hana went off to fulfill the lactose-intolerant customer's order. So I wouldn't dwell on disappointment, I grabbed fresh pastries from the warmer and methodically moved the older ones to the back of the window display.

Without Paris here, maybe I could take the risk and go put my costume on. With the courage of my mask, I could sneak away for a minute to the bookstore on my break and say something sexy to James, like . . . like . . .

"Excuse me, miss, where is the bathroom located?"

No, I could come up with something better than that. The

8

teenager who had asked the question peered at me from behind thick glasses. I straightened and placed the pastry tongs back in their spot. "Around the corner; the code's 4563."

"Thanks."

He left, and I froze. Because behind him was my dream, standing within reach.

With a calm I didn't feel, I approached the counter, wiping my hands on my apron. James smiled down at me. "Hey, Sonia," he said, in the deep voice I knew well. I'd spent enough time in class hoping he'd raise his hand to answer a question so I could hear that voice.

Tall and lean, he was dressed in tight black leather and rubber. Did I mention his damn costume was tight?

So tight. Holy crap, that bodysuit was tight. That body was tight.

I tore my gaze away from his stomach. His mother was Indian, his father Black. His skin was a deep, rich dark brown, and it gleamed, the dying sun reflecting off his shaved head and high cheekbones. He had a strikingly perfect face, all interesting hollows and sharp angles. It wouldn't be a problem to stare at that face for hours, to trace his nose and his firm jaw.

Or his lips.

Nope. Forget his lips.

He *smelled* so good, like peppermint. Not that I smelled him. It was more like the smell had found me.

Forget the peppermint too. "You're Batman," I managed, then I mentally kicked myself.

"That's right," he said, and tapped his naked temple. "The

mask smelled weird, though. Couldn't keep it on. Don't know how Bruce Wayne does it."

"The real Batman's costume is probably made of something better than cheap plastic." Why was I talking about Batman. Why hadn't I just said hi.

A dimple popped into his cheek. "The real Batman, huh?"

"Obviously not the real one. Batman's not real." A child dressed like a bat at the table closest to the register turned toward us, eyes wide. I tucked a strand of hair behind my ear and wished I wasn't wearing it in a limp ponytail. "Hey. James. You look great."

"Thanks." He looked me up and down, and I felt every inch of my baggy comfort clothes and lack of makeup. "Guess you're too cool to dress up?"

I nearly laughed at the idea that I was too cool for anything but caught myself. "Not at all. I love cosplay."

He brightened. "Yeah?"

"Yeah, I used to go to comic cons all the time when I lived in Cleveland." All the time was probably an exaggeration, but my mom had occasionally gotten tickets from one of her favorite customers. I'd gone mostly to gawk at the cosplayers and learn what I could about crafting. Unfortunately, the opportunities had been more limited since we moved to this much smaller western New York town a few years ago.

"So where's your mask?"

I tried to look casual and lean on the counter, but I accidentally jostled the stack of cups next to the register. I righted them as unobtrusively as possible. "My boss is anti-costumes."

"That sucks. It's been fun seeing people from school. It's like Halloween came early."

My shoulders lowered. Had he invited everyone at school? "I bet. Um, what can I get you today? A drip coffee?"

"Hey, you remembered my order."

Another kick. Why couldn't I be unbothered like him? Oh, right, because I was an awkward mess who loved him, and he was a track star usually surrounded by equally graceful people. "I'm, yeah, I'm really good at remembering orders, and yours is so easy." One of those things was true. My crush on him wasn't entirely due to the fact that he ordered a simple drink, and not a complicated viral hack someone put on the internet, but it wasn't hindered by it either. "Do you wanna try something else?"

"Nah, that'll do."

"Cool." I turned around and quickly poured the coffee.

"To be honest, I'm glad to see you today. I hoped I would."

I nearly dropped the hot coffee, but caught it in time. I carefully put the carafe down and picked up the cup and brought it over to him. Thank God Ilana was busy on her phone, so her too-observant eyes couldn't see my internal meltdown over James thinking of me at all.

He pulled out his credit card. "You tutor, right?"

I met his eyes, though it was hard. Like looking at the sun, if the sun was two warm brown pools of chocolate. "I do." I'd only ever had one paying student, so *tutor* was probably a stretch. I had decent grades and a fairly good affinity for math, so I periodically posted messages in our class group in the hopes

11

of some nibbles. I hadn't expected James to nibble, though. Not on anything of mine.

"I'm not doing so hot in calc, and my dad gets on my case if I get anything lower than a B." There was a slight strain around his eyes, like he had a headache, and I wondered if his dad was tough on him. "I'm sure you're busy, but do you have room for any students right now?"

The card reader beeped and I pressed the button for a receipt, on autopilot. Meanwhile, my mind short-circuited. "Um. Sure."

"Cool. It would be convenient, since we work so close to each other." He tucked his change into the tip jar, because he was a *perfect* man who tipped service workers. "Want to meet up on Monday around four?"

That was two whole days away. Today. Tomorrow. Monday. Yes, that was how days worked, last time I'd checked. "S-s-sure," I managed. "Where do you want to meet up? Here?"

"I was thinking my family's restaurant. It's a couple blocks over. Gulab?"

I knew of the Indian restaurant, but I'd never been to it. In Cleveland, we'd known a lot of South Asian families, but the community was smaller in Rockville. Since we'd moved here, my mom had been too busy working to socialize anyway. "Yeah, I know it."

"My mom's short-staffed, so I have to help with a catering gig later in the evening. We can work in the back office until I'm needed, though?"

"Sounds good."

"Give me your phone, I'll put my number in."

My fingers tingled when they brushed his. Probably because his hands were unexpectedly cold, but I'd chalk it up to pure chemistry.

James handed the phone back to me. "Gotta get back to work. Thanks. See you soon, Sonia." He gave me a sunny smile.

"Hmmn," I gurgled. I stared at his back as he walked away. *Hmmn.*

Thank you for thinking of me. Thank you for knowing my name. Your brain is in good hands with me. Are you in the market for a girlfriend? To be honest, I have basically zero parental supervision now, so we can make out if you like.

I rubbed my temples. Any of those words would have worked. But no. All I'd had was *Hmmn.*

My face was all hot, my limbs tingling. And here I'd hoped the best thing that could realistically happen today was him noticing me. Oh no, the tornado of passion had come true, in the form of consensually sharing a table with him soon!

"Ma'am, the toilet's clogged."

Crash.

I refocused on the teen who'd asked for the bathroom code. "Um, thanks for letting me know." I looked around for Hana, and found her half-heartedly cleaning the espresso machine. Either she hadn't seen James come in or hadn't cared or didn't know him, all of which were fine with me. I had no desire to engage her in any conversation after she'd been so snotty about me taking over for Paris, but here we were. "Hana . . . ?" I motioned her over. "The toilet's—"

13

"Nuh-uh." Hana shook her head. "Not in my job description."

I set my teeth in frustration. "Watch the register," I called out to her, and grimly made my way to the bathroom. Going from a tornado of passion to the vortex of a toilet. Yup. That sounded like my life.

CHAPTER
Two

As much as I'd resented both opening and closing the place on this particular day, there was something nice about having the café to myself after the last customer left. The dying sun slanted across the empty bakery displays and the almost eerie quiet played its own song, different from the clash of voices that filled the space during the day.

The traffic had slowed once the bookstore closed, so I was already ahead of the game when it came to cleaning up. I went through the ritual of closing out the register and turning off the lights, made sure all the food was stored in the kitchen, then hauled the trash to the back room. I hated the garbage part of closing more than anything, and today the bag felt extra heavy, filled with all the fun other people had enjoyed while I was being a dutiful contributing member of my household.

You had fun, too. You talked to James! Literally you said more to him than you ever have before. Don't be greedy because it didn't play out like your grand nerd fantasy. Life rarely does.

I dropped the trash on the floor and pulled my bag out of the locker. I unzipped it and pulled the top of my cute costume out.

Work is over. You can wear it now.

Ha ha, for who?

It's for you. Make yourself happy. You spent so long on it. There's no one here, no one who will barge in on you and tell you to take it off.

I could wear it home. Plenty of people had left the bookstore and gone home dressed in their costumes. It was, as James had said, kind of like Halloween. Nobody would recognize me.

I laid the outfit on the tired table taking up most of our break room, then stripped off my jeans and shirt and tossed them aside.

The costumes I'd made and worn to cons in the past had all been copying off existing comic book characters. They'd been nicer than store-bought, but nothing that had gotten me stopped for photo ops in the hallways. Since my budget and time had been limited this week, I'd scoured my closet for inspiration and decided to be an original character.

The black faux-leather leggings were a thrift store find I hadn't had to alter. The top was another story, a bodice I'd cut out of a hideous old Regency dress I'd found in the Halloween clearance section at Target last year. I'd dyed it black and replaced the ugly sleeves with tight lace down to my wrists, ending in points over the backs of my hand. In a moment of whimsy, over my left breast, I'd embroidered a small *S* in block print.

I'd found clunky old black leather boots at Goodwill, too,

and I pulled those on. They were too big, but it wasn't like I was running a marathon in them.

I stopped and stared at myself for a moment in the mirror mounted on the wall. This was the first time I'd seen the complete look.

Forget tutoring. If James had caught me in this, he would have gotten down on his knees, grasped my fingers, and begged me to go out with him.

I twisted. I'd attached the narrow, short cape to the shoulders of the shirt. I'd struggled with getting the fabric to lay flat, but I liked the way it had turned out.

I smoothed my hand over my round stomach. I'd gained weight in the past year, and between flashes of insecurity over my new appearance, I was mostly puzzled as to how to display it. I tended to treat it like I treated anything I wanted to procrastinate confronting: I hid it.

That might have been an error, though. Maybe instead I should only be dressing in clothes tailor made to fit me by my own hands. The top nipped in at my waist, hugging my breasts, accentuating my curves.

I swiped at my eyes, surprised to find some leakage there. Partially because this was the first time in a while I'd looked in the mirror and felt right in my own skin, but mostly because this was the first clothing I'd made on my own since my mom was deported.

Trying to distract myself, I dug out my makeup pouch. I wasn't a cosmetics expert, but my hands were steady enough. I studied my eyes and the cheap liner and gold eye shadow

I'd applied. The thick wings weren't perfectly matched, but I resisted the urge to redo them and make them equal. "They can be sisters, not twins," I whispered. That piece of advice had come from one of my favorite beauty influencers, and I thought about it whenever I picked up eyeliner. To be honest, my eyes looked more like second cousins twice removed, but surely the final costume touch would distract from that.

I let my hair loose and finger-combed it, grimacing. I'd been so happy this morning when I'd woken up to smooth curls courtesy of a bathrobe tie and a heatless curls tutorial, but hours up at work had knocked the cute ringlets right out, leaving frizzy waves. Into a messy bun it went.

I'd opted for a mask covering the bottom half of my face instead of the top half, solely because I could do eye makeup better than lips. I put on the gaiter and pulled it up, leaving only my eyes and forehead visible.

Ahhhh. I blinked, the eyeliner heavy. I looked . . . different. I looked good. *Winter Soldier meets Wanda Maximoff.*

My phone buzzed on the table, and I checked it. Kareena.

Do the dishes before I get home

I didn't reply. It had been so long since my sister had texted me something other than a command to do something. What I wouldn't give, sometimes, for a *where are you because I'm worried about you* text.

I threw my phone and my street clothes into my bag. I'd probably be cold, but I didn't want to cover up my outfit before it was necessary.

I grabbed the trash bag and left through the back door,

making sure it locked behind me. My mask was a blessing in the cool October air. My cape caught the wind, and the fabric lifted away from my back, my spirits lifting with it.

I flew unnoticed, tucked under the radar. But some days, I got to wear a cape.

And take out the trash.

I wrestled the Hefty bag over to the dumpster and hoisted it in, then took a second to sanitize my hands.

I wasn't sure what prompted me to look up right then— some noise that didn't belong in the evening air. The back of the shops in this plaza faced a path, and a steep embankment to a canal. The other side of the canal was dotted with lights and the backyards of small tidy homes. Bicyclists often rode there during the day, and it was a handy way to cut through the city.

There was James, sitting on the ground, gazing down at the water, his face in profile to me. The sun was mostly gone now, and the streetlight above him touched on his proud nose and chin and lit his dark hair with fire. He wore black jeans and a sweater. They weren't nearly as tight as his costume had been, but just as flattering.

God, he was so perfect. True, he wasn't good at math, but he was beautiful and uncomplicated, while I . . . well. I was wearing a cape I'd sewn myself.

Horror filled me. I was wearing a *cape* in close proximity to my *crush*.

Are you there, God? It's me, wearing a cape *in front of the* man I love.

Isn't that what you wanted? To get attention for your skills?

Yes, but he'd seen me wearing street clothes before! He'd know that I changed into this after work, after the bookstore closed, like a total nerd, while he'd done the normal thing and changed out of his costume.

I spun around and flattened myself against the dumpster, my usual fear of germs temporarily suspended. It was fine. This was fine. I'd simply . . . I don't know.

I felt in my shoulder bag and groped for my sweatshirt, my thoughts only on covering up. While I tugged at the stubborn fabric, I dared to peek around the corner.

James straightened and rubbed his hand over his face. I stopped. Even from far away, there was something odd and sluggish about his movements. Was he okay?

He made his way to his feet with some difficulty, like he was groggy. He staggered back a step, shook his head, and then took another step, this time forward toward the water. His foot found nothing but air, and he dropped out of sight. A loud splash followed.

The seconds ticked by as I waited for him to jump right out, shaking the water off. Only he didn't reappear. I looked around, but there was no one here. *Except you.*

I opened my mouth, but nothing came out. As icy cold as my vocal cords felt, I knew my limbs weren't frozen, because I launched myself in his direction, scrambling down the unpaved path, my footsteps louder than my heart.

Time slowed. Every second beat for half a second longer.

Even as I sprinted, I scanned the dark water in the canal. Where was James's head? Surely he could swim; the canal wasn't that deep. I'd learned to swim at the Y when I was a toddler, and I wasn't the athlete he was.

I skidded to a stop at the spot where he'd fallen in and fumbled with my phone to turn on the flashlight. I played it over the water, but the surface was still.

Oh shit, oh shit, oh shit.

I jammed my phone into the hard dirt of the bank for an extra light source, threw my bag on the ground, and dove in.

I immediately regretted two things, and one of them was the fact that I'd attached this cape. That damn thing tangled right up around my arms.

The other thing was not having great night vision. The water was darker than I'd anticipated. I surfaced, shoved my hair out of my eyes, and blinked, treading and scanning the water again. There. Was that movement? I dove again and kicked off, my hand making contact with . . .

Oh, thank God. It was an arm.

I held on tight and kicked upward, and sent up a brief prayer this arm belonged to James and not . . . well, any other idea was horrifying.

I nearly cried when I saw James's beautiful face as we surfaced, but his eyes were closed, his head lolling on his shoulders. I grunted and moved my grip to his middle before awkwardly swimming to the bank.

"My God—are you okay? Is he okay? We saw you jump in—" Hands grabbed my burden and lifted him away from me and up the bank before someone else hoisted me out of the water. Something sharp lanced my arm, but I was concentrating too hard on inhaling air to pay attention.

"Help him," I gasped, but I didn't have to prompt her, because with brisk motions, the lady next to James was already tilting his head back to start CPR.

"It's okay, you're okay now," said the older woman next to me. She patted my shoulder, then cursed. "You're bleeding."

I followed her gaze to my arm. My new shirt was ripped. Blood oozed out, staining the lace.

Air rushed through my open lips, halted by the wet fabric of my mask covering my mouth, my head growing light. I didn't do well with blood. I shook my head, but then couldn't stop. All of me was shaking. That blood was so thick and red. Like Kareena's blood whenever we'd had to go to the hospital. Having a sister who had had leukemia meant I was intimately acquainted with blood.

The woman with me pulled off her scarf and wrapped it around my arm tight. "It doesn't look too deep, but it's bleeding fast. It's okay, sweetheart. It must have been some debris, something sharp. You're both okay."

"Is he . . . ?"

"Yeah, my friend used to be an EMT. And we called 911. An ambulance is coming. They'll take you to the hospital to get checked out too. What happened? Did he jump? Or fall? We saw you dive in, we had no idea what you were—"

An ambulance is coming.

I inhaled so hard my nostrils burned, and in that inhale, I smelled astringent and alcohol and sickness.

We called 911.

An ambulance meant sirens and sirens meant authorities, and authorities were to be avoided at all costs.

I began to shake harder, horror at the ramifications of this situation slamming into me. "No," I whispered, my voice small and broken, like me. "I, um, I can't afford a hospital." That wasn't entirely true. One of the reasons we'd moved to New York was so Kareena and I could get health insurance through the state.

The bystander patted my shoulder. Her eyes were kind. "Honey, if money's the issue, I'll pay any bills. Why don't you lie down?"

"Sal, he's breathing, but give me a hand over here," the woman sitting next to James said with a level of calm I did not feel.

Okay. He was fine. He was breathing.

Which meant I had to go. Now. Now, now, now.

I patted my sopping-wet mask. It wasn't comfortable, but I could remove it once I got away from here. In a daze, I grabbed my phone and walked over to my bag, where I'd tossed it on the ground.

Pain shafted through me again. It wasn't pain from my wound, which was weird. I should feel something if blood was seeping out of my arm, right?

"Sit down, sweetheart," one of the Good Samaritan ladies said. "You're injured and in shock."

I was in shock, but not so shocked I couldn't hear the whine of sirens in the distance. The ambulance, but police too?

I pivoted on my toes and started to walk away, my feet

23

squelching. My cape slapped against my back. Ugh, I'd have wind drag slowing me down. Why had I just thought of that? Someone who needed to swim *or* run shouldn't have a cape.

Well, I'd get rid of the cape as quickly as I could.

God, I was cold, but I couldn't take the time to put on my sweatshirt, not that it would help much. A stealthy escape might have worked if I were dressed as plain old forgettable me, but I wasn't. "Hey, where are you going?" one of the women shouted. I didn't turn around.

Those sirens were getting closer.

I grasped my bag tighter and flew. More shouts came from behind me, but I ran in the only direction I could.

I crossed Elmwood, then Franklin, then Delaware. The street names blurred, and so did the stores and houses and any people I passed. It was full-on dark, and I was drenched with sweat by the time I started recognizing some of the houses I was passing.

Whatever lizard part of my brain had been guiding me had directed me away from my house, away from Kareena. Instead, I'd gone to the neighborhood I knew second best.

The houses here weren't like mine. They were spaced farther apart and had lavish front yards, with well-cared-for gardens.

A faint siren echoed, and my adrenaline spiked. They were chasing me. Of course they were. I was a witness to an accident. How hard would it be to follow reports of a wet, bleeding girl in a cape?

I had to change. Maybe even hide out for a while. Luckily, I knew where I could do that.

I jogged down the street, though my abused feet protested with every step, and darted across a lawn, sticking to the shadows of the side of the house. I knew this house well. I'd been to birthday parties and slumber parties and study sessions here since I was in eighth grade and we'd moved to this town. Until they'd stopped.

I slunk around the stained fence. It took me a second to stretch over the fence behind the house and undo the latch there. The gate swung open, and I crept inside, closing it behind me.

I paused. It was the first second I'd rested since I'd started running, and I pressed my hands to the tops of my thighs, drawing in deep breaths. It was okay. I wasn't dying.

James. Was he okay? What had made him fall in? It hadn't looked at all like a deliberate jump into the water, but like he'd passed out and tumbled in. He'd been breathing, though, so he'd be fine, right?

My knees turned to water, and I fell into the grass, tumbling onto my butt. My neckline cut into my skin. My cape was caught in the gate. *Stupid cape! Never again.* I jerked, and the fabric I'd so painstakingly sewn on ripped, the seams popping.

I shoved my mask down and drew in great gulps of air. If I'd died when I'd jumped in, what would have happened to Kareena when she'd come forward to claim my body? Would she have even claimed it? Or would I have been buried somewhere by the state, alone and abandoned and—

Stop. Breathe. You can't spiral right now.

I rested my head against the fence and stared up at the sky. My teeth were chattering, an involuntary physical reaction to how freezing and wet and miserable my body was. What time was it?

I checked my phone, surprised to learn it wasn't even nine. Barely any time had passed since I had thrown that trash bag away.

I had hours, but it was essential I beat Kareena home from her night shift. It wasn't like she checked in on me, but if the dishes weren't done she'd come stomping to find me, and if I wasn't there she'd be so mad when I did get home. She'd look at me in that resentful way she had and maybe she'd say something terrible. Something like . . . mocking me for the weight I'd gained since Mama had left.

I kept waiting for her to cross that line. I don't know what I would do if she did, or why I thought that was the worst thing she could say to me. I maintained all sorts of imaginary goalposts in my head, the product of endlessly imagining worst-case scenarios for everything. It was like a million ifs without thens.

I'd go. In a second. After I caught my breath. After the sky stopped spinning. After I took care of my injury. I peered at the scarf, stained red. It was just a graze, right? Some nail or glass bottle.

I tugged at the knot and peeled the makeshift dressing off. Nausea roiled in my belly. Those words, *just a graze*, always sounded so nonthreatening in movies and television. This didn't look nonthreatening.

A sharp gash ran along my upper arm, though the blood had slowed. The edges were gross and ragged.

You could die from this. Infection.

Carefully, I pulled my phone from my bag and opened my video call app.

I pressed Mama's photo. "Pick up, pick up. Please, Mama." Mama had worked whatever job she could find here, but once upon a time in India, she'd gone to nursing school. Combined with having one sick daughter, she was pretty well versed in medicine. She'd know what to do. She'd freak out and cry that I was hurt, and try to make me go to the hospital, but she'd know why I was too scared to do that.

Also, I just wanted my mama. I was sixteen, but I felt like I was six. I wanted to see her thin face and dark eyes, even if she couldn't hold me and tell me I would be okay and rub Tiger Balm on me to make me all better.

The phone stopped ringing. I licked the salty tears from my lips and stuck my phone back into my bag. The time difference. She was probably fast asleep, an ocean away from me.

My brain was probably exaggerating it, but the pain was growing worse, radiating out from the wound, all the way up to my shoulder and down through my fingers. I kinda wished the shock would come back.

I scanned the yard. The little garden shed was right where it had always been. Candice's parents were doctors. So long as they hadn't changed anything, there would be a first aid kit neatly tucked away on a shelf. I could fix myself up and change and go home.

Maybe you need stitches.

Yeah, maybe I did, but there wasn't anything I could do about that. If I was lucky, the kit might have some of that liquid bandage stuff in it. If not, I could at least clean the cut and put pressure on it. I knew enough from TV to do that.

I tried to get to my feet, but fell back onto my butt. I tried again, but only made it to my knees.

What was wrong with me?

Just a graze.

Grazes *hurt*.

A light went on upstairs in the house, and I froze. I had to get in that shed now. I was way too exposed out in the open like this. I wrestled my torn cape away from the gate and made my way to the shed, grimly focused on my quest.

I quietly closed the door behind me and used my phone's flashlight in place of the overhead light. Nothing had changed since I'd been here over a year ago. The steel shelves were neatly stocked with extra nonperishable goods and household things like toilet paper and dish soap. When I'd first met Candice, I'd been awed by the mini store in her backyard. Her mom was an extreme couponer, she'd told me, and rolled her eyes. I'd thought it funny then that someone who didn't really need to be thrifty saved money like a hobby. Stockpiling goods was a luxury when you lived paycheck to paycheck.

The first aid kit was exactly where I'd remembered it. I stripped my mask and my shirt off. The bleeding had slowed almost to a stop, but I hissed when I cleaned it with alcohol. The liquid bandage, and then gauze, wrapped tight. I had to hold my breath when I was finished in order to hear above my heartbeat, but no one was rushing the door.

My head was spinning, and it was from adrenaline now, not

necessarily pain. Thoughts of multiple people drifted across my consciousness, each one bringing a new set of worries and fear.

Unable to resist a moment of respite, I toed off my wet boots and stripped off my soaking leggings. Naked except for my underwear and the bandage, I slumped against the wall of the shed and slid to the floor.

Two seconds of rest. I turned off the flashlight. Two seconds, and I'd leave.

I was so cold. I wanted my mama.

My head tilted back. And my world faded to the vast emptiness of nothing.

CHAPTER

Three

Waking up Sonia is like waking up a bear.

I swatted at the memory of my mother's exasperated tone. Yeah, waking up was hard. Nothing good happened early in the morning.

Mama's laugh echoed in my ears as the layers of sleep peeled off me like an onion. I blinked up at the wooden ceiling above me for a second, confused. This wasn't the bunk bed I usually woke up to.

The strangely musky odor snapped my brain into focus, and I jackknifed into a seated position. I put my palm on the floor to steady myself, and the pain that shot through me knocked away whatever traces of sleep clung to my subconscious.

I cradled my arm to my chest and took stock of my surroundings. Moonlight seeped through the small gaps in the wood doors, and fall air along with it. I shivered and looked down at myself. No wonder I was freezing, almost naked on cold concrete.

My phone vibrated on the floor where I'd dropped it and I shifted a little to read the screen. Two missed calls from my mom, and one from Kareena. It was half past ten. Aw, crap.

This was not an ideal situation. At any moment, my former best friend or her parents could come barging in here to get toilet paper, and I was too woozy to try to BS my way through this one. *Oh, hi, Dr. and Dr. Carter. No, I'm totally fine. Don't worry about me. Just naked and stealing your medical supplies. Why haven't I been by lately? Ask your daughter.*

The gauze on my wound was still white, so that was good. Despite the pain and stiffness in my arm, I pulled my jeans, sweatshirt and tennis shoes out of my bag, and replaced them with my damp costume. Thank God I hadn't left my street clothes at the café.

I carefully replaced the first aid kit I'd used. I yanked my sweatshirt hood up over my head. A disguise it wasn't, but it was definitely less eye-catching than my costume.

I peeked out of the shed. The backyard was quiet. The light in Candice's room was off, but the kitchen and living room were all lit up. Her parents worked long hours, but they were probably home by now.

I snuck out of the shed, sticking to whatever shadows I could find. On the street, I tempered my desire to sprint and casually strolled down the sidewalk, trying to look like I belonged. Once I was out of view of Candice's home, I called a rideshare. It always felt like a luxury to call one, but though I had my license, Kareena needed our car more than me.

Prices were surging right now, because of course they were.

31

Story of my life, paying 1.5 times the fare right after I saved a life.

The car came quickly, which wasn't always the case here, and it was a good thing it did, because my phone died as soon as I checked the plate and got inside.

Which meant I couldn't call my mom or Kareena back. I plugged the phone into the driver-provided cord and tried not to rip my nails off in agitation on the ride home. My thoughts were all jumbled, not helped by the physical discomfort I was in. My arm was aching and I was cold. I touched my hair and grimaced at the rat's nest. Also, my curls from the morning were definitely gone now.

The driver pulled up in front of our town house just as my phone powered on, and I got out with a mumbled thanks. I locked the door to my house and collapsed back against it. The place was quiet and still, and for a second, I allowed my brain's spiraling hamster wheel a moment of peace as well. It was shattered when my phone vibrated with a text.

Is everything okay?

Mama.

No, everything was not okay. *I jumped into the canal to save a boy I love and I think he's okay but then I had to run away because the authorities were coming and I hurt my arm and you know I don't like blood and I had to go to Candice's house and that sucked because of my* feelings. *Oh, I didn't tell you, but Candice hasn't spoken to me since I told her you were deported. My feet hurt. I miss you. Come back.*

I took a deep breath and texted back. **Yup, everything's fine.**

The phone immediately rang with a video call from Mama. I hesitated a second, then hit the audio. She'd get more worried if I didn't answer, but there was no way she could see me like this. "Hello?"

"Are you sure everything's okay?" No fooling Mama. Her lightly accented English was heavy with worry, but that wasn't new. Mama hadn't been dealt an easy hand in life: she'd become estranged from her family when she married my dad against their wishes; had a daughter diagnosed with a rare form of infant leukemia; had come to America from India with said daughter on a medical visa for medical trials and treatment; prematurely gave birth to another child (me) all alone here in America because my father went and died in India and the shock sent her into labor; gotten financially and emotionally cut off from her in-laws once her doting mother-in-law died in the same year because they irrationally blamed her for their family's bad luck . . . her life was about as well written as an Indian soap opera, and that didn't include her getting deported. No wonder she always sounded like she was braced for yet another catastrophe.

And you think you have problems. "Yes. Why?"

"I can't see you."

"Bad connection," I lied, and thumped up the stairs. Though it was peeling and rickety, I liked this two-bedroom house. Mama had gotten an amazing deal on the place, the owner a friend of one of our aunties—no blood relation—in Ohio. She was one of the few people who knew about our situation, and she'd immediately halved our rent.

"You called me. It's not like you to call so early in the morning like that."

Her early morning, my evening. "I'm sorry, I wasn't thinking." I went into my bedroom and kicked a pile of clothes out of the way. Kareena had snagged the master once it was empty last spring. It had been weird that first night, to sleep alone. For as long as I could remember, I'd always been able to time my breaths to my sister or my mom.

I pushed aside another pile of clothes. The one upside of having my own bedroom was letting my inner slob out.

I plugged the phone in on my nightstand and put it on speaker while I pulled off my shirt. The pain in my arm throbbed again. I looked in the mirror. The white bandage was stark on my brown skin. "I was actually calling because my . . . friend, her arm got injured. Like cut by something sharp. And I wanted to see if you knew how to fix it."

"What did she get cut by?" Mama's voice turned brisk, the same way it had whenever Kareena had been sick as a kid.

"I don't know. Glass, maybe. It was dark, she didn't see it. Just like scraped up on it."

"If it was glass, she should make sure there are no tiny pieces left in her wound."

I recoiled. Ew. Gross. Surely I'd be able to feel that, right?

"Or if it was something rusty, she should make sure that she has her tetanus shot up to date."

Did I? "Is that something most people have?"

"You got yours when you started high school, so it depends on if she regularly sees a doctor."

I breathed a sigh of relief. One less worry. I would pray it hadn't been glass, and roll the dice.

"The most important thing is that the bleeding stops and it's cleaned and wrapped and then kept clean. Infection can always pop up later. Honestly, she should just go to urgent care and get it looked at to make sure there's no issues and she doesn't need stitches. Is this Candice? Should I call her parents?"

"No," I said quickly. I didn't know if Candice's parents knew the truth about my family, but I'd rather they didn't, given how Candice had iced me out after she learned it. "Okay, thanks. I gotta go do the dishes before Kareena gets home."

"Are you two doing well? Are you getting along and not fighting?"

"Define fighting. Is it when she yells at me and I take it?"

My mom clucked her tongue. "Sonia. She has a great deal on her shoulders. She loves you very much."

I knew what love was. My mother loved me, and when we were young, Kareena had loved me. She'd heated up food for me, and done my hair, and read me stories, and invited me to play games with her.

Love wasn't the mean way she treated me now. "I'm nice to her. I'll try to be nicer."

"Hmm." She didn't sound like she believed me, but she let it pass. "Divya Auntie is going to be coming through town soon. She said she would stop in and check on you."

"Great," I said, barely paying attention. The more time I spent on the phone, the less time I had to hide my evidence. "Gotta go. I love you."

35

"I love you, beta."

I hit the end button and finished stripping off my clothes. There was an empty plastic bag on the back of my door and I stuffed the pieces of my costume into it, along with the boots. The lack of care I took was a marked difference from when I'd left this room with every piece packed in my bag this morning.

My hands faltered on the black top I'd so painstakingly put together. There was a ragged row of torn stitches on the back.

The cape.

I frantically retraced my steps in my head. It had ripped off in the gate. I would have seen it on my way out if I'd dropped it in Candice's yard, but it was entirely possible I'd left it in her shed.

My hands shook as I knotted the bag. There was nothing I could do about it now. I couldn't exactly go back to Candice's neighborhood and skulk around at midnight. How many of her neighbors had one of those doorbell cameras? It was a scrap of red material. It didn't prove anything.

I shoved the costume into the back of my closet. It would be nice to throw it out, but any rookie knows that's exactly how things get found. I'd hide it for now. Hopefully everything was dry enough so it wouldn't start to smell.

I kept my arm out of the way of the water while I showered and pulled on sweatpants and a long-sleeved shirt after. They were nice and loose, not an inch of my body visible, and that was a relief. Maybe if I hadn't felt so confident in my custom clothes, I wouldn't have gone off and done something so foolish as risking my and my family's life. Back to hiding for now.

I checked my socials. I was a lurker more than a poster, but no one was writing any tributes or well wishes to James yet. His stories were blank, though I didn't entirely expect him to have regained consciousness and posted an immediate photo of the ambulance.

I grabbed my laptop and went downstairs to the living room. I turned on the lamp and sat on the couch. It took a couple of minutes to find a story about the canal on our local news station's site.

It made my stomach lurch, though I'd expected this. Ours was a sleepy town. Any accident or violence made the news. I hit play on the video. "Breaking news tonight, a tragic incident and a local high school student's dramatic rescue—"

I choked, as hard as when I'd been gulping water. Tragic? Did tragic mean dead?

The man's eyebrows drew together in scripted concern. "The unnamed student is in stable condition, but there's been no further official news on the minor's condition or what exactly caused him to fall into the canal. Witnesses claim a young woman rescued the boy from the water."

One of the women who had helped James came on the screen, her breath short, ambulance lights painting her face red and blue, a giant mic thrust in her face. This must have been filmed at the scene. "We just saw her dive in, no hesitation, and grab the young man, swim him to shore. I'm worried for her. She was bleeding."

Oh crap. Me. She was talking about me.

"Do you have any information about this hero? Did she give

you a name?" the reporter asked.

"No. All she said was that she couldn't afford a hospital, and she booked it." The woman's face was creased with concern. "She was about my height, dark hair, there was an *S* on her shirt."

The stupid *S* I'd embroidered on my costume. Because it had looked too blank. I'd thought I was so clever, using my first initial.

Oh no no no no no no.

I dropped my head into my hands, my ears buzzing too much to listen any longer as the anchor in the studio took over.

Now you've done it. You're going to be the reason the police show up at the door and Kareena gets caught.

I was an American citizen literally by accident. Kareena was not. My status hadn't stopped my mom from getting arrested at the dry-cleaning shop she'd worked at, and it wouldn't stop Kareena from being deported if anyone probed a little too deeply into my family.

Keys jangled at the door. I slammed the laptop closed as Kareena entered, then stopped in the entryway. Her sharp gaze ran over me. "What's wrong?"

Not even the purple circles under her eyes could detract from Kareena's beauty. She was eighteen, barely a year and a half older than me, and an ocean away in looks. She was tall and slim, her long black hair spilling almost to her butt. She literally woke up like that, along with flushed cheeks and goop-free eyes.

No wonder my grandma—my dad's mom—had seen

Kareena, their perfect first grandchild, as the source of all their family's wealth. She'd moved heaven and earth to get her into a trial in the US when her first two rounds of chemo in India hadn't worked.

I'd come into the world premature and red-faced and screaming, and split my family. I was the bad luck charm. No one had told me that, but it made sense in my head.

I couldn't let Kareena scent any blood in the water, or she'd take relentless enjoyment in cutting me down. We'd been friends once. Since our mom had left, every interaction between us had ended in a fight. "Nothing."

She placed her purse on the desk in the corner of the living room. It was ruthlessly organized, with a stack of paid bills on one side and mail still to be opened on the other. "Why are you sitting here in the dark, like a weirdo?"

"It's not dark." *I am being a weirdo.*

Kareena had never been a weirdo. Two years ahead of me in school, she hadn't exactly been a social butterfly, but that was only because we were conditioned to fly under the radar. After her cancer had gone into remission at twelve and she'd been able to regularly attend school, she'd been popular and maintained a solid group of friends. Her sunny and kind personality had drawn everyone in close. It was only in the last year that her attitude had grown so snappish, and then mostly just with me.

She hit the switch for the overhead light, which was much harsher than the lamp. I winced, and cradled my hand protectively over the laptop.

She didn't miss the gesture. She took her coat off and placed it on the coatrack. "What were you looking at?"

"Nothing." Ah, damn. Could I sound any more guilty?

"I don't believe you." Kareena took a step toward me. "Let me see."

I clutched the computer to my chest. "I don't think you want to do that."

"Oh yeah?" She took another step.

I tried to think fast. "It's an ingrown toenail."

"Excuse me?"

"I like to watch this channel where they remove impacted nails. It's relaxing. So if you want to see, fine, but I know you don't like graphic stuff." I made like I was going to open the laptop, but she lifted her hand.

She stared at me for a long moment, and I started to sweat. "Are you actually okay?"

I couldn't blame her for asking me that. I did occasionally watch dermatologists popping pimples, but the toenail thing was gross, even for me. "For the millionth time, yes."

"So freakin' weird," she muttered as she stomped away.

I breathed a sigh of relief. Better she think I loved foot health than the truth.

That I could have possibly endangered her life here. If Kareena was deported, she'd have to go navigate a country she didn't know. She might technically be the adult in the house, but she wasn't that much older than me. Trying to figure yourself and your identity out in familiar surroundings was hard enough.

And I'd be left alone. The state would finally realize I'd slipped through the cracks all this time and they'd either put me in the system or I'd have to go live with one of my mom's friends. Start high school somewhere else, try to fit in in another environment. Just because I had no friends here didn't mean I wanted to go have no friends in another school!

You're getting ahead of yourself. They don't have a description. They have a letter that they don't know is an initial. Dark hair. A scratch on the arm.

It was fine. James was stable; he would be okay. No one would come looking for me. Everything was fine.

I sat there for a while, so lost in my thoughts that I barely paid attention to the sounds in the kitchen. Until the garbage disposal whirred.

Oh damn. The dishes.

I cringed and got to my feet, and made my way to the kitchen. Sure enough, Kareena was at the sink. "I can do that."

She didn't look up from the cup she was scrubbing, and she didn't respond either, which wasn't a good thing. Tentatively, I walked up behind her. "I'm sorry. I completely—"

"Forgot," she finished crisply, and placed the last dirty dish in the drying rack. "Figures."

"I'm sorry," I repeated.

She wiped down the empty sink and faced me. "I am exhausted," she said, enunciating every word. "I asked you to do one thing." She stripped her yellow gloves off, one finger at a time, and slapped them down on the sink.

I was busy nearly jeopardizing our lives. "I know. I'm sorry. I won't forget next time."

She inhaled through her nose, then exhaled, her narrow

nostrils as dainty as the rest of her. "I have to shower and go to bed. Some of us have to work tomorrow. Have fun at school."

There was an extra bite in that last sentence, and it hovered in the air as she sailed away. School wasn't really fun for me, but it was definitely less work than her multiple menial jobs. Not for the first time, I wished I had graduated already. I had floated quitting, but it had made Mama cry so much I'd given up on that possibility.

My mission was crystal clear. I went to a fancy honors school here, better than any school I could go to if I lived with one of my aunts in Ohio. After graduation, good college, good job, be somebody with enough power and money that I could pay it back and help my mom and sister.

That was the dream. It was a dream my sister hadn't been able to take advantage of. She'd been accepted to three state universities when Mama had left. She'd had to defer, mainly because of money. She wasn't eligible for federal aid, and without Mama working here, she couldn't afford it.

I asked you to do one thing.

I picked up the gloves and hung them on the sink, just so I'd feel useful. Right. I'd helped James, and that was good, but from now on, I'd be laser-focused on doing what I was told to keep our small family chugging along. If that meant coming home straight after work to wash dishes, then fine.

No mistakes. No distractions.

CHAPTER
Four

I *heard he had a seizure and fell in.*

He was mugged, my mom said.

He hit his head and would have definitely drowned if he hadn't been rescued.

I grabbed my lunch from my locker, my resolute stance on distractions having crumbled as soon as I set foot in school that morning. James's name had leaked at some point, and everyone was abuzz.

Which made sense. I was pretty sure that if anything bad ever befell me, few of my fellow students would be able to recall what I looked like, but James was popular. His mom owned a business in the community. He was a track star. Of course people were talking.

I'd heard every speculation possible whispered over the course of the morning, while I tried to keep my head down and my mouth shut. So far, everyone seemed to be focused on what had caused him to fall into the water. I hope they stayed worried about that and not about who had pulled him out of the water.

I shut my locker with my injured arm and winced at the slight reverberation through the cut. I'd changed the bandage this morning and had been relieved to see the skin looked healthy. I didn't want to go to urgent care at all if I could help it. Even a true crime amateur like me knew the dangers of creating a trail.

Though I was braced for the worst, I faltered as I made my way to my lunch spot and caught sight of a familiar blonde head in the hallway, surrounded in true queen bee fashion by half a dozen of her minions.

Sam.

I tried not to say her name with an air of disdain, even mentally, but that was in vain. Candice's and Sam's fathers had been college roommates, and owned a practice together, so Sam and Candice had been thrown together since they were babies. Candice and I had become instant friends when I'd transferred here in eighth grade, and she'd spent way less time with Sam after that. Candice had never had a bad thing to say about her former bestie, but I hadn't been able to pinpoint anything great about her, and I'd tried.

Sam wasn't quite influencer-level famous, but she had more followers than anyone else at school. After Candice had ghosted me and run back to her old friend, I might have watched a couple . . . hundred . . . of Sam's videos to try to figure out the magic. All I'd gotten was tutorials on blow-drying her already perfect hair, fast-fashion and designer clothing hauls, and gossip. The tea was always scalding hot, covering hookups, betrayal, and love. She never named names, though, and I wasn't in the know enough to guess who she was talking about.

So, no. I didn't like her much. And the fact that Sam had dated James until they broke up a couple months ago, hadn't made me like her any more.

Candice wasn't around Sam today, though. My ears pricked up as I passed her. "I haven't heard anything more than what I said on my page," Sam said loudly. In her annoying voice.

"Are you going to go visit James in the hospital?"

Sam paused, and I did too. Too long, perhaps, because her gaze passed over me. Her cheeks were rosier than normal, and the tip of her upturned nose was, too, like she was a perfect fairy elf who had gotten her nose rubbed in a pink dirt pit.

Was that my personal fantasy? Maybe.

Her gaze didn't stop on me, though, which was standard. Nobody could bully you when they didn't know you existed. "Yeah, soon, I hope."

I hoisted my bag higher on my shoulder and kept walking, trying to suppress my annoyance. She had every right to want to visit her ex in the hospital. It wasn't her fault that she had the privilege of not caring about what authorities would be there.

I stopped in front of my math class and pushed open the door. I paused to find Mr. Walsh behind his desk. "Oh, sorry. I didn't know you'd be here." I raised my brown paper bag. "I was hoping to, ah . . ."

My calc teacher looked up and peered at me through his

gold-rimmed spectacles. He wasn't a big guy, but he walked with a heavy tread. He was balding and kind and he always smelled vaguely of butterscotch candies. "Ah, Sonia. No worries. You know you're free to eat in here if you like. Grab a seat."

Mr. Walsh had been my algebra teacher my freshman year and I'd been so excited to have him again this year. Though I didn't have a lot of friends my own age, I did have good relationships with almost all my teachers. Being a teacher's pet was a safe form of attention, I'd learned early. Positive attention, because I was a good student who didn't cause any waves.

I put my lunch sack on a desk. "Are you sure? I don't want to disturb you." I'd casually asked Mr. Walsh to let me use his classroom for tutoring during lunch once, and that had transformed into me eating in here most days, since he was usually gone this period. The prospect of having to meander through the lunchroom five days a week, trying to figure out where to sit and avoid Candice, was exhausting.

And that went double on the day after I'd broken into Candice's shed to steal her first aid supplies. Seeing her would make today the Mondayest of all Mondays.

"No, you're not disturbing me at all." There was a stain on his tan wrinkled shirt and a smile in his eyes. "Just prepping for the next class."

He did turn to his work, and the only sound in the room was the scratch of his pen on paper. I pulled my sandwich out, and also grabbed the comic I'd been carrying around in my backpack for the past couple of weeks. *Makeshift.*

Heroes aren't born. They're made, the tagline proclaimed.

Though my last cosplay adventure had ended in disaster, I traced my fingers over the heroine's purple-and-yellow costume on the cover out of habit. Simple lines and construction in the leotard and tights. Something plain could look really good when it fit right and was made with fine materials.

I opened the book. Might as well try to get my mind off James.

I nibbled my peanut butter and jelly sandwich and tried my best to focus on the text introducing Mirabel Morris, a nerdy orphaned physics prodigy with no friends except for her lab partner and her tuxedo cat, Puddin'.

The cat was drawn cute, with a little jaunty tail. I'd always wanted a pet, but my mom was allergic. Or at least, she'd said she was allergic, but I suspected she just didn't want another creature to be responsible for.

When I read, I could easily get lost in the pages. On a normal day, I would have inserted myself into the well-drawn frames, replacing the dark-haired Mirabel. I was the loner who went for a drive to shake off the sorrow of losing my parents; I was the one who hit a truck and woke up in a high-security hospital; I was the one who ran away and found that my molecular structure had changed, so I started wildly shape-shifting into every single person I'd ever met, unable to control it.

Only it wasn't me, it was still perkily drawn Mirabel, because today wasn't a normal day. I closed the book and rolled my shoulders, trying to ease the tension in them.

I haven't heard anything more than what I said on my page.

Ugh. I didn't need to give Sam more views, did I?

Yes, I did, because it wasn't like I was going to get any more reading done, and *Makeshift* deserved my full attention.

I cast a surreptitious look at Mr. Walsh, but he was still lost in grading exams, his tongue caught between his teeth. I pulled my earbuds out and stuck them in my ears.

I didn't have to search for Sam's name. Her latest video popped up on my For You page as soon as I opened the app. I could hide my stalking from her, maybe, but not from the algorithm. It knew what I wanted to see.

"So I'm sure you've heard about James." Sam's face was somber, and her whole demeanor seemed wilted, even her silky blonde hair limper than usual. She sat on her bed, where she filmed all her videos. Her bedroom was white all over, and I was almost positive she must fiddle with the color levels in post to make it so starkly pristine. No way anyone could have such a perfect space.

"Pause to read." She lifted her hand, and a news story about James filled the screen temporarily. I didn't need to pause to read it. I knew what it said. "I am, of course, worried and heartbroken. James was—is!—one of my best friends. We dated for almost two years, and though we've been on a break for the last few months, I love him dearly. This accident has wrecked me." Her lip trembled, and tears formed in her blue eyes.

Of course, they didn't spill. They wouldn't dare disrespect her by making her an ugly crier.

Wait. On a break? They hadn't broken up?

"I hope and pray he's okay, and I'm sending healing thoughts

48

to him. As soon as I find out anything more about his condition, I'll post a part two. Let me know if there's anything else you want to know." She reached out and turned the camera off.

My eye twitched, and I wasn't sure why. Of course she had a level of familiarity with and access to James that I didn't have, so she could find out stuff about his condition. That made sense, especially if they were *on a break* and not *broken up*.

I paused the looped video and opened the comments. Most of them were standard *so sorry, hope he feels better* platitudes, but one made me sit up.

Can you talk about the people who saved him?

And under that: *Heard there was a third lady who ran, why?*

And then under that: *probably shoved him in first*

Even if I could dismiss the third comment as a troll, the first two had a lot of likes. My heart thundered in my ears. No, no, no. The last thing I wanted was Sam doing any videos on me. Or my alter ego.

"Sonia?"

I yanked my earbuds out and jerked my gaze away from my phone, up to my teacher's desk. Mr. Walsh had a slight frown on his face. He glanced at my hand, and it was only then that I realized I'd strangled my lackluster PB&J.

"Did something exciting happen in that book? I know how much you love your comics."

"I, um, no. I haven't gotten to the exciting part yet." I released what was left of the sandwich and tried to unobtrusively wipe my hand on the paper bag. Mr. Walsh slid out his drawer, grabbed something, and walked over to me. I accepted the wet wipes with a murmured thanks.

I kept my head lowered and focused on cleaning up the sticky mess on my hands, which, unfortunately, left my phone faceup on the desk.

"Ahh," he said knowingly. "I've seen Ms. Larson's video on a number of phones today. A shame, James's accident. I was planning on talking about the situation in class, but how are you doing?"

I nearly rubbed my still-aching arm before I caught myself. "I'm—I'm fine."

His dark eyes probed mine, as if he were looking for a lie. Luckily for me, I was good at lies. He drew back and pulled a butterscotch out of his pocket, unwrapping it even when I refused with a shake of my head. "You sure? I've seen you two chatting."

Mr. Walsh really wanted all his advanced calc students—his mathletes, he called us—to be a tight crew. We were, too, at least in class. It wasn't like James sought me out to talk to me outside it. *Except yesterday at the café.* "Of course I'm worried about him. I hope he's okay." I didn't know why I said what I did next, except perhaps because I wanted someone to feel some of my emotions with me. "We were supposed to have a tutoring session today."

Mr. Walsh sucked on his butterscotch. "I didn't realize you were tutoring him."

"We started recently." Like a few hours before he took a tumble into the canal.

"I see. I'm so glad to hear that he came to you. Hopefully,

you'll be able to resume sessions soon."

I straightened. It was entirely possible the teachers knew more than the students did. "Do you know that for sure? He's doing good?"

"Ah, no. But I saw his brother earlier today. He stopped by to collect some stuff from James's locker, and he said James was stable."

I hadn't known James had a brother. *There's a lot you don't know about him.* Argh, I needed more information.

Mr. Walsh's face turned gentle. "In any case, if you need to speak with someone, we do have guidance counselors."

"I'm fine, really. I don't need a counselor." Well, maybe I did, but I wasn't about to see someone through the school.

Mr. Walsh nodded. "Very well. Just know you have someone here if you need it, okay?"

"Sure."

"In the meantime, if you talk to James before I do, please let him know he needn't worry about class. Once he's better, I'm sure your notes and help will have him caught up in no time. He's in good hands with you."

Our teacher was making it sound like James and I were closer than we were, but it felt kinda nice, so I didn't correct him. I gave Mr. Walsh a weak smile. "Thanks."

He gave me a final nod and trundled to his desk. I turned back to my book, but I didn't open it. Instead, I stared at Sam's paused face.

I wasn't Sam. Sam could go to the hospital and check on him. I could not.

Except . . .

I didn't have to work at the café today. I was supposed to have tutored James. It wouldn't be absurd to check in on him at the hospital under the guise of dropping off my notes or something.

I rejected that thought almost immediately. There was no way in hell I was going to the hospital, for the same reasons I hadn't wanted to go before. There could be cops there. I was sure this was still an open investigation.

But they're not looking for you. They didn't see you. Neither did James.

The other witnesses had.

Your mask was up. They only saw the top half of your face. It was dark.

I'd walk into the hospital room, holding flowers and a balloon with a teddy bear on it. James would be fast asleep, a white bandage wrapped around his head. His long lashes would slowly flutter open when my sneaker squeaked on the tired linoleum floor, and he'd turn toward me. Our eyes would lock across the hospital room, and his heartbeat would increase, something I'd be able to see, thanks to his heart monitor . . .

No. I raked my hair back from my face, so as to rake this new fantasy away from my mind. Going to the hospital was way too risky. I was putting my foot down on myself.

CHAPTER

Five

I really needed to stop finding loopholes around the feet I put down.

The rideshare dropped me at the strip mall and peeled off. I shivered as the wind cut through my sweatshirt. At some point, I'd have to start wearing my winter coat, but I really didn't want to. Donning it felt like an annual defeat, especially given how sad I knew I'd be during this holiday season, my first without my mother.

"Hi, I'm in class with James. I was dropping off my notes for him and I wanted to convey my best wishes for his recovery," I whispered. Simple, short sentences that I'd mentally rehearsed on my way over.

You are bold. You did something much braver than this a couple days ago. You got this.

"Why didn't I text him my notes? My handwriting isn't so clear. I thought this would be best. Why did I come here instead of the hospital? We were going to meet here for tutoring. Yes, I'm his tutor. How's he doing?" I nodded to myself as I walked up to the restaurant at the end. *Gulab* was etched into the window in white script, a rose unfurling under the text. I had this.

Before I could stop myself, I opened the door and walked inside.

The entryway was beautiful, a round space filled with plants and mirrors, the floor made of snowy-white marble. There was a substantial seating area through the arched doorway. The tables were draped in red linens, and gold charger plates decorated each place setting.

It was also vacant, though, which was odd. I checked my watch. It was only 4:00 p.m., but surely there was some waitstaff around? "Hello?" I called out, embarrassed to find out how weak and trembly my voice was. I cleared my throat, and tried again. "Hello?"

You tried. You can go home now.

Instead, I wandered into the dining area. A giant mirrored elephant mosaic was hung on the wall, and I took a second to admire the artwork.

The black double doors behind the bar opened, and a small man came scurrying out. His gaze fell on me, and he nearly dropped the plates he was holding. "Who are you?" he exclaimed.

I linked my hands in front of me. "Um, my name's Sonia—"

"Sorry, ma'am." The man shook his head, placing the dishes on the sideboard. "We're closed on Mondays."

"Oh." My face turned red, and I took a step back. "I didn't

realize. The door was open."

The man looked stricken. "I must have left it open by accident."

"No problem. I'll head out." Before I could leave, though, the kitchen door slammed open. At any other time, I would have jumped at the sudden noise, but I think I was just all out of startle.

A large figure came through the doorway. I was also all out of saliva, it seemed. I swallowed. Then swallowed again.

Who was this?

He was my age, or a little older, and so big and tall and broad that I took a step back even though there was a good amount of space between us. His skin was a rich brown, the undertone a deep warm bronze. His cheekbones were high and sharp enough to cut a girl, and his tight black curls gave me immediate hair envy.

His dark eyes narrowed when he spotted me. In an odd way, this brought me some comfort. I was used to people not knowing who I was, if they saw me at all. "Um, I'm Sonia. I'm—"

"I know who you are," he finished.

Wait, he did? How?

His long legs ate the distance between us. He wore all black—black jeans, a black T-shirt, a black apron on top. The severe color worked for him. "I'm so glad you're finally here." He held out his big hand, and I shook it automatically, nearly jumping at the tingle that ran through me.

His words sank in, and I frowned. "Uh, thanks?"

"Come with me." Without another word, he turned and

walked away. He nodded at the server. "Is everything okay, Raju Uncle?"

Raju looked back and forth between us, his face reflecting my confusion. "Uh, yes. I'm just going to go lock the door. Do you know when your mother will be in?"

"Soon, I hope," the guy I was with said shortly.

We entered the kitchen and I found the saliva that had deserted me upon seeing this guy. It smelled like heaven, like spices and rice and chicken and home. My mom hadn't been a gourmet chef, but she'd been good at putting together delicious meals with whatever was in the house and her silver tin of spices.

I missed our home-cooked Indian food, even the dal and rice that had been our standby meal on nights when she was tired. Since she'd left, we mostly ate fast food, sandwiches, whatever Kareena brought home from the diner, and various types of pasta, with a heavy emphasis on ramen. We didn't tell my mom that. If anything sent us back to Ohio to live with her friends, it would be my mom's concern that we weren't eating well.

"I'm Niam."

I refocused on the guy, though my stomach gave a quiet rumble to remind me of what I wasn't eating. "Um, hi."

"I'm so glad you could make it."

"I . . . you are?"

"Of course. I thought I'd be here alone."

What did that have to do with me?

Niam walked over to the big industrial sink. Everything in the kitchen gleamed. It was way more professional than the tiny space I used at the café to make acai bowls and bake premade muffins and doughnuts. "Here, wash up first."

Wash up? That was odd. But perhaps he was a germophobe?

Not wanting to be offensive by asking, I washed my hands, singing "Happy Birthday" to myself twice. When I dried off, I noticed him watching me. "That was thorough," he said.

"Thanks." Though I wasn't sure if it was a compliment or an observation.

He handed me a neatly folded piece of fabric. An apron. "Here you go."

Oh dear.

The puzzle pieces fit together, bringing with the realization a sense of embarrassment. He thought I was staff? I tried to hand the apron back to him. "I'm not here to cook."

Niam nodded and walked to the counter. It was overflowing with vegetables. "Of course you're not. I know you were hired for prep and cleaning. You're kind of young, aren't you?"

"Not that much younger than you," I said, and wondered at the touch of defensiveness in my voice.

"I suppose that's true."

"Also, I'm not—"

"We're behind. A little less talking, a little more hustling." He snapped his fingers, and my spine straightened.

A finger snap?

Who did he think he was? If nothing else, I was a guest in his kitchen. We may not have had much money, but my mom had taught me about hospitality.

Are you a mouse?

57

I carefully placed my folded apron on the counter. "I'm sorry—"

"It's okay. Let's just get to work, we don't have much time."

That's what I got for starting a blistering retort with *I'm sorry*. It had been meant to be an *excuuuuuuuse me* type of *I'm sorry*, not an actual *I'm sorry*, but I should have launched with *who do you think you are?* "Listen, I wasn't hired for this."

Niam's shoulders slumped, and he put his knife down. He turned to face me. "Sonia, right?"

I raised an eyebrow, his suddenly humble tone taking the wind out of my sails. "Yes."

"Sonia, I apologize. That was really rude. We have a big delivery for an event tonight. One of my mom's chefs is sick, and the other one could only come in earlier. She did a lot of the heavy lifting, but there's still a ton left to do to get everything packaged up and out the door." He rolled his neck. "I've never been in charge of anything this big. I'm stressed, but that's no reason to take it out on you."

"Your mom's chefs . . . ," I said slowly. "Your mom owns this place?"

He nodded. "Yeah. But my little brother's in the hospital, and my parents are with him."

His brother. I should have known he was James's brother immediately. He looked a little like him, especially when he was being kind instead of finger snappy. Same-ish build, same general face shape.

I pressed my hand over the apron and studied him. "How's your brother doing?"

Niam blinked at me. "He's—he's well, thank you for asking. He's awake and he should be coming home soon."

Relief ran through me. There. My objective was completed. I knew how James was doing. I could leave, satisfied, even if I didn't yet know what my fate was.

"Not soon enough for my mom to get here, though. I told her I could handle this, and . . ." He winced. "I don't know if I can. I've never organized a catering delivery this big."

I gave a mental sigh. *Sucker.*

I could explain that I was James's classmate, but that would embarrass Niam now, and given his sincere apology, I didn't want to do that. There was borderline desperation in his voice at having to work this event he didn't feel qualified to handle. I'd felt desperation and worry like that before.

Food service was nothing new to me. I shook out the apron and tied it behind me. It was thicker and nicer than the one I wore at the café. "What can I do to help?"

Visible relief brightened his eyes. "Can you chop cauliflower?"

I was pretty good at cutting up fruit and whatnot at the café, so once he showed me how he wanted the cauliflower chopped, it was a painless chore. I moved on to the cilantro, the tomatoes, the potatoes, and every other vegetable and herb he put in front of me. While I'd never set foot in a real restaurant kitchen, he was patient, and I was good at taking directions.

He only stopped me when I sliced an onion. "This needs to be smaller. I can do it." He touched my left shoulder and I jumped. It was barely a glance, but his finger was a little too close to my injury for comfort.

He removed his hand immediately. "Sorry."

"No, it's fine. You startled me." I handed him the knife.

There was no doubt that he was much handier with a knife than I was. His hands moved so fast they blurred.

"Can I do something else?"

"Yes." He nodded at the pan. "Put all those ingredients in the blender, and make sure they get pureed well."

The ingredients were already sautéed: onions, tomatoes, cashews. I could smell the spices wafting from them, though I wasn't sure what they were.

While I blended, he heated up some oil and added cloves and peppercorns and what I was pretty sure was garam masala. Then he took the thinly sliced onions he'd finished chopping and put them in, as well as the potatoes and cauliflower. The pan hissed when the ingredients hit.

I handed him the blender, and he poured the curry on top. He gave it all a good stir.

I knew I was gawking, but I'd never seen a chef work so close. Plus, I was hungry. That peanut butter sandwich I'd had at school was a long-ago memory by now.

He either didn't mind or didn't notice me staring at him. Niam handed me a bunch of cucumber and gestured with his fingers. "This small, okay? Real tiny." He turned to the stove.

I went back to the cutting board. "Did you go to cooking school or something?"

He gave a half laugh. "No. I'm a senior in high school. I've been helping my mom cook since I was about twelve, though."

So I'd been right. He was around my age. "Oh. Which school do you go to?"

"Rock. You?"

Rockville was the public high school. "Sutherland."

He paused. "Like my brother. You're a junior?"

I nodded.

"Do you know him? James?"

"I know of him." Funny how I hadn't minded Mr. Walsh thinking James and I were besties, but I was in too deep with Niam now to come clean. Besides, I was, oddly, enjoying the anonymity of this time with Niam. He had no idea who I was, like most people, but it felt vaguely comforting in this instance. Like I could be anyone, instead of no one. I deliberately changed the subject. "Do you think the people who eat this will be happy to learn that two high schoolers with no culinary background made their dinner?"

He smiled, and a dimple popped into his cheek. Ugh, why didn't I have dimples? Dents in the face were so cute. "The chefs made the entrees. This is the small potatoes stuff."

"Did your mom go to some fancy cooking school?"

"Not formally. She actually went to law school, and then came right back here to run my grandparents' restaurant before I was born."

I concentrated on cutting the cucumbers into the tiniest diced pieces, as he'd shown me. "Oh, wow. So you guys have been here for a while."

"Yeah. Fifty years, my family's been in Rockville." He checked on the potatoes.

"That's so cool."

"I'm surprised I've never met you, actually. I thought I knew all of the Indians my age in town."

I scraped the cucumber into the bowl. "We only moved here a few years ago." And then only because my mom had lost the job she'd had in Ohio that had given our family private health insurance. New York was one of the few states that didn't require documentation for kids to get state insurance. My mom hadn't cared so much about herself, but she'd been insistent that Kareena and I—especially Kareena, given her history—be covered at all times. Kareena had been in clinical trials, but she'd still had extensive bills.

We can survive without friends in this country, but not without health insurance, my mom had explained when we'd protested moving. She hadn't liked it either, leaving the community she'd built, but she'd done it, and I didn't blame her now that I was older. I'd been mostly happy in New York, until she'd left.

"Ah. That explains it." He bustled around behind me while I cleaned off the tables I'd been working on. A steel sectioned plate with a hot buttered naan, a green dish with cubes of cheese, and a bottled Coke slid in front of me. "Take a minute and eat."

I would happily fight him for this food, but I tried not to let that show as I took a sip of the Coke. "Thank you."

"I should have offered you food before I put you to work. My bad. We can have a bigger meal when we're done."

"Is this spinach?" I said the words before I could censor them, and flushed immediately. The last thing I wanted to do was put all my ignorance of our shared culture on display.

"Yeah. It's saag paneer."

There was no inflection in his tone, but I didn't meet his eyes. I didn't know the names of every Indian dish, only the stuff my mom made or we'd had at friends' homes. Mama was lactose intolerant, and Kareena was particular about textures, so paneer had never been stocked in our house.

It's okay if he thinks you're whitewashed. He doesn't know you.

I dipped the naan and took a bite, and had to bite my tongue to hide my moan of pleasure. "This is delicious."

He smiled. "Glad you think so."

I ate my snack quickly, shoveling the food into my mouth. Niam moved around me, filling containers and trays and wrapping things in plastic and foil.

I was still hungry when I finished, but I wasn't working this fake job to sit around and eat. After I washed up, I came back to Niam.

He was hunched over a stand mixer, his thick eyebrows drawn together. He looked more engaged and in the zone than he had while making the rest of the food.

"What else can I do?"

He glanced up. "Everything for tonight is done. Just working on my own thing now."

I looked inside the bowl of bright yellow meringue, whipped into stiff peaks. "What's that?"

"Saffron macarons." He said it with the French pronunciation. He placed the meringue into a pastry bag and started piping it onto a vinyl mat. "They'll have a whipped shrikhand filling in them."

"Fancy."

He smiled, though he kept his gaze on the pan. "I actually pitched them for an event next week, but my mom said they still needed work." He continued to make those circles, each one identical to the last. It was like ASMR, watching him pipe perfect spheres. The kitchen was quiet, except for the sound of something simmering on the stove and our breathing.

His face was so . . . content. I didn't think I'd ever looked that content, but maybe there was nothing that made me as happy as this seemed to make Niam. He finished piping the third sheet, and he lightly tapped the trays on the counter, making me jump. I'd been so engrossed in watching him that I'd forgotten that I was merely the hired help. "Gets the bubbles out," he explained. He placed the trays in the oven and went to wash his hands. "I need more flour when you get a chance, if you can grab it from the pantry for me." He jerked his chin at a pair of accordion doors.

"Sure thing."

Before I could move, he turned off the sink and leaned against it as he dried his hands. There was a subtle smile in his eyes. "You were a huge help, Sonia. I can't thank you enough for staying. I'm sorry I was such a jerk when you got here."

"The finger snapping was a little absurd," I dared to tease him.

Niam groaned and closed his eyes. "I'm sorry, again."

"No worries." My smile faded. "I know what it's like to be worried about a sibling." I hadn't understood what it had meant when I was young, all the hospital and doctor trips, just that

Kareena was often too tired to play with me. It was only as I grew older that I'd learned that fear for someone you loved.

And now look at us. She and I barely talked.

Niam nodded and folded the towel into a precise square. "Yeah. We've never had one of us land in the ER like this. It threw my family for a loop." He hesitated. "Do you need to leave? You're welcome to stick around. I could use some more cleaning help once Raju gets the order out of here."

"I don't have anywhere to be."

He glanced at me from under his long lashes. "If you have some time after, too, we can go grab a bite to eat for dinner, my treat."

I paused. His treat? Kind of like a date?

I rejected that thought immediately. James's cool older brother was not asking me out on a date. And even if he was, I wasn't going to be happy about it because the love of my life was still in the hospital, and I still didn't know when the cops would come knocking on my door. Right? Right.

I looked into his dark eyes. Before I could answer, the back door opened, bringing a swirl of fresh air into the hot kitchen.

A tall Black man entered the room, and I knew by his face, an older version of James's, exactly who he was. His arms and legs were more powerfully built than his sons'. He wore a suit, but it was wrinkled, the jacket gone. There were deep lines around his eyes and mouth, like he smiled a lot, but right now his cheeks were gaunt, his lips pursed.

The worry he undoubtedly felt for his son was reflected in the face of the slender South Asian woman a step behind him.

Her hair was in loose curls and the reddish brown strands tumbled to her waist. She wore dark skinny jeans with a colorful sweater. Her earrings were dangling pieces of resin cake.

"Mom. Dad. What are you doing here?"

His father shook his head. "James made us go home. He said, and I quote, *You look like crap. Go get some sleep and let me watch TV in peace.*"

"He sounds like he's getting back to himself," Niam said.

Or at least someone who wasn't at death's door. My shoulders relaxed.

"Oh, he's more than getting back to himself." Their mom hugged Niam and sighed. Though she was tall, she only came up to her son's shoulder. "I had to come and check on my other baby. I'm so sorry I left you here alone to deal with everything."

"I wasn't alone, luckily." He gestured to me, and two pairs of dark eyes turned to me. I shrank back slightly. "Sonia was here."

There was a long pause, and finally his mom spoke. "Oh. How nice. Um. And who is . . . Sonia?"

"Sonia," Niam repeated. "The help you hired for the evening."

His mother slowly stepped in front of him, like she was protecting him from me, and my cheeks burned. "Niam, the girl I hired was named Janice, not Sonia. She texted me that she wouldn't be able to show up. I left you a voice mail. I don't know who this is."

I cleared my throat and straightened my shoulders. Now it was three pairs of eyes staring at me. "Um, hi. I go to school with James. I just came by to see how he was . . . and you're right, I wasn't hired, but I never said I was. You assumed." My voice trailed off at the continued attention, even though I was telling the truth.

"Why didn't you correct me?" Niam demanded.

His disbelief verged on anger, and anger always made me shrink, but I stayed upright. "I did. Or I tried, but you were in such a hurry, and you seemed like you really needed help." I rolled my shoulders. This was so uncomfortable, I wanted the floor to open up and swallow me whole. This was why it was better to not do things. No one was ever mortified while staying at home and practicing invisible seams. "And then I felt bad for you, so I . . . I figured I'd lend a hand."

I waited a beat. This was so weird. They'd call me weird, and then James would hear how weird I was and he'd never love me. *Or* they'd tell James, and he'd be like, oh yeah, Sonia jumped in the water to save me, and then the cops would show up and Kareena would get in trouble—

"That's so—"

Niam's mother placed her palm on his chest, cutting him off. "Kind!" she finished. "That is the kindest, most wonderful thing I've heard. You say you're friends with James?"

"Um." I licked my lips and launched into my spiel. *You got this.* "Actually, I'm James's calc tutor." I was claiming too much familiarity with that, but just because we'd never had a lesson didn't mean I wasn't his tutor. "I was supposed to come for a lesson today, but—"

"Oh my gosh, of course. Yes, I told him he could use the back office." She came forward, arms outstretched, and grasped my hands. I jumped. I wasn't accustomed to casual touch anymore.

"Hi, Sonia." She said her *a*'s flat, which I'd come to recognize as a common western New York accent. Her eyes wrinkled up at the corners. "It is really too bad we're meeting under these circumstances."

Did this family meet each other's math classmates regularly? Her smile was so infectious, I couldn't help but respond despite my nerves. "Hi."

"I'm Pooja. And this is my husband, George."

"Hello," George said gruffly. "Always nice to meet a friend of James's."

"Hello," I managed, still awkward despite their kindness. "Well, I should probably head out."

"Oh, no. You can't leave." George straightened. "Not after all the work you did here. Have dinner with us."

Pooja jumped in. "Yes, of course. And we will pay you for your time, of course."

"No pay necessary."

She beamed at me. "We'll discuss that. Dinner, definitely."

"I should actually get home. . . ."

"It would be so nice to have a full table." Pooja's lips trembled. "It's so hard with James's seat empty."

Just like that, I caved. If staying would help this poor family . . .

Or maybe you're justifying this to yourself so you can feel comfortable staying and eating more of that delicious food.

Well, whatever it was . . . it beat going home to an empty

house with a sister who wouldn't be home till late and would probably berate me for not doing the laundry or something. "Sounds great. I'd love to stay, ma'am."

His mom clapped. "Wonderful. Do we need to call your parents?"

"No, ma'am. My mom's working." Not a lie. On the other side of the world, Mama probably was getting up soon to get ready for work.

I didn't stutter when I made excuses for my mom anymore. It didn't feel like lying to me, just creative . . . truth telling. That was probably an issue, but one I could deal with in therapy down the road.

"Please, call me Pooja."

My discomfort with that request must have been apparent on my face, because she laughed. "You're not accustomed to calling adults by their first names? You can use Pooja Auntie, then."

I relaxed. "Yes, Auntie."

Pooja turned to her son. "What do we need to finish up here, Niam?"

"You needed flour." I didn't know why I cared if Niam was annoyed with me or not. Perhaps because I was a people pleaser or . . . No, it was the first thing. "Let me get it for you." I scurried away, into the large closet off the kitchen that served as a neatly organized pantry. I turned the light on and took a second there to catch my breath.

"What on earth were you thinking?" I heard Pooja say to her son.

"You have to admit, honey, it's kind of funny," George said. He didn't bother to whisper. There was an undercurrent of laughter in his voice.

I found a plastic container of flour and picked it up while Pooja continued. "It is not funny. It doesn't reflect well on us, and James will be so embarrassed when he finds out."

"Why would he care what his tutor thinks about him?" Niam asked.

Yeah, why would he care? If anything, he might find this funny too. Best-case scenario, he'd also be impressed with my selflessness in helping his family out in a pinch. *Okay, rein in the fantasy.*

"She's not just his tutor," Pooja hissed, her voice too confident to not carry. "She's your brother's girlfriend."

CHAPTER
Six

Whaaaaaaaaaaaat.

 I had to consciously close my jaw.

"James's girlfriend?"

"Do you have more than one brother?" Pooja snapped.

Niam scoffed, which would have hurt my feelings if I wasn't so shocked. "James doesn't have a new girlfriend. He's still hung up on Samantha."

He was? Why? Ugh, why was my hearing so good, I thought as I plastered myself against the door to hear them better.

"He told me he was seeing someone in his calc class."

"He told you he was seeing *Sonia*?"

Pooja paused. "No, he wouldn't tell me her name. He said her family was conservative and wouldn't like her dating, so they were keeping it quiet. But why else would she show up here?"

Because I'm in love with him.

Conservative? Not me then. I didn't think my mom would have cared if I dated someone, but then again, it had never really come up. Now she might be more concerned, since she was so far away and worried about us more in general, but me kissing boys was probably low on her priority list of things to fret about.

I had seconds to make my decision. I had a few options:

1. Stay in this pantry forever, until these people's great-grandchildren found my dusty bones when they excavated this kitchen from the ruins of a solar flare;
2. Emerge from the pantry, admit I'd heard, and confess the truth to Pooja; or
3. Walk out all casual with the flour and act like nothing had changed since I'd gone inside the pantry.

The third was cowardly and avoided all confrontation, and it was exactly what I was going to do.

It felt like a lifetime had passed since Pooja had decided I was James's girlfriend, but it was probably more like seconds. I tried to exit the storeroom as nonchalantly as possible. I placed the flour on the counter and gave Niam and Pooja a faint smile. "Here you go."

"Excellent." Pooja smiled. "Why don't you go have a seat at the table over there in the corner? It's where we have our family meals. We'll help Raju load up the van and join you shortly."

Sure, and I'll just go ignore this whole weird thing about James telling you he was dating someone—me!—because the guy's incapacitated and I don't even know what's happening.

I sat at the long table in the corner of the kitchen, as tucked away as I could possibly get. I couldn't help but watch the little family. They were efficient as they finished up their work and put their meal together.

There was respect in the way the elder Coopers spoke to each other and their son. Sometimes, they all talked over each other. It was a mundane thing to notice about a family, but it had been so long since I'd experienced that dynamic. Talking over each other meant familiarity, like they could anticipate what the other person was going to say.

Once Raju had left, Pooja and George loaded down the table until I thought it might groan. The food Niam had given me earlier was like a distant memory as far as my belly was concerned. One by one, Pooja filled our plates. "Any dietary restrictions, Sonia?"

"No, ma'am."

"Would you like a soda?"

"Yes. I can get it, though." I knew where the fridge was now.

Niam spoke from where he was placing his macarons on a plate. "I'm up anyway. Fountain or bottle?"

"Whatever you're having. Sprite is fine."

He came back with two icy cold bottles and popped mine open for me before I could ask.

I took a sip, mainly so I wouldn't dive headfirst into my food. There was chicken curry, aloo gobi, and lamb biryani, with two folded rotis barely hanging on to the overflowing plate. I was pleased to note that I could identify most everything on the table this time, even the yogurt with cucumbers in it, though I couldn't remember the name for it until Pooja asked her husband, "Raita?"

I waited for the elder Coopers to take their first bite, and then did the same. The flavors exploded on my tongue, and I tried not to inhale the rest.

"Tell me about yourself, Sonia," George said.

This was the question the school career counselors had told us to be prepared for in interviews, and I high-key hated it with the power of a thousand suns. What the heck was I supposed to say? "Um, what would you like to know?"

Pooja linked her hands together loosely and braced her elbows on the table. "Are you involved in any sports or anything? James is, despite my encouragement to challenge gender norms."

My shoulders lowered. Pooja's smile was extremely non-threatening. "Not really into sports, no. I'm sorry, I wish I could challenge the norms more."

"I assume you're probably deep in SAT studying right now."

"Yes, ma'am." I was, though I'd just checked out books from the library. No fancy test prep companies involved here.

I had no idea what I was going to do the year after next. I knew my mom wanted me to go to college; unlike Kareena, I could qualify for federal financial aid to pay for it. Still, the thought of making myself so vulnerable and accessible on applications made me want to claw my skin off.

Plus, there was the fact that I didn't know what I wanted to be yet. The things I did love—sewing, crafting, comic books—everyone knew those didn't exactly lead to a stable job.

"So is James. I'm hoping you can get his calc grade up so he can end this semester on a better note than he started it." Pooja's words were light.

"Me too. I enjoy calc." Or at least, I was good at it. I took another bite, and had to close my eyes for a second.

I swallowed, then opened my eyes to find Niam watching me with a considering look on his face. I flushed and blotted the corners of my lips with the napkin.

"I'm surprised I haven't seen you around town before this, Sonia." Pooja tore a roti in half. I was eating my rice with my fork, like George and Niam were, but I wished I were comfortable enough to use my hands like Pooja. My mom had always said food tasted better that way, and I agreed. "Did you move here recently?"

"A few years ago, from Cleveland."

"Where are your parents from?"

I was sure my dad had been nice and all, but since I'd never met him, it was always jarring to hear the plural *parents*. "Mumbai."

She gestured to her and her husband. "We're first generation, too. My parents are from Delhi."

"And mine came here from Liberia." George helped himself to more rice.

"That's cool." Weird to think I had something in common with people who were so much older than me.

"What do your parents do, Sonia?"

I wasn't ashamed of my mom's work as a seamstress. It had put food on our table. "My mom works for a tailor." She'd been a seamstress for ages, including at the dry cleaners where she'd been arrested.

"Ah, interesting." George steepled his hands under his chin. "I suppose she's very . . . clothes minded."

It took me a second to get the joke, but Niam's groan assisted me. "Dad, stop," he muttered.

George shrugged. There was a twinkle in his eye. "Suit yourself."

I couldn't help my giggle. Pooja rolled her eyes. "I'm sorry, Sonia."

"No, no. That was great." Dad jokes were a foreign phenomenon to me, probably because dads were a foreign phenomenon to me. Kareena claimed to have one or two vague memories of our father, but she'd barely been a year and a half old when she'd left India, so I didn't fully believe her. I was kind of okay with having never met him. Better to not know what you were missing.

"So . . . you know James really well, huh, Sonia?"

I met Niam's eyes. They were different now, more assessing than curious. Like he was sizing me up. "I don't know about *really well*. We're in the same class and we work near each other," I said, answering without answering.

Just make it clear you're not dating.

Sadly, I had no idea how to do that, given my relative lack of experience in anyone wanting to date me ever.

"You work at the bookstore? In addition to tutoring?" Pooja beamed at me. "You're so hardworking."

Since I spent most of my life trying not to tell myself how

lazy I was for not accomplishing simple tasks, the praise was welcome. "Thank you. But I work next door at the café, actually."

"Did you hear about the hipster who burned his tongue? He sipped his coffee before it was too cool."

This time I laughed out loud first at George's terrible one-liner.

"Honey, I know this is your coping mechanism, but some of us are trying to eat." Pooja nudged her son for another roti. "Why don't you come with us tomorrow to the hospital, Sonia?"

Yikes. "Oh, no, I don't want to bother James." Imagine him waking up and seeing me there and then having to explain to him how his mom had gotten our relationship wrong? No, that was too embarrassing.

Also, he might somehow recognize you as his savior.

Oh, right, the original thing I'd been worried about when I came here.

"He won't be bothered. He'll probably be groggy. But you can talk to him, at least," Pooja insisted.

I thought of Sam. Would she go see him? Was anyone visiting him? Surely he had other close friends? "I . . . can't. I have to work after school."

"Of course. Once James is home, too, you can always visit him there."

I smiled, and I hoped it wasn't as forced as it felt. When James's family told him I'd come to the restaurant, I hoped they also made it clear I didn't know what his mom had assumed about me.

The conversation flowed for a while after that. I let them talk over each other, and my gaze slid along the wall. Photos of the Cooper kids were lined up, from baby to more recent. Over the door was a large framed photo of an older couple with a garland over it.

"Those were my parents," Pooja said, noticing my attention. "They started this restaurant."

"That's cool, that your roots run so deep."

"Yes. I was so happy we decided to move back here after law school, so we could make some more memories with them before they were gone. I'm hoping one of the boys wants to come into the business after college."

I didn't think I imagined Niam's fingers tightening on his bottle.

George's phone rang, and he grabbed it out of his pocket. He glanced at the screen, then silenced it. "Work," he responded to Pooja's questioning look. "Don't worry. Not the police."

I took a long sip of my drink. "The police?" I hoped my tone was as casual as humanly possible. "Hope everything's okay."

Pooja nodded. "Yes. Standard in these kinds of accidents. There was another witness when James fell in, one who ran away. The cops are trying to find her. Do you want more food, Sonia?"

Another witness. "No, thank you."

"Not just a witness, a hero. I would love to speak to her as well. So we can thank everyone who helped James." George took a sip of his water.

"She ran and hasn't come forward," Niam said flatly. "What does that tell you?"

That I'm wary of police, and I panicked.

"Running isn't what?" George leaned forward and cupped his ear at his son.

Niam rolled his eyes. "Running isn't a sign of guilt."

"Exactly." George pointed his fork at his son. "No matter who she is, or why she ran, she helped save your brother's life. Don't forget that."

"I'll throw her a parade," Pooja chimed in.

I guzzled the rest of my drink to hide my hot cheeks. My love of praise was very much warring with my need for secrecy.

Why do you need the secrecy? They'll be happy to know you saved their son.

Because I'd just heard them talking about the police looking for me. Kareena could be deported. I'd go into the system. The stakes were too high.

Niam got up and walked to the counter. He came back with a tray of the yellow macarons he'd made. "These'll probably taste better tomorrow, but we can have some now," he said gruffly.

I picked one up and sank my teeth into it. Oh, holy crap. The cookie almost melted on my tongue, the lingering taste of saffron and almond somehow mixing together to create heaven. "Wow," I said. It was all I could say, really.

Pooja took a delicate bite and cast her gaze upward while she chewed. "You were right, Niam. These are excellent. We can add them to the menu next month."

Niam brushed back the curl that fell over his forehead. "Oh, okay. Cool." But I could see the excitement in his eyes.

This was so . . . domestic.

The bolt of loss hit me harder than I'd expected. I was surprised it took this long to smack me across the face.

I didn't want to leave. I wanted to stay with this family.

I thought of my mom in India, and the shame for my desire nearly strangled me. *Disloyal.* "Um, I should go. It's getting late." Phone in hand, I rose to my feet and gave them all a strained smile. "Thank you so much for having me."

George placed his napkin down. His eyes were tired, but his smile was vibrant. "Thank you, Sonia."

Niam echoed his dad, though his words were a little more grudging. "Yes. Thanks. You were a big help."

"Immeasurable," Pooja said.

"You're welcome. See you all around." *Probably not, though.*

I called my ride and almost made it to the front door of the restaurant before I heard Pooja say my name. I turned around.

"Here. Take this."

One thing that Pooja and my mom had in common was giving guests too much food. I accepted the bulging bag she handed me. It had more than a few containers in it. "Oh, thanks. You didn't have to do that."

She ignored me. "I hope to see you very soon." Pooja clasped my hands together and looked down at me. Then she did something I hadn't experienced in a long while.

She hugged me. Real tight, so tight I almost couldn't breathe. "Thank you for staying," she whispered. "It was so nice to have one of James's friends here. I almost felt like he was here."

Since she wasn't letting go, I thought it was okay to slip my arms around her too and return her hug. "Thank you for having me." I hesitated. "Auntie."

She sniffed and took a step back. "Do you need me to call you a cab?"

"No, thank you, I have a car coming." I wiggled my phone.

"Very well." Pooja's gaze was warm. "I probably shouldn't say anything . . . but, well, I do know about you and my son, Sonia."

Oh no. "I don't know what you're talking about. We're only friends," I said slowly. Friends was probably a lie, too, but much less of one than the alternative.

"Right!" She hugged me again, then winked at me. "You're only friends."

Not *wink* we're only friends; we're only friends. "No, we—"

"Is that your ride?" She nodded at the parking lot.

I checked the Camry's license plate. Yes, damn it, it was mine. "Yes, but—"

"You don't want to keep them waiting."

No, and mostly because I didn't want to pay the extra waiting charges. Mentally, I threw my hands up in the air. This woman wasn't going to believe me even if I stayed longer to explain it.

I got inside the rideshare and slammed the door shut, then opened it, pulled my bag's strap out from where it had gotten caught, and shut it again. I adjusted the bag at my feet. "Sorry I made you wait," I mumbled.

"That's okay," the long-haired driver muttered back. He glanced at me in the mirror, and I instinctively stiffened. "What's your name? Sonia? Pretty name."

I slipped my fingers into the front pocket of my bag to curl around my phone, my pepper spray in easy reach. "Thanks. It was really popular the year I was born. *Sixteen* years ago."

The driver coughed and returned his gaze to the road, silence descending on the car. I may not have the highest self-esteem, but I learned quick working in the service industry that I look older than my age, and full-grown men aren't always the brightest.

My gaze slipped over the back of the leather seat in front of me. There was a stain on the headrest, a tiny thumbprint of a thing. I kept one hand on my phone and let my mind wander, misery slowly filling up the empty spaces inside me.

That hug replayed on a loop in my brain. I could pull it apart and analyze it like a math problem, dissect it like a pattern.

You didn't want to explain that you and James weren't a couple. You felt like you belonged somewhere for the first time in a long time, and you wanted to keep up the charade of belonging to someone. To a family.

Pooja's arms had been strong yet feminine. She hadn't hugged like my mom, but there had been something maternal there. . . .

Guilt stabbed through me. I wouldn't compare the two.

Just to calm my conscience, I pulled out my phone and sent a couple of heart emojis to Mama. She'd respond tomorrow.

Kareena was already home when I got there, playing video

games on the couch. She didn't greet me, and I nearly walked right past her before I thought of how it had felt to be at that dinner table, all those voices talking over each other. My house was silent now. So was my phone.

My sister hadn't even texted to see where I was after school, though I didn't have work penciled in on the calendar stuck to our old fridge. Still, I stopped. "Do you want some food?"

Kareena looked up, mild interest on her face. "What kind of food?"

"Indian." I lifted the bag of neat plastic containers.

Kareena blinked. "Where did you get it? You went out to eat?"

I tried to head off her annoyance at me wasting money that way. "No. At a friend's."

"Candice?"

Ouch. I may not have had any friends other than Candice, but she didn't have to rub it in. "No, not Candice. It's a friend whose family owns an Indian restaurant, and I helped out today, so they sent me home with food. Do you want some or not?"

The sharpness in my tone didn't seem to bother her. She turned back to her game. "Put it in the fridge. I'll eat it later."

"Okay." I carefully loaded the containers in the fridge and closed it. Then I neatly folded the bag and placed it inside the bag that held all the other plastic bags under the sink.

I went upstairs. I caught a glimpse of myself in the mirror over my closet and paused, startled. God, had I looked this awful for the entirety of my dinner with James's parents and brother? My hair was half out of the haphazard ponytail I'd stuck it in at some point during the prep work. Whatever eyeliner I'd put on in the morning was long gone, rubbed off.

But worse, I hated my clothes with a sudden, undeniable passion. The sweater I wore was too snug across my chest, smashing my breasts down. My jeans were fine, but boring. I was boring. And stuck. I'd changed over the past year. My body had grown and morphed. Why hadn't I?

I flung my closet door open. My bag o' shame in the back caught my attention. *Remember what happened the last time you felt good in something you wore? You created a giant mess.*

Okay, but surely that had been a coincidence, and I couldn't let that incident stop me from being a little less boring. I contemplated burning the damn costume, but we lived in a townhouse, not on a farm. I couldn't exactly start a fire in the garbage can and not expect it to literally blow up in my face.

I shuffled through my disorganized closet and came up with the dress I'd bought at the thrift store last week. It was a shapeless sixties housedress, but it had been $2 on clearance, and I liked the blue embroidery around the neckline.

I grabbed the big tote from under my bed. There were dozens of patterns in there, ones my mom had bought over the years, also on clearance. She was the one I got my big chest and my big hair and my love of a deal from.

She was my mother. My only mother.

I found the pattern I was looking for and laid the pieces out on the floor. It *was* disloyal to even think of enjoying being hugged by another maternal figure, wasn't it?

I heard a noise downstairs, and I went to my door. I only

meant to close it completely, but the happy murmur I heard made me curious.

I went to the stairs and looked down. I had a fairly good view into the kitchen from there.

Kareena stood in front of the fridge, holding the container of chicken. She took a bite, and her face smoothed, some of the perpetual strain disappearing.

I took a step away from the landing, feeling like I was intruding on a personal moment.

I wouldn't go back to the restaurant. It was too risky to trail around the family of the guy I was actively trying to distance myself from. If Pooja or anyone else really did believe I was James's girlfriend, then that was their problem, and one that James would surely be able to clear up when he was whole and healthy.

And if I felt bad that I'd never go over there again, that was my problem. I couldn't adopt a family. I had a family.

It was just a little fractured right now.

Seven

J ust because I'd nipped my feelings for James's family in the
bud didn't mean I couldn't still be invested in James—or
invested in my own safety. Sadly, nobody at school the next day
had any news about him, and that included Sam's socials, which
I may or may not have been stalking.

A low hum of tension ran through me for the entire day,
the threat of the cops showing up at any moment hanging over
my head. I was ready to snap by the time I got to work, especially after I found Hana and Paris huddled together behind the
counter, peering at Hana's phone.

Suspicious. They were hardly besties. "Hey, guys," I said,
tying my apron behind my back.

Hana shushed me. Her hair was pulled into a high ponytail,
and her makeup was flawless and elaborate, bright blue shadow
fading into a gradient of purple and teal and gold over her eyes.
"Someone released video of that kid who fell into the canal."

What.

My hands curled into tight fists, so tight my nails cut into my skin. I barely noticed. Without waiting for an invite, I crowded around the phone as well.

The video quality wasn't the best, from some home's grainy doorbell camera. Only the canal path lamps illuminated James, showing the second he stumbled. I held my breath as he took a step, slipped on the mud, and teetered.

James hit the water with a splash. The frame was empty, but then in came . . .

Me, running to the edge of the canal, my cape a flag of red in the wind. My mouth fell open as I watched myself launch into the water in what was probably the only graceful move I've ever accomplished in my life.

Holy moly, this all looked way more dramatic than it had felt at the time. Probably because of the cape. Capes made everything more dramatic. Okay, I'd rethink my slander of the garment.

It was actually . . . kinda cool to see it like this. Like a movie.

My origin story.

It was all there. Me and James getting pulled out of the water, the women trying to help him, me running away. I leaned closer to the phone screen. The video replayed, pausing on my back. My chest grew tight.

There wasn't much light, I tried to tell myself, and I never fully faced the camera. Half my face was covered, even if I had.

"The police are looking for her," Hana said, and I lifted my gaze at the subtle awe in her voice. "What a badass, whoever Shadow is."

"Shadow?"

"TikTok named her."

I'd been off social media for literally the hour and a half it had taken me to go home and change, and this had already hit TikTok? Long enough for people to give me a *name*?

I caught movement out of the corner of my eye and forced a smile for the customer standing there. Since Paris didn't seem to have any interest in helping him, I stepped up and took his order, my brain working in overdrive.

When he returned to his seat with his coffee refill, I went back to my coworkers, who were giving the video poster endless views. I cupped my elbow. "I'd already heard there was someone else there. This doesn't seem like that big of a deal."

"Can't believe we have our own vigilante in this sleepy little town," Paris said, and leaned against the counter. Her light brown hair was loose today, parted in the middle and carelessly wavy.

I toyed with my own hair, which I'd left down today. It had been plastered to my head in the video. Surely the wet bun wasn't an identifiable hairstyle. "Vigilante seems excessive. At best she's a witness to an accident."

"We watched this one video of a doctor who went through it frame by frame and said James probably had a seizure," Paris volunteered.

He could have. I'd only ever seen seizures in movies.

"Hopefully someone's able to identify her and the authorities can talk to her, mystery solved, everyone's life will go back to normal. Especially poor James." Paris said James's name like they were buds. As far as I knew, they'd never talked to each other.

I carefully took a step back. How to explain that if Shadow was found, it was her—me—whose life would never go back to normal again?

I had to do something. But what?

What if James recognized you from the video and has already told everyone who you are?

What if his family tells him his girlfriend came by and he's mortified they mistook you for someone he might actually date?

What if he realizes you knew his parents thought you were his girlfriend and you said nothing, thus confirming his suspicion that the occasionally frizzy-haired girl in his class had a crush on him?

Which one was more mortifying and terrible?

The first, dumbass. The first could get your sister deported.

"Are you okay?"

"Uh-huh," I managed. Except I wasn't. I felt like I was standing on a shore, post-earthquake, watching the water recede. The tsunami was coming, but I had no idea how to stop it. It was going to engulf me for sure if I didn't do something.

"You look queasy. Want some Pepto? My dad always keeps a bottle in the back office," Paris offered.

"No, I'm good." *Does your dad keep a lawyer in the back office?*

The back office.

There were cameras in the café, and on the building. The ones in the back were pointed straight at the dumpster. I'd put my costume on and then walked right out of the place in it.

If the police asked neighboring businesses for their camera

89

footage, it would take two seconds to connect the employee wearing a red cape leaving with a bag of trash and the girl in a red cape who jumped into the canal a few minutes later. Paris's dad would happily offer up my identity.

"Well, I'm going to head out." Paris untied her apron, though it was still fifteen minutes from our shift change time.

I opened my mouth, then closed it again. There was no way I could ask Paris for access to the cameras casually. But I had to get at them. "Paris, did you get a chance to adjust my hours for the shift I took for you a few days ago?" *That* day.

"Oh, no." Paris shrugged. "I'll do it tomorrow. My boyfriend's outside waiting for me."

"I can do it." I held my breath. I'd done it once before, though it was when Paris had sprained her wrist and gone overboard in using me like a servant to do her menial tasks for her.

Paris's forehead wrinkled. Changing the shifts required the computer in the office, her father's computer. As our de facto manager, Paris was the only other person with access to that. "I don't think—"

I pulled out my big guns. "Or I can call your dad and ask him to change it."

"No, no, no." Paris glanced at her phone and shuddered, like she was imagining her dad annoyed at her. I'd be annoyed too, if I paid my daughter to manage my store and she wandered off to go to parties with literal kids. "You can do it." She leaned forward and whispered in my ear. "The password is ParistheBeautiful!, uppercase *P*, uppercase *B*, exclamation point at the end."

Of course it was. "Got it."

After Paris left, I addressed Hana. "Can you cover the register for a minute? I'll just do that before my shift officially starts."

"Sure, but I'm not really supposed to work the registers anymore after what happened yesterday."

Oh lord. "What happened yesterday?"

"I made a customer cry." Hana furrowed her brow, like she didn't understand how one lady's tears were her fault. "I didn't mean to. She kept leaning over the register and yelling at me, and I finally told her to back off because I could feel her spit in my eyeballs and her breath smelled."

Legend. I might still be miffed at Hana calling me a mouse, but this was cool. How many entitled customers had I wanted to tell off over the past year, and here was Hana casually mocking a woman's spittle. "She started crying?"

"Immediately. Paris took her side. She said we're lucky we're understaffed, or I'd be fired." Hana didn't sound like she cared much about that. "Underpaid, more like it."

"So . . . you can handle the register?" I ventured.

"Yeah. I'll try not to make anyone cry."

That wasn't really a ringing note of confidence, but I didn't have time to worry about that when I had evidence to destroy.

I went to the back office. Paris's dad was disorganized at best, but it wasn't my place to tell the mostly absent owner how to run a business.

I changed my hours, then clicked around the computer and thanked God it was simple enough, because a hacker I wasn't. I

91

found the right archived footage quickly, cringing at the sight of myself prancing blithely along in my costume. Luckily, the back camera was poorly angled, and only caught me leaving the café, and not running to help James.

Nonetheless, I deleted everything. Then I jumped up from the desk like it was on fire. Was what I'd just done illegal?

You can't be worried about that now. It's done.

As if to underscore the finality of my actions, the office door closed behind me with a thud as I left. My face was hot. I needed a second before I returned to Hana, or she'd be able to tell that I'd just done something shady.

I went to the bathroom and entered a stall. The door to the restroom banged open, and two pairs of feet came into view. "If one more person asks me if I'm going to see him soon, I'll scream." The speaker's voice was thick with annoyance, but that didn't totally disguise it.

I stiffened and raised my head. Aw, jeez, I was the queen of bad luck.

One of the people walked into the stall next to mine. I stared at the wall separating us. "I know. I'm sorry."

"My dad doesn't even have a Facebook account, and he texted me to ask about *that guy* I used to date. Ugh, it's embarrassing, Candy."

Candice. *Candy.* My hands curled into fists. I don't know why I was so annoyed that Samantha called her Candy now, but I was.

He's still hung up on Samantha.

Why wouldn't James be hung up on Basic Barbie? My best

friend had been hung up on her.

You're being irrational. You can't feel so angry that Candice stopped talking to you and went back to her. It's not Samantha's fault.

Candice flushed her toilet and opened the stall door. "You have nothing to be embarrassed about."

I could only catch a glimpse of a beige wool coat between the slats. It was Candice's coat. She'd bought it two springs ago on sale, I'd been with her. She'd had a crush on the girl working the register at the store. We'd gone into that boutique multiple times, just so Candice could flirt with her.

After she'd bought the coat, we'd sat in the food court and debriefed, analyzing whether the woman had smiled at Candice a beat longer than necessary.

I stared at the tile between my feet and wiggled my toes in my Converse. She'd probably been with me when I got these shoes, too.

"I can't help how I feel. It would be different if we were still dating. . . ." Sam turned the water on, muffling whatever else she said.

Candice clucked. "Come on, why don't we go home? I know you said you'd feel better with a mocha, but there's too many people who know you here."

"No. No." Sam took a shaky breath. "Didn't you see the girl at the register?"

Me?

"I forget her name, but Gerald felt sorry for her 'cause she was new and invited her to my house at the beginning of the year. She hooked up with him and wouldn't take his calls the next day. I made one little post about it, and she got all bent out of shape, confronted me at school."

Not me. She must be talking about Hana.

"Sam, what did I say about these videos?" Candice sounded disappointed in Sam, which gave me some hope that the girl I used to know was still in her somewhere.

"Not all of us can be on a phone diet or whatever."

"It's a social media fast, and just because I'm not chronically online, doesn't mean I don't know what you're posting."

"I didn't use her name! No one would have known it was her or Gerald if she hadn't stomped up to my locker the next day and told me I was a bitch. Also, I took it down, which you know I never do. Only a few hundred views on it anyway."

Gross. I didn't think I'd seen that video, but I felt a moment of sympathy for Hana. Even with names stripped, it must have been jarring. A few hundred views was obviously nothing to Sam, but my skin crawled at even a hundred strangers thinking about me.

"Ugh, Sam," Candice echoed my thoughts.

"You know how loyal I am."

"You are loyal, but you take it too far." There was a hint of amusement and admiration in Candice's voice, and it made me want to leap over the stall door and confront her.

First I'd pull up my pants, though.

Loyal? What did Candice know about being loyal? Candice and I used to joke about being ride or die. Then my mom had gotten deported.

I tried not to think about that day very much, mostly because

94

so much of it was blank in my mind, which scared me. The parts that weren't came in flashes of emotions more than memories.

Like the weird feeling I'd had when my mom hadn't picked up when I'd phoned to tell her I'd be staying late at school. Or how panicked Kareena had been when I'd finally gotten home and Mama was missing. Or how that panic had made it hard to breathe, had left me curled into a ball in my room, leaving Kareena to take charge and figure everything out.

Mama hadn't even been the target of the raid at the dry cleaner's where she worked. She'd just been a lucky extra nab for them.

I do remember seeing Candice later that week and sobbing my heart out. She'd comforted me and told me everything would be all right. We'd talked for a long time, and I'd finally fallen asleep after telling her everything, save for my fears that Kareena would be next.

I didn't hear from her again. I didn't notice for a while—I'd missed classes, trying to figure out where Mama would be and what we'd do next. Kareena couldn't go visit the detainment facility, for obvious reasons, so I'd accompanied our mom's friend. I'd hated it so much I'd had to read up on ways to mitigate panic attacks, because the last thing I wanted to do was fall apart in front of my visibly scared mom.

Immigration cases don't get legal aid. The attorney my mom had hired the previous year to try to sort out our situation had disappeared, with the thousands in savings she'd given him. We were only able to scrape together enough for a cheap lawyer, who advised Mama that it would be better to voluntarily deport, that it would preserve some of her rights.

With the benefit of time to scour the internet, we'd realized she might have been better off with a court trial with a good attorney, but by then she was already gone. As it was, though, I only had a month or so with her before she left. And when I reached out to Candice, she didn't answer. Phone calls, texts, she was Casper.

And now she was complimenting someone else on their loyalty?

"I only take it as far as I need to, to protect my friends. Come on, I don't want that girl to think I'm scared of her," Sam said. The door slammed shut behind them. I left the stall and washed my hands. I splashed some cold water on my face, and it felt heavenly against my hot cheeks. "Pull yourself together," I whispered to myself in the mirror. The anger, jealousy, and worry weren't a good mix for decision-making.

Case in point: when I walked out of the bathroom and saw Hana helping Sam at the counter, my brain snapped.

Candice wasn't there, and maybe I should have taken a beat to wonder where she was. Instead, I strode up in time to hear Sam say, "Hana, right? Gerald says hi, by the way."

That bitch.

I didn't know what had gone down with Hana and Gerald, I barely knew who Gerald was, and Hana wasn't exactly my favorite person, but I wasn't about to have anyone, especially this demon girl, throwing a hookup in my coworker's face. I nudged Hana aside and accepted the iced coffee and tea she had ready. "I can take over now, thanks."

Hana's eyes were downcast. Timid wasn't a good look for her, and it made me even angrier. I spoke to Sam. "Hi. This is yours?" I checked the cups. My voice hitched on the first one, because I knew who it was for. "Mint green tea and an iced brown sugar coffee with three pumps of pumpkin, two pumps of cinnamon, oat milk, a caramel drizzle, and pumpkin pie spice on top?" One of those annoying viral drinks that were the bane of our existence.

Sam's blue eyes left Hana, like she was wistful about the fact that she hadn't gotten to take her bad mood out on the new girl. She turned to me. She was conventionally gorgeous, dressed in pink and white, her pale cheeks flushed, her long blonde hair falling on either side of her face in perfect curtains. "Yeah." Samantha reached out for her coffee.

I shouldn't have done what I did next. But I told myself it was in solidarity with Hana. And a little bit for my own personal satisfaction.

I handed the coffee to Sam and let go a split second too soon. The plastic cup slipped and hit the counter, a wave of iced coffee rising up and slapping against Sam's pink cashmere sweater, though sadly her Patagonia vest took the brunt of the liquid.

"Watch it!"

"Oh my God. I am so sorry." I pulled out a stack of napkins and handed them to her, and then grabbed a rag from under the counter to mop up the mess.

"You should be. Do you have any idea how much this sweater costs?"

Uh-oh. Genuine worry pierced my rage. "Um."

"More than you make, and I'll want it replaced."

A twenty materialized in front of me, and I followed it to Hana's hand. "The stain will come out with some dry cleaning. Here. It's on me."

Sam swatted at Hana's twenty, and it was only my coworker's quick reflexes that prevented her from getting slapped. "I can afford my own dry cleaning, thank you."

"Then there's nothing to worry about, is there? This is a minor inconvenience for you." Hana braced her hand on the counter.

"I want to speak to your manager."

"She's the manager," Hana said casually.

I almost looked behind me for Paris, and then I realized Hana was talking about me. "Oh, um. Yes. I am." I mean, I had the password to the computer. I'd doctored the video footage. Standard managerial duties.

"I—"

"What's going on?"

I froze. Candice came to stand next to Sam. She'd always been pretty, with her healthy brown curls, heart-shaped face, and doe eyes, but she'd upgraded her wardrobe since she'd upgraded her friend. The dark jeans and sweater were designer. "Sonia. Hi. I . . . didn't know you worked here."

It was the first time she'd addressed me in six months, and it only made me more furious. *What is wrong with you? Calm down.* "Hey," I said, as shortly as possible.

"It's good to see you."

Liar.

Sam pursed her lips. "Wait a minute. I know you." She looked between me and Candice. "You two hung out a little last year, right?"

And the year before that and the year before that.

The fact that Samantha didn't know made me angrier. Was I that invisible, that she didn't even know who her childhood friend had been besties with for years?

At least you know Candice hasn't been talking about you to her.

"Yeah," Candice said. "It's been a while."

"A while, yes," I added woodenly. *Whose fault is that?*

Candice's gaze lingered on my face for so long, I thought the tension in my body would give an audible snap. What was she thinking?

Perhaps she's thinking of a red scrap of fabric you left somewhere on her property.

I mentally slapped myself. Crap. With all the emotions from seeing her again, I'd almost forgotten about that piece of evidence.

If she did find it, how long would it take Candice to connect James's savior to the torn piece of fabric in her yard? Especially with that new video?

My knees almost buckled.

Perhaps she already knew, despite her phone fast, and she'd been quiet for the last couple of days for reasons known only to her. Maybe now was the moment, with her new best friend at her side, that she'd choose to announce that I was the mysterious girl who had saved James. *Shadow.*

And then she'd go one step further and tell everyone that my mom was gone.

Candice's gaze slid right off me, like water droplets on oil, and went to Sam. "Is there some kind of problem?"

Sam took a deep breath and shook her hair out. A switch flipped, and I wondered if this was the switch that she used to get into character for when she went live or posted videos. It was like a more humanlike mask slipped over her angry face. "No, no problem. We had a little accident, but . . . Sonia? Sonia apologized. In fact, she's comping our drinks." She gave me a tight smile that might have fooled Candice but not me. "Such good customer service."

Ugh. If Paris caught me comping drinks due to my own error, she'd take it out of my pay. But it wasn't like I had much of a choice. There were only three other customers in the place, and at least one of them was a regular, who had seen the entire incident. If Sam made a scene, Paris would also be pissed about that.

The bell over the door jingled. Strike that: four other customers.

It was only a desire to be away from this group that made me look over. For a second, my heart got lodged in my throat at the tall, dark, and lean boy standing in the open doorway, taking stock of the place. What on earth was Niam doing here?

Oh no. What if he talked about me being James's girl-friend . . . in front of his actual ex-girlfriend?

Black spots danced in front of my eyes. Time slowed to a crawl.

"Hello . . ." Sam snapped her fingers in front of my eyes. "Are you paying attention to me?"

"Yes. Of course." I quickly typed my employee code into the computer. "The amount will be refunded to your card."

Sam tossed her head and glanced over her shoulder, then did a double take. "Niam?" she breathed.

Niam's gaze arrowed over to us. His dark eyes met mine, and I grabbed hold of the counter to steady myself as he walked over.

He nodded at me, then looked at her. "Sam. You got some coffee on your shirt."

Her eye twitched. The rest of us forgotten, she waved her hand. "Gosh, I know, I'm just so clumsy, can't take me any-where."

How quirky of her.

"How are you? How's your brother?" Sam placed her hand on her chest. "I'm a positive wreck, so worried about him. I tried to go by the hospital today, but your mom said he was sleeping."

"He's good. Stable. Nothing to worry about. We're trying to limit his visitors right now, yeah, to family."

Pooja hadn't let her see James? After the family had invited me to the hospital? Well.

Well, well, well, well, well, well.

Sam pursed her lips. "I mean, I'm hardly a stranger. James and I are extremely close."

How close?

Niam shrugged. "If you want to talk to him, you can text

him. He'll probably be discharged tomorrow."

Before Sam could reply, Hana shoved the girl's replacement iced coffee over the counter. "Here you go, Sam."

Candice put her hand on Samantha's arm and picked up her tea. "Come on, I got us a table outside."

"I'd rather go home." Sam gave Hana and me pointed, angry glances, and picked up her coffee. "I'll talk to you soon, Niam. Tell James everyone at school is dying to see him again."

My former friend gave me one last unreadable look, but I had no idea what the meaningful eye contact meant. That she was waiting to spill the beans? That she was going to keep mum? That she had no idea who I was? It was pretty annoying that a person who hated me enough to drop me cold knew at least one, but possibly two huge, damaging secrets about me.

The anger and jealousy leaked out of me quickly, like a punctured balloon, as the girls left, but I couldn't slump, not with Niam right there. "Hey," I managed. Hana bustled away, probably assuming I could handle this new customer without spilling his drink on him.

"Hi." He watched Sam leave, then turned to me. "Sorry. That must have been weird for you."

"Why?"

Niam cast me a strange look. "She kept talking about James. And they used to date."

And you're supposed to be dating him. I rubbed the side of my nose. The last thing I wanted to do was get into this with Niam. Pooja hadn't believed me when I said James and I were just friends. I doubted Niam would now, and even if he did, Hana might overhear and then it would become a thing. "It's not a big deal. What can I get you?" Perhaps he was only here to grab a coffee or talk to his brother's boss next door.

He squinted at the menu above me. He wore more black today—a black hoodie that had faded to a dark gray and a black puffer jacket. His jeans were dark blue, though. They fit like a glove. Not that I was looking. It was an observable fact, like the grass being green or Sam being the spawn of Satan. "What's good here?"

I asked my usual question for indecisive customers. "Classic or viral?"

"Are those my two choices?"

"Lately, yes."

"What's the difference?"

"Viral is stuff that may or may not taste disgusting but looks good. Classic is what's on the menu."

Niam nodded at the baked goods. "What about the desserts?"

"The cookies are my favorite," I confessed.

"Oatmeal raisin?"

I couldn't help but wrinkle my nose. "Only when I hate myself. Raisins are depressed chocolate chips."

He chuckled. It was a nice chuckle, a low, throaty one. "I'll take a chocolate chip, then."

I grabbed the chocolate chip cookie and stuck it into a sleeve, then rang him up. He paid with his credit card, then reached into his jacket pocket. I wasn't sure what I expected, but it wasn't the envelope he pulled out from there. "Here you go."

"What's this?" I found a check inside, made out to me.

"Pay for working yesterday. I found your full name in my brother's school directory. Hope that's okay."

"Um, that's fine." The check was a decent one, more than I'd ever made in one shift at the café. "But I can't accept this when your mom already fed me dinner." I was supremely conscious of Hana wandering around behind me in earshot.

"I'm under strict orders not to come back home with it, so you can either cash it or tear it up."

Like I could ever tear up money. I folded the check and tucked it into my pocket. "Thanks. And thank your mom."

"I've also been told to tell you you have a job whenever you want it."

My mouth opened. "Oh."

"Yeah." He drummed his fingers on the counter. He had really long elegant fingers, like a musician. "Waitstaff, kitchen, whatever."

"Cool. Well . . . I'd have to see if I could swing another job." As much as I disliked Paris, there were benefits to having a mostly apathetic boss. Unlikely that I'd be able to erase security footage around Pooja.

"Great." He stuffed his hands into his pockets. "Also, I wanted to apologize . . . again. My mom pointed out that I was kind of huffy with you yesterday. The truth is, I got embarrassed over the mistake I made, thinking you were someone else. If you felt like I was short, I'm sorry."

My shoulders lowered. "That's the second apology you've given me."

His smile was slow and lit his eyes up. "I'm hoping it won't be an ongoing thing."

"I hope so, too. Thanks. I appreciate you saying that." We didn't really apologize in my family. Even my mom, on the few times she'd unfairly snapped at me, used to simply bring me fruit a few hours later. This was refreshing. "There was no need to be embarrassed, though. I was happy to help."

"Then cash the check." He slid the cookie back to me. "That's for you. I hate chocolate chip."

I stood there holding the cookie and watched him leave.

"Damn, that was smooth."

I jumped and turned around to find Hana. "Um."

"That's the brother of the canal kid? The one who works next door?"

"Yeah."

Her dark gaze switched to me. Surely she'd heard everything, including about the check, but she didn't question me, which was nice.

I automatically accepted the new apron Hana handed me. "What's this?"

"You got some coffee on yours."

"Oh." I looked down at the apron, which had indeed gotten a splash of coffee on it. I quickly changed.

"Thank you."

I paused at the sincerity in Hana's tone. My coworker was fiddling with the broken clasp on the pastry display. "For what?"

"For shutting Samantha up."

"I don't know what you're talking about. The spill was an

accident." And I only wished I'd been so noble as to only lose my temper over the way she'd talked down to Hana and not my own anger over her relationships with James and Candice.

"Right. An accident." Hana rocked back on her low boots. She wore a slouchy neon green dress. "Her friend invited me to a party the first week of school. He cornered me and was pushing me for more than I wanted to give. I asked him to get me a drink, left, and ghosted him. And then Sam posted a video about it. She said I, like, broke his heart."

I winced. Hana recited what had happened without inflection, but that sort of situation would have been rough for anyone. To have it happen on your first week at a new school, all the way across the country from everyone you knew, would have been devastating for me. "I'm sorry."

"Did you see it?" Hana's fingers twisted together. "The video?"

I gentled my voice. "No."

"She took it down after I yelled at her. But she also told me she could say anything she wanted, and people would believe her, not me. Which is probably true."

How interesting that Sam had conveniently left that part out when she'd explained the situation to Candice. "Samantha's . . ."

"A caricature of a mean girl, I know."

Surely she had some redeeming qualities. She had to have some, or Candice wouldn't be friends with her.

Or, or, or, you're such a crappy person, that she'd rather hang out with someone who's only mildly crappy. I shushed my insecurities.

Hana looked around the almost empty café, a calculating expression on her face. "Do you ever feel like we're all just playing a role?"

I adopted a breezy, bored tone to match hers. "Totally," I agreed, even though I had no idea what she was talking about. "Uh, what's my role?"

She studied me. "I don't know yet. You're weird."

I deflated. "Oh."

"I thought you were aggressively passive, but now I'm wondering if you're passively aggressive."

I paused. Neither of those sounded good. "Um."

"I don't think it's a bad thing to be weird. I'm kind of obsessed with that."

I perked up. "Oh?"

"Weird people are interesting." She took a sip from her water bottle. "Back to work, I guess. Did you get your hours taken care of?"

The hours, right. The reason I'd gotten the computer password. "Yes." Among other things.

Hana stared at me, her gaze laser sharp. "That's a nice shirt."

I looked down at myself. I'd thought about turning that striped cotton sixties housedress into a better dress, but instead I'd upcycled the material into a shirt. I'd cropped the hem so it ended at the waistband of my pants, and added loose long sleeves from the discarded material. It wasn't the best project I'd ever done, but it hadn't taken me very long.

And more important, it was different. My jeans might still be boring, but I was wearing something, anything of interest.

Better than being a person of interest. "Thanks."

"I owe you. Maybe I can buy you lunch sometime."

"You don't have to do that."

She cocked her head. "My mom caught my dad cheating on her with my stepbrother's violin teacher."

My mouth opened, though I was unsure how to respond to that.

"Also, my dad invented a chip that's used in most fast-food self-pay kiosks. Between his job and the guilt money she got in the divorce, I do okay, is what I'm saying. I'd pay a lot more to see Samantha soaked in coffee." Hana nodded at a customer who walked in. "Try not to drop a drink on this guy." Her smile was a ghost, but there. "Unless I hate them, in which case go for it."

chapter Eight

Heroes aren't born, they're made. Made of building blocks of matter, arranged in a certain, precious way.

My matter's arrangement isn't static anymore. One minute I'm me. The next I'm you.

Become a hero, they say. Nice in theory, using these powers for good. How am I supposed to do that when I can't even get a handle on them?

I need answers, and there's only one person who can help me now. The one who made me.

The knock on my door had me snapping my book closed. Focusing on *Makeshift* had been easier this morning. Probably because the shape-shifting girl's struggle to contain her newfound power was less stressful than my current life. "Yeah?" I called out, though Kareena opened the door before I could finish the word.

"You're up."

I rose up on my elbow. It was odd that I was alert this early. It usually took five alarms for me to barely make it in time for school, and last night, I'd barely slept. I'd been too busy scrolling through every social media app I had.

What might have been a minor local news story over the weekend had turned into a national and international one with the release of the video. The internet loved visual aids. I was everywhere, cropped, written on, enlarged, sharpened, hashtagged.

> Get you a girl who dives into water to save you
>
> Who is this mystery woman
>
> She's a runner
>
> Does she have a GoFundMe?
>
> She's definitely trafficking kids. The others scared her off.

Even the compliments had stirred panic in my brain. When the sun rose and my eyes had hurt too much from the screen, I'd switched to reading my comic book.

Kareena glanced around the room. She held a red shirt in her hands. "I need to use the sewing machine."

"Oh . . . sure." I nodded at my desk. The big Singer dominated the space. "Did you rip it?" I asked, because I felt like I had to.

"This has gotten too big. I wanted to wear it tomorrow." She plugged the machine in and threaded the needle.

"That's a white thread in there," I said.

"So?"

I came to a seated position and checked that my shirt still covered my injury. I'd taken the bandage off last night, and the healing scar was way too big and noticeable for bare arms anytime soon. "So there's red thread in the box, if you want."

She shook her head. "It's not that big a deal."

Okay, that was fine. I cracked my neck when she missed the shuttle on the threading apparatus. That was also fine.

"You doing SAT studying?"

I gently tried to push *Makeshift* under my pillow. No need for Kareena to have the chance to mock my reading material. "I've done some," I said noncommittally.

Why was it that Kareena only talked to me when she was checking up on me? Couldn't we have a conversation where she wasn't making sure I was constantly on the straight and narrow?

"You're using the books I used, right?"

"Yup." They were here . . . somewhere.

She put the fabric under the presser foot and didn't lower it. I almost jackknifed out of bed, but the machine refused to move when she pressed the pedal, and she figured it out, snapping the foot down. "I got a perfect score using those prep materials. It's worth it."

My belly sank. I would not have a perfect score, probably. I was good at math and English, but I was perfectly average in every way.

Kareena muttered a curse and picked up her shirt, but it was attached to the machine, the thread from the bobbin knotting under it. "What the hell?"

This time I did come to my feet. "It's not threaded right. It does this sometimes." I walked over to her and gently tugged on the shirt, then grabbed the tiny scissors from the drawers I'd set up next to it. I carefully cut the shirt free. "Do you want me to do it?"

"You know how to take a shirt in?"

I tried not to bristle at the doubt in her tone. Of course she was skeptical. As far as she was concerned, I was incompetent at everything. "Yeah."

She rose to her feet. It took me a couple of minutes to re-thread the machine, because I would not be using white thread on a red shirt.

"When did you learn how to do this?" she asked.

"I remember from watching Mama." I glanced over at her. She was lying where I had been a few minutes ago, on the bottom bunk.

Déjà vu. Reality split into two timelines, one where Mama hadn't been deported, where the lawyer she'd hired hadn't vanished, where we'd managed to find a way to keep our family together.

Maybe that reality would look like this. Both of us still sharing a room, hanging out while my mom bustled around the kitchen or watched TV downstairs. Kareena would be in college, instead of busting her ass working multiple jobs.

We'd never been the kind of siblings who could tell each other anything. Kareena might be close in age to me, but I'd always viewed her as a semi-authority figure, and I think she saw me as a child. She'd come out to me and my mom when she was fifteen, but she'd definitely never told me about girls she was into, and I'd saved my giggling over crushes for friends like Candice.

But we'd been friendly. She'd been in and out of the hospital, and I'd been in and out of hospital waiting rooms for the first twelve and ten years of our lives, respectively. We'd learned to spend a lot of time together playing quietly. "Do you remember the planes that would fly over our place in Ohio?" I blurted out.

She rolled over onto her side. "Yes. You were so scared of them when we were little."

We'd lived in that apartment for four years. For the first half of our stay there, Kareena had been ill, still a few years away from the bone marrow donor who would put her in remission. She hadn't been very strong physically, but I'd trusted her to protect me, and I used to crawl into her bed as soon as the lights turned out.

Part of me wished we'd never come to New York. I understood the practicalities of us needing health insurance and a good job, but we'd been so happy in Ohio. And maybe if we hadn't come here, Mama wouldn't have been deported, and that second more unified reality could have—

Nope. Don't do that.

I took in either side of the shirt. Though she hadn't asked me to, I also eyeballed it and fixed the arms.

When I was done, I swiveled around in my chair. "Here you go."

She dropped *Makeshift* like she was ashamed to have been caught reading it. "Thanks." She held on for a second longer when she took the shirt from me. "Why'd you ask about the planes?"

"No reason."

She nodded slowly. "You might want to do some laundry. Something smells musty in here."

I hid my flinch. After she left, my attention reluctantly went to my closet. I'd avoided looking at the thing for days, dressing in the wrinkled clothes I jammed into my dresser. Master procrastinator, that was me.

I went to the bifold doors, inching them open. A couple of things tumbled off the too-packed top shelf, but I paid them no mind. I reached into the very back and yanked out the bag I'd stuffed there.

I wrinkled my nose at the mildew-ish smell, but brought the costume to the bed and laid it out. I couldn't believe that just four days ago I'd had such a childish plan to . . . what? Seduce my crush with my perfect seams and clever bodice construction?

I knew I should have come up with a safe way to destroy the evidence, but I couldn't quite bring myself to do it. As long as it was in my possession, I felt like I could exert some control over the situation. That was probably a silly thought, but those were all I had these days.

I checked the time. I had a good hour before school still. I grabbed a bunch of my other clothes for camouflage, threw everything in the wash downstairs, and flopped onto the couch while the cycle began. I'd camp out here till it was done. No way I was risking Kareena switching the load over to the dryer. For one, she'd bitch about having to do it. Second, how did I know she hadn't seen the video and wouldn't recognize my costume from it?

Just like James might.

Sadly, there was no way to confirm that he'd keep mum, or at the very least, not fan the flames of discovering my identity.

You could text him. You have his number. How he responds might be a good indicator of whether he knows it was you.

That was some anxious pestering, though.

I opened his name in my messages. I couldn't possibly do this. Right?

Hey, James, it's Sonia. Heard about your accident—

No, no, no, of course I'd heard about the accident. He'd know everyone had, especially if he had his phone on him.

Hey, your brother said you're coming home soon—

No, then I'd have to explain in detail everything I knew about his brother.

It's Sonia. I would very much appreciate it if you could go back to forgetting my existence for the time it takes for this to blow over.

Ha, no.

Hey, it's Sonia. Hope you're doing well and that you'll be back at school soon.

I hit send and slapped my hand over my mouth, though I had typed instead of spoken.

Who's aggressively passive now?

Ugh, why had I done that? I should have—

My phone chimed and my breath stopped in my throat. Oh no oh no oh no.

I picked up my phone like it was a snake about to bite me. His words were right there, in a green bubble. **Sonia who?**

Aghhhhhhhhhhhhhhhh.

My heart attack only lasted a few seconds, though, because another bubble popped up. **Just kidding. Of course I know who you are.**

I tried not to read a secret, hidden meaning into those words.

Another bubble. Oh, he was one of those type-in-multiple-texts people.

Thanks for checking in. Going home today. Probably won't be at school for a few.

I bit my lip and typed. **SO glad to hear you're well.** Okay. This was calm and nice. He didn't know anything. Right? Right?

The three dots indicating his typing appeared, then disappeared. Then they appeared again.

Disappeared again.

WHAT, JAMES?

Another green bubble. **Probably best if we talk soon.**

I slid off the couch. Fuck.

Sleeping in school wasn't something I did on the regular. In fact, I'd never done it; I was too desperate for teacher approval. But then again, I'd never tried to function on twenty minutes of sleep before.

The bell rang and jerked me out of my doze. I slowly gathered up my stuff as everyone scurried, all of them eager to get out of our last class of the day. I'd take a nap when I got home. I needed it before I tried to formulate a response to James's ominous text.

Who texted any variation of *we need to talk* with no further elaboration? A sociopath?

A pen dropped onto my desk and I blinked blearily and looked next to me. Hana. I'd known she was in my English class, but we'd never acknowledged each other. She usually sat in the back.

"I needed a pen, so I took yours while you slept," she said.

I tried not to look too embarrassed, but I failed. "Oh."

"You working today?"

"Um, no. I'm off. Paris actually cut my hours this week." I was supposed to get at least three shifts, but that always depended on Paris's whims.

"Okay." She zipped her bag. "I would have offered you a ride, if so."

"That's . . . that's nice of you." Too nice. Surely she wasn't ready to be my friend now, just because I'd spilled a little coffee on Sam?

I didn't know how I felt about that. I hadn't been in the market for any new friends, especially ones who had called me a mouse less than a week ago.

She leaned closer. Her hair was pinned up on the side of her face today, revealing a shaved undercut. "Word to the wise, next time you nap, put your head forward and let your curls cover your eyes. If I had that much hair, no one would ever catch me sleeping."

Before I could answer, Ms. Hawley's voice chimed in from the front of the room. "Ms. Patil? Can I see you?"

Hana grimaced at me. "Good luck."

I gathered up my stuff more slowly, dreading this conversation. Once most everyone had left, I walked up to my teacher's desk, backpack in hand. "Yes, hi," I said.

"I noticed you were distracted in class today," Ms. Hawley said. Normally she was reservedly friendly to me, but there was a bite in her tone now.

I flushed. Hana was right. I should have used my hair to hide my face. I'd been too tired to do it right. "I'm sorry."

"I expect better of you, Sonia. This isn't like you."

I jerked back and turned cold. I hated being told by an adult that I'd fallen short of their expectations. Damn it, I was going to turn her words over in my head for days, taking away from the quarters of self-esteem in my mental bank. "Yes, ma'am," I echoed.

She played with a pencil. She was a younger teacher, and she leaned into the role of being a cool adult, though she definitely tended to play favorites with the more popular kids in class. "Part of being in school is learning to be a grown-up," she lectured.

That . . . made no sense. I had to learn how to be a grown-up and grown-ups never took naps? As far as I could tell, grown-ups regularly took naps! Arguably, I needed a nap more than they did. My brain was still growing.

Why isn't she asking me if something is wrong? Sleeping in class is so uncharacteristic for me, right? She could ask.

Not her job, even if a teacher like Mr. Walsh would have been more concerned than irritated. She was my teacher, not my therapist. It wasn't her job to make sure I wasn't being hunted by the internet or getting foreboding texts from a guy I'd rescued.

"I know we all have off days and stress outside of school, but if you're not feeling well, it would probably be best to see the nurse instead of napping in class, okay?"

I scuffed my shoe. What would the nurse do, call my mom? "Yes, ma'am."

"Good." She turned back to her computer. "Have a good afternoon."

I left quietly, trying not to let my annoyance show in my footsteps. I was mostly annoyed at myself, which was probably the worst kind of annoyance to have.

I tried to shake it off as I got my things from my locker and headed home. There were still gossiping knots in the hallway, but no sign of Sam, thank God. The last thing I wanted to see was her smug, eight-hours-of-sleep, well-rested face.

I hated taking the bus home, but it was quicker than walking. What I wouldn't give for a car of my own.

We should talk.

Should we talk? Probably. Did I want to? No.

I got off at my stop and walked to my front door. As soon as I opened it, I stopped.

Things had changed while I was at school. The place was spotless, a blanket folded neatly over the back of the couch, fresh vacuum marks in the carpet. We weren't slobs, especially with Kareena around, but we weren't this clean. I sniffed the air and closed the door. Was that a candle?

Kareena came out of the kitchen and did a double take. "Thank God you're home."

I almost looked behind me, but she was definitely talking to me. "Um, hi."

"Where the hell have you been? I've been texting you for hours. Mom said she texted you too."

My hand dropped to my bag. "I had my phone off." I hadn't wanted to see any further texts from James.

Kareena inhaled, and I half expected to see smoke fly out of her nostrils when she exhaled. "Are you kidding me? Have you not learned yet that it's important to be reachable?" She took a step forward. "What if something happened to me? What would you do? How would I contact you, Sonia?"

"I—I don't know." Fear bloomed inside me. "Did something happen? Is everything okay?"

She bit her lip and closed her eyes. It looked like she was counting to herself. "Divya is coming."

Some of the tension melted out of me. Our aunt, visiting from Cleveland. "Oh. Mama said she was coming this week."

Kareena raked her hand through her hair. "And you didn't think to tell me?"

"I assumed she told you." My mom usually talked to us separately. There wasn't enough communication between Kareena and me for us to talk to each other.

I put my bag on the ground and she snatched it up and shoved it into my hands. "Go put this upstairs. And clean your room."

"You think she's going to come in here and inspect our bedrooms?" I asked. I didn't mean to be sarcastic, but . . . really.

"I don't—"

The doorbell rang, and we both froze. "I think she's here," I whispered.

Kareena shooed me aside and looked through the peephole.

She set her shoulders and opened the door, a smile fixed on her face. "Divya Aunti—oof."

"My girls!" A sturdy woman careened through the door, tossing her bag on the floor and wrapping Kareena up in a hug. Divya Auntie had been one of my mom's first and best friends in America. She'd been a visa overstay, too, but she'd been lucky enough to find a path to citizenship through a job.

Despite her good luck, Divya hadn't forgotten my mom. She'd been the one who had organized the local temple twice to find Kareena a compatible blood marrow donor, and who had found my mom a job with private health insurance, the holy grail for undocumented folk who couldn't get on state health insurance. When that job had fallen through, she was the one who had helped us research our options.

She'd also been the first one we'd called when Mama had been arrested. Unfortunately, her husband had just been laid off then, so she hadn't been able to spare much money, and there hadn't been enough time for her to rally the rest of the community. Afterward, though, she had made sure our rent was reduced, and offered to let us come live with her as long as we liked. There was no doubt in my mind that if we'd stayed local to her, she would have been able to do a lot more to help us.

So I really had no idea why Kareena was so freaked out about her coming to visit.

Divya Auntie released Kareena and beamed at me. "Come here, my love!"

This hug felt different from Pooja's. I didn't feel guilty about this hug, possibly because Divya was our mother's friend.

She pulled back and looked between us. "My girls," she repeated. "How nice it is to see you."

"It's good to see you," I said, and Kareena murmured the same.

She pulled away and looked around, bright eyes curious. She'd always reminded me of a plump sparrow, and not only because of her tendency to choose floaty brown fabrics. "The house looks nice," she exclaimed. She drifted into the living room. "A little bare on decoration, yes? But of course you two poor girls have had so much on your minds to worry about that. Are the bedrooms upstairs?"

Kareena shot me a dirty look. "Um, yes, they are. Do you want some chai, Auntie?"

We had chai?

Divya Auntie touched a framed photo of us on the side table. It had been taken when Kareena and I were in middle school, at an Easter egg hunt in the park. My dress was torn and dirty, my rabbit ears askew. Kareena had been picture perfect, the shawl wrapped around her head neatly tied. Both of us had our arms around our mom's neck. I hadn't seen that photo in months, but then again, I hadn't seen the surface of that table in months. It was usually covered in junk mail Kareena hadn't gotten around to tossing out.

Auntie didn't precisely inspect her fingers for dust, but she did rub them together. "Yes, chai would be nice."

Kareena jerked her head at me meaningfully when our aunt's back was turned. "Um, I'm just going to go put my bag away,"

I said, like that was something I actually ever did.

I ran upstairs and put my bag under my desk. I made my bed in record time, then shoved as much stuff as I could under it. The laundry I'd washed that morning got tossed in the closet. With one arm, I swept everything on my desk into my drawers. A couple of spools and bobbins went awry, but they were too small to be noticed, even by an eagle-eyed auntie.

I glanced around. It wasn't the cleanest bedroom I'd ever seen, but it was okay. Surely it would pass muster, on the chance Divya Auntie did come up here.

I jogged back downstairs in time to find Kareena handing Divya Auntie a mug. "If I'd known you only had Lipton tea bags, I would have brought you some Wagh Bakri from home," she was lecturing my sister.

"You've already brought us so much."

I raised an eyebrow at the bags on the counter. That was indeed a lot.

Divya shook her head. "I did what I could with my free checked bags. Your Indian grocery stores here are not so good." She took a sip from her mug. To her credit, she didn't make a face, but she did put the mug down.

She caught sight of me and beamed. "Come here, Sonia. I have some things especially for you." She rummaged around in her bags and pulled out a bunch of bottles. "Here."

I accepted the bottles, confused. "What's this?"

"My Neeraj—you two remember your cousin, yes?"

We both nodded. Divya Auntie had two kids, boys about my and Kareena's ages. I think our moms had hoped the four of us would become best friends, but it hadn't happened. They were kinda obnoxious, especially when we were younger.

"Well, after he started college, he decided to let his hair grow. The most beautiful curls, this boy. Your mother said you were self-conscious about your hair, Sonia, so I brought you some products that worked for him."

What was she talking—oh. I had chopped off all my hair in a fit of depression after my mom had left, and it had turned me into a poufy triangle-head for a month or so. I'd told Mama about how much I'd hated it, but what hadn't I hated then? It had grown out since, and I'd spent more than enough of my own time on the curly hair forums. "I'm actually happy with my hair now. And it's not curly, just like wavy," I said, but she shook her head.

"Try these, you'll be so much happier with your appearance. You want to look tidy, don't you?"

Damn, had the haircut not grown out as well as I'd thought? I resisted the urge to check my reflection in the toaster. I'd braided it last night, and I thought the waves had looked pretty nice today.

Great, now I was self-conscious. I'd forgotten how good Divya Auntie was at delivering backhanded insults wrapped in good intentions.

Kareena was conspicuously silent. Jeez, had she thought I looked like a mess, too?

The internet doesn't think you're a mess.

Correction: the internet didn't think Shadow was a mess. "I guess not. Thank you for thinking of me," I added politely.

"I brought you this, too." She pulled out a box.

"A doll," I said, with as much enthusiasm as I could muster. "How nice."

"It's an Indian Barbie," she said. "I brought one back for all my nieces from my last trip home."

No matter their age? I would have far preferred a Makeshift action figure over this blonde doll in a sari.

"That's really nice. We'll put it in the living room for decoration." Kareena took Barbie Does India from me and examined it with far more appreciation than I had. She'd always liked dolls.

Divya Auntie turned to the bags. "Come, help me take out the food. I made enough for a few meals for you, but we can eat the chicken and the rice now."

When she said a few meals, she actually meant enough to keep us fed until the next Ice Age. By the time we were done emptying her bags, our freezer was full of plastic and glass containers. It was almost enough food to make me forget she'd called my perfectly adequate hair untidy.

But not quite. I'd caught a bit of Kareena's anxiety, and I pulled out our blue and white Corelle plates. We all sat down to eat at our rickety table, and I dug in. "So how come you're in town, Divya Auntie?" I asked.

"Oh, my sister over in Buffalo is pregnant with her fourth child. Fourth! Can you believe it? I told her, she's too old to have any more at this age, but does she listen to me? Never." She leaned forward and launched into gossip about her sister, which segued easily into gossip about our old friends and acquaintances in Ohio.

"Anyway, that's why I'm here," she finally finished, ten minutes later. "I figured, since I was so close, I would check in on my best friend's poor daughters."

I put my last bite of rice in my mouth. I'd forgotten what I originally asked her, but I nodded.

"Eat more. That's not nearly enough," she scolded me, and put a full second serving on my plate. I sighed mentally. Rookie move, cleaning my plate. Now I'd have to eat another serving. Throwing food away wasn't a possibility.

"Well, it's nice to see you." Kareena pushed her food around her plate. Smart.

Divya Auntie helped herself to some more chicken. "And how is everything going for you two?"

I sensed an important undercurrent in the seemingly casual question, and I stilled. I looked over at Kareena, who had also paused in eating.

I let her answer, because I didn't know what to say.

"Everything's going great."

"Is it?" Divya Auntie's gaze cut between the two of us. She took a sip of her water.

"Yes." I filled the pause. "School's good, work's good." *I saved a boy like a damn superhero and now there're hashtags about me.* You know, Divya Auntie, the usual.

"Hmm." Divya Auntie put her water down. "I will be honest, I worry about you poor girls up here, all alone. No family, no friends."

It would be nice if she could stop referring to us as *poor girls.* That wasn't great for morale.

"We're doing fine," Kareena repeated.

"I still think you should have come live with me after your mother left."

Neither of us had wanted that. Divya Auntie was the closest thing we had to family, but she wasn't family. I didn't think I could deal with her well-meaning insults on a daily basis. Plus, she couldn't offer Kareena health insurance, and I'd have to leave my honors school.

"I know this has been so hard for you. Harder than anything girls your age should go through. Why, look at how both of you have physically changed. You've wasted away, and Sonia—"

Oh. Line crossed, or it would be. That imaginary line of what-ifs, only it wasn't Kareena commenting on my changed body before I had figured it out.

How was Divya Auntie going to pile more food on my plate and fat-shame me in the same conversation? Make it make sense.

I didn't move, but I mentally turtled in on myself. So much so that I barely noticed Kareena putting her fork down, though I did hear her words, cutting Divya off. If I hadn't already been stunned, her calm, measured defense would have sent me there.

"We have both changed, because that's what bodies do. They gain and lose weight, and both those things are morally neutral. Sonia's appearance, in particular, is not up for discussion."

Divya Auntie's face puckered up. "I didn't mean to be rude, dear. . . ."

Kareena spread her hands out. "I know. I'm laying out our house rules." She put a subtle emphasis on *our*.

We finished dinner quickly after that. I tried to contribute to the conversation, but it was hard. Too much of my brain was busy worrying.

Divya Auntie gave us big hugs as she left and promised she'd come to visit before she left her sister's.

The house was quiet after the door closed behind her. Kareena turned to me, like she'd been waiting for the chance. "Are you okay?"

"Sure." No. I rubbed my nose, but I couldn't stop my next words. They came in a rush. "Mama wouldn't have allowed her to say anything about our bodies." Our mom was supremely body-positive, and she was always telling us we were perfect at any size. My anxiety around someone commenting on my weight was probably in relation to that, actually. It was like a tree falling in the woods with no one around; without her here to tell me I was beautiful as I was, was I? Or would my insecurities grab on to a new way to tear me down?

A muscle ticked in Kareena's jaw. "Yeah, and Divya doesn't know what she's talking about. We're both perfectly healthy."

I bit my lip. I hadn't been the only one Divya Auntie had poked at. "Um, are you okay?"

"Yeah. I have lost weight. She was stating a fact. I don't care."

I took a step forward, because the extra-brusque way she was speaking told me that maybe she did care? I thought of the shirt that she'd tried to take in. Was she struggling to readjust to her body changing so quickly too? "Good."

"You can throw her products away, too, if you want."

"I don't mind learning about my hair," I said diplomatically. Preferably in a less patronizing way, but I'd look up the stuff she'd given me. I knew the cheap stuff we had in our shower wasn't ideal for my hair type, but I also hadn't wanted to waste money on a whole slew of new items.

"Sometimes I watch YouTube at night, and I've gone down some of those hair tutorial rabbit holes. If you want links I can send them." She gave me the world's most awkward pat on my shoulder. "But, uh, I wish I had hair like yours. Being pretty isn't the most important thing, but you're, like, really pretty. Okay. Bye."

"So . . . are you." She left me standing there in the foyer, bemused, as she ran up the stairs.

I'd accepted it as fact that I'd never be as conventionally pretty as Kareena. She'd trade in her smooth silky hair for my ambivalently wavy/curly strands?

A little bubble of amazed joy expanded inside of me. I shouldn't be so happy that Kareena was being mildly nice, but the camaraderie we'd just shared were like Band-Aids to the small wounds Divya Auntie had casually and thoughtlessly inflicted.

If I looked hard enough, I could see in Kareena's compliments and defense tiny shards of hope. That she loved me and wanted me.

Sometimes I watch YouTube at night.

I stiffened. That comment was what I really needed to focus on, though. If the algorithm was really good, it would serve me right up to Kareena.

I pulled out my phone. What had I missed during dinner? When I opened TikTok, I nearly dropped my phone.

James's face filled my screen. He looked tired and exhausted, with cuts on his face, but from what I could see of his shoulders, he was wearing a white T-shirt, not a hospital gown. "Hey, guys. Wow, I didn't expect what happened to blow up like it did. Thanks for all the new followers. I'm totally fine." He put his arm over the back of the chair next to him and slouched. "You all have a ton of questions about what happened. To be honest, it was a silly freak accident, and I'm home now and eager to put it behind me. I'm so grateful for all the well-wishes, and for the people who helped me. I know you also want to find out about the woman in the cape. Trust me. I do, too." His eyes warmed. "I'd love to talk to her. Thank her. Hopefully, I can, soon." His gaze was piercing, like he was looking straight at me through the screen. "In the meantime, I'll see you later."

I hit pause on the screen and went to the comments. There was Sam, at the very top, the most liked comment. *Love you, boo boo* it simply said.

Gross. I scrolled past her.

Are you two back together?

Cute

I exited out of the comments and stared at James's paused face. I knew that gold chair he was sitting on. I could see a snippet of the corner of his grandparents' framed photo behind him.

Of course he was at the restaurant. I doubted his mother

wanted him out of her sight, even if he was apparently well enough to sit upright and address the world.

I navigated to my texts and tapped my finger on his name.

We should talk, he'd texted to me, Sonia.

I'd love to talk to her, he'd said to the world, referring to Shadow.

Did he know that he was talking to the same person? How was I supposed to live my life simply waiting on James to figure things out and for everything to come crashing down? A crash of my own making.

The opening music from the fighting game Kareena especially loved drifted down from her room. The faint sound of flesh hitting flesh followed.

She'd defended me. It might have been in a small way to an outsider, but stopping Divya Auntie from crossing that imaginary line was a very big deal. Now it was my turn, to make sure that the mess I'd created didn't splash back on her. I couldn't simply wait around. I had to do something.

This was, without argument, the most ridiculous thing I'd done. Why had I thought this was a good idea?

You wouldn't recognize a good idea if it bit you in the ass.

I didn't try to silence my critical internal voice this time, because based on my current behavior, that was a fair position to take.

I turned off the car engine. I'd taken the Camry without asking Kareena, which I didn't do often, but she was home for the night. She wouldn't miss it, or me.

I didn't drive often. I'd only learned last year, shortly before my mom left, and I hadn't gotten a lot of practice since I'd gotten my license. I'd made my way here carefully, making sure to stick to the speed limit. It was only eight, but it was full dark, and I hadn't wanted to risk being pulled over or getting into an accident.

I'd parked in the back alley, a couple of stores down from the restaurant. This had seemed like a really good idea an hour ago in the comfort of my own home.

Hide your face, go talk to him, make sure he doesn't know anything, and vanish.

In all the best comics, the main character's superhero alter ego was able to speak to their love interest with more freedom. That made sense to me. I felt like a different person when I pulled a mask on. If I talked to James as Shadow, I'd thought, it would be easier for me and for him.

I nervously tightened the cords on my sweatshirt. I'd donned my now cleaned leggings and the top I'd sewn and pulled up my mask. Unfortunately, it was too cold tonight to wear the costume by itself, so I'd put on my hoodie. Once I pulled up the mask and hood, I could let my face recede into the shadows of the sweatshirt. No cape this time, obviously. I looked ridiculous, but all that mattered was how little I looked like Sonia.

Comic books never considered the logistics. How was I going to lure him out of the restaurant? Also, what if he did know who I was? What if he'd left? He might have been here only long enough to film that video and then gone home to get in bed.

Dumbass.

It was much quieter at the restaurant than I'd anticipated. I stuck my hand in my pocket and curled my fingers over my pepper spray. Okay, I needed to head home. There was no need to see this foolishness through.

I stiffened when the back door opened and a man came out. He was tall and built, and when he walked out, the light above the door fell on his red-and-white jacket, one I'd seen James wear more than once. If he did have injuries, they weren't affecting how he was moving.

He threw a bag of trash into the dumpster in the shadows and then turned away, checking something in his hand. His phone, perhaps?

Oh my God. Could it be that easy?

Before I could think myself into a grave, I got out of my own car and slowly and quietly approached him, sticking to the shadows as best as I was able to. I stopped about twenty feet away.

Then I stalled. If I spoke, wouldn't he know it was me?

I swallowed. When I spoke, I was impressed by the deep, unfamiliar voice that emerged. "Don't turn around."

James froze.

"I'm the person from the canal, the one who jumped in the water." As I rasped the words, I flexed my fingers against my faux-leather-clad thighs. I stood up taller. I wasn't me. I was a role now. The baddest superheroine who had never existed.

He turned his head slightly. "Is that right?"

"I won't take up too much of your time. I just wanted to ask . . . tell you to not talk to the police about me. It's important they not find me. A matter of life and death," I tacked on, eager to impress the seriousness of the situation on him. It might not literally be life and death, but it was life as I knew it.

He slowly turned to face me, and I backed up. "Stop moving," I ordered, though he didn't listen.

He took a step toward me. The light fell fully on his face

and I breathed in a strangled gasp. "Life and death, eh?" Niam shook his head. "Super girl, has anyone told you you're really dramatic?"

Oh no. I'd royally forked this up. "What are you— Where's James?"

"James is in my mom's office, sleeping, like anyone else who came home after a hospital stay for a concussion and a near drowning might be. I'm James's brother, Niam."

I deserved the amused condescension in his tone. I licked my lips, inadvertently getting a piece of lint from my mask. "Oh, um. My mistake. I'll, uh, just go."

"Not so fast," he said softly, and I stopped midstep. He didn't sound mad, only slightly curious, and very amused. "I have some questions for you. One, are you aware what era this is? Waltzing up to someone in a dark alley is a good way to get the cops called." He held up his hand, revealing the emergency call screen on his phone.

I stiffened. "Did you call the cops?"

"No." He pocketed the phone. "I guess I have more curiosity than sense."

I'd hoped to solve a problem tonight, and now I'd created a bigger one. Where was that aggressive passivity when I needed it?

His tone turned more businesslike. "How do I know you're really the one who saved my brother? I can barely see you. Come closer."

I braced, ready to run. "No."

He craned his neck. "Where's your cape? Or is this your post-rescue look?"

My heart was racing in my throat, and he was making jokes. "Capes are overrated."

"If you're really her, tell me what happened that night."

"You know what happened. He fell in the canal."

"And your first instinct was to jump in to save him?"

My head itched, like I was falling underwater again. I'd scratch it, but I didn't want to pull back my hoodie. "Yes."

"Why were you disguised?"

"There was an event at the bookstore."

He rocked back on his heels. "So you're not some masked vigilante running around. That's why you're scared my brother could recognize you."

That was a pretty good summation, actually. "Yeah."

He cocked his head, that curl falling over his forehead. If the lighting had been better, I would have noticed immediately that James and Niam weren't the same person. They even carried themselves differently. "Okay. I guess that's plausible."

"I—I don't think it's a lot to ask, for your brother to say nothing to the police about what he may remember about me."

He crossed his arms over his chest. They were big arms, capable of crushing me. Or capable of creating teeny tiny macarons. "Is there a particular reason you don't want to be identified?"

I scoffed. "Have you seen the internet? Would you want to be the focus of it?"

He chewed on that for a long moment. "No."

I twined my fingers together, the thought of all those eyes on me making me want to claw my own skin off. "All I want is to be left alone. I'm glad your brother is okay. We can all move on now."

He was silent for so long I wondered if he'd heard me, but then he stirred. "Interesting."

"What do you mean?"

"You're really the girl who saved my brother."

He said it differently now, without any hint of mocking. So I responded in kind. "Yeah."

He nodded once. "Thank you. I appreciate it."

The simple thanks had me relaxing my shoulders, especially when he continued. "My brother has no idea who you are. He already spoke to the police. He doesn't remember anything about the incident."

My sigh of relief came from my toes and echoed up through me. Oh, thank God.

But then he continued. "The eyewitnesses are a different story. They saw your face briefly. I met them to thank them for what they did for my brother, and they told me they gave the police a rough sketch of what you looked like. I don't know how helpful it was, or how detailed, beyond the video."

Fantastic. I'd been so worried about James's cryptic text, I'd temporarily forgotten about the helpers.

But it had been dark and shadowed. Ugh, the loose ends! There were too many of them outside of James, between the eyewitnesses and Candice. And now Niam. "Do you think the police are looking hard?"

Slowly, he shook his head. "They have bigger fish to fry than a missing do-gooder. Personally, I think they lost interest once they figured out it was just an accident."

I let out a deep breath of relief.

"I know I'm not an expert on covert ops like you are, Supergirl, but I'd be real careful about stalking all these people and asking them to not snitch on you. I could have easily overpowered you tonight. You might have some swimming lessons under your belt, but I doubt you've got any real powers."

I wish. I rubbed my temples. "Don't worry, I won't be trying this again."

"Good." He straightened. "Not sure why, but I'm kind of on your side." And then he smiled.

It was a big ear-to-ear grin, one I hadn't seen him give up until now. It was the kind of smile I imagined he gave to people he really liked. It was the kind of smile that distracted me from what he'd said for a long moment, until I shook my head and came back to reality. "Uh, thanks." Did that mean I had nothing to fear from Niam?

He gestured. "What do I call you?"

"Call me?"

"Shadow?" His smile flashed again. "Sounds pretty silly, but I'm game."

It did sound silly, but there was no other hope for it. "Um, Shadow is fine."

"Okay, then." He studied me. Though I knew it was too dark for him to see me properly, his gaze made me feel like he was stripping me bare.

I shook my head. Where on earth had that thought come from?

He took a step toward me. "I don't know what your deal is, but I see your fear and I owe you for what happened with my brother. James listens to me. If he does remember something about you, I'll keep him quiet."

I wanted to cry with relief, but I managed to bite back the tears. Heroes didn't cry. "Thanks."

"I can't speak for the internet or the news, though. The devil works hard, but social media works harder."

"Something else will come along and take their attention." I said it with more confidence than I felt.

Niam looked similarly doubtful. "I don't know about that."

It was time to go, before James or someone else did come out here. "I'd appreciate it if you could go inside now."

"I'd like a number."

"A number?" I couldn't help but laugh. "Um, why?"

"What if I need to warn you?"

My laugh died an abrupt death. "Would you warn me?"

"Yeah."

I didn't want to give him my phone number. It would be painfully easy to trace that. Still, I warmed at the thought that he'd protect me—Shadow—like that. "I'd rather not, thank you."

His grin flashed again in the darkness. "You're a smart cookie."

The last thing I felt tonight was smart.

He climbed the steps and opened the door to the restaurant. Before he went inside, he looked over his shoulder. "Goodbye, Shadow."

How anticlimactic. He was just going inside and I'd drive away.

You don't want any more drama, remember? Going home knowing that the key person in this whole fiasco remembers nothing about you is good. "Bye."

I waited for the door to close before I went to my car. I was parked far enough away, but I checked over my shoulder constantly.

After I had gotten home and put the car keys back where they belonged, I pulled my phone out and powered it on for the first time since I'd gotten James's fateful text. I had a bunch of texts from Mama and Kareena from the day, and one from Mama that had come in the last hour. I heard from Divya Auntie. I'm sorry if she upset you about anything. If you're not asleep, can you call me? Or call me in the a.m.

I hesitated over her text. I didn't want to respond right now.

Instead I clicked over to James. We should probably talk soon.

The words still struck fear into my heart, but less so, now. I could ignore them, but I wanted to make absolutely sure that his brother was right. A response would be like an anxious litmus test. I needed the confirmation from James's mouth. Sure, that would be great.

I held my breath after I hit send. I didn't have to wait long. I probably won't be back at school till day after tomorrow. How about you drop off your notes after school tomorrow and give me a rundown on what I missed so I'm not too far behind?

I let out a deep exhale. That didn't sound at all like someone

who knew I'd saved his life. That sounded like a normal classmate who cared about his grades.

How odd, he wanted me to come to his house? When I
could just send him my notes via email or text?

I didn't want to go. I badly wanted to go.

My hands shook a little at the invitation, but I was proud of
myself for replying quickly. **Sounds good. Text me the address.
See you then.**

I sank down on the stairs, relieved for the first time in days.
It was silent upstairs. In a second I'd go change out of my costume, but for now, I'd take a breath. This might not have gone
exactly according to plan, but I felt hopeful for the first time in
a week, like this really might all blow over and everyone would
leave me alone.

Please let nothing kill that feeling anytime soon.

Ten

M y mom had called me twice by the time I left school the next day, but I ignored her. The more hours that passed, the less I wanted to talk to her, which didn't make me feel great. As inconsequential as it was in the grand scheme of things, I felt a vague sense of betrayal that she'd told Divya Auntie about my bad haircut. I didn't think I needed to tell her not to blast my insecurity to her friends.

I could hear her worry in the missed calls, though, so I sent her a text: *tutoring today, call you later.*

I shook off my guilt and stared out the window as the city rolled by. I'd splurged on a rideshare to James's home, though it wasn't far. I hadn't wanted to show up sweaty. My nerves would make me moist enough.

I was at the Cooper home far too quickly. His home was nice, cookie-cutter, similar to every other two-story house in this cul-de-sac. It had green shutters on every window, and a fall leaves wreath on the white door.

He opened the door the second I knocked, like he'd been waiting for me. I gave him my very best smile and tried not to look like I was cataloging everything about his appearance. Despite his injuries and his drawn face, James looked as good as ever today, in a red T-shirt emblazoned with our school's name and a pair of gray sweatpants that looked soft enough to cuddle up to.

He gave me a beaming smile. "Sonia! You're early."

I fiddled with my hair. I'd tamed it into a French braid today, a skill I'd learned after watching YouTube for three hours straight last night. Little wisps had popped out to tease my cheeks, but I rather thought they were pretty. I'd considered putting on some lipstick or eyeliner, but that was far too much for a simple notes drop-off. "Thanks. I mean, I know. Sorry. Do you need some time?"

"Nah, I like to be early to things too."

How to explain that I didn't like to be early to things, I had just wanted to see him? "Mm. Yeah." My words sounded rusty, but they were words, and that was a win, as far as I was concerned.

"Come on in." He stepped aside, and I entered, doing my best to not get too close.

I gave his home, or what I could see of it, a cursory glance. It was decorated in soothing greens and blues, with comfortable furniture in the living room. "Thanks for having me over."

"Thanks for coming."

I cleared my throat. "You look well."

"It's good to be home. Not good to be back to worrying about calculus, but nice to see my friends." His smile grew warmer, and I shrank back a little.

What did he mean by that? Was he joking about how his family had thought I was more than a friend?

"Yeah," I said, like a fool. "I bet you've had a lot of visitors."

"Not really." His lips twisted. "Nobody I wanted to see. My ex took the majority of our friends when we split up."

That sounded right. James had seemed more solitary since he and Sam had broken up. Gone on a break. Whatever they wanted to call it.

"Are you hungry? Want something to drink? A Coke? I think my mom made me some mango lassi before she left for work. It's the only sweet thing I like."

My mouth watered. "I'd love the lassi, yes."

He tipped his head toward the kitchen. "Come on."

"So you don't like sweets at all?" Who didn't like sweets?

"Nah. I'm more a salty guy."

I trailed after him as we went to the kitchen. As befitted a family that owned a restaurant, it was big and beautiful, with sparkling stainless steel appliances and dark granite countertops. "Nice kitchen."

"My mom insists on it, though my dad and brother usually do the cooking at home."

"Really?"

"Yeah, she's always too tired. It's okay, my dad's a big foodie, too, and it's nice to break up the Indian food."

"Does he cook Liberian food?" If James's dad hugged me, I

144

wondered if I'd feel as disloyal as I did with his mom doing it. I didn't think so. Probably because I only had a big question mark in my brain where the memory of a dad would go.

"Sometimes, though my grandparents do that better. He's a fan of just dumping things in a pot. It usually works out okay. When it doesn't, we get to have pizza." He pulled out a pitcher with saffron-tinted liquid in it and poured two glasses for us. He slid one over to me.

I sipped the lassi slowly, though I wanted to guzzle it, both because of my nerves and because it was delicious.

"Let's go to the living room," he suggested.

I trailed after him, past the beautiful wrought iron staircase. The floors were a warm yellow hardwood, covered with rugs. "You have a really pretty house."

"Thanks." He directed me into a room with plush honey leather couches. "Have a seat."

I chose the sofa, since it was what he gestured to. I expected him to sit in the armchair, but instead he sat right next to me. I placed my bag on the floor and leaned over to pull my notebook out of it.

I had to shake my hair out of my eyes when I straightened. I should have used pins to keep the braid in place.

"Oops, hang on." His finger caught a strand of my hair and pulled it away from where it had stuck to my lip.

I tried not to expire on the spot. Why didn't my hair have nerve endings, so I could have felt that? "Um, thanks. So here are my notes. I could have emailed or texted them to you."

"I prefer paper notes." Yet he didn't look at my notebook or make a move to take it. James inched closer. "I heard you came to the restaurant while I was in the hospital."

Oh no, no, no.

I swallowed.

He looked up at me from under his lashes. Despite all the cuts and bruises, he was still super attractive, with his sculpted face and full lips. "It was nice of you to stick around and keep my family company like that. I've been in the hospital before, but I get why a concussion stressed my mom out more than a broken wrist."

I wanted to know why and how he'd gotten that broken wrist, but it didn't seem like the time. "No problem. I didn't plan on staying for dinner or anything, but . . ." *I fell in love with your mom and the way everyone talked over each other. Sorry, I'm starved for family.*

That sounded pathetic.

"They're persuasive. I know." The lines around his eyes crinkled. "I heard there was a mix-up."

Oh nooooooo.

"My brother had a task to do, and he gets tunnel vision when he's stressed out."

The anxiety left my body in a silent whoosh. He was talking about Niam confusing me for staff. "No worries. It's totally okay."

He finally took the notebook from me before it slipped out of my sweaty fingers, and flipped through it. "My mom really loved you, by the way. I haven't heard her gush that much about anyone, not even about her own kids. You know you have a standing job offer, right?"

I flushed. "She's really cool."

His smile grew. "She is."

I pointed to the notebook. "We're going to have a quiz next week, by the way—"

"I'm surprised you haven't asked me what happened to me, exactly."

"I, um, I was mostly happy to hear you were okay."

"Never thought I'd be a national news story. The *Today* show wanted to interview me."

If there was anything that would get my attention off math, it was that. "Wow." The last thing I wanted was any more coverage. "What did you say?"

He scoffed. "Of course I said no. There's nothing more to say. I don't remember much about what happened. One minute I was walking, the next, I was in the hospital."

Navigate this carefully. "Must be weird."

James fiddled with the notebook. Then he closed it and put it aside. I guess we were not doing math now. "Why did you come to the restaurant, Sonia?"

What an incredibly loaded question. "Just . . . we were supposed to have a tutoring session."

"And that's the only reason?"

"What other reason could there be?"

His dark eyes penetrated my soul. I'd always thought he was kind of a surface-level always-happy guy, but in this moment, he looked more like his focused, serious brother. "I thought you were worried about me."

"I mean, s-s-sure. I'd worry about any of my classmates."

"Hmm." He took a sip of his drink, and I did the same. "Do you save any of the others from drowning?"

I inhaled so hard on my drink, I choked.

"Whoa there." James put his drink on the table and swatted me on the back. Unfortunately, a simple back swat wasn't going to stop me from expiring.

I finally swallowed past the obstruction and tried to breathe, but it wasn't easy. "What did you say?" I'd misheard him, surely. He'd asked if I'd ever saved anyone else from frowning, which, while weird, did imply that my sunny disposition was sparkling.

James let out a long exhale of breath, then surprised me by moving even closer, until our knees nearly touched. "I saw the video. I know what you look like." He playfully tugged on a strand of my hair, a move I was too shocked to enjoy. "And the sweatshirt you put on before you ran away, I've seen you wear it before. That bag you were carrying, that's your bag."

I doubted my own mother had an inventory of the sweat-shirts or bags in my closet. How did he? "James—" I furiously blinked back the prickle of tears. "No one can know. It's a secret. You can't tell. . . . If you do, you don't understand what's at stake. I can't have anyone look—"

"Hey, take a deep breath." James gathered my hands in his and squeezed. I looked down at his big hands and breathed, trying to trace the heavy ring on his finger with my gaze. I had to keep myself grounded. Bad enough that I'd been found out. I couldn't become incapacitated here with a panic attack too.

Niam had lied to me. James had known who saved him.

"I haven't told anyone that I suspected it was you."

I tried to get my racing heart under control. "Suspected?"

He made a face. "Well, yeah, but you just confirmed it."

Ugh. How could you be so utterly foolish?

"I haven't told anyone," he repeated. "Not the police, not my family. I didn't want to say anything until I was sure."

So Niam hadn't been lying. "Now that you're sure, though, you're going to tell them?" My voice was raspy with unshed tears. I was terrified I'd start crying, because then I'd never stop.

"Not if you don't want me to."

Bullshit.

I hadn't realized I'd said the word out loud, until he scooted closer. "I'm serious. I figured you had a reason to run. I wanted to give you a chance to explain first."

I couldn't tell him. There was no way. "It's family stuff."

His gaze seemed to tap into my soul. "Your parents?"

"Yeah."

I hated the undeniable pity that touched his eyes. "Would they be mad at you for being out that night, or . . . ?"

I remembered what Pooja had told me, about her parents being conservative. "Yes." Fine. That was a good enough answer as any. Let him think I lived in such a strict household that my mom would be furious that I was out and about after dark.

Yet my strict parents let me work late and go over to boys' houses for tutoring?

No need for the story to be ironclad. People believed stories

149

with the consistency of Swiss cheese all the time.

"Gotcha. I'm so sorry."

A little smidgen of hope rose in my chest. "It's fine. But . . . but no one can know, okay?"

"I—"

"I saved your life." That came out more forcefully than I'd intended. So forcefully, James drew back. I immediately missed the warmth of his hands. "I'm sorry."

"Don't be sorry. You're right. I owe you, big-time. If that means I have to keep my mouth shut, that means I keep my mouth shut."

"Even to friends," I stressed. I thought about Sam, and how she'd said they were on a break. "Or girlfriends."

"I don't have a girlfriend, and even if I did, I wouldn't breathe a word." James mimicked locking his lips. "I'll keep it a secret. I promise. Trust me, I want this over, too."

I studied him, finally calm enough to moderately assess the situation. "Why do you care?"

He squirmed. "Did you see the TikTok doctors analyzing what might be wrong with me? Saying it was epilepsy or that I was drunk?"

Which doctor? There had been a few viral videos. "I might have," I murmured. "I don't think it's anything to be ashamed of, though. My uncle has epilepsy." Divya Auntie's mild-mannered husband, though I'd never seen him have a seizure.

"I don't have epilepsy, and I wasn't drunk. I have a condition where my body produces too many platelets."

"That sounds . . . scary."

"It's really not. It doesn't have a huge impact on my life. So long as I take meds and get enough sleep, I can keep things pretty well in check. If I don't, I get headaches or faint. I've been slacking lately, because . . . well, stress."

I thought of how his hands had been so cold that fateful day, and the strain in his eyes. If I'd had an idea, I would have said something. "It's still nothing to be ashamed of."

"I know that. It's just that it's my condition to tell people about."

I picked up on his frustration immediately, and nodded in empathy. "I get it." When Kareena had been young and sick, she'd never wanted anyone to know about her cancer. Now that I was older, I understood that it hadn't just been about not attracting attention. It had been a form of exerting some kind of control over a situation that was wildly out of her control.

He touched his head. "Anyway, I'm happy to forget this ever happened and keep our mouths shut." He held out his hand. "Pact?"

I didn't hesitate, but I met his handshake. "Pact." His hand was dry and warm, the calluses papery soft.

Would it be better for him to not have realized I was his savior at all? Sure. But if a pact of mutually assured destruction was the best thing I could hope for, I'd take it. "What about the others?" The witnesses. Candice. Niam, after my foolishness last night.

He was still holding my hands, and he didn't pull away, so I didn't either. "They didn't see your face well, right? And if anybody does somehow connect you to Shadow, deny it. I will, too. No one can prove it."

Except Candice. I'm sure my DNA was all over her shed.

Still, though, I supposed without physical proof, I could confidently deny everything. I'd have to practice that in my bathroom mirror.

"Don't stress about it. No one would ever suspect you."

I shrank a little. It was the assurance I wanted, but not because it was so far-fetched for mild-mannered me to be a hero.

"They said you got hurt. Were you okay?"

It was nice of him to ask. "Cut my arm." I gestured to the general area, safe and hidden under my long-sleeved shirt.

He surprised me by raising his hand. I held my breath. His fingers hovered over the spot, and then dropped away. "I'm sorry to hear that."

I let out my breath. "It's healing fine, no big deal. A first aid kit did the job."

"I'm glad." His smile started around his mouth, but it hit his eyes pretty fast. "Unrelated, but want to hear something funny?"

"Sure."

"When you came to the restaurant, my family actually thought we were dating."

"Oh." I thought of how a genuinely surprised person might react to this revelation. "Oh my goodness, I cannot believe it."

"Yeah." He wrinkled his nose. "It's my fault. I heard last week that my ex was talking to someone new. So I told her I was talking to someone, too. She asked me who it was, so I figured it would be fine to just say that she didn't know her. My mom overheard me on the phone. I was so ashamed to admit that I'd made it up to make Sam jealous so I, uh, told Mom it was someone in my math class, and the reason I'd never brought her around was because her parents were conservative.

"My mom must have decided on her own that my imaginary girl was South Asian, probably because she didn't tell my grandparents about my dad until they were engaged."

All the dots were connecting. I had two choices here: pretend I had no idea what he was talking about or admit that I had known what his whole family had assumed.

Or fall in the noncommittal middle, which is what I did. "So that explains some things."

He chuckled, but his cheeks were a little red. "I'm so sorry."

I could afford to be magnanimous now. "Listen, no worries. This happens."

"Does it?" His laugh was hoarse. "Getting mistaken as a guy's girlfriend while he's in the hospital might be a first. Maybe a second, max."

"No harm done."

"Right, right, right." He glanced away. "It was nice for my parents to actually like someone I was dating for once. That hasn't happened ever."

"I liked them too." More than liked them. That hug . . . I cleared my throat. "They're really nice. You're super lucky."

His face softened. "I am, yes."

Before I could respond, a door opened and closed, and loud footsteps echoed through the house. Niam appeared in the doorway, and I instinctively scooted backward on the couch. I wasn't too worried about appearances in front of James's brother, but I also wasn't used to sitting on a couch with a boy.

Niam paused when he noticed me, surprise in his face. "Sonia. I didn't realize anyone was here."

I wriggled my fingers at him, and hoped I looked totally cool and blasé and not like someone he'd talked to in a parking lot under the cloak of darkness. I deliberately notched my voice up an octave higher, the better to distance it from Shadow's—uh, my—throaty drawl. "Hi."

He switched his attention to James and scowled at his younger brother. "You're supposed to be resting in bed. Why are you out?"

"Because I couldn't answer the door from my bed." James's tone was pleasant, but there was a bite under it. "Sonia came by with notes." He lifted the as-yet-unopened notebook as proof.

Niam ignored me. "None of your teachers will expect you to be up to speed yet. Go back to bed. Sonia, it's nice to see you, but do you mind . . . ?"

"Niam, quit it." James's face darkened. "I'm fine."

"It's not a problem at all," I said hastily. I came to my feet. "I'll see you in school tomorrow, James."

James grumbled, but he walked me to the door. "Thanks for coming by," he said. "We're still on for tutoring, right?"

I paused. I hadn't thought about it. "I didn't realize . . . I mean, sure."

James slid his brother, who stood behind us, an annoyed glance at his obvious hovering. "Great. We'll talk about it tomorrow." He surprised me with a hug.

It was odd to be hugged by someone taller than me. My face smooshed up against his chest, and his big hands rested on my back.

I should have felt fireworks exploding in my belly. Or butterflies, or something. But oddly enough, all I could wonder in that moment was whether it was cologne or gum that always had him smelling like spearmint.

"Pact," he whispered in my ear, and I couldn't help but shiver at the rush of air over the little hairs on my earlobe. I gave him a nod and happened to glance over his shoulder. Niam stood at the base of the stairs, his eyes narrowed on us. When he noticed me watching, he turned away.

I licked my lips. "Pact."

CHAPTER

Eleven

"I—I don't understand."

I turned myself back, but that didn't stop Trish from staring at me in pure horror. No doubt it was jarring for your best friend to see you shape-shift into your own cat. Puddin' meowed at me and ran away. "This is who I am now. I can't help it."

"How? When?"

I told her everything. The accident, the strange hospital, the unbelievable ability I was left with, the shadowy scientist in charge of it all.

"They're after me now. They'll stop at nothing to get their investment back."

"Then we have to stop them."

I snapped my comic closed when my phone rang as I walked to the bus stop. If I had any superpower, it was walking and reading at the same time.

156

I tucked *Makeshift* into my bag and pulled out my phone. My mom. In the beginning after she'd left, Mama had called Kareena and me daily, but lately she let us initiate contact. She said it was because she didn't want to bother us while we were busy, but I think she also didn't want to serve as a constant reminder of our loss. Or I was projecting, because talking to her was often a reminder of my loss.

So the fact that she'd called me so much in the last couple of days meant she was really desperate to talk to me, and I couldn't ignore her forever.

"Hi, beta." Her voice was warm and soothing, and I let it flow over me in place of one of her hugs. "How are you?"

Annoyed at you. Sleepless because I saved a boy, sleepless because he knows, sleepless over a hug and his soft eyes and what it all means, but finally feeling a measure of peace that someone shares my secret. "Fine."

"You didn't call me back."

Guilt ran through me, both at the thinly veiled anxiousness in her voice and at the statement. "Sorry, it's been so busy with school and work, and the time difference." Time zones were a handy excuse.

She made an understanding noise that compounded my guilt. I shuffled the phone so it rested between my shoulder and ear and readjusted my backpack on my shoulder as I walked. "How are you doing over there?"

"Good, good. I have some news. I found a better place to work. More than double the pay, a designer with a store in London, too."

I momentarily forgot my irritation with her. My spirits

brightened. "That's fantastic." My mom had no immediate family, except for a brother who had stopped talking to her when she'd married my dad against his wishes, so she couldn't count on them. She did, however, have a few cousins who lived in Mumbai. They didn't have much, just a one-bedroom flat, but they were willing to share.

She'd found a decent place working as a seamstress in India, but it had paid way less than she'd made here for the same work. Mama enjoyed sewing, and she'd passed it on to me, but I'd never glamorized her profession or wanted to do it for a living. There was a big difference between dealing with cranky customers all day and taking raw fabric and turning it into something beautiful as a hobby.

I hoped one day she'd be able to go back to school and finish her nursing degree, since I know she only tailored because it paid the bills, but until then, a better-paying job was a good thing. "I'm so happy for you."

"I am happy, too. I'll be able to save even more now for my own place to live."

"Have you spoken to any attorneys?" I kept my voice low as I walked down the block.

She switched to Marathi. I could mostly understand our language, though I couldn't speak it. Mama often went back and forth during our conversations.

But she always, always, spoke in her native tongue when we talked about immigration. It had been a secret code here, not so much there, but she hadn't lost the instinct. "Nahi. It's much too expensive."

"More expensive than your own flat?" I regretted my words immediately. It wasn't Mama's fault that she didn't have a lot of discretionary money. It also wasn't her fault that she hadn't been able to afford a good attorney after she'd been arrested. That was the reality of the American immigration system. You weren't entitled to representation, and charlatans flourished in the space.

"You know my coming back there will be difficult, if not impossible," she added gently. There was a hint of uncertainty in her voice, one I hated.

There had been something she'd always liked to say to us, a proverb, about how rubbing grains of sand together for long enough could produce oil. If you worked hard at something for long enough, it would come to fruition.

For so long, I'd just assumed my mom could do anything, and it was jarring to grow up and realize she couldn't accomplish miracles, no matter how hard she worked. Some things were out of everyone's control.

"If I can get a good job and a nice place to live, I'll be able to properly provide for the two of you if you come here. So I think it is better to save the money."

I stopped in my tracks and looked up at the tree above me as I processed her words. My mom had been hinting about us coming there for a couple of months. This was the first time she'd said it outright.

Part of my fear about Kareena's status being discovered was how it would affect me and where I lived, and I was well aware that that was selfish as hell. There were a few possibilities of

159

what my future would look like. One, Kareena and I lived in America forever, while my mom was in India. I'd be able to go back and forth to see Mama, but if Kareena left the country, she wouldn't be able to come back in.

Two, somehow Kareena and my mom got American citizenship, and we could all live together here. That felt like a far-off pipe dream, especially if we couldn't afford attorneys anytime soon.

Or three, Kareena and I could go to India, and we could all live together there.

The third wasn't a bad plan. We wouldn't have to skulk around like we did here. We wouldn't be apart. If my family came first, as it was supposed to, I should be eager for that.

But . . . I didn't want to go. I was disappointed in America a lot of the time, but I still wanted to stay here, in the country I knew, with the language I knew and the culture I knew.

I was precisely what some people might call whitewashed. I didn't *feel* any connection with my mother's—and technically my sister's—birthplace the way I saw other hyphenated American kids connecting with it. My mom had been so busy making sure we fit in that I'd assimilated almost too well.

"I guess you're right. I hoped—" *Things could go back to the way they were.* I wanted door number two with all my heart.

My mom took a deep breath and changed the subject, but not to one I cared for. "I wanted to talk about Divya's visit. I know you're upset."

"Kareena told you that?" I hadn't really seen my sister since the night before last.

"No, Divya did."

I kicked a rock. It was gloomy today, and I'd finally caved and pulled out my coat, albeit my lightest one. I'd gotten the red wool piece for a steal at the thrift store. I'd only had to fix the wrists. I didn't know if the boxy coat was trendy, but I liked the way it looked on me. It was the only piece of my outfit that I liked. "I didn't want her to point out I'd gained weight."

"I understand," she said immediately. "I know she's blunt, but I was very disappointed she even tried to comment on your body. She knows better. I have spoken to her and will speak to her again."

Relief. Though my mom wasn't here, she was still defending me. "I also wish you hadn't told her how much I hated my last haircut."

She paused. "Did I?"

"Yes. She brought me some stuff and said I could look more tidy."

I could swear the words my mom muttered under her breath were a curse. "I may have told her about your cut, yes. I was sad that you were upset and I wasn't there. Sometimes Divya hears a complaint and tries to find a solution, instead of simply listening. She means well, but I'll talk to her about that, too."

My shoulders lowered. "Thanks."

"You have your father's curly hair, you know. It was the first thing I noticed about him. I think it's perfect on you. Not messy at all, it's full of life."

My mom didn't talk about my dad very often. I think it hurt her too much. I hadn't realized I had my dad's hair, but when

161

I thought back to the few photos I had of him, I could see it. I pushed a strand out of my eyes. Full of life, not a mess. "That's cool."

"I'll speak to her," she repeated. "I'm sorry."

It was nice knowing that even if my mom wasn't here, she had my back. Her validation flowing over me, healing those cuts as well as Kareena's compliments had.

Speaking of Kareena. "You may want to talk to Kareena, too. Divya also told her she was too skinny."

This time, I knew her mutter was a curse. "I will, thank you for letting me know. I'm glad you're looking out for her."

I was trying. We hadn't really spoken since the night before last, and I wondered if I'd dreamed her defense of me, but I'd still protect her from my own actions.

I reached the bus stop and sat down on the curb. I was one of a handful of people still picked up here. Everyone else had graduated to driving themselves to school.

The wind blew harder, so I pulled the strings around my hoodie to tighten it. Winter was actually kind of nice, in that I could cover up more without anyone giving me a second glance. "My bus should be coming soon."

"How is school? Have you made any new friends?"

"I have friends. I totally have friends." If I sounded more defensive than I wanted to, that was my problem.

I was friendly to lots of people. Wasn't that the same thing as having friends?

"Of course you do. Candice is lovely. I want you to have more."

I ran my tongue over my teeth. My mom *had* always been on me to be more outgoing, to be more like Kareena. I'd never really understood it, because between work and us, it wasn't like my mom had had a huge social circle. In fact, I couldn't remember a time when she had even gone out without us. "I don't see what the big deal is with not having a ton of friends."

"I want you to have a community. You don't have anyone there."

My nose twitched. Way for my mom to drive my loneliness home.

I thought of James, and his hug. Would I see him at school today? Would he look at me with the same softness as he had yesterday? Would he acknowledge me at all as his friend? *Safer if he didn't.*

My sorrow over that made my words more accusatory. "Do you have anyone there?"

"Of course. I have your masi. Some old friends."

I knew about my aunt, my mom's fellow black sheep cousin. My chest tightened at the way she said *friends.* A man?

My mom had never shown any interest in dating here. The few times she'd spoken of romantic love for herself, it was always in the past tense. She'd loved my dad deeply, and he her.

If she fell in love with someone there, and they got serious, she could get remarried. They might have more kids. She'd have a whole new family. And here we'd be, all the way across the ocean. Forgotten.

Then go live with her. Guilt over my selfishness ripped through me. I didn't want that either!

Breathe. Mama had never even indicated to me that she might be starting something new or that she was even looking at any men. I was creating problems. She hadn't been away from us long enough to gestate a half sibling for me.

"You need to have companionship in your life."

I heard her worry without her saying it. *You're already alone, and you have your sister there. What will you do if she leaves?*

Sometimes I felt like all roads led to me alone. No matter what country I might be in. Fingers of fear ran over my spine, making my tone sharper than I intended. "I'm fine."

She hesitated. "Okay, Sonia. Don't get upset."

Shame instantly followed my fear. I didn't want her to be so worried about me. "I'm not." A rumbling sound came closer, and I glanced up to see my bus coming. "I gotta go."

"Sonia—"

"My bus is here."

My mom sighed. "Will you please call me later?"

"I'll try. It'll probably be tomorrow. I'm trying to sleep earlier lately." If James was right, the coverage would die down soon . . . and I'd be able to stop doomscrolling for hours in bed.

Her voice softened. "I do want you to be sharp in school. I love you, Sonu."

I didn't know if it was my imagination that she said the words with a little more emphasis now than she used to, but I'd take it either way. "I love you."

J ames was back.

The gossiping was so loud today, I didn't have to strain to listen.

I saw him with Sam. I hope they get back together.

Did anyone ever find out what's wrong with him?

I actually think the bruises and cuts are a good look.

My first few classes flew by without a sighting, but that wasn't unusual. Our school was large enough that we wouldn't cross paths until calculus.

I saw him earlier than that, though, right before my lunch period, leaning against the locker right next to mine. He was talking to a couple of guys I recognized as part of Candice and Sam's friend group. One of them was on the track team with James.

Someone bumped into me, and I realized I'd frozen. I started walking, albeit slowly. James caught sight of me, and a smile bloomed across his face. "Sonia! Hi. There you are."

I gave him a small smile, though my heart was pounding. What did he want? "Hey."

"You know Travis and Asuelu, right?"

I nodded at the guys. I didn't actually know them, except by sight. They gave me curious looks but said hi.

"See you two later," James said. He turned to me as they left, and I tried not to drown in his dark eyes.

"How's your first day back going?"

"It's . . . going." James shrugged. He'd worn a brown shirt today, and I wonder if the neutral color was an effort to make himself look as boring as possible. It didn't work. He was too striking.

"That doesn't sound good." I spun my lock and opened the door.

"It's like everyone wants to talk to me all of a sudden."

I couldn't relate to that, though my empathy was ready to crawl out of my body at the distress in those words. I softened. "It's because everyone likes you."

"Do they? Or do they want to be around me because I went viral for something ridiculous?"

I tossed my books into my crowded locker and pulled out my lunch. "I suppose it could be that. How's your follower count?"

"Much higher than it was before." He rolled his neck. "People have nothing better to do than be curious about strangers. Like I'm a character, not a person."

That sounded awful. Positive attention from a small group of people was one thing; becoming the internet's darling was another. "That sucks. I'm sorry."

He readjusted his backpack on his shoulder. "No big deal. You have lunch?"

"Yup."

"Good. Can we go through your notes before class? There were a few things I didn't understand."

"Oh. Now?"

"Yeah, that would be great."

I stuck my tongue in my cheek while I tried to figure out what to say to that. "Um . . . I guess we could go to the classroom."

James cocked his head. "You mean Mr. Walsh's classroom? Let's just go to the cafeteria. I have to buy a drink. I forgot my water this morning."

Noooo. "Um."

"You got something against the cafeteria?"

I glanced around, but no one was looking at us. Or rather, no one was looking at me. "Seems like a bad idea, for us to be seen together, yeah? Might get people talking. Draw more attention to us?" Someone could connect the dots, realize that I was the one who had saved him.

James scoffed. "I've talked to dozens of people today, and we have an actual reason to sit together. If anyone looks at us, they'll just see you tutoring me. I got help from Lin a few periods ago for history class. It's normal."

I wasn't special, was what he was saying. I chewed on that. "I guess you're right."

"Besides, we're friends."

We were?

He talked while we walked, which was good, because I was too busy internally freaking out.

The cafeteria was a big space with round tables, and a place so terrifying I hadn't entered it since last May, since Candice and I had quit each other.

Where were we going to sit? The tables arranged and re-arranged themselves every few months as people broke up and got together. Nothing was static in this room. It was enough to give anyone an anxiety attack.

I got milk just to have something to buy while James bought his drink. He joined me and we walked toward the back-ish. We were pulled up short by a feminine call.

"James!"

We both turned to the table, and the blonde standing there. Asuelu was also at the table, and a couple of kids I didn't recog-nize. No Candice, thankfully. "I saved you a seat, James," Sam said sweetly. She was dressed in expensive jeans and a baby-blue top that showed a faint sliver of her belly.

I was proud of my coat, but that was currently in my locker. My worn tie-dyed shirt couldn't compare.

Her gaze drifted over me, and I tensed, but she dismissed me. Did she . . . not remember our last encounter?

"Aw, thanks, Sam. But Sonia and I have to do a little study-ing," James said easily. "We'll grab a table over there. See you later."

Sam blinked, and she looked at me again. This time her eyes hardened, though the same smile stayed on her lips. For her friends' benefit? For James's?

I'd seen the meanness she was capable of, and how quickly she could switch in and out of it. The last thing I wanted was for it to be directed at me again.

"How nice of you to help others," she said, saccharine sweet.

"Sonia's actually helping me with math." James touched my elbow. "Come on, Sonia."

"I told you people would think this is weird," I muttered as we walked away.

"No one thinks it's weird. Just act normal."

What even was normal?

Except . . . maybe he wasn't entirely wrong. We got a couple of curious glances as we walked to the empty table, but they were directed at him, not me. I was, as ever, invisible, even with him by my side. Maybe more invisible with him by my side.

"Is this table good?" he asked over his shoulder.

"Um, yes." I sat down, and he surprised me by grabbing a seat right next to me instead of across the table.

"I'm starved," he said, and opened his lunch bag.

He unwrapped his neat foil-covered sandwich. The ciabatta bread looked fresh and beautiful. It was pierced in the center with a toothpick. Bright red chicken peeked out from the sides. "That looks good."

He grinned. "Restaurant kid. I get leftovers for lunch. This is a tandoori chicken sandwich. My brother baked bread last night."

"Lucky." I pulled out my slightly smushed peanut butter and jelly from its Ziploc bag.

169

"I am." He handed me a container. "Want dessert?"

I almost fist pumped when I opened it and saw the same macarons Niam had made earlier in the week. "I would punch you for this."

"No violence necessary."

I ignored my sandwich and sank my teeth into the sweet. "Did it ever embarrass you to bring your mom's food to school?"

"You mean 'cause it's different?"

"Yeah." We'd gone to a mostly white elementary school, and my mom had tried to pack me and my sister, like, aloo gobi wrapped in rotis. Now I regretted the protests I'd mounted to get Lunchables instead.

He lifted a shoulder. "When I was really young, probably, but my parents always told us to eat what we liked. And now, people are jealous that I get gourmet lunches that they have to pay for."

Damn. I wished I'd had that kind of attitude. I could have had so many more meals cooked by my mom's own hands. "Right."

He took a large bite of his sandwich. "I remember your sister. Kareena?"

A lot of people remembered my sister, though she'd been two grades ahead of us. "Yup, that's her."

"She was cool. She was salutatorian last year, right?"

"She was," I murmured. She'd missed valedictorian by like half a percentage point.

"That's a lot of pressure on you."

"I'm already far from the top two spots." I had good grades, not perfect ones. I finished the rest of my macaron and took a drink from my water bottle.

"I know what it's like to have an overachieving older sibling."

"Oh?" I tried not to think of how I'd cornered Niam in his parking lot like a third-rate superhero. "Is Niam a genius too?"

"Nah, he actually hates school. But he's always been my mom's right-hand man in the kitchen."

I slid the container of macarons back to him with great reluctance. "He definitely makes a mean dessert."

James smiled. Someone came up to tap him on the shoulder, and he turned his attention away from me, which was good, because I didn't want to scarf down my gooey peanut butter sandwich right in front of him.

I was able to get a couple of bites down as he talked. There was a slight itchiness between my shoulder blades, like someone was looking at me, so I glanced over my shoulder.

I met Sam's narrowed blue gaze. She maintained eye contact for a solid minute.

When the person next to her spoke, she turned away, and I did too.

Welp. That was scary.

James's friend left so I felt free to ask, "Um, do you usually sit with Sam?" *Is that why she's giving me a stare of death?*

James finished his sandwich. "Not since we broke up. Today was the first day she's spoken to me in public since then, actually. Most days, I've been running during lunch."

So we both avoided eating in here. I put down my sandwich

and wiped my fingers. "What questions did you have about my notes?"

"Just needed a couple clarifications." But he didn't pull out my notebook. Instead he leaned closer. "Hey, can I ask you something?"

Since I couldn't hear him well over the din of other students, I had to sway his way. "Sure."

"Where did you get your costume? That day?"

I stiffened and shot a look around the cafeteria. "Jesus, James."

"No one heard us. I'm curious."

"I made it," I said shortly.

"No way! How?"

"With fabric and a sewing machine. Just the top; the pants were bought," I added, lest he think I was any kind of pro.

"That is so cool." He popped open a bag of chips and offered them to me. I shook my head. "I should have known from the letter on the front."

I took a bite of my sandwich and chewed determinedly. "I don't think you know the meaning of a secrecy pact."

"Relax. No one's even looking at us. But they might if you keep looking so stressed out."

I made a conscious effort to relax my face. "You're going to kill me, James."

"I hope not." He grinned at me, and it was annoying how disarming it was. "I'd rather keep you alive."

"In that case, maybe pipe down,"

James took a swig of his water. "You're really good. It was

better than my store-bought Batman."

I paused. "Thanks."

"Do you cosplay?"

"I've been to a few cons."

"I didn't know that. You read comics?"

I tensed up a little. I was a lurker for a reason. Talking to fellow fans intimidated me. "Yeah. I like movies more than books, though."

"That makes sense, if you're into cosplay," he said easily, and I relaxed. "All this time I've been working at the store, you should have told me you like comics. I could have set some aside for you. What are you reading now?"

"*Makeshift*. I'm enjoying it."

It made me happy that he nodded immediately. "Yeah, she's cool. Did you get to the part where Puddin' shapeshifts into goo to get her out of prison?"

I tried not to grimace. Spoilers, James. "No. I did not. I'm on the first volume."

"Oops. Sorry. That was in the second." He mimed zipping his lips. "I won't say another word, but let me know when you're there."

"Sure."

James crumpled his foil up. "You could make me a costume."

I gave him a quizzical smile. "What kind?"

"I don't know. I like superheroes too. Or you could make me a suit. We got that dance next week."

I stilled. I'd seen the posters in the hallway for the pre-Halloween dance. "The Harvest Festival?" It had been called the Halloween Ball until some religious moms got mad we were celebrating the occult or something, and they'd swapped out the costumes for semiformal wear.

"Yeah. You going?"

"I . . . don't really care for dances." Last year for the festival, I'd stayed home while Candice had gone. Kareena had offered to drive her, since she hadn't gotten her license yet. My mom had helped them both with their outfits, sewing Kareena a gorgeous pants suit from scratch. I wished I'd gone now, if only to have some good memories from last year to outweigh the bad.

"We could go together. That would be nice, yeah?"

The air sucked out of my lungs. I opened my mouth, but James's gaze dipped over my head and stopped me. "Hi," he said.

"Hey." Hana stopped next to the table. Her gaze went back and forth between us. "You're that kid who fell in the canal."

James's smile didn't slip, but his eyes turned a little cooler. "Yeah. James."

"I'm glad you didn't drown."

"Uh, thanks?"

"I'm Hana. Hi, Sonia."

"Hi," I murmured.

"Nice to meet you." James checked his smartwatch and got to his feet. "Ugh, I have to go meet with Hawley to get my missed work. I'll see you soon." He gave me an easy smile, and then did something that shocked me.

He touched my shoulder.

It was the lightest touch, a squeeze, really, there and gone, but it froze me solid, even after he walked away.

Hana dropped her tray on the table. The chair slid out in a screech, then screeched again when she slid back in. "Well, well, well," she said in a not-very-quiet voice. "You're hooking up with the canal kid."

I jerked. The people at the table next to us glanced over, then put their heads back together. Oh no. "I'm *not*." I tried to be just as loud as her, but I doubted it would help.

"I didn't know you guys knew each other."

Uh-oh. "I tutor him."

"You didn't tell me that you tutor the canal kid the other day."

The other day, when we'd watched the video. Yeah. Any rational person, if they were friends with James, would have mentioned it then. Why hadn't I? "He has a name, you know."

The diversion worked. "James." She frowned. Her lipstick was a cool-toned pink that I coveted instantly. "I'm not a huge fan of *J* names, but maybe he'll surprise us."

"We're friends."

"Uh-huh."

"We are." Why I was having to defend myself to my coworker, I didn't know.

"Friends don't ask each other to dances." She took a bite of her pizza. "Just FYI."

I licked my dry lips. "Sure they do." Did they? What about friends who were grateful that their friend saved their life?

"Uh-huh." She opened her milk.

"Hana—"

"Okay. Okay. Sorry. Whatever you say."

I crumpled my garbage together, fully intending to leave. She took a swig. "I wouldn't get up yet, if I were you."

I paused. "Why."

"The Queen of Vipers over there is watching you from her table. She won't come over and bug you as long as I'm sitting here, but she might confront you on your own. Do you have a coffee to drop on her?"

I made sure I was fully seated. "Why would Sam confront me?"

"Because you're hooking up with her ex."

I shot another look around, but luckily, this time Hana had whispered. "I'm *not*."

"Do you want to be?"

I opened my mouth, then closed it. Like, yes, I wanted to hook up with James, but he couldn't possibly want to hook up with me? "I—I . . . I'm not really the hookup type."

"Meaning you want to, but you don't know how." Hana nodded, like she'd gotten her answer. "Either way, Sam's a little erratic, and I wouldn't want to be in her crosshairs."

That wouldn't have been a word I'd apply to the Samantha I'd known the last couple of years, but she had looked more mean lately. I tried to relax in my hard plastic chair. "Fine. I'll stay here."

"Good plan." Hana took a bite of her apple and studied me. "If the zombie apocalypse happened tomorrow, what would you do?"

I carefully folded up my napkin. "I beg your pardon?"

"Everyone in this cafeteria turns into a zombie, right now. We're running for our lives, become a tight group of survivors. What are you going to contribute?"

This felt oddly like a job interview question, but a more fun one than "tell me about yourself." I thought for a second. "I'd steal stuff."

"Ahh, the procurer. You'd build our stash."

"Yeah, but . . ." I took a sip of my water. "Do we make it out of this zombie apocalypse?"

"Sure, rebuilding can be a spin-off show."

"Then I'd loot and hoard things so I could be on top when our new barter system emerges."

"Interesting. What things? Expensive jewels?"

"Nah. Things people don't realize they need until they need it. Contact lenses, entertainment stuff, soap."

"Hmm." Hana chewed on her pizza for a long moment. "Fascinating. Criminal, but make it practical."

"Why are you asking?" I couldn't help the suspicious tone in my voice. I didn't really think Hana would bring about the zombie apocalypse for fun, but I wasn't about to become an unwitting accomplice.

"I think we should be prepared, is all." She took a sip of her milk, her eyes a little too focused on me, like she was already evaluating me for her merry band of apocalypse survivors.

"What role would you be?"

She tipped her head. "What do you think?"

I hesitated. For all her toughness and brains, Hana wasn't sociable enough to be a leader, so . . . "I think you'd be the healer."

She blinked. Her makeup was flawless as usual today, the liner two perfect wings. Her eyes were twins, not cousins. "What?"

"You'd be the one who patches people up and sends them back into the zombie battlefield." I crumpled my napkin up and dropped it on my paper bag.

Hana's lips twisted. "I have no desire to go into medicine."

"Yeah, you'd be like a field medic." I was starting to enjoy this. "You know, the person who has no training, but rushes out and learns under a kindly old doctor who's eventually decapitated by a bad guy? That kind of healer."

"Oh, that kind." Hana almost smiled. "Gotcha." She ate in silence for a moment. "How come I never see you in the lunchroom?"

Nobody had ever asked me, and I didn't want to lie. "I usually eat in a classroom. Read or work on projects."

"What kind of projects?"

I shrugged, trying not to be ashamed of my grandma hobbies. "Like, embroidery."

She raised an eyebrow. "Did you embroider that shirt you were wearing the other day?"

"No, that was actually an old housedress I turned into a shirt."

"You thrift flip?"

"I—sometimes."

Her critical gaze ran over me. "Where are the things you flip, though? You don't seem to wear them."

My face burned. "In my closet, mostly."

"Hmm. You should wear them. That shirt was cute."

I shrugged, unsure of what to say.

"Do you want to go to a party tomorrow?"

I blinked. It had been so long since anyone had asked me to go anywhere. "I, um . . ."

"Unless you're working."

"No, I'm off the schedule for a few days. Paris's cousin is home from school, and she always gives him shifts."

"So let's go."

"Where's the party?" I asked cautiously, still hedging. The introvert in me didn't want to go to any damn party.

"There's this kid I take virtual piano lessons with, Remy. He goes to Xavier."

The private Catholic school. The boys there were a little wild, but I could always leave if I hated it. "Will it be a big party?"

"We'll know when we get there."

It would be a different group of kids than the ones I saw every day, which might be good. It would take my mind off James's weird behavior for a night.

James, who asked you to the dance. Even though you both know you shouldn't even be seen together.

This man was a conundrum.

Maybe he fell for you. Like, he realized in the hospital that he adores you, and even though being together could blow your pact out of the water and draw attention to both of you, he can't help himself—

"Sonia?"

Right, the party. "Um." The thought of hanging out with

Hana wasn't unpleasant, though I squelched any budding excitement. I wouldn't get my hopes up for a grand friendship. I wasn't looking for one, after all. But maybe I wouldn't have to lie to my mom the next time she asked if I had friends. "Okay," I said slowly.

"Cool. I can pick you up at eight."

Eight! That was so late. *You already told her about your grandma hobbies, you can't have a grandma curfew too.* "Sure. Sounds good."

"Want to text me your address? You should have my number from work, right?"

The bell rang, and I got up from the table. I almost backed out right then and there, but my mom whispered in my ear. *You need companionship.* "Sure."

"Good." Her smile was slow and easy, and one of the few real ones I'd seen on her. "We'll have fun."

Not for the first time, I wished I had half the confidence she did.

Thirteen

The place is like a fortress. The employee badge I have only gets me so far, and it's taking all my concentration to focus on keeping my face right.

Especially when I turn the corner and see Reyes. Why does the love of my life have to work for my new mortal enemy?

He looks up and smiles at me. Of course he does. He thinks I'm Sally Jones, receptionist, not Mirabel from physics.

The timer on my phone rang and I pouted as I closed *Make-shift*. I normally would have finished by now, and I was close, with Mirabel about to head into the inner sanctum of the bad guy in disguise. But it was almost five, so I needed to shower if I wanted my hair to dry before the party. The thick strands took forever.

I eyed my SAT prep workbook. I hadn't cracked it open yet, and that would have to change soon.

I'd do fine on my SATs, but I had to do more than fine. It wasn't enough for me to go to an okay school. I had to go to the best college I could possibly afford.

The mounting pressure made my head hurt, and I shoved the prep book away, burying it under a little mound of paper on my bed. I could spend tomorrow doing SAT stuff.

I felt better after my shower. I rough-dried my hair with a towel and made my way back to my room.

I could still cancel. Instead of going out with Hana, I could stay home and . . .

And what? Think about my bloodstained cape at Candice's? Or how James had lost his mind?

Had he meant it? What *had* he meant?

It had been a joke. That was the conclusion that had allowed me to fall into a restless melatonin-induced sleep the night before. He hadn't actually meant it. It wouldn't have made sense for him to mean it.

If he had meant it, I'd have to think about what had brought his sudden interest about.

Stop it. Focus on your hair. You can control your hair even if you can't control confusing boys who say one thing and then do another and then kind of casually ask you out, undoubtedly because—

Nope, nope, nope. Not going there.

On my phone, I opened YouTube. I kept one eye on the curly-haired woman in the video, and after adding gel to my strands, I rolled a T-shirt into a doughnut, tied the ends together with a scrunchie, and placed it on top of my head. Then I carefully wrapped triangle-shaped sections of hair up and over it.

I'd disappear hovering next to Hana anyway, but primping was nearly as soothing as watching a seam form under the light of the old Singer. When I was finished, I smoothed the hair carefully and went to my closet.

Forty-five minutes later, I wanted to scream.

Nothing looked good on me. It either didn't fit, or fit a little too well. I stared at the pile of clothes in the middle of my room. If I'd had any energy, I would have gotten a plastic garbage bag from the kitchen and filled it up with all of them. Start fresh.

I went back to my closet and riffled through what was left. A bunch of clothes I hadn't gotten around to flipping yet, and a few Indian dresses that no longer fit but the fabric was too nice to toss. I fingered a sunny yellow lehenga, the skirt and top a hand-me-down from some auntie's daughter, that I'd worn to a Diwali party when I was eleven. Then there was the cerulean anarkali, also a hand-me-down, that had gone to a wedding the year before.

We hadn't gone to any functions since we'd moved to New York. Even if I had any Indian clothes that still fit me, I wondered if I'd feel comfortable in them anymore.

Since I didn't know what else to do with it, I'd folded my now-infamous costume and placed it on the top shelf. A sleeve peeked out, and I stuffed it back. If only I could wear that. It had been the first thing I'd donned in a while that had made me feel good about myself.

A knock came at the door, and I spun around guiltily, glad I'd tucked my incriminating outfit away. Kareena stopped when she saw me. "Oh, sorry."

I glanced down at myself. I was only in a bra and panties and a big T-shirt, and was too apathetic to care.

She took note of the rest of my room and came in. "What are you doing?" Then, before I could answer, continued, "What happened to your hair?"

I didn't need a mirror to tell me I looked like the brown Bride of Frankenstein. "It's a heatless curls method I saw on TikTok."

"You could have used my curling iron."

"I don't know how to use a curling iron. Besides, heatless is better, right?"

Kareena cocked her hip. She wore her pink diner uniform. It said *Kelly* on the name tag on her chest, and I wondered if she was the one who had anglicized her name or if it had been her boss. "I would have showed you."

You would have? Since this was the first time we'd really spoken since Divya Auntie's visit, I didn't want to start a fight, so I shrugged. "Thanks, but it's fine. It was an experiment." I turned away and faced the mirror and tested my hair for dryness by patting it.

"Are you going somewhere?"

"I was going to go to a party." I said the words without thinking, and then I rolled my lips tight. No, no, no, now Kareena was going to make me feel terrible about going to a party while she went to work. "I don't know if I still will."

Instead of stomping off or saying something biting, though, she leaned against the door. "A party where?"

"At the house of this kid from Xavier. You don't know him." I pulled out the scrunchie holding the T-shirt in my hair together.

She scowled. "Xavier boys are wild. You can't trust them."

"I wasn't planning on trusting him, just going to his party."

"You're going with Candice?"

Could everyone just stop bringing up Candice? "No."

"I haven't seen her around lately."

"I don't really talk to her anymore. And don't worry, I'm not going now. I don't have anything to wear."

My sister was quiet as I pulled the shirt out of my hair. The strands tumbled down to my shoulders and I nearly reared back. Was that all it took to turn my waves into lustrous locks? A T-shirt and some product?

"Wow. Your hair looks amazing."

I was, indeed, amazed. So much volume. I touched a strand, momentarily forgetting my frustration over my wardrobe. The dab of coconut oil at the ends of my hair after my shower had worked wonders, defining my curls.

I used to hate when my mom sat me down and rubbed the oil into my head, because I could never get it all washed out the next day and kids would ask me why I was greasy. Who knew I'd come full circle. The slight scent of coconut was nostalgic now. "It's so . . . smooth." Light bounced from the almost-black strands in a way I'd never seen before, like it was a reflecting pool.

"Do you have hairspray?"

"No."

"Hmm. Come on, then." She turned on her heel.

"I'm not going out, though." I was talking to air. I gave my wondrous hair one last glance in the mirror and followed her to her room.

I didn't go inside the master bedroom much anymore. Kareena hadn't changed things since my mom had left. It was still neat as a pin. The bedding was the same pretty red-and-pink-rose quilt, the same mismatched lamps sitting on the mismatched nightstands.

But the clothes in the closet were all Kareena's, not my mom's. We'd packed most of hers up, at her direction. Some we'd shipped to India, her favorites she'd taken with her.

There was a neatly stitched embroidery hoop on the wall. It was from a kit someone had given her when she'd first come here and had to pass the time in the hospital, pregnant with me, at Kareena's side. It said *LOVE IS* . . . in big cursive letters, with little blue forget-me-nots dotting each letter and tiny roses underneath. I hadn't known what it meant when I was young. I still didn't, not really. Why wasn't it finished? What *was* love?

Kareena walked over to the vanity and picked up her hair-spray bottle. My mom had never worn much makeup, but she'd liked to sit at the little fancy table and brush her hair, and I had liked to watch her comb through the waist-length strands. Her hairbrush was gone, and so were her lipsticks and perfumes. Some of those things were in my room.

"Turn."

I bit off my instinctive contrary protest. What did it hurt to try to preserve this hair as long as I could?

She tousled my hair, working her fingers through it as she sprayed. "Sit down."

"Why?"

"Just sit down. I'll do your makeup."

I eyed her closely. Was she ill? Why was she being so nice to me? "Didn't you hear me? I'm not going."

"Then you can sit around the house with your hair and makeup done."

That seemed like a monumental waste of both our time. "Don't you need to go to work?"

"Not yet."

If I were a tougher person, I might throw her offer in her face, but I was so confused and eager for any crumb of affection, I sat. Before Mama had left, Kareena had occasionally done my makeup for fun. It was from her that I'd learned which YouTube channels to watch for tips on brown skin. We'd giggle on the bottom bunk of our bed and gossip about people at school.

The last time she'd done my makeup had been for her senior awards banquet. Mama had been arrested two weeks later.

I almost flinched when she touched me now but forced myself to relax while she dabbed lotion and foundation on my face. "Who are you going to this party—sorry, who were you going to go with?"

"A friend from work, Hana."

"How come you don't talk to Candice as much anymore?" she asked as soon as I closed my eyes for her to apply eyeliner.

Because she's an asshole. You know what? I was tired of pretending Candice hadn't disappeared on me. "She stopped talking to me last year, after Mama left," I said shortly. "I told her Mama was deported. I guess she didn't care for that." Though she'd eaten at my mom's dinner table so many times over the course of three years. That hadn't been enough to humanize us.

Kareena's hand froze in midair.

Even at my saddest and most vulnerable, I wouldn't have risked Kareena's safety. "Don't worry, I didn't tell her about you."

Kareena went back to the eyeliner. "You didn't tell me that she ghosted you."

I couldn't identify what was in Kareena's tone. "You didn't ask." Anyone else would have been able to figure it out, but Kareena hadn't been interested in tracking my friendship habits.

Kareena was quiet as she finished brushing shadow over my lids and outlining and filling in my lips. I blinked my eyes open at her direction.

I inhaled as I turned to the mirror. "Hey. Wait a minute."

"I didn't do much. You look good."

I . . . did? The shadow she'd brushed on was dark and smoky, though she'd also packed on a glittery highlight at the inner corner of each eye. My skin glowed, smooth honey brown. My lips were a deep, burnt red, perfect for autumn. It was like me, but a more artistic me, one that had needed the bare minimum of coaxing to come out to play. That it was Kareena who had brought this stranger to the surface was the real surprise.

This person didn't look like she could ever be invisible.

"You should go to that party."

I flexed my hands to rid myself of the slight tingling in them.

"I told you, I have nothing to wear." I wish I had time to make something.

Kareena turned away and went to the open closet. "I don't think your clothes will fit me," I murmured.

She rummaged around and came back with a simple black T-shirt and a pair of boots. "This shirt is bigger in my chest. It's supposed to fit loose. Wear some jeans under it."

I accepted the offering. The shirt was soft and supple, and mildly sheer, and it probably would fit me. "I don't think—"

"You're basically ready. Why wouldn't you go?"

I bit my lip. How to explain my anxiety about making a new friend without sounding foolish? Especially to someone who had never had trouble making friends.

If she hadn't also wanted to keep a low profile, Kareena would have been prom queen in addition to salutatorian. It had been work for her to be invisible, unlike me. "Why do you want me to go?"

She tugged on her skirt. "Mom said you need to make more friends."

I cast my gaze down. "Oh." So it wasn't because she wanted me to get out and ostensibly have a good time. She'd been guilted into being kind. "Right."

"Is Hana picking you up?"

"Yes." I got to my feet.

"Wait." She picked up a bottle of perfume and held out her hand.

I gave her my upturned wrist. She spritzed a spray on each wrist and rubbed it in with her own. Roses filled the air, and

189

mildly lifted my spirits. "That's nice."

Kareena lifted the bottle to her nose and inhaled. "It was one of Mom's."

My heart seized up. I breathed again, trying to capture the memory that went with the scent. It was there, just out of reach, teasing me. "I don't remember it."

"She used to wear it when we were little. I think you have the one she wore more recently. You know she could never throw anything away."

There was a heavy silence following her words, and then Kareena cleared her throat. "Okay, I have to head out for work or I'll be late. Be careful."

"I will." I trailed behind her to the door, and watched her go downstairs. How long had it been since she'd told me to be careful?

Far too long. I looked down at the shirt she'd handed me. It was possible she'd changed, or she'd come out of the traumatic fog she'd been in since Mom had left long enough to revert to my bossy but kind older sister.

Yet I was terrified to trust in her. How did I know she wouldn't switch back and hurt me again?

There were no guarantees on anything. So I'd keep my guard up. But in the meantime, I'd definitely wear this shirt. It wasn't anything special or unique, but it was soft and comfortable, and nicer than anything I had in my current rotation. It was also the most thoughtful gift my sister had given me in a while, and given to me freely.

I was still ambivalent when Hana pulled up in front of my

home, but I patted myself on the back for at least being out-side and waiting, and not hiding under a blanket with books. I forced a smile, because normal people smiled at the thought of going to a party.

At the very least, my ride was pretty. I opened the door of the red Tesla and got in, pushing the passenger seat back so I could fit my legs. "Hi."

Hana ran her gaze over me. Her aesthetic tonight was a nineties schoolgirl, in a short pleated plaid skirt and tied-off crop top, with bubble-gum-pink lipstick and light eyeliner. "You look good."

"Thanks. So do you. Nice car."

Hana glanced around the vehicle as she pulled out of the driveway, like she was just seeing it now. "Thanks. My dad gave it to me when I turned sixteen."

"That's so nice of him." I clutched my belt at the way she handled the wheel with one hand. Personally, I wasn't confi-dent enough in my own skills to drive our Camry with two hands.

"It's his guilt gift for cheating on our mom, so don't be too impressed." She threw the car into drive with more force than I would have.

I was as nonplussed as I'd been when she'd thrown out the same information earlier. "Oh."

She shot me a sideways look. "Sorry, my therapist told me I shouldn't lead with how my dad's a two-timing asshole."

"It is a little jarring," I admitted.

"It's been less than three months, so it's still pretty new."

"You guys found out your dad was cheating, they got divorced, and you moved across the country in three months? Phew. That's a lot." No wonder Hana was so brusque. What had she been like last year? I knew better than anyone how big life changes could mess with your head.

"Yup. My mom grew up here, though, so not a lot of changes for her. Just for me and my brother." Her fingers tightened. "Parents, am I right? Can't live with 'em, legally can't live without them."

I crossed my legs. That was both true and not true as far as I was concerned. I tried to sound similarly breezy. "Uh-huh."

"Enough about me. Thanks for coming with. Do you mind if I stop at that grocery store on the corner? I didn't have dinner, but I don't want to spend the time waiting at a restaurant, and I've been eating too much fast food lately."

Hm. I hadn't banked on dinner one-on-one. Did we have enough to talk about? On the other hand, I hadn't eaten anything since lunch, and it was probably best to not walk around nauseous in a social situation that already made me kind of nauseous. "That sounds great."

We settled into a mildly awkward silence, but it wasn't so bad that I'd tuck and roll out of the car to avoid it.

When we got to the supermarket, we circled the deli and she picked up a sandwich. I did the same, and also grabbed a California roll. She wrinkled her nose at that. "Grocery store sushi?"

I put the sushi in the cart. "Trust me, it's really good."

"I'll reserve judgment." Hana added another sandwich to

the cart and tossed in a few bags of chips.

We walked down the aisle, and I grew tense when I noticed her perusing the wine and beer. I couldn't be in the car with her if she was going to drink. I hadn't spent this long avoiding police attention just to get pulled over for a DUI.

Luckily, she passed the alcohol by and moved on to the mixers. Hana grabbed a soda. I swiftly calculated the cost of my meal, came in under budget, and then added my own drink.

I didn't need to be so cautious, though, because Hana waved me off when I tried to separate our stuff at checkout. "It's on Daddy." She smirked and tapped a heavy black card on the reader.

I was really glad Hana was in therapy, because her family trauma seemed almost as big as mine, but in a different way. Though I'd trade *deported mom* for *cheating dad*, especially if it came with that credit card and a parent in the same country.

Hana paused outside the entrance of the store. I didn't know what she was doing until she fished a sandwich, chips, and a drink out, and held it out to the homeless person camped on the curb, in the shadows. "Do you want this?" she asked, no inflection in her voice.

The man took it with a thanks. I waited till we were out of earshot to speak. "That was really nice of you."

"Just trying to make up for having more money than I need."

"Still . . ."

She opened her car door more aggressively than necessary. "Don't worry about it. Come on."

It didn't take a genius to see that Hana didn't want a big deal to be made about her good deeds. Why, I wasn't sure, except that she might feel it detracted from her tough persona. I fell silent and got into the car. "You want to eat in here?"

"Yeah. Let's find a nice view. You know any place?"

"Sure." I directed her to the nearby park. There were no beautiful views in Rockville equal to what Los Angeles probably offered, but there was a bluff with a well-lit road that overlooked the midsized town.

She parked her car, and I handed her the food. Before she could open the sandwich, she cracked the top of her soda and chugged a good bit of it. Then she pulled off her scrunchie. To my amazement, she unscrewed something on the side and tipped the hair tie over the bottle's mouth. Clear liquid poured out, into her Coke. The scent made my nose wrinkle. "Is that vodka?"

"Grey Goose, no less."

My love of spy gadgets and functional accessories warred with my fear of the police. Though I was impressed by the ingenuity, I had to be the wet blanket. "I can't be in the car if you drink and drive. I'll get in big trouble if we get pulled over."

"You have your license?"

"Yes."

She tossed me the keys. "Then you drive."

I caught them against my chest. Anyone else our age might be thrilled at driving a state-of-the-art Tesla, but I wasn't anyone else.

However, short of knocking the drink all over the leather

seats and flinging her scrunchie flask into the night, I didn't have much of a choice. I couldn't exactly get a rideshare all the way up here. I placed the keys in my lap. I'd be fine. I was a good driver. A Tesla was basically a Camry with a nice dress on. "Okay."

"I was going to offer you some, but I'll refrain now. Good for you, being so responsible." She took a big drink.

I opened the sushi. "Yeah, I'm responsible all right."

"I mostly need a little courage before we go to Remy's." She shifted. "Thanks for coming with me tonight. I probably wouldn't have gone if it was just me. It's less stressful when you're walking in with someone else."

I mixed wasabi with soy sauce. I'd never thought someone as self-possessed as Hana would be nervous about anything. "Do you like Remy?"

Hana took a bite of her sandwich and chewed for a long moment. "He's better than most of the straight guys here. Their interest feels like some new-girl fetish."

I'd met my fair share of creeps, and I believed her. "That sucks. Was it different in LA?"

"Probably not, but it was bigger, and I had pretty protective friends." Hana took a bite. "You don't seem to have a lot of friends."

Ouch. "Yeah." I squirmed at her extended stare. Her bluntness was a feature, not a bug, like Divya Auntie. Unlike Divya Auntie, I hoped Hana knew or could learn which lines were not to be crossed. "Not really."

"Don't look so sad. It's not a reflection on you. I don't have any friends here, and I'm awesome." Hana popped her chip bag open and offered it to me. I passed. "Someone said you used to be tight with that girl who hangs out with Samantha. Candice?"

"I used to."

"What could you possibly have in common with someone who likes that evil witch?"

I almost laughed. "First of all, I think Sam hides her true nature really well. She's good at playing people. And Candice and I . . . we had a lot in common." A similar silly sense of humor, a strong sense of justice, a deep love of reading and movies.

More than anything, she'd been accused of being a romantic space cadet a time or two, just like me. We'd spent hours in her room daydreaming about some guy—and/or, in her case, girl—and where our lives might take us. We were going to go to college together, and then get married and have houses right next to each other so our kids could play.

So much for dreams.

"What happened? Did you break up or something?"

I'd never heard anyone but me call a friendship ending a breakup, but it was so accurate. Being ghosted by Candice had felt just as, if not more, painful than any romantic relationship imploding. "Yes." I focused on picking up my grocery store sushi with my chopsticks.

"Why?"

I told her the truth about my family and she didn't want to be my friend anymore. I wasn't enough. "I think we grew apart."

Hana nodded. "That happens."

"Has it happened to you?"

"Yeah, after I moved here. My old friends cut me out of the group chat."

I paused. Not texting Candice immediately all the time had been incredibly hard, maybe even harder than not being with her in person. "I'm sorry."

"Eh. Life happens." Hana's tone was the same as always, but I caught the little dip in it. "Since we both have no friends, maybe we can hang out like this. Outside of work and school."

My gut instinct was to say no, and it was so strong I had to stop and wonder why. Why hadn't I wanted to come out tonight? Why hadn't I made any friends to replace Candice's role in my life after we broke up last year?

Because she hurt you too much.

Yeah. That was it, and it was a foolish fear. It wasn't like I'd be as vulnerable with anyone as I'd been with Candice.

Mama was right. I'd be careful and cautious this time, but it would be nice to have a new friend. Or at least, the promise of one. "On one condition."

She raised a perfectly plucked eyebrow, but there was an air of stillness about her, like she was waiting for me to reject her.

I offered her my last sushi roll. "You try western New York grocery store sushi."

She grimaced, but she ate it. I watched her face as she chewed and swallowed.

Hana looked at me, and it was with great pity. "Sonia . . . that was terrible."

It startled a laugh out of me. "Was it?"

"Yeah." She finished her spiked soda. "Next time we hang out, we're getting delivery from whatever passes for a real sushi restaurant in this town. My dad's treat."

CHAPTER

Fourteen

Okay, so driving a Tesla was very different from driving a Toyota.

I breathed a huge sigh of relief when I pulled up in front of Remy's house, and unclenched my hands from around the steering wheel. A more chill girl than me might have been excited to cruise around in the expensive car, but I've literally never been chill a day in my life, so why start now.

I parked on the tree-lined street in the upscale cul-de-sac. The driveway was full, and I didn't want to get blocked in. What if I did want to leave early?

"There's something I should tell you." Hana unbuckled her belt. Her words were clear and her motions smooth, in spite of what had looked to me like a generous pour of vodka.

"What?"

"James miiiiiiight be in that house tonight."

If I'd been drinking something, I would have done a spit

take. "What? What?" I had to repeat it, because she was already out of the car.

I wrestled with my belt, then tumbled out of the car. "Hana, what the hell?" I hissed over the car.

She adjusted her top and waited for me to catch up with her on the sidewalk. "This is what friends do."

"Blindside each other?"

"Nope. Help each other. Push each other out of their comfort zone."

"Is this related to that aggressively passive thing you said about me?"

Hana shook her head. "What do you mean?"

I'd been thinking about her words nonstop and she didn't even remember? "You said you thought I was passive aggressive, but then you decided I was aggressively passive."

Hana rolled her eyes. "Oh, that. I still don't know if you're aggressively passive, but I've obviously changed my mind on whether that's a bad thing. I like you."

I stopped. Liking me was implied by her asking me to be her friend, but it was still nice to hear it.

"And you clearly like James. He clearly likes you—"

"You only saw us interacting for two minutes. You can't possibly know that."

She held up one finger. "One, you didn't mention you tutored the canal kid when we were watching that video. Why? Because you were upset about him being hurt, because you liked him."

And because I was also in that video!

But I couldn't say that. Damn it.

"Second, I heard him ask you out."

"He wasn't asking me out."

"He was."

"It was a joke."

Hana rolled her eyes. "Who would joke about that?"

"He couldn't have been serious."

"Why not?"

Because I saved his life so he thinks he owes me.

There. There was the thought I hadn't wanted to admit to myself, the reason I hadn't wanted to unpack James's behavior. How could he possibly feel anything more than gratitude or pity for me? My dreams weren't meant to come true like that. My lips flattened.

At my silence, Hana raised an eyebrow. "Or do you have an avoidant attachment style, and the minute you realized he was interested in you, you lost interest in him?"

I didn't know! Did I have a . . . whatever that was?

"Look, who cares how he feels. You like him, you don't like him, either way, no harm done on you going in there."

My nose twitched at her superior attitude. "Are Candice and Sam in there, too?" This house was only a few streets over from Candice's. The reality of a midsized town was that no one really lived that far from anyone else.

The benign calmness slipped off her face. "If they are, we can leave. I wouldn't force you to stay around an ex-friend."

"You wouldn't?"

"No. I'm not trying to make you miserable. If you genuinely

want to leave now, we can go back to my house and watch movies. I don't care."

I wrestled with a decision for a moment, but I sighed. As outspoken as Hana was, I believed her. Anyway, I was driving, so I did have the upper hand on when we left.

I grumbled, but fell into step up the pathway. The house was big and brick, and had huge windows in front. I zipped my jacket up as we walked to the door. The fall air was cutting right through it, and the closer we got, the more I worried about how sheer my shirt was.

We stepped past a trio of fall leaves and pumpkins. "Can't believe we're only a few months away from Christmas," Hana remarked.

I didn't want to think about it. It would be Thanksgiving before I knew it, and Christmas a minute after, and then my birthday a week later, and it would be my first holiday season without my mom. We didn't celebrate Christmas, really, but I liked twinkly lights enough that my mom had always indulged us with a tree and a few presents. Our Christmas Day tradition had been to go to a movie together and get Chinese food.

I didn't imagine we'd take the tree out this year, though it was still in our storage closet. My nails dug into my palm. Should I get Kareena a present? Was she getting me one? I didn't know which was worse: the day passing unacknowledged and in quiet or getting my sister a present and nothing in return.

Not now. Don't get distracted by these thoughts now. Focus on the party.

"Yeah, the year is zooming past," I agreed, and knocked on

the door. The sound of music was louder now.

There was a huff of impatience behind us, and I turned to find a kid behind me. "Is the door locked?" he asked pointedly.

Ah. I didn't know the party etiquette. My idea of a party had been a few people over at Candice's house. Her parents would have answered the door and gestured us in, then stayed upstairs and out of our way. If there was surreptitious drinking or weed, I would busy myself with taking the family dog for a quick walk.

I tried the doorknob and it opened under my palm. The guys crowded us into the entrance. "Watch it," Hana warned them softly when someone bumped into me. One of them turned to us with a cocky look, took stock of Hana's arched eyebrow, and they wandered off.

I flexed my fingers. Were there any pets here that I could use for my light social anxiety?

"Come on," Hana said, starting after them. "The party's over there."

The party sounded like it was everywhere, but I followed along to the kitchen. There were about a dozen people crowded around inside, including a lot of boys who immediately caught sight of us and straightened when we walked in.

I expected the attention to go to Hana, since she'd left her jacket in the car and was seriously cute in her outfit, but I was surprised by how much of it was directed toward me. I fiddled with the zipper of my red coat.

How did I absorb her level of confidence? Because I could really use it.

There was a mess of beer and cider and alcohol on the table and the fridge was open. I knew I was out of my comfort zone here because my immediate worry was for the power bills. "Want something to drink?" Hana asked, apparently oblivious to the guys looking us over.

Before I could answer, a giant redhead walked into the room. He was built like a linebacker, and his nose looked like it had taken a few hits. His gaze brightened when he caught sight of Hana. "Hana? You came!"

She cocked her head, and her hair slipped over her shoulder. "Remy."

Remy? This giant was the one she took piano lessons with? If I didn't know Hana liked him, I wouldn't have guessed it from her blasé attitude. She surveyed the room with her calculating gaze, like she was looking for something to be disappointed by. "It was a last-minute decision. I had nothing else to do."

I watched in amazement as Remy immediately fell over himself to impress her. What was Hana's power? Just acting like she didn't give a fuck? Was that the ticket to being someone everyone was in awe of?

She gestured to me standing behind her. "This is my friend Sonia. Sonia, this is Remy."

Remy turned his blue eyes to me and smiled, and I couldn't help but smile back. There was a sweetness in his expression at odds with his massive size. I could see why Hana liked him. "Let me get you both a drink."

"I'll have a Corona," Hana said.

Remy's brow creased as he rummaged through the beer in the ice chest. If he didn't have it, I half expected him to run to the store to get Hana one. "Ah, here it is."

Hana looked at me. "What do you want?"

I was grateful to her for including me, but I wasn't about to be pulled over on our way home with even a hint of alcohol in my system. "Coke is fine."

Remy found that quicker. He popped the top on the can and handed it to me.

I took the can from him and muttered a thank you, but he was already turning back to Hana. "So, new girl, what made you decide to come over to my house?"

She took a swig, not breaking eye contact. Cool power move. "I told you, I literally had nothing else to do."

Remy nearly melted. "I'm honored anyway."

"You shouldn't be. It was this or do my nails."

I shifted. This flirtation could go on for hours.

As if he sensed my distraction, Remy pulled me into the conversation. We chatted for a few minutes and I was just starting to get relaxed when he invited us into the living room.

That was when I saw a familiar dark head. Hana and Remy faded into the background.

James, chatting with a big group of people, holding center court on the couch. Though Hana had prepared me for his presence, I nearly choked on my Coke.

You like him. He likes you.

Did he, though?

I took a step back, but James looked up. Our eyes met, and he broke off mid-sentence. His eyes widened, and he sprang to his feet. "Sonia!"

His reaction shocked me, and so did his hug when he reached me. My hands dangled limply for a moment, but then I put my arms around him and returned the embrace. Like last time, it was over and done too quickly for me to experience it as well as I should have, beyond appreciating the faint hint of peppermint. "Hi."

He pulled away and smiled down at me. "I didn't know you were coming. God, I should have invited you."

"That's okay." Hana edged her way into our personal space. "I took care of that. Hi, James."

Was it my imagination, or did Hana place slightly more emphasis on the *J* in his name?

James nodded at Remy and gave Hana a friendly smile. "Hey. Glad you made up for my mistake."

I chugged my Coke until it was like half gone. My mouth was inexplicably dry.

Hana looked him over. "You look well."

His bruises had healed remarkably, or . . . I peered at him. Was he wearing makeup? If so, it was blended impeccably.

"Thanks. Getting back into the swing of things." He tilted his head at the gaggle of people who had surrounded him. They'd gone back to chatting with each other, but I noticed a couple of curious gazes our way.

Hana's gaze dragged between the two of us. "You sure are."

She might as well have wiggled her eyebrows. I pulled my

jacket zipper down, suddenly hot.

"Tired of your fame yet?" Hana asked James.

"A little," he said. His tone was light, way lighter than it had been when we spoke privately.

"Did they find the girl in the video?"

I stiffened. James, thankfully, did not. "Nope. She did her good deed and vanished, and I wish her the best." His smile was easy, like he'd said the same thing more than once. Not even with a glance my way did he betray my secret. Slowly, my shoulders relaxed.

He might be behaving in a rather confusing way, but he was keeping to the pact.

Luckily, Remy chose that moment to step in. He held his hand out to Hana. "Hana, want to come check out my new gaming setup?"

I could sense her hesitation in leaving me, but she was also looking at Remy with no shortage of interest, so I gave her an encouraging smile. I might be awkward, but I wasn't about to require Hana to tie herself to me for the night so I wasn't lonely. That kind of demanding shit was for a lifelong bestie, not a new friend in training.

As soon as she left, James surprised me by slinging his arm over my shoulder. "Look at you, mathlete, at a party." He gave me a little shake and released me.

I rubbed my arm. "It is a Saturday night," I said, like that meant something to me. I might as well ask, lest I be waiting for Candice to jump out of the shadows. "Is anyone else from school here?"

"Chandra. Do you know her?" He nodded at a girl sitting on the couch. "Otherwise, no. I know Remy because he used to ride the bus with my brother."

I'd seen Chandra around, and she seemed benign enough. "Ah. Gotcha." Thank God.

"I'm glad you're here, though."

Be like Hana. Don't give a fuck. "Yeah, figured I'd come last minute. Hana asked."

"I wouldn't have pegged you two as friends."

"What does that mean?"

He chuckled and held his hands up. "Nothing. Just that you're very different."

"We are, but she's been kind to me." After she'd insulted me a little here and there.

"That's all that matters." Someone called James's name and he waved. "Come meet some of my friends." He led me to the group on the sofa. "Guys, this is Sonia. She's been getting my grades up in calc." He introduced me, too quickly for me to actually catch any of their names, save for the one I vaguely knew.

I nodded and smiled, though I was lost. "Hi, nice to meet you."

Chandra waved. "I've seen you around school."

I automatically smiled back. Was I not completely forgettable, then? That was good. "Right. Nice to see you."

We chatted for a while; or rather, James chatted and told stories and we were there to laugh and cheer him on. I got pulled into the conversation nonetheless, and the more we talked, the more relaxed I became.

After a while, though, my introvert tendencies kicked in and I started to grow a little weary. I surreptitiously checked my watch, surprised an hour had passed. Perhaps there was a reason I'd only ever had one real friend at a time. It was too exhausting to have a steady conversation with more than two people.

"James, how are you doing?" A new guy walked up to the group.

"Hey, man." James did that weird side hug thing men did. "What's up?"

"What's up with you? How are you feeling?"

"Great!"

The new guy gave him a sympathetic look and leaned in. "You sure? I heard you were in pretty bad shape. It's only been a week, right?"

This time, I caught the twitch at the corner of James's eye before he answered in the same relaxed tone. "I'm fine. Really."

"That video was so wild, man."

"It was awful to watch it on the news," Chandra chimed in.

"I saw it for the first time on Twitter," said another guy. "Couldn't believe it was you."

James's smile was tight, and my heart gave a jump, despite myself. Clearly James didn't want to talk about the rescue or being hurt. Whether it was because it made him feel weak or because it was lingering PTSD, I didn't know, but his so-called friends ought to respect him when he obviously didn't want to discuss it. "I have a question," I blurted out, and then stilled when everyone turned to look at me.

Yikes. "Um . . . what role would you play in the zombie apocalypse?"

James blinked twice. Everyone was silent, similarly confused. Then James's lips curled up. "I think I'd be in charge of our new government."

That made sense. James had a politician's air about him, like he was running for senator of nothing. I wouldn't be surprised if he kissed babies and shook hands when everyone else was running from the zombies.

In a meta twist, the others followed his lead, and after someone said they'd be the muscle, they started discussing some dystopian show they were bingeing. I tried to pay attention and look interested, though I hadn't watched a ton of television lately.

After a few minutes, James surprised me by taking my hand and squeezing it. He leaned in close and whispered in my ear. "Thanks."

I should have shivered, but none of the little hairs stood upright this time. "No problem."

He used his grip to draw me away from the group. "Want to come play beer pong?"

I tried to hide my grimace of disgust. Did I want to play a game where a ball bounced all over a table and a floor and then fell in someone's cup, which they then drank? Seemed less gross to just lick each other's faces. "Ah, no, I'm actually designated driver."

"You don't have to drink. Or you can drink water."

I'd still have to touch that icky ball, though. I smiled. "Aw, thanks, but I'm really saving myself embarrassment for when you find out how uncoordinated I am and laugh at me."

"I'd never laugh at you!" He winked at me. "I owe you."

James, watch it. I glanced around. "Pact," I reminded him, in a lower tone.

"Pact, right. You want to at least come watch me play?"

I never thought a pout could be attractive. And I was right, it wasn't super hot, but James was still cute. I shook my head with an indulgent smile. "I'm going to get another drink."

Someone called James's name again, this time more insistently. He looked torn for an instant, then he patted me on the shoulder. "Okay, sure. Don't take too long." He loped away. I only spent a split second admiring the lope and then returned to the kitchen.

Hana wasn't there, so she and Remy were probably still upstairs. A couple of guys smiled at me, but I avoided their eyes. I needed some air, and I needed to think.

The dance. The hugs. The way he was looking at me.

Oh man, James was flirting with me. And I wasn't falling over myself to stay in his company? Had I gotten a concussion too when we were underwater?

Or did I really have that avoidant attachment style Hana had thrown at me? I'd google it later to really find out.

I grabbed another Coke and wandered through the double glass doors to the patio. I assumed Remy's parents were either not home or the most understanding parents in the world, because there were a lot of joints strewn over the abandoned patio table.

My nose twitched at the smoke. Every now and then I wonder if weed might calm my anxiety, and then I remember no temporary high is worth getting caught and my mom deciding all of her sacrifices were useless.

I was about to go back inside when a bark stopped me. I glanced over my shoulder to find a curly-haired dog bounding around the corner of the house. It cocked its head at me, then ran away the way it had come.

Puppy!

Helpless, I followed the creature. "Here boy! Come here, little cutie. You're such a cute little—" My excitement turned to dismay when I rounded the corner. The dog sat on a stone bench in the landscaped garden. Right next to Niam Cooper.

"I 'm assuming you're talking to the dog and not me."

I swallowed past my lump of embarrassment. "Uh, yes. I was."

Niam arched a thick eyebrow. He wore jeans and a blindingly white T-shirt tonight, topped with a maroon bomber jacket. The moonlight burnished his brown skin and tight lustrous curls with a silvery sheen.

Lustrous? Had I inhaled some of the weed secondhand?

I was positively destined to keep running into this man in the dark. Reflexively, I raised my hand to my chin. When I didn't find a mask there, I dropped it away guiltily. I wasn't Shadow this time, I was myself, and I better act like it. Mild, well-mannered, Sonia.

He didn't seem that surprised to see me, but I imagined it took a lot to shock Niam. "We have to stop meeting like this."

Buddy, you have no idea. "I was thinking the same thing. Ha ha."

"What are you doing here?"

I gestured to the dog. "I, um, heard the dog. Wanted to make sure it didn't run away." *I wanted to play with it, because animals are more fun than people.*

"I meant, what are you doing at this house? Remy's never mentioned you."

I doubt he would, even after tonight, given how laser-focused he was on Hana. I slipped my hands inside my jacket. I'd close it in a second, but a part of me wanted Niam to get a glimpse of my cute casual outfit, one that fit my body a little better than usual. He'd seen me behind an apron twice, and once cloaked in a baggy sweatshirt and the disguise of darkness. Pride alone demanded he know that I could clean up. "My friend's friends with Remy. What are *you* doing here?"

"Remy and I used to ride the bus together."

James had already told me that, and that was common for the area, where the public school buses also took kids to other area schools. I'd only asked to deflect from me being out of place.

"But I'm mostly here to make sure my brother doesn't mix too much alcohol and prescription meds. Parties aren't really my thing."

They weren't my thing either, but it was weird to have something in common with James's taciturn older brother.

Niam's words sank in, and I frowned. I hadn't thought about James's pain meds. "Um, I don't mean to snitch, but I should probably tell you he's playing beer pong inside right now."

Niam muttered a curse, and he shook his head. "Should be okay. My friends are under strict orders to water down all his drinks. I'll give him a few minutes and then I'll drag him away."

I drifted closer, charmed despite myself by Niam's gruff affection for his younger sibling. Probably because it felt foreign to me now.

Kareena did do your makeup today. She told you to be careful.

Yeah, crumbs of affection. After months of a starvation diet.

Niam nodded at the puppy. "Did you want some time with Benny here?" The dog perked his ears up at hearing his name.

"I wouldn't mind it," I admitted. "I'm not much of a party person, either, and my friend's off somewhere with Remy."

"Ah, then she'll be a while." He paused. "If she wants to be, that is. Don't worry, Remy's a good guy."

"That's great to hear." I wasn't sure if I could trust Niam entirely, but then I thought of the way he'd promised me that he'd keep mum in that parking lot.

If I could trust James to keep a pact, I supposed I had no choice but to trust his brother as well. At least until I was proven wrong.

I sat down on the opposite bench and placed my Coke next to me, then snapped my fingers. "Here, Benny. Do you want to come here?"

The dog gave me a confused whine and didn't budge.

Niam patted his butt. "Go on, buddy. Go to the nice lady." His tone was low and more gentle than I'd ever heard it. The fall air whispered over my neck, making goosebumps break out. Or at least, I'd tell myself it was the fall air.

Benny hopped off the bench and came to sit next to me. I ruffled my fingers through his fur and scratched him, trying to make it worth his trip over.

"You look nice tonight."

I flushed and sat up, lest my cleavage hang too far out of my shirt, but he didn't seem to be looking there. His eyes were on mine. "Thanks."

He gestured at his face. "You, uh, did something different with your makeup?"

"Yes." I paused. "I put some on."

"Oh." He rubbed his hands over his thighs. "Your hair is shinier than usual. But in a good way."

I blinked at him, and it was in that second that realization dawned over me.

Holy shit. This big, tall, handsome man from a perfect family with a gruff attitude and competent hands was kinda awkward. He'd fooled me with the self-assured, no-nonsense manner in the kitchen and with Shadow, but he'd been in his element there.

Not at a party. Alone with a girl he'd mistaken for an employee.

And that was all I needed to calm down. Where James's smooth flirtation made me antsy, Niam's word vomit made me feel in control. "Thank you," I said gently. "It's coconut oil."

"My grandma used to scrub our heads when I was young."

I smiled. We had at least this cultural marker in common.

"Yes. My mom did too." I ruffled Benny's fur and he put his head on my lap in adoration. "He's a good dog."

"Yeah. I've known him and Remy for a while. This is a really a small town underneath it all."

"And you have deep roots," I guessed.

"Yup. Second generation. Our dad's family all lives in New York City, but our maternal grandparents lived here from the time they came to the country."

"That's so nice." I wished I had that kind of connection to anywhere.

"It is. Except for the whole everyone knowing you and your business thing." His smile was faint. "Speaking of businesses, I know it's short notice, but do you want to pick up some extra cash tomorrow? We're booked for a party at the restaurant. My mom asked me to text you, and I didn't have a chance to ask James for your number."

Hmm. The pay was good, and I didn't mind being back in the warmth of the Cooper restaurant. But then again, the more time I spent around this guy or his family in well-lit conditions, the more I might reveal.

"It won't be like last time. We actually have help tomorrow. You'd mostly be doing prep work, washing dishes, and helping my mom with whatever back-end stuff needs doing."

Oh, so his mom was going to be there. The *hug*.

The speed of my affirmative was pathetic, and I'd analyze what it meant later. "Okay."

"Give me your number?"

I rattled it off, and he nodded. Working at a restaurant must have honed his memory, because he didn't write it down, just absorbed it into his brain.

"Do I need to wear anything special?"

"Not really. The servers wear all black, but you can be comfortable."

We enjoyed the silence for a while; it might have been ten or fifteen minutes or even longer. My weariness melted away as we sat there, like my battery was being recharged with every tick of the clock. Finally Benny got tired of my love and jumped to the ground.

Niam broke the silence. "I saw you inside," he finally said. "Talking to my brother. Before I came out here. You looked happy to see him."

So that's why he hadn't been surprised when I turned the corner. "I was happy."

"You know, our family thought you and James were dating at first. He told us you weren't when he came home."

There was no point in pretending. "I know," I admitted. "James told me."

"I knew you weren't. I said you weren't my brother's type."

Ouch. I might be collecting way too many blunt people in my life.

His brow furrowed, like he was debating what to say next. His words came in a rush. "My mom initially thought you were dating because she heard him talking to Sam, trying to make her jealous. He's been bummed since they broke up, not really taking care of himself."

What was he saying? "I don't think I understand."

"Just telling you to watch yourself, Sonia. My brother's a good person, but he's kind of in a weird place right now and recovering from a traumatic event. I don't want to see you get accidentally hurt."

My face flamed as Niam's meaning sank in. He was saying that James was only flirting with me to make Sam jealous. Sam wasn't even here, though. "That's not very nice," I said, and I was proud of how firm my voice was.

His thick brows drew together. "What?"

"That you think your brother wouldn't want to be with me for any real reason." It was one thing for me to think it. Another for him to.

"I didn't—"

Before I could answer, my phone buzzed and I groped for it in my pocket. James, like I'd conjured him. **Where are you?**

I texted back, eager to get away. To prove Niam wrong, despite the niggle of doubt that already lived in my brain. *That would make sense. That he's using you to make someone jealous. Why else would he show interest? Pity. Gratitude. Or as a tool.*

Outside, in the backyard. "I have to go," I said to Niam.

"Sonia, wait."

I stood my ground as he came closer, reminding myself that I was dressed as Sonia, and not Shadow. I didn't have to run.

He bent down and picked up Hana's keys. They must have fallen out of my pocket. "Here you go."

I accepted the keys, and our fingers touched. An odd burst

219

of electricity went through mine, tingling up my arm and into my brain. I jerked the keys away from him, startled. What was that? "Thanks."

"Sonia?"

I found James a hundred feet behind me. He glanced between his brother and me.

"I'm sor—I'll see you later," Niam murmured.

I shook my head and walked toward James. He smiled easily at me, though there was a tightness around his mouth. "What are you doing out here with my brother?"

"Nothing," I said shortly, then glanced over my shoulder. Though the dog was still there, passed out on the grass, Niam had vanished.

Okay, Batman.

James's face relaxed. "I thought he'd already gone home."

"Sounds like you wanted him gone." *Because he's mean and too honest?*

"I didn't want a babysitter."

"Does he usually babysit you?" We entered the sliding glass doors. The party had quieted down some.

"He and my parents have always been overprotective of me." He poured both of us a Coke without asking what I wanted. He doctored the one in front of him with a liberal splash of Jack Daniel's. I hadn't realized there was hard liquor here.

I accepted the fresh soda. "That sucks." I didn't know how genuine that sounded, because I'd occasionally kill for someone to be overprotective of me. Not Niam, though.

James leaned against the counter. "You okay?"

I met his gaze. "Sure. Why wouldn't I be?"

He sucked his teeth. "Come with me. I want to show you something."

No. Tell me what your brother was talking about.

But that aggressively passive trait reared its head, and I walked with him down the empty hallway until we got to a door. It seemed vaguely illicit to wander around someone's house like this, but Remy was otherwise occupied.

I forgot about etiquette when I got a look at the basement. "Wow." It was set up like an old-timey movie theater, complete with plush leather seats and a huge movie screen.

He placed his drink in the arm of one of the seats. "Hang on, let me get the lights."

I stared at the drink he'd left behind, and then at my drink. They looked identical.

Prescription drugs.

The guy had just had a head injury. I wrestled with myself for a second, then switched our drinks. Niam—that too-real jerk—had said his friends were watering James's drinks down, but James had poured his own whiskey into this glass. It might be more of that babysitting James hated, but I also didn't want to have to rescue the man a second time, if his drugs interacted with the alcohol.

The lights dimmed, and LEDs popped up on the floor and on the wall. I forgot my angst for a minute. "This is so cool."

He came back from the wall and flopped onto a two-seater couch. "It is, isn't it?" He patted the seat next to him. "Take a load off."

I sank down gingerly. "You, uh, want to watch a movie?"

He tilted his head back. "I just wanted to get away from everyone." He took a sip of his drink. Er, my drink. "Ugh, I swear, all the liquor is weak here tonight."

I didn't pick up my drink. Er, his drink. Instead, I changed the subject away from his glass. "It wasn't the accident that made your family more protective of you?"

"Nah. It's rare to get diagnosed with this platelet condition so young, but I was doing a pretty good job taking my pills. My getting dizzy and passing out like that, in the worst possible way, is, like, confirmation for them that they need to hover over me." His lips twisted. "They're not wrong, I suppose. I should have been more compliant with my meds."

"You said you were stressed out, too. Don't be too hard on yourself." Stressed out because he and Sam had broken up. Niam's words traveled through my brain.

James had used a fictional stand-in to get Sam to feel jealous. Could he have realistically flipped his emotional switch over to me so quickly and completely?

He placed his arm casually over the back of the sofa. It wasn't quite over my shoulders, but it was close.

Part of me wanted to encourage that touch. I was starved for physical affection. When my mom had been here, she'd hugged and kissed us every day.

"My family will loosen up as time goes on." He gave me a shadow of his smile. "Don't worry about it. I'll be fine, Sunny."

He probably would be. He had the support and protection of an amazing family.

Wait a minute. Ew. Ew. Until now I thought I'd be okay with James calling me anything in that sexy low voice, but . . . Sunny?

I cleared my throat. "Sunny?" I asked.

He gave me a sheepish look. "Do you have another preference for a pet name?"

"Are we giving each other pet names?"

"No? No. You're right. Way too juvenile." He scooted closer, and I grew tense. Our thighs pressed against each other, and his arm dropped, so it was right over my shoulders. His fingers stroked my shoulder, and I shivered, a natural physical response, despite the unease in my brain.

I wanted to believe that yes, he obviously liked me, that this was just low self-esteem making me hesitant, but I didn't fully believe that. I wasn't the only one seeing red flags in this behavior, and as angry as I was at Niam for saying it, his brother knew him.

He gazed at me through half-closed lids. "I like your hair like this," he said.

You look nice tonight.

James hadn't complimented me once until now, or noticed anything was different about me. Even Niam had been more effusive.

Those sleepy bedroom eyes had probably charmed more than one girl, but they left me, who had been desperately in love with him a week ago, unmoved, and that told me better than anything that I needed to listen to my instincts. Especially when my instincts had me turning my head at the last second, so his kiss bounced right off my ear. Which was gross, crush or not.

"What are you doing?" My voice wasn't as clear as it had been with Niam, which was annoying, because this felt like a more important time to be firm.

"Um, I'm sorry. I thought you . . . I must have misread . . ." James shifted, until a good leg's worth of space was between us.

"I mean, what are you doing, in general?" I waved at the basement love nest. "Asking me to a dance, eating lunch with me, trying to kiss me? What's your game?"

"There's no game."

"Do you feel bad for me?" I rose to my feet and paced away. "Do you feel like you owe me?"

He sat forward on his seat. "What are you talking about?"

I thought of what Niam had said. "Are you just trying to make Sam jealous?" I asked softly. I felt foolish saying it. I doubted there was a timeline in the multiverse where Sam would be jealous of me.

"No, of course not. Don't be silly. You took my breath away the first time I saw you. When I was in the hospital, all I could think about was you. You saved me physically, and then emotionally."

Only, of course he didn't say that, because that would have been a wild fantasy come true. He said nothing, and the silence was my answer. *Crash.*

I faced him, even as my heart hurt. "I have to go," I said quietly.

He spoke when I was at the base of the stairs. "Sonia! I don't

224

see what the big deal is. I thought you were into me."

I stopped at the stairs and searched his pale face. He hadn't said it as a question. He'd said it as a statement. This was just my night to be embarrassed, I suppose. "You've . . . you've known I liked you? All this time."

He opened his mouth, then closed it.

Mortification threatened to keep me right there, but I forced myself to stomp up the stairs.

Chandra was in the hallway when I opened the door, but I ignored her greeting. I pulled my phone out of my pocket and texted Hana. *I'd like to leave now. I'll be by the car.*

Thank God no one stopped me as I made my way outside and to the Tesla, especially anyone with the last name of Cooper. I was very much over them.

"Sonia?"

I looked up to find Hana traipsing across the neatly mowed front lawn. Her hair was rumpled, and her clothes were slightly askew, but she looked concerned instead of annoyed at her night being interrupted. "Everything okay?"

"Yeah, I got really tired."

Her lipstick was smudged all over her lower chin. "Why are you out there? I thought for sure you and James would be in one of the rooms upstairs, too."

I straightened away from the car. "He actually showed me the basement."

She frowned at me over the hood of the car. "That sounds serial-killer-ish."

"It's a movie theater." I shook my head. "It's not important.

Nothing happened. James isn't into me like that."

"If he's showing you basements, then—"

"He was trying to make Sam jealous." I said the words louder than I should have, but thankfully, no one was around.

She stared at me for a long moment. "He admitted that?"

I lifted a shoulder. "Basically."

Without another word, she did an about-face and started walking back to the house.

Wait, this didn't bode well.

I had to trot to catch up to her longer legs. "Where are you going?"

"He can't use you and get away with it. I'm going to slap him silly." Her calm response was terrifying.

"Ah, no need." I stepped in front of her, then placed my hands on her shoulders when she tried to go around me.

She scowled down at me. "You're unexpectedly strong."

"I know." I shook my head. "Hana, get in the car."

"But it's not right," she insisted. "He can't treat you like that."

Warmth bloomed in my chest. It had been so long since anyone had defended me in any way, and Kareena and Hana had both stepped up this week. "I know. But going in there and punching him would only make more gossip fly, and I'm not about to let Sam hear that he and I are fighting. It'll just make everyone think what he wants them to think, that there's something between us."

She subsided and glared at the house, like it was the building's fault James wanted to use me.

226

Ouch. *Use* was such an ugly word, and I really didn't want to think it in context with my love life. "Can we go, please?" I said quietly. "I'd like to forget this happened."

She huffed, but she turned around.

We got in the car, and I fastened my seat belt. "How was your night? I'm sorry for pulling you away early." It had actually been kind of her to abandon her guy for me.

Another little firework in my chest. That was, like, real friend behavior there.

"No, it's best you did. I wouldn't want Remy to think he's that important."

That didn't sound incredibly healthy, but I wasn't exactly the poster child for healthiness right now, so I couldn't call her on it.

"I think Remy might have some real potential in my rotation."

"Rotation?"

"Harem. Make-out buddies. It would be a rotation of one, but you have to start somewhere."

"Oh. That's good." I wondered if Remy might have long-term potential, but I think as far as Hana was concerned, it would also be okay if he was for the short term.

"I think so. Do you mind driving me home? You can take the car to your place, and I'll arrange to pick it up tomorrow."

I was curious to see where Hana lived, so that was fine. "Sure, but I'll tell you right now, I don't love driving your car."

"Why?"

"What if I bang it up?"

"Eh." Hana yawned. "I really wanted a Mustang, so if you total it, you'll actually be doing me a favor. I might finagle a gas guzzler from my dad for Christmas." She rattled off the address, and I put it into my phone.

I glanced over at Hana, but her eyes were closed, and her head rested against the leather seat. I was just as tired. Too tired to think about either Cooper brother. I started the car and peeled away from the curb. Tomorrow would be soon enough for that.

CHAPTER

Sixteen

There was a moment between sleeping and waking up when I could pretend that my world wasn't chaotic, and everything wasn't life and death. When a Sunday could mean that my mom was home, cooking something delicious for breakfast while my sister and I slept in like normal teenagers and not a guardian and her ward.

I sniffed the air, confused, as I came further out of sleep. Was that . . . pancakes? Waffles? I hadn't smelled that in this house for months.

I blinked up at the sun-filled room and rolled over onto my side, stretching. The book on my chest fell off me. I'd finished *Makeshift* last night as I was trying to sleep. She'd shifted into the villain to gain access to his inner sanctum, manipulated him into a fight, and celebrated his defeat with her friends and Puddin'. I'd drifted off with the last sentences rattling around my brain.

I might be wearing other people's faces, but my voice remains my own.

Everyone has a voice, even if they don't have superpowers, so anyone can be a hero. When we can speak up for ourselves, we can speak up for others.

I picked up my phone from under my pillow and checked the screen, the sleep in my eyes blinding me at first.

Then I read the text, yelped, and dropped the thing. So much for dreams.

The message was from a number I hadn't saved in my contacts. **This is Niam. Confirming that you're coming to work tonight?**

Aw, crap. I'd forgotten that I'd be going to Gulab tonight.

Niam texted like he spoke, brusque, to the point. He hadn't talked like that to Shadow, but I wasn't Shadow. Well, I was, but he didn't know that.

I opened the message and started to reply. **I can't come in today because . . .**

Because what? Because *you were right, and your brother's a fickle asshole who I have no wish to ever see again?*

But that wasn't their mom's fault, and she was the one who would be left shorthanded if I didn't come.

I deleted the text. I bit my lip and asked the most pertinent question I had, too tired to care about how it sounded. **Will your brother be there**

Niam's reply was instantaneous. **No. Just me.**

I wrestled with that. I didn't want to see Niam either. James's behavior was his own issue, but Niam had been right. I didn't think he would gloat, but it was still embarrassing, damn it.

I thought of the money I'd make tonight. I would avoid Niam as much as I could and keep my head down and do my job.

His next message came before I could say anything. I'm sorry I overstepped last night. It's none of my business. I won't bring it up today, promise. We can keep things professional.

I nearly chewed my lip off. That was a nice apology, though I didn't know if I could trust any Cooper right now.

But wouldn't it be suspicious if I didn't come after I said I would? It was a few hours. I could do this. Yeah, I'll be there.

He didn't reply verbally, but he did like my text. I nearly tripped on the discarded clothes in the middle of my room when I got up. I was still wearing Kareena's shirt from yesterday, though I'd put gym shorts on when I'd gotten home.

As I brushed my teeth, a million and one thoughts slammed through my brain, firing every neuron up so they were annoyingly alert.

How could James think he could use you?

Because you're a mouse.

Pathetic.

What if he tells everyone about you being Shadow now?

He said he didn't want the attention. He won't drag this out any longer.

You can't trust him anymore. He probably just agreed to that pact because he thought he could use you to make Sam jealous.

I pulled the scrunchie around my hair off, and my hair tumbled down. It was still in pretty good shape from yesterday, though flyaways had started to pop up around my hairline. I'd remembered to wash my makeup off last night, but the bags under my eyes were so dark they looked like smeared mascara. I was going to have to pat a good amount of concealer under there before I went to work tonight.

Work at the Coopers'. I shuddered. *The money. Think of the money.*

I came out of the bathroom. The sound of laughter caught my attention, a laugh I hadn't heard in a long time, light and tinkling. It should have made me happy too; there was a time when it would have.

I followed it and that unusual smell of pancakes to the kitchen to find Kareena sitting at the breakfast table, phone in front of her, my mom on the screen.

"Is that Sonia?" My mom's voice carried through the phone, so loud and strong she might as well have been in the room. Except she wasn't.

I stepped forward from where I hovered in the doorway. "Good morning."

Kareena flipped her hair over her shoulder. Her smile had faded, but it lingered at the corners of her mouth. "Morning," she muttered.

"Did you make pancakes?"

"Yeah, but I didn't want to make yours and have them get cold. The batter is over there, though."

I didn't know if I believed that Kareena had given me that much thought while making her own breakfast. I looked at the bowl of batter. It was nice of her to have at least saved me some. Putting batter to pan wasn't a lot of effort, but unfortunately, I had zero motivation this morning.

"Your hair looks so nice, Sonia," my mom enthused.

Though it killed me a little—I was still annoyed about the almost weight comment—I gave credit where credit was due. "I used Divya Auntie's products. I'll thank her for them."

My mom smiled. "I'm glad they worked for you. You are up early."

I checked my phone. For a Sunday, it was early for me, barely ten a.m. "Yeah."

"Surprising, since you got home so late yesterday," Kareena remarked.

Damn it, Kareena. I didn't mind my mom knowing I went to a party, she wasn't strict like that, but then I'd have to answer questions about who was there and why I was there and what I did, and I was tired.

"Were you out last night?" Mama's voice rose in surprise, and I couldn't blame her. *Pathetic. Mouse. Who would go to a party with you?*

"Yes, I went to a party." I grabbed a bowl and spoon and the box of cereal from the top of the fridge and came to the table to sit next to Kareena. Normally I'd sit across from her, but then I wouldn't get to see our mom.

"Oh, a party. Who was there? Candice?"

The last thing I wanted to do was talk about Candice. "Um—"

"We're out of milk," Kareena interrupted.

I looked down at the Frosted Mini Wheats in my bowl. "Fantastic."

"Sonia?"

I dug my spoon into the bowl and ate a big bite of dry cereal. It tasted like straw. "Candice wasn't there. I went with my new friend, Hana."

"Oh, that's so nice." Mama sounded happier than she had in a while, which cheered me up, despite how crappy my night had been. "Who's Hana?"

"I work with her. She's new in school." If I'd been alone with my mom, I would have gone into a bit more detail, at least about the dinner we'd had and how Hana was a little too honest, but seemed to have a good heart, but I felt odd baring so much with Kareena sitting there.

Mama leaned closer to the camera. "Were there any boys there, Sonia?"

I avoided looking at Kareena. "A few. Don't worry, none of them were there for me." I kept the words as expressionless as possible. So long as I didn't think about it too hard, I wouldn't fall apart.

James had never been mine. There was no reason to feel this sense of loss.

My mom hummed. "I wouldn't mind if they were. I'd rather you tell me. I'm not one of those moms, you know."

She was a cool mom. Yet again, we were out of step with other diaspora kids I knew, whose parents wouldn't entertain the thought of them dating before marriage, but I appreciated Mama for this. While she'd never explicitly encouraged it, she had bigger fish to fry than us kissing someone in high school. "I know. But there was no one there."

Despite her words, my mom looked relieved. "None of my friends believe me when I say my daughters are so focused on school and not interested in boys at all. Or girls," she said hurriedly. "I'm sorry, Kareena."

Kareena lifted a shoulder, face bland. Her being gay had never been a big deal in our little family, because my mom was, again, a cool mom. Though Mama occasionally misspoke, she usually caught herself and apologized when she did. "It's okay."

"What have you got planned for today, then, Sonia?"

"I'm going in to work."

"Oh, the café."

"No . . . I started helping out at this Indian restaurant. They have a party today."

"Which restaurant?" my mother immediately demanded.

"Gulab," I said.

"Ohhhh. I drove by that place a few times." Mama sat forward. "Have you met the owners? Are they nice?"

"Really nice. Her name's Pooja."

"I'm glad you're spending time with some people in the community. Does she go to the temple? You could go with her. Meet more people."

I exchanged a look with Kareena, and for once I could read her perfectly. "Oh, I don't think we need to do that." We were technically Hindu, but I didn't think I was a religious person. We'd lucked out in Mama not really being one either, but she'd considered the temple a handy place to find a community.

Mama didn't press. "Well, be on time and do a good job."

"What time do you have to go in?" Kareena asked me.

"Four. I figured I'd walk."

"No, you can't walk," my mom interjected. "Did you know one of your classmates was in the hospital? Someone tried to mug him, and he fell in the canal. He could have died."

Of course this news had made it all the way to India. I looked down at my cereal. The cut on my arm may have faded to a thin red line, but it ached now in remembered pain. If she saw that video, would Mama be able to tell it was me? Didn't mothers have some kind of sixth sense about their kids? "He didn't get mugged. It was an accident. He fainted and fell in."

"Either way, you can't walk around town." The wall behind her was cracked, though she'd hung a wall hanging over it to pretty the place up. Her home with her cousin was fairly sparse, but she'd decorated here and there. More than she'd decorated our home when she was over here. Guess without kids she had more free time.

I slapped that cruel thought out of my head. "We have one car. I have to get around, so I have to walk."

She scowled at me. "Sonia. Take the car if possible, or call a ride."

Kareena busied herself with cleaning up her plate and silverware. I took another bite of my dry-as-dust cereal. "Okay, fine."

"I'm pulling a double shift, starting at three. Why don't you drop me and take the car?" Kareena offered.

I raised an eyebrow. She so rarely volunteered to let me have the car. "Um, sure."

"Come get me at midnight is all. Don't forget."

"I won't."

Mama smiled, but there was a tiredness around her eyes. "So happy to see you working together. I should get to bed. I have to be at work by five."

"They better be paying you for all the extra work you're doing at this new place," Kareena said over the rush of water in the sink.

Mama didn't say anything about the pay, which told me they probably weren't. "Good night, girls."

"Night, Mama," I said.

After she hung up, I rose and took my bowl to the sink. If Kareena hadn't been there, I would have dumped my bowl and left, but I caught her side-eye and picked up the sponge.

She grabbed the cereal box. "Who's the guy?" she asked, and I nearly dropped the bowl. We'd never talked about love interests before in all our years inhabiting the same house, and I didn't know how to start now.

"What guy?" I stalled.

"The guy you definitely saw at the party last night." Her tone was dry. "Mom may not have caught your blush, but I did."

"There's no one."

"Is he a she or a they? Obviously, that's cool."

"No, he's a he—" I caught Kareena's smirk too late. Damn it. There was no point in lying. "It's no one you know."

"I might know him."

"You don't." I scrubbed harder at the bowl. Who would

237

have thought I'd suddenly yearn for the Kareena who didn't care about me?

"Oh. Is he fake?"

I shot a look over my shoulder. "Like I made up an imaginary boyfriend?" My voice was testy, but only because she was frighteningly close to the truth. "Please."

"Okay, okay. Just checking." She hesitated. "Do you know about condoms?"

This time, I did set the bowl down. "God. Yes. We're not . . . I'm not having sex with anyone. I barely talked to him, and we left things on not-so-great terms."

"Well, good. Tell me if you are so we can get you on the pill. The last thing we need is a baby."

I took some minor comfort that she said *we*, but it wasn't much. "Don't worry, there's no babies on the way. I know how they're made, I took health class." Kind of. My health class had been a phys ed teacher more focused on tossing deodorant and tampons our way than actually getting into the nitty-gritty of sex. But I had the internet and no supervision. I was aware.

"Hmm. Fine. What are you doing before work?"

"I should probably study. We have a test this week."

She nodded. "If you need any help with SAT stuff, I can give it to you."

Ms. Perfect Score would be a better tutor than any fancy SAT class, but I was confused. Why was she being so nice to me? "Um, thanks."

Hope began to flutter alive, and I did my best to crush it. There was no way we could go back to the before times. If I hoped, then I'd have to deal with another crash back to reality, and that was the last thing I wanted.

"I'm glad you're working at this place. They seem to pay well, given the check you deposited the other day."

"They do, yeah. Thanks for letting me borrow your shirt last night."

"No problem. Listen, uh, whatever you make tonight . . . use it to buy yourself some new clothes."

I tensed. Here it was. An insult about my clothes. "You think my wardrobe's so bad?"

"No, but you're unhappy with it. If making a few tweaks here and there will make you more confident, well, you should do it, because then you'll be putting that confidence out into the world. Go buy some clothes. Ones you actually like."

I closed my jaw. That might have been the most impassioned advice Kareena had given me in like six months. That it was to tell me to spend money was bizarre. I took a small fraction of my pay for incidentals like going out with Hana last night or my various crafts. The rest went to our household budget.

Mama must have told her to be nice to you. That's all this is. "I might use some of it—"

"No. All of it. And ask if you need more." Her eyes finally met mine. "Things might be tough, but we should still get to feel good about ourselves."

The hope fluttered alive again. It was buried beneath a mountain of regret and words unsaid, so it was fragile and couldn't quite fly. But this time, I didn't immediately crush it. "Okay. Thank you."

She pivoted, her silky hair fanning around her in a semi-circle. "I'll let you know when I'm ready to leave."

I hurriedly dried my hands. If Kareena's goal was to make sure I was never able to figure her out . . . well, she was doing a great job.

Seventeen

My stomach was a ball of knots by the time I got to Gulab. One would think, after a week of this, I'd be used to the feeling of wanting to throw up due to the string of awkward situations I found myself in, but no.

Though I was running late, I dug into my bag and pulled out my phone. Still nothing on James's feeds exposing me. That was a good sign, though he could have still gone to the cops.

I got out of the car and adjusted my crossbody purse over my chest. I'd worn my only nice pair of slacks, but they were snug in my waist. Hopefully, my loose long-sleeved shirt and oversize cardigan hid that. Buying new clothes was sounding better and better.

I walked to the front door of the restaurant. I'd considered going in from the back, but only Shadow knew where that was.

I thought I'd have time to prepare myself to face Niam, but

there he was, right at the hostess stand. He glanced up, and our eyes met.

I let the door close behind me, the jingle loud in the silence. I searched his face, looking for signs that James had tattled on me, but there was nothing unusually knowing in his eyes. He spoke first. "Sonia. Hello."

"Hi."

He adjusted the cuff of his long-sleeved button-down black shirt. He wore his gray apron over it, but unlike last time, it was still spotless. "Can you lock the door behind you? I kept it open for you."

I turned the lock on the door. Had he been waiting here for me? "Sorry I'm a little late, I had to drop my sister off first."

"No problem." He tilted his head. "Follow me, and we can get your paperwork in order."

"Paperwork?"

"Yeah. So we can get you on the payroll. I assumed last time you'd already done all that, but of course, you hadn't."

Even though I was documented, the thought of paperwork always made me a little nervous. Paris's dad paid me under the table, but I knew most people didn't do that.

I followed Niam into an office. It was relentlessly neat, with a big desk and comfy armchair, as well as two computer monitors. There was a big couch there, with a blanket folded over the back. Maybe this was where James had rested when he'd come home from the hospital. "Is your mom here?" I asked.

"She is. She's in the kitchen, getting everything together. Have you ever worked catering before?"

"Other than last week, you mean?"

He glanced up from the computer. There was a hint of sheepishness in his face. "Yeah."

"Nope."

"Really? You're pretty good at knife work and taking direction."

His tone was friendly, kind, like last night hadn't happened. Had James said something to him? Did he realize there was nothing to worry about, because his brother wouldn't be flirting with me any longer?

It doesn't matter. You are in the restaurant, he is a coworker, and that is how you're going to treat him, regardless of what's transpired between you and him or Shadow and him in the past. "I do some food prep at the café. What kind of party are you hosting tonight?"

"It's a pre-wedding event."

Another thing my mom hadn't had time or money to do was go to people's weddings. In the beginning it was because Kareena had to be extra protected from germs, and then it had become habit, and we'd only gone to a couple of celebrations. The result was that I probably knew more about Western wedding traditions from TV and movies. "A sangeet?" I guessed.

"Kind of, but it's a fusion couple, so it's more nontraditional. Like a rehearsal dinner with dancing."

"That's cool."

Niam nodded. The light slanted across the desk, making his dark hair and skin glow. His hair was shorter and sharper, like he'd gone to a barber between last night and today.

Last night, when he made it very clear that his brother wouldn't

243

seriously be interested in you. And was then proven right.

I wanted to shrink, become tiny, but science hadn't figured out how to do that yet, damn it. Instead, I stiffened my spine.

He clicked the mouse, unaware of my unease. "Okay, come fill this out."

I rounded the desk, pulled out my identification for him, and quickly typed my information into the forms he'd pulled up for me, trying not to notice him standing near me.

He closed out of them. "Perfect. Let's head to the kitchen."

I was braced for him to break his word and say something about the party or James, but Niam was all business as he hustled me to the kitchen. The awkwardness he'd displayed last night was gone.

We entered the kitchen, and it was an entirely different scene from when Niam had been trying to furiously hold everything together and get the order out the door by himself. Pooja stood in the center of the chaos, directing the half a dozen chefs and employees in the place. Everywhere I looked there was something either bubbling or cooking or cooked, all manner of foods and colors and spices.

I momentarily forgot my worries. "Wow. It smells fantastic in here. I could eat everything."

Niam smiled, and it was the kind of smile he'd given me when I was Shadow, full of pride and without reservation. "It does, doesn't it?"

I met Pooja's gaze. "Sonia," she said, and dropped what she was working on.

Don't expect the hug this time. James had told her we weren't

244

dating. Surely she wouldn't—

But then she did. She wrapped her arms tight around me and pulled me close. I tried not to be a creeper, but I inhaled her scent anyway. It wasn't floral, like my mom had favored, but cinnamony. "It's so good to see you again."

"Good to see you, too," I murmured.

"Who is this?" one of the chefs asked. He was big and burly, and sounded stern, but he had nice eyes.

"One of my nieces," Pooja said. My surprise must have been obvious, because she winked at me once he was out of earshot. "Niece in spirit." Pooja kept hold of my arm as she led me to the counter. "I can't thank you enough for your help tonight. We are perpetually short-staffed."

I didn't know why, if they paid everyone as well as they paid me. "How can I help?"

"Since you're new, you're going to copy what I do, to start. You were pretty good on prep, so we'll have you shadow one of the chefs, too. And then you'll fill in wherever anyone needs you. Sweeping, dishes. I know you're used to facing customers at the café, but it'll all be back of the house tonight. Sound okay?"

"Sounds perfect." I suspected that I would much prefer helping out in the back to having to deal with someone mad because they thought I'd skimped on the brown sugar syrup in their chai latte.

"Excellent. Come, you can help me with the samosas."

"Those are my favorite thing to eat, so that works." I glanced over my shoulder, but Niam had left us. He wasn't working the stoves today, but laboring at the cutting board. When his mom was around, I supposed he was relegated to prep as well.

She waved me over to the counter and handed me a potato and a peeler. "Go on, peel all of these for me, really well, okay?"

I barely had time to think over the next six hours, because the work ramped up fast. I'd never been in a professional kitchen as it catered an on-site event. It was one thing to pack up dishes for a driver to take. It was another to send out a hundred appetizers, soups, salads, entrees, and desserts on a timed schedule.

There was a lull for a beat once the five courses were out. I finished sweeping the floor for the millionth time, then heard my name called.

I glanced up to find Niam hard at work next to the stand mixers.

I mentally took a deep breath. How I'd managed to avoid him this long, I didn't know. I checked around, hoping someone would need me as well, but everyone was busy. I walked over to him. *Keep it professional.* "What's up?"

He glanced at me. Sweat had made his dark hair even glossier. "We ran short on the dessert table. Can you fill the cupcake trays while I make batter?"

"I think I can manage that."

Niam placed one bowl of batter next to an already lined cupcake tray. "Here you go. About three-quarters full."

I stepped aside as one of the other chefs darted around me. My nose twitched at the heavy scent of cardamom. "What kind of cupcake is this?"

"Rosewater. It's gulab jamun inspired. My mom's signature dish."

I knew what that was, at least. My mom had loved the syrupy, sticky fried balls of dough. "My mom always got gulab jamun for us when she was around."

I tried to focus on filling the cupcake tin uniformly and without spilling, though it was harder when he spoke over the whir of the mixer. "I'm so sorry."

I gave him a wary look. "For what?"

"You said . . . I didn't realize she had passed away."

I replayed my words in my head and nearly slapped myself. *When she was around.* It must have been the tiring heat of the kitchen that had caused the slip. Silly, silly me. "Um. She hasn't. My dad did." I hurried to reassure him when he grimaced. "But I didn't really know him. She's . . . she's in India. Visiting." Or so I hoped.

"Oh. Who do you live with?"

I concentrated very hard on my job. "My older sister."

He brought a big tin of pistachios to the cutting board. "Is she much older?"

"A couple years."

He paused. "She's eighteen? And you live with her? Both of you, by yourself?"

Oh crap. We hadn't gone through any kind of legal process for Kareena to be appointed my guardian, because, well, for obvious reasons. The system had overlooked us, and it wasn't like I was a toddler or a child. I'd be considered a full adult in a little over a year. What did it matter if Kareena was my unofficial guardian for a minute? "Temporarily," I lied. "My mom will be back soon."

He opened his mouth, and fearing more questions, I changed the subject, though I would have loved to simply walk away from him. "You should be a baker."

His hand flew as he chopped the pistachios. "Yeah?" He scraped the chopped pistachios into a bowl and came toward me. I took a giant step back because he was, well, giant. He picked up the filled cupcake tray and placed it gently in the oven. Then he wiped his hands on the towel over his shoulders. His muscles flexed. It was a subtle flex, like he didn't want to quite overwhelm my poor delicate lady sensibilities, but I saw it.

Whoa. I shouldn't have seen it, though. I glanced around.

"Can you help me make the syrup?" He jerked his chin at the stove.

So I wasn't going to be able to wander away from him.

The syrup was relatively easy, melting sugar and water and adding spices, all of which he did. I was grateful he handled that part of it. I didn't know much about cooking, but I knew that saffron was expensive.

He stirred for a moment, then handed the spoon to me. The syrup was fragrant, but the scent of cardamom seemed to have gotten under his skin, because it grew fainter when he stepped away. "Stir it for five minutes."

I glanced around at the room. "Is there a clock in here?"

"No, here." He handed me his watch. "Use that."

I accepted the gold-and-black watch automatically. It was all scratched up, but the heft told me it was expensive. "Oh, I don't want to be responsible for this."

"It's old, don't worry about it. It was my dad's. Put it on if you're worried about losing it."

I slipped it on my wrist reluctantly. I had thick wrists, and the band wasn't that loose on me.

We worked in silence for a few minutes, and then he cleared his throat. "Listen, about last night . . ."

Before I could clearly say *you said we wouldn't talk about last night*, he continued. "Your friend, Hana . . ."

Ah. So that was why he was being nice to me. Nothing new. Guys and girls had always been nice to me to get Candice's number. Candice had always been more interested in crushing on people than she had been in dating them, so it had been fruitless on their part. "What about her?"

But Niam surprised me. "My buddy Remy's kinda into her. She seems cool. Do you think she's into him, though?"

"Did he ask you to ask?"

His smile was reluctant. "No, but I know I'd want him to, if the roles were reversed."

"The roles?"

"Like if I was into you, and he found himself alone with Hana."

I leaned over the pot to hide the weird thrill that ran through me. *It's only because no guy has ever said he's into you. Even a hypothetical into you. Calm down.* "Hmm."

"Well, what do you think?" He squatted and opened the oven, pulling out the finished cupcakes.

I tore my gaze away from the strong, clean line of his back.

249

"I—I think Hana's her own person, so if she likes him, she'll let him know."

"I just don't want him hurt, you know?"

"She's not a cruel person." She could be too direct, but not out of malice. If I'd told her she'd hurt me when she'd called me a mouse, she probably would have given me a confused look but apologized.

"That's good to know."

I almost didn't hear him, because he'd stepped closer to me. He took the spoon from me, his long fingers brushing over mine, and stirred the syrup, the threads of red saffron floating in the sticky mess. He picked up the pot and poured the mixture over the cupcakes.

I licked my suddenly dry lips as the syrup cascaded over the golden-brown domed tops of the cupcakes. It drizzled down to pool a little on the pan, but the cake soaked the spiced sugar water up immediately.

"Want one while it's hot?"

I tore my gaze away and brought it up to his face. I'd never noticed the tiny beauty mark on his cheek, near his ear. I focused on it, so he wouldn't see that I'd been weirdly fixated on him pouring syrup on the cakes. As if he was pouring it on himself.

Mentally, I reared back. *What is wrong with you. Stop noticing things about him. This is James's brother, the same one who couldn't believe you and James could be a thing.*

"Sonia?"

Yes, I wanted one, but some self-control was called for right now. "No thanks."

250

He picked up the conversation where we'd left it, which confused me for a moment. "I was only concerned because Hana's not Remy's usual type."

I stiffened. *You said I wasn't your brother's type.* "What do you mean by type?"

He poked a toothpick into each cupcake. "You know."

"I don't know. Everyone uses that word, but does that mean that there's types of women? How many types are there? Two, three? Eight?"

He raised his hand in the universal gesture to slow down. "I didn't mean anything by it."

Sure he didn't. *Keep it professional.*

He was the one who had brought up unprofessional things!

"Sonia, can you please help me with this?"

I turned away. "Your mom's calling me."

I had to check myself from stomping off, because I didn't want Pooja to realize I'd just lost my temper at her older son. Or rather, taken out my temper at her youngest son on her oldest.

I was zero for two on not being angry at the Cooper boys, while falling in like with their parents. Good times.

CHAPTER

Eighteen

The party wound down around ten, and for this, my feet were extremely grateful. One by one, the staff finished their duties and closed everything up. I spent a long time mopping the floor, probably longer than I needed to, but I didn't want to miss a spot.

I put my tools away, grabbed my sweater and bag, and went to the office. The door was slightly ajar, and my feet faltered when I heard the loud voices spilling out of it.

Niam.

"I don't see why I can't work the next few weeks."

"This is not a punishment, son."

"It feels like one."

"You have to get your college applications out. We want to make sure you have the time to do them. I know you like the money, but if you need cash for something, we can—"

I'd never heard Niam sound so agitated before. "It's not

about the money! I—I like working!"

"I know you do, and I appreciate that so much. It's a joy for me that you love being here as much as I do." Pooja sighed, her weariness apparent. "Can we please discuss this at home, Niam?"

"No. Because you and Dad will gang up on me, and suddenly we'll be talking about how my grades aren't great, and how if I applied myself I could have gone to Sutherland and had a shot at a better college, like James."

I winced. I'd been too young to understand the importance of the entrance exam for our honors high school when Kareena and I had moved to New York, or I would have been stressed out too, that she would be admitted and I wouldn't. Getting into our high school didn't mean you were smarter than the kids at the public schools. It meant you were good at taking tests, and sometimes all siblings weren't good at taking tests.

"We have never compared you and James. You two do that, and I don't know how to make you stop." Pooja's voice was stern now. "I lost out on opportunities, working at this restaurant when I was in high school. I resented it and my parents for years. I don't want that for you."

"I won't resent it. You said I was good, and you're finally letting me cook more and—"

"Niam. I'm so tired. Please."

"You know, whatever. Fine. I'll work on my college apps." The door opened without warning, and I jumped.

I cleared my throat as he stared at me. *We have to stop meeting like this* was what a sassier version of me might say, but all I could come up with was "Uh, hi."

His nostrils flared, and he stepped around me. I wished I could moonwalk away, but the time for that had passed. I peered inside the office to find Pooja rubbing her temples. She smiled at me, but her face was strained. "Hello, Sonia, are you all done?"

"Yes, ma'am. Um, Auntie."

"Fantastic." She nodded at the brown paper bag on the desk. "I was about to come get you. I made you a bag to take home. Leftovers."

I adjusted my bag across my chest. "Oh, I don't need anything."

She waved that away. "It'll go to waste if you don't take it."

I entered the room and peeked inside the bag. I should have been sick of the smells since I'd been inhaling them all day, but they wrapped around me. "Thank you. I really appreciate it."

"There's samosas and some of Niam's cupcakes, as well as tandoori chicken and chole bhature."

I closed the bag. "Is that chickpeas?"

"Yes. You've never had it?"

Oops. My ignorance was showing. "No. Sorry. I'm, like, a little whitewashed."

Pooja didn't lose her smile, but it did become quizzical. "I don't understand."

"Whitewashed?" I shrugged. "It just means I'm not super Desi."

"No, I know what you mean by it. I've never cared for the term. Our diaspora is vast, and individuals are a product of a

254

lot of different factors. You're still the ethnicity that you are, even if you don't feel like you fit whatever mold you think you should."

I squirmed. How did she know I often felt like a square peg in a round hole? "Thank you." I didn't think I believed her, but it was a nice thing to say.

She walked over and laid her hand on my shoulder. Her wedding ring was cold, but her skin was warm. "Thank you for your help today. I'm so glad Niam suggested asking you to come in."

For once, I didn't focus on her touch, but her words. Niam had suggested I come work here? Why had he couched it as his mother's idea?

She released me. "If you'd like to come by next week, we could talk about putting you on the schedule. We also have an opening for waitstaff, if you'd prefer that."

Could I come work here when I wasn't on speaking terms with her kids? "I'll think about it."

"Don't forget the leftovers."

"I won't." I backed out of the office and went to the kitchen. It was sparkling clean and empty, save for a busboy. *Don't worry about where Niam is, or whether he's okay. What had that fight been about?*

I tried to think of Kareena telling me not to work in order to focus on my college apps and I couldn't quite picture it. But then again, I also hadn't pictured her telling me to use all my money from the restaurant to buy new clothes either. I supposed anything was possible.

I groaned when the light flashed off the watch on my wrist. Niam's watch. I'd completely forgotten about it. I could leave it with his mom, but then I'd have to go back into her office and do that awkward *and one more thing*. I wrestled for a second. My feet hurt, my back hurt, and no one would blame me if I forgot and returned this later. . . .

Except me. This was his father's watch, after all. "Excuse me, do you know if Niam left yet?" I asked the busboy.

"He's up on the roof." The kid nodded at the double doors on the side of the kitchen.

I hadn't even realized you could go up to the roof. I went to the doors and climbed the stairs to the access door.

It was a flat rooftop. The red–and–gold sign of the restaurant spilled over the concrete space, making it far more magical than it probably was during the day.

Niam sat with his back to me, in an outdoor lounge chair. Another was open next to him. A can dangled from his fingers. "I'll go home soon."

His words were so cold I almost turned around and backed out, but I remembered why I'd come up here. "I wanted to return your watch."

He stiffened and rose up on his elbow to turn around. The moonlight and the neon played over his features, casting him in crimson and yellow. "It's you."

"Yes. Hi. Um, I'm happy to leave you alone, I just forgot to give you this." I walked over to him.

He took the watch. "I thought you were my mom."

"I'm not."

"I can see that. You don't have to leave." He nodded to the other chair. "Have a seat, if you want."

I would have declined, except the air was calm, the weather unseasonably mild, and there was a tightness around his mouth and eyes that I hated.

He did you a favor yesterday, whether you like it or not. "Um . . ."

"I was going to show you this place after work, anyway. I thought you might like it."

"Why'd you think that?" Because it was heavy, I dropped the bag of food on the table between the chairs and my bag on the floor. It spilled over, and some of my things fell out, but I left it.

"Because you're kind of introverted. Like me." He handed me a plastic bowl.

I didn't dispute that assessment. I was kind of introverted. Inside the bowl were what looked like caramels, round disks with a divot in the middle. "What's this?"

"A dessert."

"But what is it?" I sat on the chair.

"Milk candy. My grandma, my dad's mom, she used to make it for me whenever we visited her." His smile was nostalgic. "She was a professor and didn't spend a lot of time in the kitchen until recently. She just retired. But this was something she always had on hand for us. It's mostly condensed milk, cooked down in a pan."

I put the candy in my mouth. It was chewy and caramelized, and the perfect level of sweetness. "It's nice."

His smile was faint. He closed his eyes. "Some foods stay

comfort foods forever."

I had comfort foods. I didn't think a big strong guy like this had comfort foods.

I studied his profile. He'd changed into a white long-sleeved Henley and jeans before he'd come up here. The ribbed shirt made his broad shoulders even broader and brought out the golden undertones in his skin. It clung to his thick biceps and skimmed his narrow waist and hips.

I swallowed, then swallowed again as I realized his eyes were open. His lips had gone soft, and they were fuller than they normally were in his seriousness. *Luscious* was a good word to describe him, actually. "I'm sorry," he said, and his voice raised little goose pimples all over my arms.

I looked away from him and ate another piece of candy in the pregnant pause. "Sorry for what?"

"When I said you weren't my brother's type, I didn't mean that you weren't good enough for him."

I was loath to ruin this nice moment with talk of James. "Listen. We don't have to talk about your brother," I said tightly. "I confronted him last night and he as much as admitted he was only flirting with me to make Sam jealous."

A muscle ticked in Niam's jaw. "Do you want me to smack him?"

That startled a laugh out of me. "What? No."

"Are you sure? It's my job as his elder brother to humble him every now and again. Clearly I've been slacking."

Privately I agreed, but I didn't want to make the brothers fight. "Humble him when I'm not a part of it."

"Done."

I ate another piece of comfort milk candy. "So, anyway, I guess you were right. I shouldn't have gotten mad at you. You did me a favor." Even if it had been embarrassing.

His words drifted along the cool night air like they were meant to be there. "I should have made it clearer that I didn't think you were his type because his last girlfriend had a severe mean streak and we didn't like her. And you don't, and we do."

It was always good to have my assessment of Sam's meanness confirmed. "Gotcha. Who's we?"

"My parents. Me."

I couldn't do anything but eat another candy after that. His words were raw and honest, and I felt my anger slipping away like water moving over stones. "Okay. I forgive you."

He let out a deep sigh. "Good. Thank you. And I'm sorry you got hurt anyway."

"I didn't get hurt." I had, but I didn't want to tell Niam that.

"You're not heartbroken?"

He didn't look at me when he asked that question, and I was grateful for that. Because this heartbreak didn't feel as big as it should, given that I thought James had been the love of my life. It was more like injured pride, and fear that he'd betray me. "No. I'm okay being his classmate." *And his occasional lifeguard, but we won't discuss that.*

"Hmm."

I placed the box on the table. "You can apologize to me in sweets anytime."

His smile lit up his eyes. "Will do."

"I should probably head out." I hesitated. "You going to stay up here? You're good?"

"Ah. You heard the fight. I wondered how long you'd been lurking in the hallway."

"I wasn't lurking, I was . . ." Fine, I'd been lurking. "Is everything okay between you and your mom?"

Niam squinted out in the distance. We weren't high enough to get a good view, but the little cars driving by did make me feel big and powerful. "Yes. It's not a new argument. I had to beg my mom to let me work here. She wants us to have options, which means college. I don't see the point. Culinary school, okay, but not college."

I paused. "You don't think she wants you to become a chef?"

"Or a baker, no."

"Your mom owns a restaurant, though."

Niam counted his mom's accomplishments off on his fingers. "My mom went to college, then law school, then came and took over her parents' restaurant. That's the recipe she thinks we should follow. She doesn't trust me to know what I want right now."

"That's a really long time to wait to do something you want to do. And a lot of money to spend on a degree you're not going to use."

"Tell me about it."

"Have you flat out told her you don't want to go to college?"

He barked out a laugh. "No. You saw how she reacted when she thought I wasn't going to work on my applications twenty-four/seven for the next few weeks. My parents are already disappointed that I'm not as smart academically as James is."

His mother had talked about James's calc grade slipping when I'd first met her. But then again, I couldn't believe the woman downstairs or the man who had cracked dad jokes to alleviate the stress of his son's accident would stand in their child's way of pursuing his dream. "Your parents might surprise you."

"Would your mom be okay with you working instead of going to college?"

"Probably not," I admitted. "But I actually want to go to college."

"You want to, or you don't think there's another choice, like me?"

I parsed his words. As anxious as the future made me, the answer was clear. "No, I want to." More than want to, I had to.

We weren't in the same position, he and I. He had options, and a solid support system. He didn't need financial stability like I did. And I wasn't sad or resentful of that; it was what it was. "There is no hobby or interest of mine that I would choose over security for me." And my family. "A college degree is the most likely way for me to achieve that, as far as I'm concerned. But that's not everyone's situation."

He looked down at the ground. Then he leaned over and picked up the comic book that had fallen out of my bag. *Makeshift.* It was normal-sized, but it looked small in his big hands. "I'm not much of a comics nerd, but James brings them home sometimes. I've read this one. It got a ton of buzz."

"I liked it, but the end was a little unrealistic."

"What do you mean by that?"

The thought I had when I'd finished scratched at the back of my brain. I was aware that this was going to showcase how big of a nerd I really was. "The final line said that everyone has a voice, has power, basically that we just have to believe in ourselves." I licked my lips. "But that's not true, is it? Sometimes it doesn't matter what you want or say or believe in. Bad stuff happens. So what's the point in loving yourself or believing in yourself, if things are going to happen to you anyway? It just seemed so . . . silly and needlessly cheesy."

Something flickered in his gaze, and he leaned back against his chair. His dark eyes were trained on me, his thick eyebrows lowered. "Have you ever felt powerless?"

I'd brought up this depressing scenario, but I grimaced. "Yes."

"Me too. When I was thirteen, my dad got in a really bad car accident. He was in the hospital for weeks. Broken bones. Head injury. Coma. I thought he was going to die. Thank God he pulled through."

I don't know why I shared the following story, except that he'd shared, and it was so quiet and calm up here. "My sister had leukemia when she was young. She was in and out of hospitals till she went into remission at twelve. Like, multiple rounds of chemo, bone marrow transfers, you name it."

"She's good now?"

"Yeah, luckily. I didn't realize until I was like six that it wasn't normal to be in the hospital all the time." I thanked God

Mama had had private health insurance during that time. You had to show that you had the capacity to pay for any medical treatment if you came into the country on a medical visa, and my dad's family had been rich enough to demonstrate that. But then we'd gotten cut off from them. The medical trial Kareena had originally come here for had only taken us so far, and after that, my mom had to pay through the nose for insurance. "See? Some things you don't have power over." Sometimes, no matter how hard you tried, you couldn't turn sand into oil. "So what's the benefit of believing in yourself?"

"What's the harm in it?" he countered. "Will it make things worse?"

I paused, thinking the words through. "It could."

"It could. Or maybe you'll start to happen to things, even if or while bad things are happening to you."

I crossed my legs. "Wow. That's really deep."

"Working in front of a hot stove for hours on end tends to bring out my deep thoughts."

I chuckled.

He tucked the book back into my bag. "I don't think it's cheesy. I don't think any kind of optimism is cheesy. You have to believe in something, right?"

My heart struggled against my brain. Daydreaming was what I did, but constant crashes back to a less than dreamy reality had made me cynical. "Maybe."

I laid my head back to look at the stars. The street was quiet around us, the parking lot almost cleared of all cars.

We sat in silence for a long time, but my phone alarm going

off made me stir. "Oh. I have to run and get my sister from work."

He got up when I did. "I'll walk you to your car."

Suddenly shy, I nodded. "Okay. Thanks."

He carried my leftovers for me, and even put the bag in my back seat. He closed the door and placed his hand on the roof. In the dark, in the nearly empty parking lot, he seemed even taller and bigger. He smelled like cardamom and saffron, and everything that made the food in my back seat so good.

Niam rested his weight against the car, leaning slightly. If I turned my head, I'd be able to watch the show of his bicep flexing without having to peek via my peripheral vision. Because I was peeking.

The shirt he wore looked soft to the touch, like he'd washed it a lot. My sweater wasn't extremely heavy, but wasn't he cold?

Because I was, suddenly. Or was it something else causing those goose pimples all along my skin?

He came closer and I realized the goose bumps were definitely from something else, because his body heat instantly warmed me up. "Can I tell you something?"

I was surprised by how breathless my response was, but he didn't bat an eye. "Sure."

His long lashes fluttered. The moonlight kissed the high curve of his cheek. "When you said you weren't my brother's type . . . I didn't only mean that you were too kind for him."

"So what did you mean?"

A ghost of a smile touched his lips. "I meant you couldn't possibly be his type . . . because you're mine."

My mouth would have fallen open if he hadn't kissed me. The kiss was fleeting, like a butterfly's wings over my lips, a sample of his taste. His fingers cupped my elbow, and the heat of his light touch permeated through the knit of my clothes to my skin. Electricity ran through me, shooting from my head to my toes, making them tingle.

I was still holding my breath when he pulled away. He gave me a deep, searching look. "Good night, Sonia. I'll text you."

I had no idea what I said in response, probably some garbled variation of *okay*, and I turned around and got in my car. He shut the door gently behind me. My brain was rioting, so many thoughts bouncing around inside it, I'd never be able to focus on one.

I drove on autopilot to Kareena's diner. My face was flushed, my adrenaline still high. A first kiss could do that to a gal. Especially when that first kiss came from the brother of the guy you'd previously liked.

I pulled up in front of the diner and flipped the visor down to examine my face. I still looked the same. Except my cheeks and lips were pink. The latter from me licking and touching them in confusion.

Caramelized condensed milk. I could taste it on my lips. I could taste *him* on my lips.

Kareena opened the passenger door and slid in. "You're late."

I glanced at my watch, surprised. I'd been so careful to leave ample time. "It's 12:03. I'm three minutes late."

"I got done fifteen minutes early."

Clearly the generous mood my sister had been in earlier

today was gone. My first instinct was to apologize and keep quiet, but then I heard Niam's voice in my head. I wanted to happen to things, damn it. No more of that aggressive passiveness or passive aggressiveness. "I didn't know that. Text me next time."

She harrumphed. We drove in silence the rest of the way. If we had a different kind of relationship, I might have told my sister about my first kiss, but not now. She'd probably only lecture me about safe sex awkwardly again anyway.

When we got home, I reached behind me for the food Pooja had given me.

I hesitated when we got inside because I was still kind of annoyed at her sniping, but my conscience whispered to me. "Here." I handed her the food.

"What's this?"

"Leftovers from the restaurant."

She opened the top box and found the samosas. "Yum." She took a bite and closed her eyes, like she was having an experience.

I thought of what Pooja had said. "They still need more help at the restaurant. I could see if they need documentation for everyone . . ." I trailed off. "What's wrong?"

Kareena carefully put down her food. "You asked if they could hire your undocumented sister? Are you kidding me?"

I flinched. "No, I didn't. I said I could ask—"

She didn't seem to hear me. "I can't believe you. Don't you understand how important it is for us to stay quiet?"

"Of course I understand that." Literally my whole life

revolved around it. It always had. Hell, I couldn't even revel in the satisfaction of saving James's life because we had to be invisible. A lot of angst could have been avoided if we'd had the right paperwork. "I'd never do anything to jeopardize things."

"*I'd never do anything* is right. God, I'm so fucking sick of this."

Resentment and anger stirred inside me. It wasn't even resentment and anger at her alone, but at the government and the world and at borders and at my dad's vindictive family and my mom's shady lawyer. "You think I'm not fucking sick of this? It's not like you're a ton of fun to be around lately." I don't know who was more surprised by my vicious reply, but it had definitely shocked me. Her eyes narrowed, and I braced myself.

But her voice was low when she responded. "You're right, I'm not," she said. "I'm tired and cranky and overworked and I would kill to go to a party. Or talk to my friends. Except there's no one to talk to, because they're all at college having fun, and I'm working dead-end jobs so we can squeak by from month to month."

I took a step forward. "Kareena . . ."

"No." Her fake smile stretched across her face and she took a step back. "Don't placate me. There's nothing either of us can do to fix the ugly way I feel." She raised the box. "But thanks for the food. I'll eat in my room."

I stood there for a while after she stomped upstairs. My fists clenched and unclenched at my sides, in time with the rapid beating of my heart.

I paced from one end of the kitchen to the other. *Be nice to her*, came my mother's chiding voice in my ear. *She's so tired and worried all the time. You have to be the strong one sometimes.*

I stopped. Yeah, Kareena had misheard me and spun out, but I could have walked away or not said anything. I'd messed up too, broken the fragile truce we'd somehow built over the last week.

My phone chirped, and I groaned. Had Kareena tattled to my mom already?

It might be Niam. The hope that it was drove me to pull my phone out.

It wasn't my mom, and it wasn't Niam, but it was, in fact, his brother.

I'm so sorry. Please, can we talk?

Nineteen

I should have known James was bad news days ago. Never trust a man who deployed cryptic texts with no follow-up.

I almost called a mental health day to get out of school on Monday, but I didn't want to have to forge an excuse note. What would it say, anyway? *I need a day off to avoid confrontation with my ex-crush whose brother gave me my first kiss. The ex-crush who may or may not blackmail me.*

I had a free period today before lunch. I tucked my knockoff AirPods in my ears, checked around me to make sure no one was watching, and opened TikTok to navigate to Sam's page. At this point, she was the top search in my history, second only to James.

She usually posted daily, or even two or three times daily, as befitted our resident influencer, but the past couple of days had been light on content. Since she'd implied she and James were considering getting back together.

Ugh, was James so dim that he didn't realize he didn't need me to make Sam jealous to woo her back? She'd happily trot back to him now that he was trending.

The next stop on my morbid tour was the ShadowSaves hashtag. Now that my immediate panic had mostly died down, I could kind of appreciate the nice things people were saying about Shadow. The general approval of the internet was a heady drug, and I could see how people could get addicted to it.

I wasn't a fool, though, and I knew this wasn't positive attention like being teacher's pet. Sentiments could turn on a dime. Which was why I was happy to note the videos and tweets under the hashtag weren't growing as exponentially as they had in the beginning. Now that the one-week anniversary of the sensational incident had come and gone without Shadow's identity being revealed, she wasn't front-page news. Everyone had moved on to shame some guy who was hooking up with and ghosting dozens of girls in Brooklyn.

She? Me. Dear lord. Was I starting to think of Shadow as a separate person? Perhaps. That might be a problem, but I was rapidly running out of bandwidth to handle any further problems.

Because I knew if James spilled the beans or Candice did have that cape, I was still in danger.

Or if Niam realizes the girl he kissed and Shadow are the same person. Or if the witnesses can somehow ID me. Or if . . .

Argh!

It was when I was walking to my locker to grab my lunch that I spotted James. Standing right in front of my locker, keeping me from my sad peanut butter and jelly.

With Sam, no less. In profile, they seemed to be in a heated conversation, with their heads together, speaking in hushed whispers. Sam looked cute today, in a skirt and an oversized cardigan, her silky hair falling over her shoulders.

I got jostled by someone walking past me. Unfortunately, the motion made James look up, and I immediately pivoted. I didn't precisely run away, but I also didn't walk.

I was starving, and sadly, my lackluster lunch was being blocked by Mr. User and the love of his life, so I had no choice but to go to the cafeteria. I only slowed my pace when I dared to look over my shoulder and realized he wasn't behind me.

Why would he be? This wasn't some romantic drama where he'd chase me through the hallways and profess his love. If he wanted to do that, he would have sent me more than another cryptic *we need to talk* text. Hell, he could have even tracked me down at the restaurant yesterday.

I was glad he hadn't. I was still too mad and antsy around him to trust a conversation. Also, I'd kissed his brother, and I didn't know how to feel about that.

I'd rather pay for terrible cafeteria food, even though I hadn't budgeted for the extra expense today. I consoled myself with the fact that it was pizza day. I did like the cheap plastic pizza. I added an apple to my tray as lip service to healthiness and paid.

I scanned the room for Hana. I could go take my hot lunch to Mr. Walsh's room, but that would involve carrying a tray down the hallway, which would draw more attention than I cared to receive.

Besides, the one thing going on in my life that could fall under normal teen drama was that kiss with Niam, which meant it was the one thing I could dissect with someone, and Hana was the most likely confidante. It wasn't like I could go spill to my mom. Easier to confess a kiss to a cool mom in person. Over FaceTime it was awkward.

I was so lost in my thoughts, I didn't even register the footsteps behind me until a hard shove knocked me forward. Instinctively, I clutched my tray closer, and the hot pizza pressed right up against my chest. "Oops," came a singsong voice. "So sorry. Good thing that shirt doesn't look too expensive."

I peeled the pizza I'd been looking forward to eating off my chest, more stunned than angry. I pivoted to find Sam standing behind me. Her eyes were bright, and her smile was a little too big. "Why did you do that?"

She lifted her shoulder. "It was an honest mistake. You know, like the time you spilled coffee on me."

Someone laughed at a table near us.

"Right?" Sam took a step forward. "That was an accident, too, or so you said."

My sense of justice agreed with her. A food product for a food product, shirt for shirt. Except she was enacting her revenge in a very public setting.

If I was brave, I would have held my ground, but I took a step back. My skin was crawling. If Sam grew any louder, she'd attract the attention of more than just the people around us. It was still early in the lunch hour, which meant the cafeteria wasn't full, but this wasn't a large school when it came to gossip.

No one knew who I was, but they knew who Sam was, and this would spread.

I imagined worst-case scenarios as a hobby, but having Princess Sam, Duchess of Assholes, berate me in front of the school hadn't crossed my mind before. Clearly, my anxiety needed to step up.

"What? You have nothing to say? You're such a—"

"Sonia. There you are, let's go." A strong hand grabbed my upper arm. I nearly cried in relief when I looked up at Hana's stony face.

My hero.

"Oh, look." Sam smirked. "Your mommy is here, Sonia."

Sam had fully taken her mask off and was in full lizard-person form. I never thought I would pray for Candice to show up, but I prayed right then.

Hana didn't react. "Watch your tone, or I'll alert the vice principal that I'm getting distracted by your short skirts. How many dress code violations does it take to score a disciplinary note, anyway?"

"You're one to talk." She nodded at Hana's sleeves. "I can see your terrible tattoos."

"Yeah, but my mom doesn't care about patriarchal and sexist dress codes. I'm guessing yours does."

Sam snapped her gum. The scent of peppermint hit me. James's scent. Either they chewed the same gum, or he'd given his lady love a piece. "Your parents might care about what you did at Gerald's house. At least, others here definitely will."

Hana didn't react. "We never had sex. If he told you we

did, he's a liar *and* a bad kisser, and I don't fuck with either of those." Hana pulled me closer, almost putting her arm around me. "Let's go, Sonia."

I followed, because I wasn't sure what else to do. As we walked, I clocked multiple sets of eyeballs on me, and the crawling sensation on my skin became worse, until it extended through my brain. Hundreds of spiders running inside me, all over me.

My breath grew more strangled, until I was nearly choking by the time we got outside, Hana's arm the only thing keeping me upright. I don't know how long we walked, but soon I was seated sideways in the passenger seat of a familiar Tesla, my feet still on the ground. At some point, Hana must have wrested my destroyed tray of food out of my arms and left it behind.

Hana stood outside the door and braced her hands on top of the car, blocking me from outsiders' view.

Blue sky. Red car. Black hair.

"Is this a panic attack?" she asked quietly.

I nodded, still gulping in air. I'd broken out in a cold sweat and my chest hurt, like I was having a heart attack. *Not a heart attack*, I said to myself, lest I freak out more. The first time I'd had one of these the week Mama had left, I'd spent almost an hour in a miserable ball on my floor, working my fear up more and more, until I'd passed out in exhaustion.

Hana held her hand out. I stared at it for a long minute, then took it. Her fingers were strong and steady, unlike mine. "You're okay," she said, in that same quiet voice. "You're here in the school parking lot."

I lowered my gaze to her arm. *Red flower. Purple flower. Black heart.*

I repeated what I was seeing again and again, a coping mechanism I'd seen in some psychiatrist's video, until the worst of the panic vanished. Through it all, Hana stood there patiently, letting me dig my nails into her skin.

I took one last deep breath and let her go, though the coldness in me craved touch. "I'm . . ." I meant to apologize for being such a silly, overdramatic princess, for falling apart because of a two-minute interaction in the crowded lunchroom. Sam hadn't even been as mean as she could be to me, why was I so upset?

"Don't be sorry. It happens." She leaned into the back seat and got a big roll of paper towels. She rolled a bunch of papers around her hand and gave them to me. "Do you want to clean up your shirt? My mom only buys bamboo paper towels, so they're kind of shitty, but they'll do."

I tried to mop up the cheese and marinara, but on the white T-shirt, it was almost hopeless. "I'll have to go back to class like this." Back to calculus, where James would surely notice and ask me about it.

"Nope," Hana announced, and motioned for me to swing my legs over. "Get in."

I complied, confused. "Where are we going?" Juniors and seniors were permitted to go off campus for lunch, but I never went.

"Let's go shopping."

"That'll take longer than lunch."

"So?" She made a face. "I'm fine with skipping out on the

275

rest of the day, are you? My mom might get a call from the school, but she's busy until after five, so I won't hear about it till the evening. If I hear about it. She's been shockingly lax since the divorce."

And my mom was gone, and Kareena was at work. If they left her a message, I'd deal with her questions then. A spurt of rebellion had me sitting up straighter. "Okay. Let's go."

We hit the McDonald's drive-through first. I used to love fast-food places, but we'd always gotten McDonald's after Kareena's chemo when I was little, so I'd lost my taste for it a long time ago. Hana chose it, though, and I was still embarrassed enough over my panic attack to not voice an opinion. I picked at my french fries and took a big chug of my milkshake. The cold, icy drink made my head stop spinning a little.

Hana took a turn. The sun glanced off her red tattoo. "I thought it was illegal to tattoo a minor," I said.

She ate the burger with one hand while navigating the car with the other. "It is, in California. And in New York, maybe. But my mom and I went to Nevada to get matching tattoos after everything imploded with the family. I don't think she would have done it had she been in her right mind, but I wasn't really in my right mind either."

"I'm sorry. I imagine all parents' divorces are hard, but it's probably worse when you know so much of what went down."

She drummed her fingers on the wheel. It was a standard bleak fall day. We were lucky there was no snow on the ground yet. "Yeah," she finally said. "I wish they'd both left me in the dark. Better to be ignorant than have to know in detail all the

276

times my dad forgot about us. But my mom decided at some point I was her therapist, so." She finished off her burger.

I waited for her to continue, but she was silent. "So, um . . . thanks for what you did today." I couldn't think too hard about what would have happened if I'd had a panic attack in front of Sam.

The girl was the evil version of me. She had my best friend; she'd had the man I loved. I didn't want to break down at her feet.

"I guess this doesn't do a lot to convince you I'm not a mouse," I continued. I kept my tone light, but I held my breath.

"Eh. Having a panic attack here or there does not a mouse make, but I haven't thought you were a mouse since you dumped a full cup of coffee on Sam's ugly sweater." Her eyes warmed. "You're a hero, and you'll be more than that after word spreads about how Sam melted down on you today."

I drew back. "I don't want anyone talking about me." Unless it was nice, but how often did that happen?

She gave me a sidelong glance that made me squirm. "Why is it so bad for people to talk about you?"

I toyed with a lukewarm french fry. "Do you like people talking about you?" I instantly wished I could retrieve the words, given that I knew what at least a few people were saying about her.

She didn't seem fazed. "You mean, do I mind that they're calling me a slut? Not really. It's lazy and unimaginative. How many times can you make fun of a girl for either having sex or not having sex?"

I scratched my head. "Are you naturally this healthy and well-adjusted or do you pay a really good therapist?"

Another almost-smile. "The latter, and I'm only healthy in certain areas. You do know why Sam smushed the pizza on you today, right?"

"Probably revenge for the coffee."

"Sure. But also because of James." Hana shot me a meaningful look and pulled into the parking lot of the local Goodwill. "His plan clearly worked."

I took another sip of my drink. "No, I think it's for the coffee."

Hana rolled her eyes. "If it was for the coffee, she would have gotten you fired. That girl wanted to *fight* you."

I thought about Sam and James's hushed conversation in the hallway in front of my locker. Had their fight been over me? "Not a chance."

"Why?"

"Because I wouldn't make a girl like Sam jealous."

Hana stared at me. "You said that was specifically what James wanted to use you for."

"Yes, but it wouldn't happen."

"Why?"

"Because she's gorgeous."

She rubbed the side of her nose. "And you are . . ."

"Not," I supplied flatly. Not like Sam, at least.

"You're really pretty. You have nice hair. . . ."

"My aunt got me some gel and I found a new curling method." I touched the strands.

"No, you had nice hair before you Curly Girl'ed it. It's thick with volume and secrets. You also have a gorgeous face, and a great body."

"I'm not—"

"Sure, you're not Sam, which is fine. You need to take a second and ask if you really think you're ugly or if you grew up predominantly around European beauty standards." Hana opened her door and got out of the car, like she hadn't just delivered the most profound realization I'd had in ages. "Come on. Let's get you a new shirt."

CHAPTER

Twenty

I t was midday on a Monday, which meant we pretty much had the store to ourselves. Hana glanced around when we went inside. "How about this? I pick out an outfit for you, and you pick out an outfit for me. That would be fun."

"Uh . . ." Hana did always look so cool, but I also was a little wary of what she thought might look good on me. "Just to clarify, are you trying to make me over?" Was this going to be a *montage* with my new stylish friend?

I wasn't firmly against a makeover montage if I looked better in the end. It would be a distraction from . . . How many issues did I have going on right now?

She grabbed a cart. "Only if you want me to."

"I don't think we have the same sense of style."

"Trust me."

It wasn't exactly a montage as much as it was Hana marching up and down the aisles, muttering to herself and giving me occasional assessing glances, but montages probably came in all shapes and sizes.

She stopped at a rack and pulled out a yellow top, then a black one. The second one was a crop top, which was pretty far out of my comfort zone, but I didn't say anything when Hana dropped it in the cart. I did find an old Metallica T-shirt on the hanger that was kind of cool, and would work to replace my current pizza-stained top. Hopefully no one would ask me to name a Metallica album. "You shop efficiently," I remarked.

"It's my hobby, to be honest."

"Shopping?"

"Yup. If I could be a professional shopper and always spend other people's money, I'd be happy." She frowned at a hole in a shirt and put it back. "We should go to the mall next time. There'd be more of a selection."

A mall would mean higher-priced clothes. I made a noncommittal noise. "I prefer thrifting." I was so happy that "thrifting" was what poor people with no money and rich people who cared about sustainability had in common. No one could tell which one I was.

"How do you feel about dresses and skirts?"

They weren't in the wardrobe that was currently dumped on my bedroom floor. "Umm, undecided."

"I gotchu." She threw a skirt on top of the pile.

"I thought we're getting one outfit for each other."

"Everything's so cheap. Whatever you don't wear, I will."

I glanced around, but I didn't see anything here that called to me. "I'm going to go look for you."

"Don't get me more than one outfit," she cautioned, though she'd just defended the pile she'd pulled for me. "I already have tons of clothes. There wouldn't be any room in my closet."

That was a really nice out to keep me from spending more money than her. I appreciated it. "It'll take me a second. I think I know what I want."

She pushed the cart as we went to the back wall, where the dresses hung. I riffled through them, discarding each one until I got to a fluffy prom dress that must have been buried in someone's closet for the past twenty years. The top was black, a boned satin corset, while the bottom was a mess of hot-pink tulle. Bows and ribbons covered up most of it, but I could see potential in the bodice.

Hana's eyes widened and she took a step back. "Um . . . I don't think that's really my style."

That was, without a doubt, the most diplomatic I'd ever heard Hana. I stifled my laugh. "Don't worry. I'm going to fix it." At the very least, I thought I could fix it. I dropped it on top of the other clothes. I searched through the rack some more until I found a burnt-umber silky slip dress. I considered it, then tossed that in the cart as well.

She looked skeptical, but nodded. "I guess I have nothing to lose."

"You don't. Should we try this stuff on?"

"Nah, dressing rooms are kind of gross. Let's buy it and go to my house. Unless you'd rather go to yours?"

If we went to mine, my lack of a parent might be too obvious, and after I'd already spilled the beans to Niam yesterday,

I didn't want to go further into detail with my new friend. "Yours is fine." I'd only briefly seen Hana's home from the outside when I'd dropped her off the other night, and the mini-mansion had fascinated me.

We checked out and stepped outside. Hana shivered. "I'm already missing LA weather. I'm not looking forward to the real winter here."

"Me neither." For different reasons, though. I liked the cold, but the days would get darker earlier, and I feared I'd get depressed then too, missing my mom so close to the holidays.

When we pulled up to Hana's home, her huge circular driveway was empty. Candice had a pretty house, but that was a firmly middle- to upper-class house. This was a rich-people house, all red brick and lush landscaping. "What did your dad invent again?"

"A chip." She held up her pinkie. "About half the size of this."

"It must be a really important chip."

Hana snorted. "Not really."

I tried not to gawk when we went inside, but it was hard. There weren't a lot of furnishings, which made sense, given that they'd just moved in a few months ago, but what there was, was expensive as hell, even to my untrained eye.

"Whoa." I stopped in front of a huge painting above the living room mantel. It was easily twice the size of me, stretching upward to the high ceiling. In it was a younger Hana, a small boy, and a beautiful woman with sunkissed tan skin wearing a big diamond necklace. No one was smiling. "This is amazing."

Hana came to stand next to me. "Um, yeah. It was a family portrait, but my mom had my dad painted out of it."

I tried not to gawk, but, luckily, she smiled. "I know. She's intense when someone wrongs her."

"Where's your brother?" I followed her up the big circular staircase.

"He lives in LA."

"Oh, I'm sorry, I didn't know that."

Hana shifted the Goodwill bag from one hand to the other, and I'd gotten to know her well enough to recognize the fidgeting as a sign of disquiet. "My parents decided to split us up *Parent Trap* style. We'll see each other on the holidays. Either he'll come here, or I'll go there."

Oh, that really sucked. "You must miss him."

"He's a booger, but yeah." She led me into a bedroom. It was as sparsely decorated as the rest of the place, but her four-poster bed was a thing of beauty. The mattress was piled high with white pillows and a white duvet, and wispy tulle hung from the posts. The rest of the furniture was equally snowy and pristine.

"I love your bed," I said, with great admiration.

"Thanks. I got to pick it." She dumped the clothes on the bed.

"You first," I said.

She eyed the ancient prom dress I'd picked for her. "I'm still not sure about this."

"I am." I was not. This could easily be a mess, but I felt that same thrill of excitement I felt whenever I transformed nothing into something. "Can you try it on?" I pivoted when she started stripping right there, my cheeks red.

"Done."

I turned around and clamped my hand over my mouth at the sight.

"Don't you dare laugh."

I cleared my throat. "Why would I laugh."

She gave me a disgruntled glare and flicked the big bow at her waist. The poufy skirt dwarfed her slender frame, and ribbons decorated her whole chest. "This is a joke, right? I look like Little Bo-Peep went to Victoria's Secret and the Pink brand threw up on her."

"Give it a chance." I walked around behind her and tugged on the ribbon lining the back and inspected the seams. Since it was an adjustable corset, I wouldn't have to do much altering, just . . . fluff removal. I could see the potential in it. "Okay, you can take it off."

I also had her try the slip dress on. "I said one outfit," she protested.

"You bought me more than one thing," I reminded her. "And this will add up to one outfit, I promise."

She smoothed her hand over her hip. "If the top wasn't too small, this one might actually be cute."

"Don't worry about that." I pinched the fabric at the small of her back and made a mental note. "Okay. Take it off. I'll work on this at home."

"Try yours on now."

I had to duck in and out of her bathroom, because I wasn't as comfortable with nudity as she was. Also, I didn't want her eagle eyes to catch the scar on my arm. Hopefully, at some point I wouldn't be self-conscious about shorter sleeves. I didn't want to be wearing chunky sweaters in July.

The shirts she'd picked for me were adorable yet comfortable and plain, mostly wardrobe staples that actually fit me properly. I would be happy to wear these. "You did a great job," I said, as I emerged.

Hana sprawled in a plush armchair next to her bed. "Then keep everything. But try that final outfit I laid out there, and let me see it."

It was the most excitement I'd ever heard in Hana's voice, and it became infectious when I donned the clothes and came out of the bathroom to show her. "Wait. This is cute." The green skirt was high waisted enough that barely any skin showed between it and the black top, just a sliver that I was comfortable with, and it was long enough that I didn't feel self-conscious over my legs. The waistband accentuated my waist and the shirt was a V-neck crop that showed off a hint of cleavage. I felt . . . sexy? Even though I wasn't showing much skin. My curves looked and felt scrumptious instead of inconvenient. Like they had in my ill-fated Shadow costume. Hopefully, this outfit didn't lead me to some crisis. "Really cute."

"You can wear it to school tomorrow," she said cheerfully.

I hesitated. I'd managed to avoid thinking about school, and James and Sam. "It's very . . . visible, isn't it?"

"What do you mean?"

"The last thing I want to do is to stand out," I mused aloud. "What if Sam confronts me again?"

Hana sighed. "Listen. Sam might pick on you no matter what you're wearing. Like, you should definitely feel like the girl who can take her man."

"I don't want her man," I muttered.

Hana shot finger guns at me. "That's the spirit."

I gave a her a faint smile. "I'll think about it."

"Let's think about how to punish James for being such a dickhead, too."

My first instinct was to defend him, but I didn't know how to. He *had* acted like a dickhead, but Niam was right—he had gone through a rather traumatic event. "He did almost drown," I said. "Maybe this was all some PTSD reaction."

"Do not forgive him."

"I don't. And I can't forgive him if he didn't apologize yet," I pointed out. "At least, not in person."

"What do you mean not in person?"

"He did send me a text. . . ."

She bounced in her chair. "Let me see it!"

I hesitated, then reached into my bag for my phone. It had been nice not to have it in my hands while we'd been out and about. Hopefully Kareena hadn't been trying to get ahold of me again.

I looked down at the screen. Not Kareena. Someone else. I read the text, then sat down.

"What?"

I looked up at her. "Niam texted me."

"I thought James texted you."

"He did. Yesterday." I read the text twice more, certain I

wasn't comprehending it properly. "Niam texted me while we were out today."

"Who the hell is Niam?"

"Niam is James's older brother. He goes to another school."

"How do you know him?"

"Um, I've worked at their family's restaurant." Once under mistaken identity, but I'd gotten paid for it, so it counted.

Hana stared at me. "Girl, how deep into this family are you?"

Deeper than I'd planned on being. "He asked me out," I blurted.

Hana raked her hands through her hair. "Who, James?"

"No!" I showed her the screen. "Niam."

She grabbed the phone and read the text. I didn't have to reread it. I'd already memorized it.

Hey, hope you've recovered from that long night. Wanted to see if you were going to the festival on Thursday and needed a date? I'm very available and would even bring a corsage.

While he didn't go to our school, it wasn't unheard of for guests from other schools to attend events.

"Oooooh . . . *Hope you've recovered from that long night.*" Hana's tone was laced with innuendo, and I flushed.

"He's talking about work."

"Uh-huh. Bestie, I didn't think you had it in you. Dating his brother is the most diabolical punishment you could come up with for James."

I flinched, thinking about the kiss. I hadn't wanted it to be punishment.

My face must have given something away. "Whoa, I was joking, but clearly I hit a nerve."

I *had* wanted to dissect this with someone. "Niam kissed me."

Hana raised an eyebrow. "You're just now telling me this!"

"It's a weird thing to bring up in casual conversation."

Hana hit reply. "Do you want to go out with him? If not, I'll help you compose a gentle let-down."

"I . . ." I did, but . . . *Why are you incapable of crushing on men outside of this family?* "I don't want it to seem like I'm just doing it to get back at James."

"Who cares if it seems like that?" Hana shook her head. "Do you want to say yes?"

"Well . . ."

"Yes or no? I mean, I was kind of hoping we could go to the festival together, but I don't want to stand in the way of true love."

True love seemed a little grandiose here, and I was flattered Hana had wanted to go with me. "You and I could still go together. I could decline. James'll be there, after all." Hana might be right about me being avoidant. If I had plans with Hana, I could sidestep this dilemma.

She gave me a look of pity. "It is not your job to manage James's feelings. You can have compassion for him, but he's gotta handle his own stuff. Come on, it'll be fun. How about we go as a group, it might take some of the pressure off. Me and Remy, you and Niam."

She said it casually, but I caught the little hitch as she said

Remy's name. She liked the guy, and this could be a way to take the pressure off her, too. I didn't want to stand in the way of that. Still. "People might stare at me if I'm with Niam." My voice shook. The last thing I wanted to do was have a panic attack at the dance like I had earlier today.

"Bold of you to assume they wouldn't be staring at me, but okay." She waved the phone. "Is positive attention fine? Like, Niam's not going to be smushing pizza on you. Hopefully. People might be curious about James's brother and you, but there's no drama involved in you dating him."

I was torn. I didn't know. I'd been raised to be scared of any attention. Who knew if my brain could differentiate the two?

At the same time, James had thought I was some pathetic creature who would fall all over herself to be his pawn, even after I'd fallen all over myself to save his drowning ass. My anger stirred alive. It would be mighty satisfying to show up there on his brother's arm.

No, Niam isn't punishment! Don't tarnish that kiss.

"If you get nervous, we can always leave. Just like the party." Hana typed. "Here, you can hit send if you want, but you don't have to." She handed the phone back to me.

Yes, I'd love to go with you, Hana had typed.

"Let Niam decide if he's cool with his brother seeing the two of you together."

I hesitated. "I don't even know what I'd wear."

"I bet we can overnight a whole haul of clothes before then. Or we can go to the mall. Want to play hooky again tomorrow?"

"I think at some point, I do have to go to class." And see James. And talk to him. I owed him that much, right? Or did I owe him anything? I'd saved him. I'd posed as his unwitting shield and sword.

Perhaps Hana was right, and he owed me.

Hana opened her mouth, but before she could answer, a knock came on the door.

"Hana, why did I get a call from the school—" An older woman stuck her head inside the room, and I recognized her from the painting downstairs as Hana's mother. Her face was unlined, but silver strands ran through her otherwise dark brown hair. Her eyes bounced over me. "Oh, I didn't realize you had a guest." Her face transformed from a scowl to a placid greeting quickly. "I'm Hana's mother. Who is this, Hana?"

"This is my friend Sonia."

"Sonia." Hana's mom inclined her head. "What a pleasure. It's so nice to meet you. Call me Tina."

"Nice to meet you, too." I tugged on my new skirt.

Tina's smile slipped as she looked at her daughter. "Hana, you know the rules."

"Mom, quit it."

"I'm sorry, Sonia, but I prefer to know someone's parents before Hana invites them over."

I opened my mouth, then closed it again. It was still too early where my mom was to even think of calling her.

Luckily, Hana piped up. "Oh my God, Mom." She closed her eyes. "It's not a playdate. I am almost an adult."

"I understand that, but those are house rules."

"My mom's out of town right now," I said. "But I was leaving anyway." I gathered up my stuff, including my ruined shirt.

Hana's mom smiled at me, seemingly relieved that I'd defused the tension. "Thank you, Sonia. I hope you understand. I'm sure your mom is just as protective."

I thought of my mom's decree that I not walk anywhere. "Yes, she is."

Hana escorted me to the door. "Let me drive you home."

"No need. I'll get a ride." I'd had a number of unexpected expenses today, but Kareena had told me to spend my paycheck on new clothes, and I was in possession of those and still under budget.

"I'm sorry my mom's so annoying."

"She's fine." I looked up the stairs. Hana's mom gave me a weak wave. "She wants to be careful. I get it. I'll see you at school tomorrow."

"You're wearing your new clothes?"

I laughed. "I'll think about it."

She squeezed my arm. "Stop agonizing over James. He's a nonentity. Enjoy Niam like James doesn't exist."

That was easier said than done, but I nodded. "I'll think about it," I repeated.

In the car, I did just that, Hana's unsent ghostwritten text sitting in my mind and on my phone. I leaned my head against the window and let my brain take over. Niam and me, walking into the school. My dress was long and red and flowy, though I owned nothing like it. My hair was loose, floating about my shoulders. His suit would fit him perfectly, and I'd rest my hand on his strong arm as we entered the dream version of my school. We would turn heads, but in a good way.

I let the fantasy spin the rest of the way home. In it, I was confident and calm. I was invincible. For once.

Twenty-One

N o one is staring at you.

I glanced around my English class, but everyone was either doodling, pretending not to be on their phones, or, in the rare case, paying attention to Ms. Hawley while she droned on about *The Scarlet Letter*.

I didn't know if I was happy no eyes were on me or disappointed. In a moment of weakness this morning, I'd opted to wear the green skirt Hana had bought me, though I'd paired it with my new/used Metallica shirt, a bulky black sweater, and black tights as a nod to the weather and in an effort to be less visibly . . . visible.

Over the course of the day, I'd found myself walking a little straighter. It wasn't about showing more skin. It was the color and the fabric and the pop of green that had brightened my mood on the dreary fall day. I'd gotten a total of two compliments from other classmates, as well as an enthusiastic thumbs-up from Hana when she'd sat down behind me right before class started, and all of those things had been lovely.

I felt good. Good enough that I could continue to follow Hana's directive and forget about James and focus on the better things in my life. Like possibly going out with Niam in a few days.

I heard a soft snort behind me, and a hand extended over my shoulder. "Listen to this."

I grabbed the AirPod from Hana—not a knockoff, of course—and put it in my ear, keeping my gaze trained on Mrs. Hawley's back while she wrote something about themes on the whiteboard. The last thing I wanted was to get chewed out again by this teacher for not focusing on the lecture.

It wasn't music, though, but Sam's voice that filled my eardrums. I stiffened. Somehow, I'd managed to avoid her and James for yet another day. I'd briefly considered that they may be hidden away somewhere, making out, but Sam's words quickly convinced me otherwise.

"Hey, guys. I know I haven't posted anything new lately, but I've just been going through some stuff." Her voice was teary, but I knew if I turned around and looked at the screen, there would be no tears or red eyes. No ugly sad faces for perfect Sam, just overblown white comforters and walls and flowers that made her rosy skin glow. And an audience that kept track of whether she was present on social media or not. As a professional online lurker, I could not relate.

"You all know that me and my guy have been through so much together, so many ups and downs. But this latest challenge we've had . . ." She sniffed. "It may be too much for us. There's another girl." My heart thumped, but she gave a long sigh. "I'll make a part two tomorrow with an update. I just can't talk about it right now."

Making an unnecessary part two? Sam was definitely a monster.

The bell rang, and I discreetly pulled the AirPod out of my ear, turning around to hand it to Hana.

"Do you think she's talking about me?" I whispered.

"Or James not wanting her back, in general." Hana wasn't discreet, and the people gathering up their stuff next to us turned to give us curious looks. "And you thought you couldn't make her jealous. This is damage control, in case it comes out that James prefers you. She also reposted her video about me."

I looked up sharply. "What?"

Without another word, she scrolled and handed me the phone and her headphones again. "It's in her stories, so at least it'll go away soon."

This was a different Sam, one who wasn't teary. Her cheeks were flushed with indignation, her eyes snapping fire. She wasn't at home, but in the girl's locker room. "Can't believe what happened last weekend, storytime. So we're at my friend G's house for a party, right? This new girl, let's call her H, she's been coming on to him all night. He's, like, wildly in love with her."

"She's the one who asked him to show her his room," came a feminine murmur from off camera. Not Candice. I didn't know why I cared, but I did.

296

"That's right." Sam nodded. "They hook up, no judgment. He comes down to get her a drink, and when he goes back, she's with someone else. In the same bed."

"Gross," came the anonymous one-woman chorus.

"So gross," Sam agreed. "And she had the nerve to run out of there like he was the one who did something to her. Now he's heartbroken, and she won't return his calls."

I pulled the AirPod out, not eager to hear any more. My stomach churned. "I'm so sorry. I had no idea she said all this." Sam had left *a lot* out when she'd recounted things to Candice in the bathroom.

"Why are you sorry?"

"She only reposted it because we're friends and you defended me."

Hana set her jaw stubbornly. "I don't care what she says about me, and I'm not going to change my behavior to satisfy her."

There wasn't a hint of vulnerability in her armor, but I still felt awful. "Ugh, Hana."

"Don't worry about it," Hana advised, because she didn't realize I had literally never not worried about everything, and got up. I realized we were the last ones left in the room, except for a couple of jocks creepily flirting with Ms. Hawley, and I rose, too.

"We're still going to the dance together?"

I tried to shake myself out of the funk of my personal soap opera. *Focus on Niam and the date. Was it a date? The date!* "I haven't texted Niam back."

"Girl. Get on that."

"I'm still thinking. But either way, you and I can still go together."

"I assumed. There isn't much to do in this town."

Not compared to LA. Her casual certainty that we'd be going together was nice. "I was thinking of working on your dress today. Might be an option for you to wear."

To her credit, Hana's grimace was barely visible. "Oh, yes, um. That beautiful dress you bought for me. Listen, no worries if it's not, I have plenty of semiformal dresses."

I hid my smile. Hana would have more faith in me when I finished de-poufing that dress. I wasn't confident about a lot of things, but this, I had a good feeling about. "You don't have to wear it, even if I finish it."

Visible relief flitted across her face. "You working at the café today?"

"Yeah. Hopefully Paris is in a good mood."

Hana walked with me to my locker, and I realized I was standing taller than I had all day. It wasn't just the outfit. It was her, walking by my side. Like I had a shield from the worst things people could do to me.

Dangerous thought. There was a reason I'd stayed friendless since Candice, wasn't there? I couldn't go relying on another girl anytime soon.

"Do you need a ride to work?" Hana leaned against the lockers.

I forced a smile for Hana. "I don't want to be a bother." I opened my locker and reached inside for my jacket.

My brain didn't process what I was seeing fast enough,

because my hand landed on it first. The silky material slipped through my fingers, as elusive as my peace of mind.

Glaringly red, my once-perfect cape, that I'd stitched ever so carefully onto my Shadow costume. It wasn't mildewed or stained but had been washed carefully and folded into a square. It sat on the bottom of my locker, on top of some books.

"Sonia?"

I snatched the fabric up and grabbed my coat too, shoving the red jacket over the incriminating evidence. I slammed the locker shut and tried not to look guilty as I stared up at Hana. "What?"

"Do you want a ride? To work? I can drop you on my way home."

I readjusted my coat to cover the cape, my mind racing. Did I want to be in a car with Hana, who saw far too much and was getting to know me a little too well, all while Shadow's cape sat in my lap?

Absolutely not. "I'm good," I said. If my words were a little breathless, Hana didn't seem to notice.

"Okay." She raised her shoulder. "See you tomorrow."

I didn't remember if I said bye or not. I was way too focused on running away. That cape burned a hole over my arm, where it rested against my bare skin, almost as stinging as the cut had been. If I shoved my sleeve up, people would be able to see that, too.

I exited through one of the side doors and made my way to a bench. I glanced around surreptitiously, but no one was paying attention to me.

As smoothly as I could, I opened my backpack and shoved the cape in there. I zipped up the bag and sat down.

Oh no oh no oh no.

But . . . how was this possible?

Candice, obviously.

I'd used the same lock since freshman year. She'd had the combination, just like I had hers. Over the past three years, we'd often used it to leave things in each other's lockers. Gifts, snacks, jokes, returning things we'd borrowed. 6-42-12. That was hers. Easier than mine.

I clenched the back in my hand. There was no one else who would leave this for me. Which meant that:

she'd had it this whole time;

known it was mine;

hadn't told anyone, and;

returned it.

Why return it? As a threat? No, that didn't make sense. If it was a threat, she would have told me she had it, or cut a piece off and left it there, like a mafia boss sending someone a bloody finger.

My breath came faster as I stared at the yellow buses in the circular driveway in front of me. One by one, they pulled away from the curb as my thoughts peeled off.

Perhaps . . . she'd meant for it to be a peace offering. A kindness. A confirmation that even though she knew, no one else had to.

I slowly reached into my pocket and pulled out my phone. I hadn't deleted her number or our message history. I had to scroll all the way back.

Thanks for being there for me yesterday gonna be busy for the next little bit, talk soon.

Want to get dinner tomorrow?

Hey. Everything okay?

I miss you.

My last few texts to Candice glared at me. All unanswered. I tapped my finger on the keyboard. My pride and fear of explicit rejection had stopped me from texting any more after that, though there had been a lot of nights when I'd wanted to.

She'd just . . . dropped me. Never told me why, or how. And I had let her, because not knowing why our friendship had imploded was better than being yelled at or told I was unlovable.

The cape was the second thing she'd dropped on me with no explanation.

Anger stirred in my chest, but I tamped it down. If I got angry, I wouldn't be able to think. I could let this go, like I'd let her ghosting go. Accept the cape, and whatever message she was trying to send.

Except, this time, it was more than my own feelings on the line. If Candice did decide to rat me out, as weird as that would make this gesture . . .

I typed a quick message. **Hey. Sorry to bother you. Did you leave something in my locker?** There. That was low-key and not incriminating.

Her response was instant, which shocked me. **Yes, but let's not talk about it over text.**

That was smart. Candice had always been craftier than I. She'd loved reading mysteries and thrillers while I'd dived into my comics and romances. It had been reading, not the subjects, that had made us friends when we'd first met. We'd bumped into each other in the school library and then had lunch after, chatting about our favorite books.

I'm on a college visit, about to get on the plane. Will be around my dad all week. Back on Friday. Talk then?

I didn't have a choice, did I? I tried to bury the thrill I got at seeing all those words where before there had been none, and replied, **Okay.**

Don't worry about anything.

What the hell kind of directive was that?

I opened my bag again and peeked in. The fabric lay where I'd stuffed it, which . . . of course it did. It wouldn't have gotten legs and walked away.

It seemed like I was destined to just consistently worry about the loose ends. Was this how all heroes felt when they were hiding a secret identity? Weren't they exhausted?

I didn't know how long I sat there, but my phone vibrated. I feared it was Candice, so I checked it, but it was Paris. **Where are you**

One hurried rideshare later, I was at the café. I jogged in, breathless, but was grateful to find the place mostly empty, save for a customer at one of the outside tables, and Paris pacing inside. "Where have you been," she snapped as soon as I entered.

"Sorry." I was only twenty-five minutes late, and she was often much later, but I wasn't the boss's daughter. "I got held

302

up at school." I readjusted my bag, that cape burning a hole through the canvas, into my back.

"Hmph. At least you're here. I need to head out for a couple hours. I'll be back in time to close."

I blinked at her. "You can't leave me here alone."

"It's a Tuesday afternoon. You'll be fine."

"You're not supposed to leave me here alone," I clarified. It was one thing to close alone, but I didn't want to be solely responsible for a register full of cash and everything else in here for hours. What if a customer came in and threw a fit over something?

"I'll pay you time and a half. This is an emergency."

"That's not—"

"Fine, I'll pay you double." Paris pouted. "I have to go get my eyebrows done and this is the only time this week my girl can fit me in. They're monstrous."

I pressed my lips tight together. "I want triple," I heard myself say.

Paris's—not terrible, but slightly overgrown—eyebrows rose. "What? That's absurd."

"I'll be doing the work of two people, and I want hazard pay on top of that for being left alone here. Triple." Who was saying the words coming out of my mouth? I didn't even know.

Paris gave a gusty sigh. I fully expected her to postpone her appointment, but she nodded. "Fine."

Oh. Cool. Wow. Was this what asserting myself felt like? Wait, what a high.

She did, at least, wait for me to go drop my bag in the back and snag an apron. God, I hated leaving that bag—and the cape—in my locker, but it was the safest place for it.

I was in the middle of restocking the cups when the bell over the door rang. I looked up, but this wasn't just any customer.

Be cool. Be cool.

I lowered my head and tried to get my breathing under control, but it was hard when my heart was racing as it was.

Son of a *bitch.*

I glared at James. "What do you want?"

He closed the door behind him and made his way to the counter, unfazed by the annoyance in my voice. "Hi, Sonia."

"Did you not hear me?" If I was going to be assertive, I was going to be assertive with everyone today.

"You didn't answer my text."

"Did you not take a hint from that?"

"It's really important I speak to you. Please, can we talk?"

"I'm working."

"So am I." He tilted his head at the bookstore. Like the café, it was similarly deserted, but I could see the owner at the register. "I only have a few minutes. I said I was coming over for a coffee."

"Your usual?" I asked coldly, then kicked myself for remembering what his usual was.

"Yes, please."

I turned my back and went to the coffee, annoyed that I'd made a fresh batch. He needed Paris's hours-old coffee.

"I am so, so, sorry," he said, to my back.

I bit my lip and stared at the swirling brown liquid.

"You have every right to be furious with me. You were right. I knew you liked me, and I used you. And it was the last thing I should have ever done, especially after you saved my life."

I finished pouring his coffee and put the carafe down. I hadn't expected such a humble, clear apology. "It seems to have worked. Sam's jealous and posting weird videos about us."

"I wasn't trying to make Sam jealous."

That made me turn. I brought the coffee to the counter. "Then what were you trying to do?"

"I was mad at her. She dumped me, took most of my friends, and then, just because I got some publicity and she'd get some clout, she went online and said we were getting back together. Making it seem like I was the one who had dumped her. I wanted to embarrass her, I think."

"I have news for you, buddy." I snapped a top on the cup of black coffee. "Being used to humiliate someone isn't much better than being used to make someone jealous."

He hung his head. His cuts and bruises had started to fade. "I know. I don't know what I was thinking."

"And you used me *after* I told you I didn't want anyone to figure out I was the one who helped you. You brought more attention to me."

He seemed to shrink. "I didn't think about that. I guess I figured if people were gossiping about you and me, they wouldn't be gossiping about my weakness."

"So you think someone who faints from a physical condition is . . . weak?"

He frowned at me. "No."

"Oh." I nodded. "Just you. It only makes you weak."

His mouth worked. "They call me fucking *canal kid*. How embarrassing is that?"

I tried to take a step back and look at this from his point of view. I didn't want to minimize his feelings just because I felt like my stakes were higher.

As far as everyone else had been concerned, he'd been on top of the world, and then an accident had shattered his public persona as the golden child. That was enough to make anyone act squirrelly. "You're not weak, but I understand the desire to not have people picking apart your life."

"Thanks." He pressed his lips together. "I didn't come over here so you could comfort me. I need you to know how incredibly sorry I am, and it'll never happen again. I hope we can be friends again. Better friends than we were, even."

"That depends. Are you going to tell everyone about me?"

"What? No. Of course not." To his credit, James looked flabbergasted that I'd even think such a thing. "I promised I wouldn't. I may have almost messed that up, but not on purpose. I'll be extra careful now."

My shoulders lowered, a slow trickle of relief coming through me. "Sure?"

"Absolutely." He gave me a long look. "You *really* want to stay secret."

"Yes." I licked my lips. "It is vitally important no one ever finds out about Shadow. Not your mom. Not your brother." Especially not Niam, not now, when everything was still so fragile and new.

"They won't. Pact," he murmured, and this time I felt like he took it more soberly.

"And if someone figures out it was me . . ."

"I'll deny it," he said immediately. "I owe you."

My sigh felt like it came from my toes. "Okay. Good."

"I don't have the right to ask, but I'd appreciate it if you never tell anyone what a dick I was."

That was easy enough. "Pact." I paused. "Did you see Sam's video today? About you two not working out?" Hana had been right. It must have been damage control, an attempt to spin opinion onto her side when it became apparent that James wasn't going to fall in line with dating her again.

His lips twisted in disgust. "Yeah. I also saw she reposted that rant about Hana. Is Hana okay?"

"Yeah, she's fine." Or, rather, she said she was fine.

"The first time she put it up, that was one of the reasons we broke up," he confessed. "I don't trust Gerald like she does. He's lied about more than one girl. We had a huge fight over it."

That was promising. I'd hate to think I'd had a crush on someone who could condone such gross rumors being spread.

"I honestly don't know what I saw in her. The girl's a walking red flag. My family was right."

And I didn't think he even knew about the pizza smushing. I couldn't tell him about it, because then I'd have to explain about the coffee tossing, and I wasn't about to do that. I scuffed my foot on the tile. "Sometimes you have to learn the hard way," I said diplomatically.

James glanced over his shoulder, but his boss was busy with

a customer. He spoke in a rush. "Speaking of family, I, ah, talked to my brother last night, and I want you to know that I'm totally cool with you two. I mean, I don't love it, because I actually think we could have—well, never mind. He's a good guy, and you're a great girl."

Oh jeez. "Niam told you?"

"Yeah."

"Oh."

"Did you think he wouldn't tell me?"

"I mean . . . I was hoping he wasn't the type to kiss and tell."

He opened his mouth. Then closed it again. "Uh . . . you kissed?"

Oh. Jeez. "What did he tell you, exactly?"

"He told me he asked you out," James said slowly. "I told him that was fine with me, and I was happy for both of you. I wasn't about to stand in your way after I was already a jerk."

"Oh."

James started to look amused. "You two, uh, moved fast."

I wished I could throw some ice water on my cheeks.

"I . . ." I cleared my throat. "It wasn't a real kiss, barely . . ." I trailed off. I didn't need to give him a play-by-play of our kiss. Even I, with my limited experience, knew that was in bad taste.

He sobered. "It wasn't to get back at me, right?"

"No! Ew. Trust me, you weren't even in my mind then." It had, in fact, been one of the few times he hadn't been in my mind in the last week.

"Okay. That's good." He dropped his hands to his hips. "Well, I'm happy for you. I bet you'll have fun together. Hey, maybe we can, ah, go to the festival as a group."

"Um, maybe." Not. I paused. "I haven't said yes yet."

"You should." He tilted his head at the window. "Or come up with some excuse before he gets in here."

I followed his nod and jumped. There was Niam, walking past the glass storefront with purposeful steps. He wore a black bomber jacket, and had a pair of sunglasses perched on his face, hiding much of it. He stopped in front of the door and raked his fingers through his hair.

Gosh, I wanted to do that.

James half laughed. "Wow. I think I'm a little jealous of my brother. I don't think anyone's ever looked at me like that."

I examined my heart for its reaction to that statement, but there was none. I couldn't care less how James felt, so long as he wasn't crushed. "You don't really like me like that." I thought it would hurt more to say that, but it didn't.

My crush on James hadn't been based on reality, but on dreams. The more I talked to him, the more I realized I barely knew the guy. I'd projected on him all the things I'd thought I wanted and fallen in like with those qualities.

He wrapped his hands around his coffee. "What are you going to tell him?"

"I think I'm going to say yes," I said, and the speed of my answer surprised me, given how much waffling I'd done over it. "I'd like to."

He gave me a long, searching look, then smiled. That smile was very bright. "Cool."

"It's just a first date." I had to regulate my fantasies before they went out of control and I imagined a white picket fence for Niam and me.

The bell above the door jangled, and Niam came in. He stopped when he caught sight of James.

James picked up his coffee. He hadn't paid for it, but it didn't matter. The drip coffee wasn't all that good here, and I hated that I had to charge anyone for it. "Hey, Niam," he said casually, like it was normal to run into his brother in the café. "Was chatting with our mutual. Come over when you're done here, I got a book you might like. I'll see you in math tomorrow, Sonia."

"Bye." Was my voice breathless? It was. And not for James.

Niam nodded at James, then sauntered over to the counter. I didn't pay attention when James left. I was too busy watching Niam's long legs.

He didn't waste any time on pleasantries. "You didn't answer my text."

Funny, how both brothers were complaining about the same thing. "Sorry. I had to think about some stuff."

He nodded. "Can I have an almond croissant?"

The non sequitur caught me off guard, but I nodded. I grabbed a croissant and bought it back to him, shaking my head when he reached for his wallet. I might get in trouble if Paris found out about all these comps, but I was getting paid triple right now. I could cover a coffee and a croissant. "On the house." It was the least I could do for leaving him on read. I imagined it took some degree of courage and initiative to ask someone out. He didn't look like he'd been sweating for my response, but when it came to Niam, he didn't lay all his cards on the table.

"Thanks." He gently tore into the croissant and looked inside it. "What bakery do you all use?"

"Uh, it's definitely not from a bakery. It comes frozen, and we bake them in the oven."

He grimaced and showed me the inside, which barely had any filling. "Figures. It's nearly empty."

I was unsurprised. "I prefer the chocolate croissants." I grabbed the tongs and brought him a fresh chocolate croissant.

He broke off a piece and gave it a grudging nod. "Edible, at least." He took a bite. "So what did you think about?"

"You know. This and that."

Niam met my gaze. "Should I have not asked you out?"

"No. You should have. I mean, I'm flattered."

"You're flattered, but . . . ?" He took another bite.

I shifted my weight from one foot to the next. "I've never gone on a date before. With anyone. I'm not used to getting asked." James's weird lunchtime invite didn't count.

Another bite. His Adam's apple bobbed when he swallowed. "That's weird."

"What is?"

"That you've never been asked out by anyone before."

A steady warmth flowed through me, echoed by the way his eyes dipped over me. "You look pretty today, by the way," he added. "Green's my favorite color."

"Thank you." I tucked a loose strand of hair behind my ear.

"I thought you were ghosting me because . . ." Niam glanced

over his shoulder, toward the bookstore. James wasn't anywhere to be seen, but I got his message.

"No. I told you, I'm not hung up on James. And I wouldn't ghost you." Not after how Candice had ghosted me. "I really was startled."

He ate the rest of the croissant in two bites, then wiped his fingers.

"You liked it?"

"No. I eat when I'm nervous. Keeps my hands busy." The lines around his eyes crinkled, though his lips didn't move. He held out his hand and without thinking, I placed mine in it. His fingers ran over the back of my hand, down each finger. The rhythmic motion was both soothing and . . . not soothing.

"I didn't know you get nervous."

"Of course."

Like me. Nice to know I wasn't the only one who over-thought everything. "If the invite's still open, I would love to go with you. That would be really nice."

This time his smile included his lips. He twined his fingers around mine. There were scars on his hand, remnants of his work in the kitchen. They scratched against my skin, but in a good way. "Okay. Cool. I can pick you up."

"Um, Hana and Remy might come with us."

"Sounds fun." His thumb rubbed against the back of my hand, and my brain shorted for a second.

We stared into each other's eyes for a long moment, and he finally stirred. "If I stay, I might want to kiss you again, and you have pretty big windows here. Don't need someone to go tattling to my mom."

And his brother and the elderly owner of the bookstore might see us. But that aside, I wanted him to kiss me again. Butterflies fluttered awake in my belly, and I welcomed every last flutter. "Um, sure."

"Day after tomorrow, though. I'll see you." He let that hang, a promise.

He drew his hand away from mine. "Yes, see you then," I echoed.

I stared at the door after he left. James melted away, and so did Shadow, and everything else. The calmness Niam infused in me lingered, even though he was gone.

Since no one was in the room, I let out a little girlish squeak. Then I quickly went to the back. I didn't have long, in case a paying customer came in.

I opened my bag and yanked out the cape. It was risky to dispose of it anywhere, but I couldn't carry it around with me any longer than I had to. Mindful of the interior cameras, I tucked it into my apron pocket, then went to the big garbage bin in the kitchen. I stuffed it inside, under a bunch of spoiled fruit. I'd take out the trash at the end of my shift. Paris would be delighted with me, and that cape would be buried in the dumpster out back.

The bell jangled, and I hurried to the register, a smile on my face for the group of middle schoolers who walked in.

Finally. I could start to breathe again. Candice might know something, but I'd ditched the evidence she'd had on me; James and I were on good terms and he was willing to keep my secret; Niam liked *liked* me. Soon I'd be able to forget all the bad things that had happened over the past couple of weeks. Things were going back to normal.

I brushed my skirt. Only somehow, it was a better normal than it had been before.

Twenty-Two

"I cannot believe you made this."

"Technically, I didn't make it. I brought out its inner beauty." I walked around Hana, trying to see if I'd missed something. When I wasn't drifting about with a goofy smile on my face over Niam, I'd spent most of the last two days buried knee-deep in fabric for outfits for her and me.

I'd done full-on surgery on her prom dress, ripping off the sleeves and ruffles and skirt. With all of that gone, what was left was a black boned corset top.

As for the slip dress, all I'd had to do was cut off the bodice and run a zipper along the side to make it into a skirt. The dark orange-red slid over Hana's hips like silk. It complemented her body just like I'd hoped it would.

She turned and admired her profile in my mirror. She'd offered to let us get ready for the dance at her house, but her mom's directive about meeting my parents first had been at the top of my mind. I'd fobbed Hana off with an excuse, because I hadn't wanted to explain that my mom was roughly ten hours ahead of us and therefore too asleep to make friends with her mom. "This is gorgeous. Truly," she added. "I feel so bad I just got you, like, shirts and stuff during our little shopping spree."

"You got me things I feel comfortable in, and that's priceless. You don't have to wear it tonight. You can wear the dress you brought," I added. To my eye, the zipper at the skirt was puckering. I could fix that, if I had more time.

"What are you talking about? This is like haute couture." She waved her hand at the garment bag that lay on my bed, the one that probably actually contained haute couture. "And it's got witchy girl autumn vibes, which are right up my alley." She turned and preened. "Look at my boobs. This isn't something I would have thought to buy for myself, but it's so hot."

"Everything looks good on you."

"You should have a YouTube or TikTok or something where you show off your flips. Which feeds into an Etsy." She gasped. "You could monetize this."

As much as I liked money, the thought of putting my stuff on sale made me want to claw my skin off. "I have no desire to girlboss," I said dryly.

"You don't want to be like a fashion designer?" She lifted her hair up, then dropped it down, and frowned at herself in the mirror.

I nearly shuddered. Take my hobby, which I enjoyed and loved, and turn it into a career? No thanks. My mom might have taught me crafts, but she'd stopped truly loving sewing when she'd been forced to hem pants all day long. "Nah. I'm fine becoming a lawyer or an accountant or something equally boring." Professions where I could get a steady paycheck and hopefully wouldn't grow terribly bored with.

She snorted. "My mom would *love* you. I told her last week I want to be an underwater nude artist when I grow up."

"Do you?"

She sighed. "Not really. I'm just a troll. Where's your dress?"

I bit my lip. I'd been feeling pretty confident over the last couple of nights as I burned the midnight oil to cut, sew, and hem this dress, but I couldn't help but fret now. "I made it, but now I'm wondering if I should have gone and bought something."

She scoffed. "Show me."

"Promise to tell me if it's terrible?"

"You know I have no filter."

That wasn't entirely true, but I did trust her not to let me walk out of the house looking awful.

"Come on."

"Fine." I got up and went to the closet, only opening the door wide enough to pull out my dress. My Shadow costume was buried deep in the void, but I wasn't taking any chances. I'd throw it out like I had the cape as soon as I got the opportunity.

Hana stared so long at the dress I pulled out, I grew worried. "Is it that bad?" We still had an hour before Niam and Remy came by. I could raid my sister's closet and cobble something else together.

Kareena wasn't home, which was good. I hadn't wanted to rub a dance in her face. We were still kind of walking on eggshells after the other night.

"No, no, no. It's actually gorgeous. I'm speechless."

"You're being honest?"

"Do you think I'd admit to speechlessness otherwise?" Hana walked forward and touched the silk. "This fabric is beautiful."

"Thanks. I actually made it out of clothes I had lying around." Two of the Indian dresses that hadn't fit me any longer, paired with one of my mom's old saris, from back when she'd enjoyed the lap of luxury as the daughter-in-law of a successful businessman. She'd given me a few of those saris a couple of years ago, to do whatever I'd wanted with them. I'd held off, because using saris for my own clothes would have been like an imposter move. Like I was appropriating, even though it was my own culture.

But I'd thought about what Pooja had said, and it had felt right when I'd started cutting and sewing and hemming. These dresses in their original state might not fit me any longer, but the material was still mine, and so were those saris.

Hana bounced on her toes. "Put it on. I have to see it." She turned around to give me some privacy, which I appreciated.

I'd started off with the outfit as a two-piece, because skirts and tops were individually easier for me, but I'd grown confident, and had decided to sew it all together at the last minute. I wasn't comfortable with the chunky golden borders or big prints—too visible—so I'd used the parts that were the plainest. It was still flashier than anything I'd worn in a long time.

The pattern was made up of carefully arranged complementary vertical strips in all different shades of blue. A patchwork gown of old, discarded, but still precious fabrics.

Before Hana could turn around, I made sure the concealer I'd dotted over my scar was still there. My injury had faded to just a thin angry line at this point, but I wasn't taking any chances on anyone spotting it.

Hana squealed when she turned around, the high-pitched noise odd and unusual coming from her. "Oh my God, I love it. Look at you. Niam is going to *die*."

I did as she directed and looked in the mirror. Niam might die. The dress hem hit just below the knee. The top had been the trickiest part. The bodice was made up of two wide strips of contrasting material, crisscrossed over my chest and fully concealing my breasts and my bra, over my shoulders, crossed over and around, and tied behind my waist. Complicated, but it was the perfect balance of revealing and modest for my taste. Still . . .

"I was thinking I could wear a cardigan," I said.

"The Second Amendment gives us the right to bare arms," Hana said, deadpan, and I couldn't help but laugh at her terrible dad joke.

What if the concealer over my scar rubs off? But I had set it with a pretty heavy-duty setting spray from Kareena's stash. It was so small, and the place would be dim.

"You can wear a jacket or sweater if it makes you feel more comfortable, but I think you look hot as hell without it." She lifted her hands. "Up to you, though."

I looked at myself in the mirror again. My body was draped and supported and caressed by that blue silk, like this cloth had been spun years ago to serve me tonight. It wasn't a stranger's form in that mirror, but my own. Why would I cover up my hard work? I'd be fine.

"Let's do makeup."

I thought of Kareena doing my makeup last weekend, and a pang of loss hit me. I kind of wished she was home tonight. "Sure."

I let Hana do my face, and it took me a second to adjust after she was finished. There were contours where they'd never been. Another version of me, a more dramatic one. "I love it. Do you mind taking a photo for my mom?"

She took a bunch, then handed the phone back to me. "You said your mom's out of town, right? When's she going to be back?"

I'd told Niam about my mom, kind of. It felt weird not telling Hana.

You told Candice and she ghosted you for months. "Not sure yet," I murmured.

"Is she coming back?"

I froze and met Hana's too-knowing gaze in the mirror.

"I know what it looks and sounds like when you're covering up for a parent," she said matter-of-factly. "And you don't talk about her like she's present."

I turned around slowly. "She . . . she lives in India now."

"And you live with your sister." Hana nodded. "Was she forced to go back, or did she leave? No judgment either way."

I cleared my throat. "Forced. She was deported."

"Ahhhh." Hana bit her lip. "I'm sorry."

"It's not a big deal. My sister's old enough to take care of me." And she did kinda take care of me. "I talk to my mom on the phone."

"I talk to my dad on the phone, but it's not the same. He wasn't, like, a great husband, but he was a good dad. It's harder when he's so far away, so I can imagine how hard it would be if he was an ocean away."

That was the first time I'd heard Hana say anything remotely complimentary about her dad. I wondered how much of her disdain for him was because he cheated on her mom and how much was because she was hurt and missed him. I swallowed the lump in my throat. "I don't want anyone to know, okay? Not about my mom, or about me and my sister living alone together."

Hana mimed locking her lips. "It may not seem like it, but I know how to keep a secret."

"I also don't want you to treat me any differently."

She cocked her head. "Why would I do that?"

Why would she do that? Hana wasn't the type to baby someone. "Putting it out there."

"Well, don't worry. This isn't a bombshell for me. I figured something was up. If you ever want to talk to me about it, you can." She gave me an awkward pat on my shoulder.

The unease inside me quieted. It would be easy to think she was placating me and that she'd ghost me like Candice had, but I was on guard for that now. "I don't like to talk about it, but thanks. And . . . if you ever want to talk about your dad, I'm here, too. Like, even just to bitch about him."

"I also don't love to talk about it, but the bitching, I can do." She gave me another pat, then grabbed her makeup bag. "I'm going to use your bathroom to do my face, if you don't mind. There's way better lighting."

I wondered if she could also use a break from this heavy conversation, because I sure could. "No problem." I sat down on my bed, trying not to crinkle my dress, and sent Mama a couple of the photos Hana had taken.

To my surprise, my phone rang and her face popped up on the screen. Why was she up so early? Or late, depending on if she'd gone to bed yet.

"Where did you get that dress?" my mom asked as soon as I answered.

I smiled at her, pride filling me. "I made it."

She leaned her head on her hand. The fan in her room made shadows on the white wall behind her. "That's amazing, beta. I'm so proud. Send me more photos, you look beautiful. Where are you going? Another party?"

There was a thread of something uneasy in her question. "A dance."

Her eyebrows climbed. "But you hate dances."

"I do, but I'm going with my new friend Hana." I licked my lips. "And this guy asked me."

She blinked rapidly. "Who's the boy?"

"His family owns that Indian restaurant I've been working at. His name's Niam." I tried not to let my tone get swoony, but

I was afraid it couldn't be helped.

Last night, he'd texted to ask me what color dress I was wearing. Blue, I'd responded.

Blue's my favorite color.

I thought your favorite color was green.

You make every color my favorite.

Then he'd followed up with questions. About the dress, and my sewing skills. Interest and listening were mad romantic on their own.

"Hmm. His family is well-off?"

I didn't understand why the thought of that had made her smile so tight. "I don't think they're rich, rich. They seem comfortable. Does that matter?"

Her laugh was forced. "No, no. Just be careful around privileged boys. They are sometimes entitled, you know?"

"Niam's not like that. He has a decent family." I didn't want to tell her how much I loved the family, especially his mother. That would make her feel terrible, and that was the last thing I wanted. "Besides, Dad's family was privileged, right? Don't tell me he was entitled."

"His brother certainly was," she said dryly. "There's a reason I'm wary of the rich. Though, if your father or grandmother had lived . . . well, you don't even know what our life was like before they passed." She suddenly looked every inch of her forty-some years. "There were so many parties and fancy clothes. I was spoiled. It's probably why I made so many poor decisions with you two."

I sat up, concerned. The rushed way she was speaking was

familiar: it was the same way my brain spewed out insults and nasty things to me. But I'd never heard my mom talk that way. "You didn't make poor decisions with us. How we grew up was fine."

"I should have returned to India as soon as your sister was in remission and begged your kaka to give us something. Anything."

I narrowed my eyes. "I wouldn't have wanted you to beg them for anything." I sometimes wondered if everyone's dad's side was as bad as mine. Though I'd never met them, the facts told me mine were evil. Who cut off a widow and kids when they were in another country? When one of the kids was sick?

She lowered her eyes, and my suspicion grew that she was wrestling with her own circular thoughts, because she hadn't seemed to hear me. "It was my mistake."

"How come you're up so late, Mama?"

"Oh, I couldn't sleep. Thinking of . . . things."

I swallowed, seeing my own anxiety reflected in her face and posture. Of course, I had to have gotten it from somewhere, right? She'd had more practice hiding it than I did. "Do you have any sour candy there, Mama?"

She wiped at her cheek. I wished the camera quality was better, so her face would be clearer. Was she crying? "I—what?"

"Anything sour?"

She glanced around her, like she was seeing her cramped bedroom for the first time. "There's some tamarind candy. Why?"

"It's silly, but I read somewhere that super-sour candy can help when you're—" *Locked in an anxious death spiral.* "When you're thinking too hard to sleep. Like it disrupts the thought processes." I had no idea if that was scientifically true or not, but the few times I'd tried it, it had helped me.

She frowned, and now she looked more like Kareena. That was good. I'd rather her be cynical and suspicious than teary-eyed. "That sounds made up."

"Well, you're thinking about it now, instead of whatever had you looking so upset, so it seems to work."

Her smile was faint. "Fair enough. Listen, beta, Divya Auntie is—"

Hana opened the door and came in, and I looked away and gave her an absent smile. "My friend's here, Mama. Do you want to say hi?"

She swiped at her cheeks again, confirming that she was indeed crying. She switched to Marathi. "Does she know I live here?"

My mom had never exactly told us to keep her deportation a secret, but she worried about bringing attention to Kareena and our unofficial guardianship. I debated lying, but keeping lies straight was exhausting. "Yes."

Mama surprised me by merely nodding. "She must be a good friend." She switched back to English. "I'd love to meet her."

I introduced my mom and Hana, who instantly transformed into a polite young woman. They chatted for a moment, and then Mama spoke to me. "Go on and have fun. You both look so beautiful."

"I will have fun. Get some rest."

My mom glanced away, then back. I could tell her smile was fake. "I'll call you tomorrow."

I raised an eyebrow at Hana after I hung up. "You're really good with parents."

She tossed her head. "It's my superpower. If she was here, she'd be thanking me for being your friend."

I snorted. That might be true.

"Remy texted me that he and Niam are five minutes away. Ready?"

I looked down at my phone. My worry over my mother's mood wasn't going to go away anytime soon, but the anticipation of seeing Niam was too big to squash. "Yup. You sure we look good?" *Do I look good?*

She smoothed her hand over her hip. "Yes. We're gorgeous. Now grab your shoes."

I'd had to steal my footwear out of Kareena's closet, and I hoped she wouldn't mind. They were simple gold shoes, but they had a chunkier heel. I wasn't accustomed to anything but flats, and I wasn't about to break my neck.

The doorbell rang as we made it downstairs. I opened the door to find Niam standing outside, Remy a step behind them.

I was gratified by the fact that it took Niam a second to speak. "Wow," he finally said. "You look amazing."

"Amazing," Remy said, from over his shoulder, but he was looking at Hana. His big face turned red, clashing with his hair.

"We're wearing Sonia Patil originals," Hana singsonged, and went outside. Remy pulled her into a big bear hug. He lowered his head and kissed her, and I glanced away, back to Niam.

"I know you said you were making your dress, but this is so good, I can't believe it." Niam shook his head. "Wow," he repeated. He held out a box, which contained a corsage: a single white orchid with a blue ribbon. "I, um, brought you this."

I had no idea anyone actually bought corsages for their dates outside of, like, movies or shows. "I love it," I half whispered, and let him put it on. "You look really nice, too."

"Thanks." His eyes warmed. He wore a dark blue suit, though neither he nor Remy wore ties. I knew nothing about men's clothes, except that the white shirt deepened the rich brown of his skin and eyes. There was a matching white orchid pinned to his lapel.

I grabbed my jacket for the walk to the car but couldn't bring myself to hide my dress. I'd rather freeze.

He held out his arm to help me down the steps from my door, and I took it, like I was a fragile flower who would tumble down the concrete stairs I raced up and down on a daily basis. Gentleman that he was, he also circled the car to hold the door open for me. I got into the passenger seat, while Remy and Hana clambered into the back.

It was quiet in the car while we drove, Niam and me because we were vaguely awkward, Hana and Remy because they were causing the awkwardness by smooching in the back seat.

I caught Niam's glance, and I relaxed at the amusement there. He held out his hand. I stared at it for a second, then took it. His hand was bigger than mine, the palm dry. His fingers curled over mine, holding me in place. "I hate to tell you this," he murmured, "but FYI, my mom's chaperoning the dance."

My first instinct should probably not have been excitement that I'd get to see Pooja. "Oh, I see," I said instead.

"She already told me she'll stay out of our way," he hurried to say. "She's excited we're going together. She loves you."

I tried not to be smug about that, but wooing someone's parents was almost as good as wooing a teacher. I hoped Candice's parents still asked her about me. "It's okay, I get it. She probably wants to make sure James's okay, right?"

"Yeah, she can be overprotective. Though she did promise to stay out of his way as well."

"We'll all be busy, I'm sure."

He squeezed my hand. "You've looked pretty every time I've seen you, but you look extra pretty tonight."

"Every time? What about when I was sweaty at the restaurant?" I teased.

"Sure. You even sweat pretty."

A groan came from behind us. "Surely you can do better than that as a compliment, Niam."

Niam rubbed his thumb over my finger. His one-handed driving should have made me nervous, but he gripped the steering wheel so confidently, I didn't worry. "You're right, Hana."

Hana dove back onto Remy's lips.

Niam and I exchanged a smile, and it was the nicest feeling in the world to have that shared moment of understanding.

My brain tried to take that smile and run with it, to create a fantasy, but I stopped it. I didn't need a fantasy. I looked out the window at the town slipping by and squeezed Niam's hand. He squeezed it back, with more feeling.

For tonight, I was going to let reality be my dream.

Twenty-Three

Our school was ambitious, and the PTA had run with the theme of a harvest festival. They'd taken over the student parking lot and turned it into a carnival . . . if the carnival was underfunded and staffed by volunteer parents. There were hay bales and booths with various snacks and drinks. We bypassed the cider and doughnuts because I was too nervous, Niam was too snotty about grocery store food, and Hana and Remy were . . . well, they were still too interested in each other's lips.

I couldn't blame Hana. If I were slightly less worried about being the center of attention, I'd be diving into Niam's mouth too.

I didn't expect to see Pooja immediately, but she sat behind the ticket desk, positioned right in the main lobby. Mr. Walsh was next to her, and they both beamed at us as we walked in. "Well, if it isn't one of my favorite students. And it's Niam, right? Nice to see you again." He gave a cheerful smile and a nod to Hana and Remy.

Niam frowned at his mom. "Mom, I thought you were going to be behind the scenes."

Pooja had the grace to look bashful. "I can't help what job the PTA president gives me, Niam."

"Right, 'cause you've definitely never gotten into a fight with a PTA president."

His mom's smile was serene. She flipped her long hair over her shoulder. She wore a trendy belted black sweater dress and black boots. "Is your brother with you?"

"No. He's coming separately. Can we get our tickets—"

"Sonia, it's so good to see you. What a cute couple you two make."

"Um, thanks."

"You look absolutely beautiful. Where did you get your dress?"

"She made it," Hana piped up. "Mine, too."

My hype woman.

Both the adults made appropriate impressed noises. "Is there anything you can't do, Sonia?"

Lots of things, but I didn't want to list all my shortcomings in front of my new date.

Mr. Walsh nodded. "I say the same thing, that her mother must be so proud of her."

I didn't react, but Hana took a step forward. "Four tickets, please. My treat."

"No, you don't have to do that," Niam protested, but Remy was quiet. That is, until Hana's head bent while rummaging around her purse. Then he smoothly put cash on the table and snagged our tickets.

"Let's go," he said cheerfully, and guided Hana away.

Mr. Walsh handed us our wristbands. "Have fun, kids. Make good decisions."

Niam offered his hand, and I tentatively took it, conscious of Pooja's speculative gaze on us.

The *ugly duckling gets a makeover and walks into a crowded room of people who never noticed her before on the arm of a handsome prince* fantasy was, like, rookie-level dreaming.

In reality, I hadn't been ugly to begin with—Hana's comment about Eurocentric beauty standards had really made me think—and I hadn't had so much of a makeover as gotten a few new hair products and had the courage to wear clothes that I loved and made for myself to embrace instead of hide my personality. Also, no one was really looking at us.

I did, however, have a handsome date.

I looked up at Niam and he smiled. His lips were so full and nice, and I wondered how they'd feel pressed on mine again. But, like, for longer.

Always eager to improve, I'd googled *how to kiss* and watched a few videos on technique and form. Our first kiss had been a good kiss, as far as fireworks, but I wanted the chance to show off what I'd learned. I could only do that if we lip-locked for longer than the sample Niam had given me in the parking lot.

"Well, I'm bored already," Hana muttered.

I tried to shift my thoughts away from kissing, though that was hard. "You said we'd have fun," I reminded her. I tucked a curl behind my ear. I'd added more oil than last time, so much I'd feared I'd get those old taunts about being smelly again, but my curls were so defined next time I might add more. Moisture, my hair had been begging for it. I was going to listen to the million wavy and curly people on the internet and drench my curls.

"We will have fun," Remy said gallantly. He offered Hana his hand. "Want to get something to drink before we dance?"

"You think the punch is spiked yet?"

"Uh, I don't think anyone usually tampers with the drinks."

Hana made a disgusted noise. "I'm living in hell."

"I didn't say *we* couldn't spike our personal beverages." He gently lifted his jacket and exposed a silver flask.

It was no scrunchie flask, but it was resourceful, and Hana clearly thought so, too, because her smile lit up her eyes. "Lead the way, handsome."

Niam touched the back of my arm. "Are you thirsty? For spiked or unspiked drinks?"

"No. I'm good."

He nodded at the dance floor. "Uh, do you want to dance?"

That was what we were here for, but there was a slight problem. I licked my lips. "I'm not really a great dancer."

"Neither am I, but the good news is, you don't have to be. No one here is."

It was a faster song. I could fake shimmy for three minutes. "Sure."

As soon as we got onto the dance floor, the song ended, and a slow dance came on. Niam's lips curled up. "Even better." He opened his arms.

I didn't have to think. I stepped inside the circle, and he closed them around me. "See? We're killing it," he said against my temple. I shivered at the warm puff of his breath against my skin. "Put your hands on my back."

I did as instructed. He still smelled like cardamom, like the baked goods he loved were somewhere on his person. His hand pressed against my lower back and urged me closer. His pinkie rubbed against my spine. "Now we sway," he murmured.

It was true, no one else was good at dancing, and no one else cared that we weren't either. I didn't know how much time passed, but after a couple of songs, I relaxed enough to lay my head down on his shoulder. Niam lowered his head and pressed his cheek against mine. His legs brushed against my thigh, and between two layers of fabric, the heat of his body started a low fire in my belly. If the night could have ended there, I would have called it all a win.

But it didn't end there.

"Sonia," he said, and my stomach turned into butterflies to hear my name uttered like that. I never thought so much yearning could ever be attached to the syllables that made up me.

"Sonia" came another familiar voice behind me. "There you are."

Niam released me too quickly, and I glanced over my shoulder. James stood behind me, uncaring of the people dancing around him. He was objectively handsome in his suit, but I was newly obsessed with Niam, so I was unmoved. "Hi, James," I said slowly. "Can I help you?"

Something passed between James and Niam, but I didn't

know what it was. James gave us both a strained smile. "I'm sorry to do this, but, Sonia, can I speak with you for a second?"

Niam took a step forward, strain compressing his lips. "We're busy, James."

"I know. Obviously. I swear, I wouldn't do this if it wasn't important."

"Wouldn't you?" Niam asked, and I gave a double take. That had sounded vaguely hostile.

James caught it too. He rolled his eyes. "Yeah, man. I told you, I'm cool with you two. I just need to talk to Sonia."

I placed my hand on Niam's chest. "Be right back." Niam subsided. I walked with James to a dark corner and he turned. Before he could speak, I raised my hand. "You don't need to keep dragging me away to apologize. You know that, right?"

He grimaced, and I realized instantly that something was wrong. His gaze was far away, and there was more sweat on his neck than dancing alone could account for. "Are you okay? What's up?"

"Nothing. I've been having some trouble in crowds since my accident, is all."

Oh, hey. "Okay, that's reasonable. But then why are you shoving yourself into situations where you're going to be in big crowds? The parties, this dance?"

He scratched his head. His hair had grown out, his skull no longer smooth and shiny. "I just keep hoping things will go back to normal."

There it was again, that compassion. "James—"

"That's not important right now. I have to talk to you about something else," he said in a rush. James shuffled his feet. "Sam posted a video."

Uh-oh. "What kind of video?"

He gritted his teeth. "One about you and me."

The Beyoncé song playing over the speakers faded out in my ears. Sam, who had all those followers, had posted a video about . . . me? "Show me."

He rubbed his hand over his face and handed me his phone. The video was up. I pressed play. I had to rely on the captions, since the volume wasn't loud enough to hear.

There was Sam, getting ready, taking her curlers out one at a time, in her nonsensically white room. "Okay, I have some tea. You want some tea about how flaky men can be?

"You all know I've been with James for the past two years. And then he had his accident. I tried to help him, I tried to be there for him, I tried to give him space. And how did he repay me? By hooking up with someone else." She lifted her hand, and I gasped. There, on the green screen, was a sharp and crisp video of me and James going into the basement in Remy's house. He had his arm around me. From the angle, things did look more intimate than they had been.

She finished unrolling her curlers. "My friend sent me this. Her name's Sonia or Sania or something. Whoever she is . . . I know relationships are hard work, but I don't know if I can keep being strong and hang in there when I see him with other girls who are clearly chasing clout. Like, that was our lunch table you're eating at with her. That's our group of friends you're bringing her around, you know? It's too much. So I'm done. I'm not running after him anymore, and if he wants to be with someone else, then he's welcome to her. I hope they're happy together, though I doubt it, because I heard she's dating his brother now."

I couldn't take any more, but luckily it was over. I pushed pause when it began to loop to the beginning, and straightened.

"What the hell is going on?"

I jumped, and turned to find Niam next to us. He glared at his brother, which made it clear that he'd seen the whole video. "You said nothing happened between you two."

"It didn't," I said, as firmly as I possibly could. "We went to the basement and talked. That was when I found out . . . well, anyway."

"Where you found out he was using you to make Sam jealous." Niam made a sharp gesture. "Well, it worked. Happy now?"

"That's not . . ." James grimaced and had the grace to look ashamed. "It doesn't matter. I'm sorry. I didn't want this."

"Well, you got it."

I rubbed my hand over my tight throat. I glanced around. Maybe it was my imagination, but it felt like the same people who hadn't paid us any attention before were watching us now. "They're talking about me."

To his credit, James looked stricken. "No, they're not. There aren't a ton of views on this; no one will pay attention."

"Hana hooked up with one guy, and she's still being mocked months later," I said clearly. "Do you really think anyone forgets stuff like this? Even when there's a plausible way to deny it?" It was like I couldn't catch a break.

Part of me wanted to shrink into myself. To dissolve and melt away, or to hide and hope this blew over.

The other part of me was enraged.

I hadn't done anything wrong here. But someone else had. James, who had used me. And Sam, who had decided to put me on blast to not just the school, but anyone who stumbled across this video.

A chill ran down my spine. And how long would it take someone to put the green screen photo of me and James side by side with the footage from the rescue? "They'll figure it out," I whispered, half to myself.

James shook his head, having understood me. "No. Pact, remember?"

Niam looked between us, and his eyebrows drew together. He took a step away from us. "What pact?"

Great. My handsome prince was rethinking his courtship.

There was that crash. Only this time, I was crashing back to reality from reality, not a dream.

I shook my head. Too much listening to Makeshift and not enough being cynical. So much for believing in yourself and everything magically falling into place.

What's the harm? Here was the harm. Utter and complete disappointment.

James and Niam were arguing in hushed whispers, but I couldn't pay attention. I searched the decorated cafeteria for an answer to this new crisis. It was like I had a homing device wired into my brain, because I caught sight of Sam immediately, walking out of the cafeteria in a pink satin slip dress.

My disappointment and worry found a target, and I'd had enough.

I ignored James and Niam as they broke off their arguing to call after me. I didn't see her in the empty hallway, but I had a hunch about where she'd be. And I knew James wouldn't be able to follow me in there and protect his precious ex.

I slammed open the door to the girl's bathroom, and it shut behind me with just as much force. Sam looked over from the mirror, pausing in lining her lips. Recognition and rage were quickly replaced by boredom, but I wasn't fooled. She might pretend to look through me, but she knew exactly who I was.

"Take it down." I don't know who was more shocked by the guttural tone of my words.

Sam turned to face me fully. Her light pink dress made her look angelic, but she was anything but. "What the hell are you talking about?"

The door opened behind me. "Hey, guys. What's going on?"

Fear and shock flirted on the edges of my anger, but that anger burned. I turned. "Candice. I thought you were out of town until tomorrow."

"I got back early. I didn't think you'd be here." Candice tried a smile. Her eye makeup was sharp and dramatic, the green eye shadow a match to her emerald dress. "You never cared for dances. Before."

Had she told Sam about the cape and me? Was it better to be known as a homewrecker who hopped from brother to brother, or the hero who had saved James? The former would bring less attention, right?

"Candice, tell your ex-bestie to get away from me. Some bug crawled up her butt."

I refocused on Sam, and my rage flared again, overpowering my concern over that cape. "Take it down," I repeated.

Candice took a step forward. "Take what down?"

"She posted a video about James and me, insinuating that something happened between us, and that I dumped him to date his brother," I said flatly. While I may have been on a date with Niam, we weren't dating. Especially after this mortifying turn of events.

Candice flinched. "Sam, you didn't."

Sam rolled her eyes. "I don't see what the big deal is. I barely mentioned her, and no one knows who she is. If they did, it's not like anyone would believe he really went from me to her."

This time I flinched. "You used my name, you cruel bitch."

"Jesus, Sam," Candice muttered. "The hell is wrong with you? Take it down."

Sam's brow crinkled. She clearly didn't like earning Candice's disapproval. "No. Now, if you'll excuse me, I have a party to get back to." She stomped past me.

I gave Candice a disgusted look. "This is who you prefer to spend your time with?"

She lowered her head, which only made me madder. I didn't wait for a response. I followed Sam. In my peripheral vision, I noticed Niam and James standing in the otherwise empty hallway, but I was so angry, my vision was clouded in red.

"You're a fucking asshole," I snapped.

She froze, and her back trembled. Slowly, she spun to face me. "Watch your tone," she bit off. "I'm not the one shoving herself into relationships where she doesn't belong."

"Guys, why don't we go into a classroom, before anyone else comes out here," James said, and we both snarled at him. He took a step back, but persevered. "That's not nice, Sam."

Dear lord, had this guy actually been fooled into thinking this girl was nice? How? Had he had a head injury *before* the canal?

Sam turned on him. "Nice? You want nice? I cannot believe you. I tried to take care of you when you were sick and I was turned away, while she got to basically come in and feed you soup."

I cleared my throat. "I didn't even see him when he was sick, actually, let alone feed him soup."

"You came by the hospital to chase publicity and likes," Niam said flatly. "My mom said you had your phone out and ready to film. That's why she told you to go home."

At least *someone* could see through Sam as well as I could.

"Sam, I can't believe you're mad at me. *You* dumped *me*, remember?" James shook his head. "I could go on my socials and tell everyone what you said to me when you told me we were over. Or when you turned most of our friends against me."

"Then do it," Sam said. "All I did was speak my truth about my feelings, and I don't have to be sorry about that. If you don't like it, don't watch."

"Listen, you can say whatever you want about my brother," Niam started grimly.

"Hey—"

Niam raised his hand at James. "He kind of deserves something for his crappy behavior. But leave Sonia out of it."

Sam's fake lashes fluttered. "Wow, you have so many protectors, Sonia. That's so impressive for a random."

"Sonia's not a random," James said firmly. "She's my friend."

"A friend?" Sam sneered. "Give me a break. She's a nonentity. You probably didn't even know she existed a month ago. If you want to make all the pathetic losers your new girlfriends, go for it, but that doesn't mean we can't laugh at them."

James took a step forward, blocking me with his body. "Apologize to her," he said sternly, and I couldn't tell for a second if he was talking to me or his precious Sam.

When Sam laughed, I realized it was her. "I will not. I may have talked about that photo, but I wasn't the one who took it. Don't you see how it reflects on me? I will not be made fun of because you decide to hook up with trash."

"Sam," Candice hissed.

"I know you have a soft spot for her, Candice, but you need to drop your blind spot around her family and see that she's an opportunistic leech. I've known it for years."

I froze. Like my rage turned into a block of solid ice, encasing me in it. What did she mean, my family?

Candice told her. About your mom. About Shadow.

"Shut up, Sam."

Sam didn't listen to her friend but kept talking. "Just because you dated her sister doesn't mean you have to keep babying her—"

The slap of flesh on flesh shocked us all. So much that it took me a second to process Sam's words.

Candice and . . . Kareena?

What? How? When?

Sam cradled her cheek and stared at Candice, her face white except for the red handprint on her cheek. "What the fuck," she whispered.

Candice shrank, but her vocal cords worked. "I told you to never tell anyone that."

"It's not like I outed you, for God's sake."

No. Candice and Kareena were both out. But that didn't mean I'd known about them together.

They'd lied to me. Kept me out of something. My best friend and my sister. "You and Kareena?" I rasped.

Candice licked her lips and lowered her head. It was all the answer I needed.

Another voice cut in. "What on earth is going on here?"

I focused on Mr. Walsh, Pooja hurrying behind him, all concern. They must have heard us.

Sam's tears developed and overflowed her eyes. The girl could cry on command, too? "Candice hit me!"

"Sam posted a video lying about me," James said loudly and clearly. "Does that go against our zero-tolerance anti-bullying policy?"

Sam's face drained of color. Had she not expected James to snitch on her?

"Hitting is also against that policy," she said, through gritted teeth.

Mr. Walsh's eyes went flinty hard, and his mustache trembled. "Let's all go to the principal's office and sort this out, shall we?"

My fingers started tingling, which was odd. I tried to clench my hands back into feeling normal.

But instead, my chest grew tight, and so did my throat. No, no. Why was this happening now? The attention wasn't focused on me any longer.

The adrenaline's leaving you, and you're processing.

But I didn't want to process, because if I processed, I'd have a panic attack. No way in hell was I going to do that in front of all these people. "I want to go home," I said, low.

Mr. Walsh cleared his throat. "Sonia, we do need to discuss—"

"She's barely a part of this," Niam said, and came closer to me. Too close. The air grew thicker, more difficult to drag in.

"Sonia didn't do anything," Candice chimed in, and Sam's lip curled.

"She can come speak to the principal tomorrow, can't she?" Pooja said quietly. Mr. Walsh pressed his lips together but nodded.

"I need to go home," I repeated.

"I'll take you home," Niam said.

The last thing I wanted was to sit in a car with Niam. If I was going to have a panic attack, I wanted to do it safely away from the guy I'd been researching how to kiss. "No. Thank you."

"Sonia, it's no big deal."

"I said no." I took a big step away. Unlike that night at the

343

canal, I didn't run, but I definitely didn't take my time getting away from all of those eyes.

Once I got out of the building, I did start jogging, and it was harder to do it in heels than it had been in water-logged boots. I made it past the low-budget carnival stalls that were in various stages of breakdown, all the way to the overflow lot. I flew past people, and I'm sure I got strange looks, but I ignored them. When I got to the drop-off circle, I hunched over and took deep, bracing breaths of the cold night air. The tightness in my chest eased, but the prickle of tears in the corners of my eyes meant a storm of emotions was imminent.

That ridiculous, poorly timed video. Niam scowling at James and I. Candice slapping Sam.

Candice and Kareena. Kareena and Candice. Even their names sounded right together.

Why do you feel betrayed? You weren't dating Candice.

But she'd been mine. My best friend and confidante. And now I was finding out that she'd had just as close a relationship—maybe closer—with my sister? The sister who only paid attention to me these days when our mom forced her to?

"Sonia!"

I whirled around, ready to cry or scream, unclear which one. But Pooja's furrowed brow stopped me from falling apart. "Auntie, I'm sorry, but I need to go home." Why was that the only thing I could repeat?

"I understand." She lifted her keys. "Come, my car's right over here. You must be cold."

I hesitated. I'd rather have the anonymity of a rideshare,

but if I waited I risked Niam or James or Hana—or Jesus, Candice—being here soon, sympathetic and curious and far too knowledgeable. Also, I was cold. "Fine. Thank you," I said, trying to swallow my emotions.

"It's okay. We all need a hand sometimes."

I needed more than a hand right now. I needed a whole different home, a whole different world.

Out there in the multiverse, surely there was a place and a time where I had a nice normal family, and nice normal friends and a nice normal boyfriend. Where the two relationships I'd grieved for the most hadn't had a secret relationship that had shut me out before I'd realized they'd shut me out.

My dress caught in the door of Pooja's car when I closed it. I opened the door, freed the silk, and closed it again. I pressed my forehead against the cold window, and stared up at sky, dotted in diamonds. If I concentrated on the stars, I could keep the panic at bay.

If your and Kareena's relationship were still the same as it had been before Mama left, would you feel this bad? Or would you have been happy to have another tie to Candice?

It was useless to ponder hypotheticals. This was now. And given the crash after crash after crash of the evening, now sucked.

Twenty-Four

I mentally groaned when we pulled up to my house and I saw the car sitting in our driveway. Kareena was home. Of course she was. Why couldn't something go my way?

"Thank you," I said woodenly to Pooja. My throat was hoarse after being silent for the entire drive. "I'm so sorry for inconveniencing you."

"It's no bother," she said gently. "Is your mom home, Sonia?"

Yikes. I rubbed my temples. "My sister is."

"Will your mom be home later?" she persisted. "I'd love to speak with her."

I looked into her kind eyes and lied through my teeth. "She works late."

"You two are home alone?"

"I'm almost seventeen. My sister's of legal age and is my guardian when my mom's not home." *A guardian who lies to me.*

Pooja lifted her hands. "That's fine. I want to make sure

you're taken care of before I leave."

"Yes, ma'am. I—I'm taken care of." That lie, I nearly tripped over.

"Let me know if you need anything. Anything at all."

I nodded. She was being so nice. "Yes. Okay. Thank you." I got out of the car and made my way to my front door. My heels thudded on the concrete steps up to the house. Her headlights flashed over me as she pulled away once I stepped foot inside.

The sound of video games hit me first. I walked right past Kareena sprawled on the couch. She said something to me, but I ignored it. I wanted to get to my bedroom and take these clothes off and sleep and not get up for as long as possible.

Actually, undressing was too much effort. I collapsed on the bed in my beautiful but now wrinkled dress and buried my face in the pillow. My phone vibrated, and I pulled it out.

Messages, from James and Niam and Hana. I didn't want to look at the content of them, but I got the vague impression of concern. Someone must have gotten to Hana to tell her what went down between the five of us in the hallway. Hopefully, she was the only other person who knew. How long would it take for everyone to know? Sam would definitely be filming as soon as it was humanly possible. Hell, she was probably setting up her three-point lighting system right now.

The last thing I wanted was for the Coopers or Hana to come here and see me. I quickly texted a reply. **I'm fine. I'm home. Please give me some space.** Then I copy-pasted it to all three of them.

Niam was the only one who immediately replied. **Space**

347

is fine. I'll check in on you tomorrow. Please don't worry about anything.

I stuck the phone under my pillow and grimaced at the stomps coming up the stairs. Not now.

There was a cursory tap on my door and it opened. I lifted one eyelid. "I'll do the dishes tomorrow."

"I already did them."

I closed my eyes again. "Sorry."

"Did you make that dress?"

"Yes."

"You did a good job." Kareena cleared her throat. "So, um . . . why does the principal want to talk to Mom?"

Oh shit. "He called?"

"Yup. I told him Mom was sleeping. He said he expected to see you in the office as soon as you get to school. That there was an altercation, and you were a witness. What did you do, Sonia?"

"Nothing." *You did it.* Okay, I'd partially done it. Sam was to blame, too.

Kareena came inside and cursed when she stepped on a pen. "This place is a biohazard."

"It's just cluttered." Why was she here? Was the video game not enough of a place to let out aggression? Did she need to be on me right now? "Look, I know you hate me, but I can't fight with you right now."

Her eyebrows drew together. "What? I don't hate you."

My jaw worked. "Whatever."

"Sonia . . . what's wrong?"

"Nothing."

"I need to know what happened."

"Why?"

"Because I'm responsible for you."

Guilt threatened to pierce my righteous anger. She was responsible for me, and that was why she had to stay here and not have any fun and had to work all the time. And why she didn't tell me anything, even back when she'd ostensibly loved me.

All those times, I'd thought back to what a good relationship we'd had, and that had been a lie too. I didn't even have nice sisterly memories to look back on.

You're acting like she and Candice cheated on you.

"Then explain why your principal's calling."

I examined the bottom of the bunk bed above me. "Why don't you explain why you dated my best friend, then."

The silence between us yawned wide, like an ocean.

Finally, she gave a long, low sigh. "Did she tell you?"

It was an admission. I'd already known it was true, but the confirmation made me tremble. "No. Her asshole friend did."

"Which friend?"

I forgot that Kareena had just attended our school last year. "Sam."

Kareena muttered something under her breath. "She's hanging out with her now?"

I covered my eyes with the back of my arm. It was easier to talk to her when I couldn't see her. "How long did you date in secret?" I thought of Kareena taking Candice to the dance around this time last year. We'd been sophomores; Kareena had been a senior. I hadn't thought anything of it. We were so close in age, we'd often shared friendships.

I didn't expect the bed to depress slightly next to me. I peeked to find Kareena sitting on the edge of the mattress. She had to hunch over. "Just a few months."

"Three?" Three wasn't so bad. Three wasn't even a real relationship.

"More like . . . five or six."

That was way more than three. "You snuck around with her for the majority of last year?"

"Don't yell at me."

I pulled my arm away to glare at her. "I'm not yelling. This is incredulous voice raising is all. But if I wanted to yell, I could."

She pursed her lips. She hadn't changed out of her godawful pink uniform from the diner. Her name tag was different tonight. Karen. "People would have talked if I was actively dating someone, especially a sophomore."

My mother's voice whispered in my ear. *You don't like attention, either. She has more at stake than you did.* Kareena had been *made* for attention. She'd been naturally popular, drawing people to her. I wondered now how much of her life had been spent downplaying her natural light, so she could fly under the radar.

Mama had been upset when Kareena had gotten a B in her history class last year, knocking her out of the valedictorian slot, but Kareena had only shrugged. The salutatorian hadn't had to give a speech in front of a big crowd. Had she purposefully taken herself out of the running?

Though understanding crept along the edges of my indignation, I persisted. "But you could have told *me*." I added, "We . . . we used to talk."

"We did. But . . . not about dating and stuff." Kareena spread her hands wide. "I didn't want to complicate your friendship if it didn't go anywhere."

"Well, guess what?" I raised myself up on my elbows. "It did complicate it, and it seems like it didn't go anywhere."

"I didn't know until recently that she'd ghosted you."

"You would have known, if you'd paid attention for the last few months."

She nodded. "Yeah. You're right."

Her easy agreement took some of the wind out of my sails, but I rallied. "You've been awful to me."

"I know. I had a long talk with Mom this morning. She . . . yelled at me."

That raised both my eyebrows. "She never yells at you."

"I know. She had good reason to. She told me how badly I've behaved toward you, and how much it hurt you."

She had? I'd known my mom was on my side, but a part of me had always felt like she was slightly more on Kareena's side. An oldest daughter/mother bond that I would never be able to puncture.

"It's like . . . like I've been in a fog since Mom left. Just shoving everyone away, without a care as to who I hurt."

I rubbed my finger over my upper lip, hating that my anger was wilting under the weight of immediate understanding. I'd been in a fog, too. "Did you love her?"

"Candice?"

"Yeah."

She rubbed the back of her neck. "I thought so, at the time. I wanted to protect her. The last time I saw Candice was a few days after Mom was deported. She was coming from your room. I could hear you crying." Kareena sat in profile to me. Her throat moved as she swallowed. "She came over to give me a hug, and I . . . I thought about what might happen if I was deported too, how much it would hurt you and her, and . . . I snapped. I told her I was dealing with too much to think about her and that I didn't want to see her anymore. I said a lot of other stuff, too."

I remembered that night. "That was basically the last time I saw Candice, too. All this time, I'd thought she'd felt some kind of way about Mama. Like she thought the deportation was a stigma."

"I don't know why she ghosted you. But I'm guessing it might have partially been because of me. I'm sorry."

I was honest enough to admit that she couldn't shoulder the entire blame for my anger. "Candice could have not ghosted me. I could have confronted her. Our friendship wasn't only your responsibility."

"I know you're mad we didn't tell you."

"I just felt left out, I suppose." *Abandoned. Alone.* "I feel left out a lot these days. Like I don't have anyone."

"You have me. I know it doesn't seem like it lately, but you do have me." The next words seemed like they were pulled from her. "I love you. I'm sorry. I didn't want to hurt you then and I don't want to hurt you anymore."

The anger melted away completely. I tried to cling to it, because it kept me warm, but it was gone on the wings of a hunger so deep I couldn't ignore it.

I wanted to be loved by my sister and have my family back. Or at least some semblance of it. It was all I wanted. "Can you hug me?" I felt silly as soon as the words left my lips. She'd never been physically demonstrative, except with Mama.

But she scooted over, and I sat up, my speed betraying my need. It wasn't a hug like the one Pooja had given me. This was rusty, and more of a side embrace, but I rested my head against her shoulder and soaked it in anyway.

We sat together for a while, and then she stirred. "I'm glad we had this talk, Sonia, but what does this have to do with the principal calling?"

Mentally, I sighed. I'd forgotten about everything else from the second Candice and Kareena's relationship had been revealed.

She seemed to brace herself. "If it's . . . like was your date mean to you? Did he do something? I know you went with that guy from the restaurant. . . ."

I could just not tell her. It would be easy to not trust this kinder, softer, apologetic Kareena.

But I was so tired of having no one. I pulled away, then dug my phone out of the hidden pocket of my skirt. I navigated to Sam's profile, then stopped. The video was gone.

Had Mr. Walsh persuaded her to take it down? Had Candice?

"Sonia?"

"Sam had posted a video."

"Candice's bitchy friend?"

"Yeah. She's the one who . . . anyway, she got mad thinking James liked me, but he didn't, and so she posted a photo of us. And I was worried someone would—"

I stopped. I couldn't tell her I was worried someone would identify me as Shadow. Our truce was too new, and Kareena would get so angry with me.

"Someone would what? This is very confusing."

I tried to relate the complicated story more slowly, skipping over the rescue and my pact with James.

"Okay, let me get this straight." Kareena rubbed her palms on her thighs. "You liked James, but he was only pretending to like you to passive-aggressively inform everyone he had no interest in Sam. But now you like his brother, and Niam likes you. Except everyone thinks you're dating James, and that you stole him from Sam. Sam got mad and posted a video calling you out. You confronted her, and she doubled down. Then Candice hit her."

"That's actually a better explanation than I could provide."

Kareena shook her head. "Girl, my head is spinning."

I clasped my hands together tightly. She had no idea how much more it could spin.

"Candice really slapped her?" A fond smile played on Kareena's lips.

Violence was wrong, and so was the smidgen of satisfaction I'd felt over that slap in the heat of the moment. "I imagine that's really what the principal wants to see me about."

"Then you're not in trouble at all. This will work itself out. Look, Sam already took the video down."

"She could post another one."

Kareena smirked. I wished I could have that kind of smirk when it came to Sam. "So? Who cares?"

I care. And you'll care if the spotlight turns on us on a global scale. "I don't want to attract any more attention either. You should empathize with that."

She paused, probably thinking of herself and Candice. "I do, but you and James aren't together, and people will figure that out."

How to explain that being linked with James at all was a bad idea? Like, I thought back to eating lunch with him in the cafeteria and I wanted to kick my past self. I should have completely avoided even being seen in his company.

"They'll talk about you for, like, five minutes, then let it go."

I squinted at her. "Have you been to our high school lately? They have nothing else to do but talk about other people."

She grimaced. "Okay, maybe they'll talk for ten minutes."

"Or longer. It could spread beyond the school."

"Why on earth would some teen drama spread beyond the school?"

I rubbed my too-gritty eyes. "Because."

"Because what?"

"Never mind."

"Uh, no. You can't say something weird like that and then never mind me."

My mom's voice came again. *She should know, so she can be prepared. What if the police do show up to talk to you?*

My shoulders slumped. I got up from the bed. She shifted aside.

Don't trust her. You're going to ruin this nice moment you're having.

I bit my lip. "You have to promise you won't yell at me."

"I won't yell at you."

"Or snap at me. Or say something mean."

"I wouldn't."

"You do. All the time." If she crossed the imaginary line in my head and said something truly unforgivable, undoing everything we'd accomplished here today . . . well, I didn't know how I'd react.

She rubbed her forehead. "I do, I guess. I promise, I won't yell at you or snap at you or say anything mean."

"And you can't tell Mama."

Kareena edged forward. "I'm starting to get nervous, Sonia."

"She'll only worry. You don't want her to worry, do you?" She shook her head. "Fine. I won't tell Mom."

The walk to my closet was the longest walk of my life. I didn't want to do this, but it also felt like I badly needed to do this. I found my costume. Carefully, I handed it to her.

"What is this?"

I tried to swallow. "I made it. I wore it . . . the weekend before last. I was working at the café, and there was an event at the comic book store where James worked."

She traced the *S* on the top. Her frown deepened, and I could tell the exact moment realization set in. She looked up at me. "Sonia, were you the one who . . ."

"Yes."

"I saw the video."

"Yeah."

Kareena rubbed her hand over her face. "That was *you* who jumped into the canal?"

I tried not to feel bad about her disbelief. "Yeah."

"But . . ." She lifted her head, her eyes narrowing. "You were injured."

I rubbed my arm, smearing the concealer. "It was a scratch."

She grasped my arm, turning it this way and that. "Sonia. You could have been hurt."

"I wasn't. Not badly."

"You could have needed medical attention. This could have gotten infected. Why wouldn't you tell me this?"

I squinted at her. "Because I knew you'd get mad?"

"Why would I . . . ?" Her voice grew louder, but she throttled it back when I took a tiny step away. "Why would I get mad?"

"Because of the publicity. The cops came."

"You didn't talk to them. You ran." She raked her hands through her hair. It was slightly greasy, like she was due for a wash. "Oh no."

"If I'd stayed, they might have wanted to speak with Mama and then dug and . . ." I twisted my hands together. "I didn't want to lead the authorities to you."

"You were protecting me."

"Yes. And me," I added, with some guilt.

Kareena clenched her fist in the fabric. "Who else knows?"

"James figured it out. And so did Candice. I—I went to her house to clean up before coming home, and I left my cape behind."

"Of course there was a cape," she murmured.

"But Candice gave me the cape back. She hasn't said anything to me, but I think that means she won't tell."

Kareena licked her lips. "Candice and I have some issues between us, but I don't believe she'd tell either. She knew about me all this time and she's kept silent. She knows what's at stake."

"She knew about your status? You told her?"

"Yeah."

There was a wealth of pain in that one word, so I didn't pursue it. "James and I have an understanding. He won't tell either."

"Can we trust him?"

"I think so. He doesn't want anyone talking about the video either." He'd had something of a brain blip, but I believed that was resolved now.

Kareena carefully placed the costume on the floor. "No one else can know about this, Sonia."

I tried to swallow. "I know. I've been doing my best to keep the secret since. It's the main thing on my mind."

"I believe you and I understand why you didn't tell me. It's not like I made myself an easy confidante."

I appreciated her taking accountability. "What do we do?"

"Nothing. This never happened. You are not all over the internet. And you're going to go into the principal's office tomorrow and only talk about Sam making videos about you, and nothing about this. Same with Mom. Got it?"

I gulped. Her bossiness wasn't so annoying this time. I'd been adrift for so long, and it was like she was throwing me a line of security by telling me what to do. "Yes. I'm sorry."

"About what?"

"Making this a mess."

"It's a mess, but you did save someone's life. That's pretty cool."

I twisted my fingers together. "Thank you. For being so reasonable."

Her forehead pleated. "Please don't thank me for doing the bare minimum after months of being a dick. I don't deserve it."

"Mama really gave you a talking-to today, hmm?"

Her smile was a ghost of itself. "You have no idea."

"I wish she could come back." My words were so soft I was surprised she heard them.

Kareena bowed her head, and her hair fell forward to hide her face. "I think Mama coming back is almost impossible."

A sharp pang of sadness hit me at her verbalizing it. "You think so?"

"Yes. But . . . if I can get some kind of status here, I could at least go visit her." Her gaze turned far away. "That would be a dream. I'm pretty resigned to never seeing her again. She can't come here. And I don't want to go live there."

Made sense that Katrina knew our options as well as I did, but it killed me that I could at least go visit. "Me either."

"Mom made it so easy for me to come out to you both. She

was so progressive. I remember how startled I was, when I was a kid, that the rest of the world wasn't like our family."

That was true. Just as Mama was ruthlessly body positive, she'd also raised us to be open and accepting of others.

Kareena picked at her nails. "It's hard enough to be young and queer here. I don't want to have to go navigate my identity in a place I don't know."

I swallowed, reality slapping me in the face. Of course this was part of Kareena's anxiety over being deported, and in the back of my head, I'd understood the magnitude of the consequences should her secret be discovered. Hearing it spelled out, though, nearly made me buckle in sympathy for the mental load she carried all the time. "I'm sorry if I did anything to add to your stress. I'll try to be better. And do the dishes," I added.

"We'll both be better." Kareena rose to her feet, and she looked up at the top bunk, where she used to sleep. Slowly, she climbed the ladder. "I'm tired. Aren't you?"

I should have taken off my dress and my makeup, but I got into my bed too, and turned off the light on the nightstand. "Do you remember what Mom used to say, about the guy who rubbed a piece of gravel until it became oil?"

She gave a huff of a laugh. "Yeah. She'd trot it out anytime I wanted to give up on something."

My words were halting. "I don't want to give up on this family. We're broken, but we still have each other. Please . . . don't go back to how it was last week." I didn't care if she was only being nice to me because Mama had chewed her out. I just wanted it to continue.

"I won't." She stuck her hand off the top bunk, and I grasped it.

I timed my breathing with hers. It had been so long since I'd gotten to do that. I thought it would take forever to sleep, but in reality, it took no time at all.

Twenty-Five

I stared at the chevron-print carpet in the main office. I'd already spent the last hour speaking with the vice principal, and then they'd put me in the little empty conference room.

Kareena had already been at work this morning when I woke up, but she'd left me a note.

> *Remember what I said.*
> *You're going to go into the principal's office and only talk about Sam making videos about you, and nothing else. You got this. I trust you.*

And that was exactly what I had done. I wondered if they were talking to James in another room, or where Candice and Sam were. At least I'd be able to get this meeting over with before I figured out whether to let my mom find out about this.

The door opened, and the secretary stuck her head in. "You

can come into Principal Ahmed's office now, Sonia."

I nodded and gathered my stuff together as the woman went back to her desk. Two familiar figures walked by, and I locked eyes with Candice. She faltered, and her mom noticed.

The elder Carter's gaze met mine, and her eyebrows lifted, her expression softening. She stopped. "Sonia. It's been so long."

"Hello, ma'am." *Thanks for the extra supplies you keep in your shed.*

"How are you doing?"

"Good, thank you." *Good, because filled with anxiety over circumstances I can't control* wasn't a valid response.

"Good, good. We miss seeing your smile around our house." Her lips tightened and she glanced at Candice. "Certainly, Candice never received any kind of suspensions for fighting when you two were closer."

"Suspension?" I took a step forward.

"A week," Candice said, her voice hoarse.

A week for one slap? I thought that was excessive, but Dr. Carter didn't agree. "We're lucky it wasn't longer or an expulsion. As it is, I'm not sure how you're going to explain this to colleges." Candice's mother gave her daughter an arch look. "I have to run to the hospital. Drive straight home when you leave here, Candice." Her heels clipped on the tile as she walked away.

I waited until she was out of earshot. "A week, huh?" I adjusted my backpack on my shoulder.

"Yeah." Candice rocked back on her heels. Her mom must have pressured her into wearing nice clothes for this meeting, because she was dressed like she was about to go into a business-casual day at the office in black pants and a blue silk shirt. "I'd like to speak to you. Can we meet at the usual spot?"

I hesitated. I didn't particularly want to speak to Candice, but then I thought of what I had said to Kareena yesterday. I could have asked Candice why she'd ghosted me a long time ago, and I hadn't. I nodded and waited until she left before I made my way to the principal's personal office.

Principal Ahmed was a skinny, tall Black man, and I'd never had a reason to be on his bad side. Judging by his smile when the secretary ushered me in, I didn't think I had a reason to be right now, either.

James was not in his office. Sam, however, sat at a round table, flanked by an equally stiff blond couple. Her parents, I presumed. I wondered if their master bedroom was as blindingly white as Sam's room was.

"Sonia, thank you for coming. Have a seat."

I gingerly sat in the chair the principal indicated. I wished I could avoid Sam, but I couldn't, not here in this small office.

"We understand there was an incident involving you and Sam yesterday at the dance, based on a particular video she posted."

"Um, yeah."

"We've reviewed the social media account, and we find it to be in extremely poor taste." Principal Ahmed adjusted his glasses.

"We are horrified," Sam's mom said. She cast her daughter a scathing glance. "We had no idea Samantha was such a bully."

Whoooooa.

Our principal frowned. "Mrs. Larson, please. Sonia, Sam has something she'd like to say to you."

Sam cleared her throat and looked me in the eyes. "I'm sorry, Sonia. I understand what I did was wrong, and it won't happen again."

She was lying. I could tell that instantly. And so could her parents, because her mother gave her a hard poke. "Say it like you mean it," she hissed.

"I cannot believe I am missing work for this," Sam's dad said. "This is something you could have handled on your own."

Her mom glared at her father. "Work isn't your child. She is."

"The reason she can afford her phone to bully people is because I work."

"And see how well that's worked out for us."

Whooooooooa.

"Mr. and Mrs. Larson. Perhaps you could step outside for a minute."

Sam had turned even paler than she had yesterday. It made me feel . . . bad? "Actually, can Sam and I talk alone?"

Principal Ahmed hesitated but finally nodded. "A couple minutes," he cautioned. I didn't know what kind of fistfight he expected would break out, but I didn't need more than a couple minutes.

Sam's throat worked, and she spoke as soon as the adults left. "You got me suspended. I'm out for three days."

"For the video about us?"

Her nostrils flared. "And your little friend Hana filed a complaint. I filmed on school grounds, so the principal thinks he can regulate it. My dad's going to call his lawyer."

Hana, I love you. "I guess they really take that no-bullying thing seriously."

"I'm not a bully. I talk about my life. It's not like I'm doxing people or something."

My anger flared. "The video about us was more than a day in the life of, and you know it. You thought you could just tell James you want him back and he'd come running. You panicked when it seemed like he was more interested in me. You name-checked us because you wanted people to hate us and be on your side." I paused for a breath. I had no idea where this confident tone and words were coming from, except that I knew for a fact the authority figures were holding her responsible for doing something bad, and that was amazing. "You got yourself suspended."

"You're not so innocent. I know what you were doing."

I tried to hold on tight to that confidence. "What was I doing?"

"You were only trying to get with James because I got Candice back."

I scoffed. "What?"

"Candice became my friend again this year, and that made you mad. So you tried to show me that James preferred you. Joke's on you, I don't care."

Survey said she did in fact care, but I didn't want to get into that. I was too shocked by her words. "I'm not jealous of you being friends with Candice."

"Why not? I was jealous of you. Candice and I were friends since birth. Our parents have been friends since birth. Then you moved here, and suddenly she never had time for me. And her parents like you more than me!"

And here I'd thought Sam had had no idea who I was until I'd spilled coffee on her.

Sam tossed her hair over her shoulder. "I hope you're happy, because Candice isn't talking to me now."

Had I developed a crush on James before or after I'd found out he dated Sam? I couldn't remember. Could my interest in him have been an odd form of revenge for Candice shutting me out of her life and rekindling her friendship with Sam?

Sam and I hadn't been fighting over the same man all this time. We'd been fighting over the same woman.

"I don't control Candice, but you might be right," I admitted quietly. "The difference between us is that I didn't try to hurt you purposefully, and you did."

That surprised her into silence.

"Candice and James are both their own people, and they'll do whatever they want to do. We can't control them. We don't own them. So maybe we put this weird feud to rest now." I stood up. "Your parents seem like dicks, but you don't have to be. Stop trying to knock everyone down so you can feel good about yourself. And apologize to Candice. A real apology, not the one you gave me. She was wrong to hit you, yeah, but you betrayed her secret, and that's really shitty. She might have trouble trusting people now, and that's on you." *Like I have trouble trusting, thanks to her.* "Oh, and I am actually sorry about the coffee."

I went to the door just as Principal Ahmed opened it. He looked relieved that we hadn't drawn any blood while we'd been left alone. "Is everything okay, Sonia?"

"Yes, sir. We had a productive conversation."

"Good, good. I left a message for your mother, by the way. If she could give me a call back soon, that would be great."

I did the mental math on time zones. "She's not feeling well, but she'll call you tomorrow, if that's okay." That gave me today to figure out how to break this to her. Mama would be stressed about a principal call, even if I wasn't in trouble.

"That's fine. Please give my best to your sister. It was a pleasure catching up with Kareena last night, though not under ideal circumstances."

Of course he remembered Kareena. "I will."

I left the office. The hallways were empty, everyone in their classes. I glanced over my shoulder at the secretary, through the wide windows of the main office. Then I walked out the doors of the school.

I found Candice at her car in the student lot. She'd been one of the first ones to get their license last year, and we'd often met up there after school so she could drive me home.

She straightened from where she sat in the driver's seat, her legs out the door, and stood. "Hey."

I stopped a few feet away. "Hey."

"Thanks for coming out here."

"No problem. I'm sorry you got suspended."

"I deserve it. I shouldn't have hit Sam. I was just so mad at what she did."

"You mean telling me about you and Kareena."

"And shoving you into the spotlight. Either one would be bad for Kareena."

I tucked my hands into the back pockets of my jeans. "Kareena said you knew about her status."

"Did she?" She scuffed the toe of her sneakers on the concrete. "What else did she tell you?"

"That you were together for six months, she broke it off, and she hadn't realized you'd ghosted me as well."

Candice was silent, eyes downcast.

"You left me."

She flinched.

"I told you my mother was leaving and how depressed I was over it, and instead of staying and helping me, you left me. I thought you couldn't stomach actually being friends with someone who doesn't have a neat and tidy family like you do. Someone whose mother did the best she could when she was all alone and desperate." The anger and sadness and grief I'd tamped down for months rose up inside me.

Candice shook her head so hard her curls trembled. "No! I don't care about you or your family's citizenship, for God's sake. I'm so sorry. I was so sad. Kareena . . . broke my heart."

"I'm not Kareena."

Candice's chin wobbled. "I know. I didn't want any reminders. I wanted to retreat."

"So you retreated from me, too."

"You would have seen how upset I was. Kareena didn't want you to know about us. I was so torn."

That tracked. Candice had always hated confrontation. Her way to deal with stress was to bury her head in the sand.

Sound familiar?

Candice looked at her fingers. "I'm sorry," she said, her voice barely a whisper. "I'm so sorry, Sonia. After a few weeks went by, I didn't know how to come back to you. So I stayed gone. I convinced myself you were fine without me."

I was not fine.

"I'm sorry," she repeated. "Please. Forgive me."

Like last night, the anger and sadness drained out of my body like a punctured balloon. "You won't tell anyone about Kareena? Not even Sam?"

"Sam and I aren't exactly on speaking terms anymore."

"You know she's a lizard person, right?"

Her laugh was on a huff of air. "I forgot that you were always a much better judge of character than I. I always chalked up her bad behavior to her awful parents."

No, I'd just been more wary of people than Candice. Not naturally, but because I'd had to be.

"I won't tell anyone about Kareena." She paused. "Or about anything. I hate to break this to you, but a mask and a cape aren't the disguise you think they are." Candice shook her head. "Did you even wipe down the outside of the first aid kit you used? Your DNA is probably all over my shed."

She sounded more disappointed in me than anything else, and to be honest, I was disappointed in myself. I'd made some airhead moves since taking up the cape. Moves I'd normally yell at a TV screen for. "I wasn't really thinking straight."

"Don't worry. I bleached everything. For you, and also for Kareena."

I didn't have to ask Candice if she still loved Kareena. It was there in her eyes, and I imagined her answer would be different from my sister's.

She played with her car keys. "Look, I know you struggle with anxiety—"

My bitter laugh surprised us both. I'd never heard that sound come from my own mouth. "No, I don't struggle with anxiety. I'm actually quite good at it. Olympic athlete level."

The lines around her mouth eased. "Is there an Anxiety Olympics?"

"If so, I get a gold in Intrusive Thoughts and Doom-Scenario Planning."

Her chuckle was warm and kind, and it flowed over me. For a second, it felt like we were still best friends. "I was going to say, I know saving James caused you a lot of stress, but you did something good. Foolish and reckless, but good. I understand you can't take the credit, but let the universe pay you back the karma."

I nodded. "Thanks."

"No problem. Um, maybe sometime . . . we can go out to eat or something, you and I."

I tried to imagine Candice and me in each other's lives again, but there was only a blank. It could never go back to what it had been. But maybe we could start small and build something new. "We can try texting each other again," I offered.

She inclined her head. "I'll take it."

We stood awkwardly for a moment, and she gave a rueful smile. "I should head out and let you get back to class."

"Sure. Bye."

I watched her peel out to start her mandatory suspension. I didn't want to go back to class. I pulled out my phone and texted Hana. Did you get a fauxpology from Sam, too?

Her response was instant. Bestie, she has to give it to me in writing! You know I'm posting that shit everywhere.

I huffed a laugh, my spirits rising. I met her parents.

omg are they also awful

Very much so.

I can't wait to hear all about it

I hesitated. I'm in the parking lot. Do you want to come out? If you have your dad's credit card, we can get some of that non grocery store sushi?

I always have my dad's cc, but it's 10 a.m.

Yeah, true. Skipping a whole day was wild. I bit my lip and regarded the building, quiet with everyone hard at work in classrooms. A car pulled into the circle. A late student jumped out and ran for the front door. My phone buzzed again with another text.

Which means we'll have to camp out in front of the restaurant till they open for lunch. Let me pull the bad cramps card and get out of here.

Twenty-Six

By tacit agreement, Hana and I didn't discuss anything related to last night during our early lunch. Instead, we chatted about more important things, like the difference between East Coast and West Coast oysters. I thought all oysters the world over were the same, but luckily I had a cosmopolitan friend like Hana to straighten me out.

I wondered if we'd go back to school after lunch, but instead, Hana mentioned a craving for bubble tea. We grabbed our drinks and she drove to the park we'd come to the previous week.

Hana shut off the car and narrowed her eyes, squinting into the distance. She moved her big straw around in her milk tea. Her cheeks pulled in as she hunted the boba. "This is not terrible," she finally announced.

I chewed my lychee jelly. "It's the best we have to offer out here, anyway."

"I miss one thing about LA, and it's the food."

I knew enough about Hana to know that wasn't true anymore, but if she wanted to talk tough, I wasn't about to stop her. "You could always move back for college." I'd never been to California, but I imagined swaying palm trees, perfect weather, and guacamole on everything.

"I don't think I'd want to leave my mom for that long. There's no way in hell she's stepping foot back in the same state as my dad anytime soon."

"I totally understand that."

"At least we've found good sushi here. We'll search for a place to elevate your boba palate next."

I patted my belly. "Yeah. You were right, grocery store sushi isn't nearly as good as the real deal."

"Right?" Hana took another sip of her tea. "You want to talk about last night?"

I wiped the condensation off my cup. "What did you hear?"

"Niam actually came and got me. He told me about the video and Candice and the slap heard round the world."

I turned my phone over in my hand. "How did Niam look?" I'd asked for space. I couldn't be upset that he hadn't texted me yet today.

"You haven't talked to him? Upset, of course. But he was real discreet about it. Anyway, as soon as he told me, I texted you, and then I went to the principal's office to file my own little complaint about Sam."

"Thanks for that."

"Eh. I did it for me, too. It did kind of bother me, the rumors she spread about me. Not that I care what anyone thinks," she hurried to add, and I nodded.

"Right, right." I took a drink. "Is anyone . . . talking about me? At school?"

"Not really. They're too busy talking about Candice kicking Sam's ass."

"It was one slap."

"It was one well-deserved slap."

"No one deserves to be hit," I said, but it was a weak protest.

She rolled her eyes. "Okay, okay, but let those of us who had to take shit from her take a tiiiiiny amount of pleasure in it, please?"

Fair enough. I was far from perfect myself. It would be hypocritical to say I hadn't felt mildly vindicated by that slap. "So no one's talking about me and James?"

She smirked. Hana was dressed in defiant spring colors, green pants and a yellow sweater over a light blue long-sleeved shirt. "Not with all the talk about Sam. Isn't it wild how so many people who are popular aren't actually well-liked?"

A tiny pang of sympathy hit me. Sam's parents didn't seem great, and while that wasn't a total excuse, it didn't exactly produce angel children. "I don't want her to be canceled."

"Eh. In this case, canceling is just another word for consequences. A suspension and some gossip about her for a change might fix her attitude. Hell, maybe she'll learn something."

I thought of how upset she'd looked, as well as her insincere apology. "I hope so."

"I wish you would have let me come over last night." Hana

poked her straw around the cup and didn't look at me. "We're friends. I could have helped."

I concentrated on my own drink, the better to hide my too-expressive face. "It's been a while since I had someone who would do that."

"Me too," Hana said softly. "I used to have a boyfriend and friends and a brother and parents who at least tolerated each other enough to live in the same house. Then I came here and I had no one."

I straightened, touched. I'd had no idea Hana could be so sentimental. I swayed toward the loneliness in her voice. "You can have me, if you want me."

Hana sniffed. "I want you. You're pretty cool."

That was high praise, coming from Hana. "So are you." I allowed a portion of my heart to crack open a little more than before. Friendship was about more than just having someone to eat lunch with or go shopping with. It was about having someone to rely on and comfort and be comforted by. It was about having a person, something I had sorely missed. "We could both probably work on accepting the other person doing friend stuff for us."

"Yeah. I'll make an effort."

"Me too." Maybe eventually, I could even talk openly to Hana about my sister, and Shadow. Not yet, but someday.

My phone messages dinged, and I looked down. Kareena.

Got a call you weren't in class. Everything okay?

Tears pricked my eyes.

"You okay?"

"Yeah." I swiped my arm over my eyes. "Uh, my sister got a call from the school and she checked in on me. She doesn't normally do that." I typed back.

Everything's fine, just needed to get out. The meeting went okay.

Okay, good. I see you're at the park, don't stay there till dark, it gets a little sketchy.

I frowned. How do you know I'm at the park

I turned your location on this morning before I left. If you're going to run around jumping into water, better I know where you are. And it's good for you to know where I am.

Another warm and fuzzy feeling. Others might be annoyed that their sister knew where they were, but the sign of caring made me feel good. I switched to my Find My. Only one person was being tracked, and Kareena's tiny dot showed up at her workplace. Got it. See you tonight. "Sorry," I said to Hana, and put my phone down.

"No problem." She placed her nearly empty drink in the cup holder between us. "Should we go to the mall? My dad sent me $500 last night."

I gaped at her. $500 was an enormous amount of money to be sending around. "For what?"

"He forgot my brother's birthday, but he thought he forgot mine. He told me to go spend it anyway. Let me buy you a new outfit."

I shook my head. "I can't let you keep buying me clothes." The thrift store was one thing. Buying new would be way more expensive.

"How about we barter? I'll blow the money, you can alter whatever I buy. That way we'll both have cute clothes that fit us. Actually, you'll be the one doing more work."

I mulled that over. "I'll think about it."

"Good. Think fast. We have to go now, so we have time before work."

I groaned. "I forgot we have to work today."

"Or we could keep playing hooky, and let Paris do our jobs for once."

"Tempting, but no. I have to clock in."

She nodded. "Don't worry. If Paris tries to browbeat you into something, I'll just make a customer cry and distract her. Actually, with my track record, I might do that regardless."

"I'm not going to let Paris browbeat me any—" I stopped in fastening my seat belt. "Wait, was there more than the one?"

Hana grimaced and put the car in reverse. "Look. They deserved it."

Paris wasn't a problem at all during our shift, because she wasn't there. A new kid named David lurked in the back, handling the food, while we worked up front.

I was at the register when the deliveryman came in, bearing a bouquet. They were beautiful blooms, an explosion of yellow and orange and red wildflowers in a red vase. "Sonia Patil?" he asked cheerfully.

Confused, I nodded, and signed the screen the man put in front of me on the counter.

"Ooooooh." Hana abandoned the espresso machine, and the

customer's drink she'd been working on, and moved around me to touch a petal. "Who is it from?"

"I don't know. I've never gotten flowers before."

"Here's the card!" Hana plucked it off the cardette and waved it at me. "Open it before I do."

Her excitement was contagious. I opened the envelope and pulled out the card. "*Been thinking about you.*" I flipped the card over.

"And?"

"That's it." I squinted at her. "Did you send these to me?"

"No. Trust me, I'd sign any flowers I sent. I like getting credit for things."

I sniffed the bouquet, the scent of carnations and mums and daisies wrapping around me. "I don't know who would send me flowers."

"Um. You *did* go on a date last night."

Oh. Right. When you spent your whole life dateless, it was easy to forget that there might be someone out there who'd send you a gift. "Niam?" A smile formed deep inside me and rose up to my lips. I'd avoided thinking about him so hard, my brain gave a sigh of relief to conjure up his dark eyes and smile.

She gave a sudden gasp, and I jerked. "Sonia! Wait. What if it's James?"

"Why would it be James?"

"Do you think he fell for you while he was using you as a pretend girlfriend?"

"Um, no," I said flatly, and moved the flowers to the other counter, far away from any potential customers and their kids.

"That's how it works. You fake date, then you fall in love for real."

"We didn't fake date, and not in this world, it doesn't."

Hana didn't seem to hear me. "I didn't think James had it in him."

"He doesn't. Trust me. These are from Niam." A little thrill ran through me. I should have called him today. Part of me had been scared, thinking of his scowl when he'd seen that photo of me and James. Even if he did believe there was nothing between me and his brother, surely he wouldn't want anything to do with me once he realized what a drama my life was. These flowers were an encouraging sign, though. Had he picked them out, thinking of me?

"I thought you liked him."

"Who?"

"James!"

"Are you Team James now or something? Because you were ready to fight him in the street last week."

"I am Team You, I just love stirring shit."

That tracked. "I liked . . ." The illusion of him, and I'd liked what he represented. I liked Niam for himself, and the way he treated me. "I thought I liked James. He's a friend now, at best."

"Hmm." Hana sounded dubious.

A gaggle of teenagers came in, and we were kept too busy to talk much after that, thank God. My gaze kept straying to the flowers. They made me happy, my first ever flowers.

I would call Niam, I decided while I was sanitizing the bathroom door handles. I would call him and thank him, and then we'd have a nice long chat.

Turned out, I didn't need to call him, because about five minutes before closing time, Niam walked in. I almost dropped the cups I was restocking.

Hana had already left for a piano lesson, so I was alone in the café. *She's going to be so annoyed she clocked out early.*

Niam's gaze settled on me. His eyes seemed darker and more focused today. He walked up to the counter on soundless feet, and I swallowed. The place was empty, save me and him.

"Hi." His voice was rumbly and deep, and somehow matched his heather-gray Henley. Thank God he was wearing a coat, so I wouldn't be distracted by his forearms. Or . . . other parts of him.

"Hi." Why did I sound so breathless?

He jerked his chin over my shoulder. "You got the flowers."

"You got them for me?" I'd known as much, but relief still flowed through me, though I didn't know why. Perhaps because it was finally one thing going the way it was supposed to go?

I liked a boy, and he'd sent me flowers. The way God intended.

"Of course."

"There was no name on them."

"Oh. They must have screwed up." He paused. "Did you think someone else was going to send you flowers?"

I bit my lip. "No. Hana thought . . . well, never mind."

"What did Hana think?"

"She thought James sent them."

The strain around his eyes grew. "Oh. Because of the video?

Is that what . . . everyone thinks? That you're with James now?"

"No. I mean, if they do, it doesn't matter. Because I'm not." I put extra emphasis on the last words.

A muscle in his jaw clenched. "That's what James said."

I raised an eyebrow. "You don't believe us?"

He lifted a shoulder. "No, I . . . that video."

"Us going into the basement. I was mad at him the next day, remember? It's because we didn't do anything, and I confronted him with what you said. Just like I explained already."

"Right, right." He shuffled his feet. "Of course."

I popped the rest of the cups down on the stack, mildly annoyed. "You can believe me or not."

He scrubbed his hand over his hair. "I believe you. I'm sorry. Sometimes it feels like James and I are always competing for the same thing."

My mild annoyance lifted to extreme annoyance. "Well, I'm not a thing, and there's no competition here."

"Gotcha. Understood." Ever so subtly, he relaxed his weight against the counter, and his body leaned toward me. "By the way, your hair looks really pretty like that."

You will not be distracted by meaningless flattery.

Um, yes I will.

I touched my messy bun. I'd made it with a rubber band, and it was going to hurt like a bitch to take it out later. "In no world does this qualify as pretty."

He looked at me from under his lashes. "It does in mine, when it's your hair."

Oh. To give myself something to do in lieu of melting into

a puddle, I pulled my towel off my shoulder and swiped at the counter. "Um, thanks."

"Can you make me a drink?"

I blinked at the rapid shift. "Sure. What would you like?"

"Whatever you like."

We'd played this game before, so I made two drinks: one that I thought he'd like, and an herbal tea for me. If I drank caffeine now, I'd be up all night.

I placed the cup in front of him and waved off his offer of a credit card. Paris hadn't got on my case about comping drinks yet, so hopefully my luck would hold. He tilted his head toward a booth. "Can you sit with me?"

I wasn't supposed to, but there was no one here to tattle, save for the cameras. I nodded.

He sat on one side of the booth and I sat across from him. My knee brushed against his, and the little hairs on my arm stood up, especially when he maintained the contact. He took a sip and raised an eyebrow. "What is this?"

"You like it?"

"It tastes like a butterscotch sundae."

"It's the latest viral drink."

He took another sip. "I thought you hated the viral drinks?"

"I can admit when the internet proves me wrong."

He smiled faintly. "I'm sorry last night sucked."

"You had literally nothing to do with the sucking." He was the only innocent party in the whole crew.

"I just wish our first date could have gone better. Hopefully, the second one will."

I took a drink to hide my excitement. Second date? Yesssssss. "Hopefully."

"James said Sam got suspended."

"Yeah."

"Good. That video was out of line."

I inhaled deeply. "I'm glad you don't think I overreacted."

"Of course not. If anything, I think you showed restraint. Given what was at stake."

I looked into his dark eyes. They were so near-black the pupils were barely visible. "What are you talking about?"

"You being Shadow."

A loud sound filled my ears, like a thousand oceans rushing over my head. "What."

He glanced around, but the café was as empty as it had been before he'd dropped that bomb. "I know, Sonia."

"James. He told you." So much for a pact.

"No. James knows?" His lips tightened. "You two are really close, huh?"

"He guessed," I snapped, in no mood for his weird jealousy of his brother. "And promised to keep his mouth shut."

His forehead cleared. "Ah. The pact."

"So how did you know, if it wasn't James?"

"It wasn't hard. Your disguise isn't that good."

I slumped. *Apparently not.* That made, what? Three people who had guessed? I was surprised Sam and Hana hadn't cracked the code yet. "So I've heard."

"Plus, there's your smell."

I pulled back. "My *smell*?"

"It's a good smell! Your scent, I should say. Like jasmine."

Mama's perfume. "How do you notice a scent?"

"I'm in the kitchen all the time," he said simply. "I have a good nose."

Could any other hero say that their downfall was a freaking perfume? This was so embarrassing. I took a big gulp of my tea. The hot liquid was no longer comforting. "When did you figure it out?"

"When you came to the alley to see me."

"That was . . . a while ago. You kept quiet, all this time?"

"Yes. I thought you'd confess and it would all be over and we could move on, but the longer it went on, the more I wondered why. Why you were so adamantly opposed to even the hint of publicity. And then I found out about your mom and listened to little things you said here and there, and I realized . . ."

I tried to swallow, but it was hard to do that while I was reading between all these lines. "Realized what?"

He pushed our drinks out of the way and grasped my hands. "Was your mom . . . was she deported?"

I licked my bone-dry lips. He was too smart, and he saw far too much. "Yes."

"You filled out the paperwork for payroll. But I'm guessing your information wasn't authentic?"

"What?"

"You and your sister. You two are also undocumented, right?"

I couldn't speak. He was wrong, but also right.

He squeezed my hands, his face soft. "Sonia, it's fine. We

can help. My mom—"

"Your mom?" I found my voice. "What about your mom?"

"She used to be an attorney. My dad is an attorney. They have connections and can help you. Hell, she's dying to help the person who saved her baby boy."

The roaring in my ears grew louder. "Let me get this straight. Your mom knows what?"

"That your family's undocumented, and that you saved James."

I yanked my hands from his. "Did you tell her?" I couldn't help that my voice rose on the last word.

He held up his hands in a beseeching gesture. "She cornered us today at the restaurant and asked about your family. She always knows how to get James to talk, and he accidentally spilled about the rescue. I figured I should try to explain why I thought you didn't want anyone to know."

Seems I had two Cooper men to kill. No wonder James hadn't texted me today. "Did she talk to the cops?" I spat out.

"No. I promise, she didn't. Sonia, everything's going to be okay. There's no point in keeping this charade going."

"Charade?"

"Yeah. You don't have to lie anymore, or fake anything."

I didn't know where the next words came from. "You can't even tell your parents you don't want to go to all those colleges you're applying to. Who are you to lecture me about faking anything?"

He jerked back but rallied. "Please calm down."

"Don't tell me to calm down!" The level of betrayal I felt.

If he'd liked me, if he'd trusted me, why couldn't he trust that I knew what I was doing? Why had he had to go in like a hero and fix things for li'l old me?

"I like you, Sonia—"

"Do you?" *He doesn't like you. No one who actually liked you would jeopardize your safety like this. He was just trying to get with you because of his weird competition with his brother.* "Or did you ask me out because you thought your brother liked me?"

He drew back physically. "That's disgusting. If there had been even a hint of anything between you two, I wouldn't have looked twice at you."

"You sure? You two definitely have a rivalry going."

"I only want to help you."

"You could have helped me by staying out of my business." I scrambled to my feet. "You have no idea what you've done."

Impatience touched his expression, and he also came out of the booth. "Tell me what I've done."

You opened up our little trusted circle to include too many others. Outsiders. My heart was racing and adrenaline pumped through me, making my stomach hurt. I had to flee, and I had nowhere to flee, so I'd have to fight. "Get out."

"Sonia . . ."

"Go away," I shouted, and immediately covered my own ears. I breathed deep, just to get my own panic and temper under control. "Go away."

"Sonia—"

"I need to think, and I can't do that with you standing here."

His nostrils flared. "Nothing bad will happen. You saved a

387

life." He gestured wildly. "You don't want help with the legal stuff, that's fine, my family can still help yours."

The legal stuff. All the things we'd wanted and scrimped and saved for, and eventually had to toss aside. He said it so casually, like it was easy, when I knew it was never and would never be easy. My heart stopped, then started again. "Get the hell out of this café."

He stumbled back. I took advantage of his stunned state to walk him to the door. I locked it behind him.

I had to go through the closing motions while crying. I sobbed while I dumped our still-full cups in the trash and wept while I threw out the trash.

I made my way to the back room and sat down on the bench next to my locker. My bones were old and tired.

Shit. Shit, shit, shit.

I didn't know what to do, or how to fix this. The powerlessness was so deep and infinite, it yawned inside me like an empty cavern. The tears wouldn't stop, and for once I didn't try to hold back my sobs. Instead, I cupped my head in my hands and allowed them to come.

Once I'd depleted every drop of moisture from my body, I was able to dig my phone out of my pocket. I checked Kareena's location and then I got up. There was only one place I could think to go.

Home.

CHAPTER

Twenty-Seven

M y eyes were gritty and exhausted by the time I walked up our sidewalk. *Sorry, Kareena, someone knows our secret. No, not that secret. The other secret. I'm sorry, I messed everything up.*

I braced myself as I entered the house, then paused, wondering if I'd walked into the wrong home, because this one smelled amazing.

The familiar trill of laughter made me tense. Oh no.

As much as I wanted to race upstairs, I reluctantly made my way to the kitchen. "Hi, Divya Auntie," I said when I came into the kitchen.

Divya turned around from where she stood at the stove and beamed at me. "Hello, Sonia. So good to see you again. Come here."

I accepted her hug. I hadn't forgotten that she'd hurt me, but I only had so much room for negativity inside me. Some things I'd have to let go.

"Sit down, sit down," my aunt said. "I'm making dinner."

I looked at Kareena, seated at the dining table, in her work uniform. When Divya Auntie turned back to the stove, my sister gave a helpless shrug. "Isn't it nice how Divya Auntie came by so unexpectedly? I tried to call you."

I had felt my phone buzz in the car ride home, but I'd been too consumed by existential dread to answer it. Plus, I'd worried it was Niam.

Be. Cool.

I took a deep breath and put the most pleasant expression I could find on my face. I'd keep it together until Divya left, and then I'd . . . well, I didn't know what I'd do. But I had to wait, and I would. Hiding stuff was nothing new to me. It was second nature, in fact.

"So nice." I went to the table and turned down the papad Kareena offered me. Normally I loved the greasy little crisps, but my stomach was still too tight to eat.

How was I supposed to say anything now? I couldn't, not in front of our aunt. She'd flip out more than anyone, and I wasn't emotionally capable of handling her histrionics right now.

"You don't have to cook for us," Kareena said to Divya.

"Nonsense. If I didn't, you'd starve. Look at all the take-out containers in your fridge." She bustled around, finding what she needed in our small kitchen. "I put instructions on the freezer meals I made for you. Make sure if there's any Pyrex, you put it aside for me, I'll pick it up next time. Mine is red, but also my name is on it."

Between her chatter, Divya finished making the roti and

brought them back to the table. She placed them in front of us with a flourish, along with two Pyrex containers filled with chicken and potatoes.

I couldn't refuse the food, so I took a bit of the chicken. Though I didn't want to eat, I mimicked the others and took small bites of my food, making appreciative noises. It was a surreal feeling, this dinner party. If I squinted my eyes, I could pretend Divya was my mom and everything was back to normal. Only it wasn't.

"So . . . what brings you here, Auntie?" Kareena asked.

"I have to get back to Ohio tomorrow. I've been talking to your mother." She focused on me, her gaze earnest. "Sonia, I wanted to apologize for being so thoughtless last time I was here. I only want to help, but I didn't mean to hurt you."

That wasn't a perfect apology, but it would do. I nodded and took a bite of my food. It sat in my stomach like a rock, but if I didn't eat, she'd think something was wrong.

She took a sip of her tea. "We've talked a lot, your mom and I, and I had a proposal for you two. Your mother said it would be your decision, but I'd love it if you'd come live with us, Sonia."

I sat up straighter. This offer wasn't new, but what was new was that it was only directed at me. I touched my chest. "Just me?"

"Well, I'd love to have both of you. But Kareena would have difficulty getting health insurance coverage in Ohio, and your mother badly wants you to be covered, Kareena, for obvious reasons. I know you go to some fancy school, Sonia, but we could certainly find you a place in Cleveland. The public school district we're in is not bad."

I was the furthest thing from hungry now.

"That's not what we all decided when our mom left," Kareena said quietly.

Divya Auntie gave us a rueful smile. "I know, but we didn't realize exactly how hard things would be then, did we? I know my friend doesn't charge you much rent, but, Kareena, you could pay even less with a one-bedroom. You also wouldn't have to worry about Sonia all the time. Sonia could have a community again. Wouldn't that be nice?"

She made it sound like a community would make up for being alone, away from every family member I had. For others it might, but not for me.

I looked at Kareena, but she was watching our aunt with an expressionless face. Our mom might have said this was okay, but had Kareena signed off on it, too? Did she want me to leave? Had she known this was coming?

Was I too much of a burden for her? "Is this what you want?" I asked her. *Was everything you said last night a lie?*

She gave a single shake of her head. "No." She set her shoulders. "Sonia's in an amazing school, and hopefully it'll lead to an amazing college. I can handle the finances. We're doing fine right now."

Divya Auntie sighed. "It's not only a financial concern I have. My cousin did hear that you're getting involved with some boy, Sonia. Kissing him in parking lots. That doesn't lead me to believe that you are able to provide the structure she needs, Kareena."

What the *fuck.*

What kind of whisper auntie network is this? Who on earth had tattled on me and Niam, so that it reached our auntie *two states away.*

Kareena straightened, and I wondered if she'd let Divya have it. Instead, she turned to me. "What! Sonia. Kissing a boy? You know I don't condone kissing boys. I cannot imagine anything grosser than kissing a boy, in fact." Her scowl was fierce, but her eyes were light.

I wanted to laugh, but I was still too stressed.

Kareena sighed and addressed our aunt. "I am sorry, Divya Auntie. Thank you so much for bringing this to my attention. This will not be happening again, and I can assure you I'll be handling this. Don't worry."

Divya Auntie pursed her lips. "I should hope so. I didn't tell your mother, and I see now that was the right call." She took a bite of her food and chewed thoughtfully. "I'll still check in on you. I think of you as family, you know. And there're others in your old neighborhood who feel the same way."

"I know." Kareena took my hand and squeezed it. "But this is my *sister.* I would be worried sick if she lived in another state. I'm capable of taking care of her. We take care of each other." She looked at me. "Right?"

I thought I'd cried myself out, but I hadn't, it seemed, because a prickle of tears came. She was saying everything I'd wanted her to say for months, and I didn't deserve it one bit. She didn't know about Niam and James telling their parents everything yet. "Maybe I should go with Divya Auntie," I whispered.

They both looked at me, Divya Auntie's fine eyebrows raised. "I never thought I'd see the day you'd be the rational one, Sonia," she murmured.

"She's not being rational," Kareena said. Her gaze searched my face. "What are you doing?"

"It . . . might be better. If I wasn't here. Messing things up." I couldn't continue. I shoved back my seat and left the room, my feet pounding up the stairs.

Kareena found me not long after flopped on my bed.

"That was interesting," she remarked. "What was that all about?"

"Nothing." My words were muffled into my pillow.

Her footsteps were measured as they came closer. She sat next to me on the bed, in almost the same position she'd sat the night before. "That doesn't sound like nothing."

I turned my head slightly to speak. "Where's Divya Auntie?"

"She left. I told her you had your period, and you were emotional and didn't know what you were saying, and we'd talk tomorrow after she got home."

I scowled. "That's misogynistic."

"She's a little misogynistic. She was always telling Mom that boys were easier to have than girls." Kareena rolled her eyes. "Like, okay, but your precious curly-haired son literally does drugs, Auntie."

My laugh was watery. "I forgot about him."

"You weren't always forced to talk to him." She awkwardly patted my shoulder. "Now. What's wrong?"

"You really want me to stay with you?"

"Of course."

I gulped. "They know."

"Who knows what?"

I told her about Niam's visit to the café. I felt a momentary pang that I'd abandoned his beautiful flowers there, but then reminded myself that he was a snake. Let Paris think tomorrow that someone had gotten the blooms for her.

Kareena was silent for a long time, hands clasped between her knees. The fragile truce between us was so new it stretched between us like a delicate string, just waiting for her words to crush it.

She puffed her cheeks out. "I don't know what to do, Sonia."

The admission scared me, as did the small sound of her voice. My fear of someone discovering our secret was huge, but Kareena had to be ten times more terrified. "Can we . . . can we call Mama?"

I expected her to say that we could handle this on our own, and that there was no need to worry her, but Kareena pulled her phone out and dialed our mom. Mama picked up on the third ring and smiled. "Oh, it's both of you." Her smile faded as she took in our faces. "What's wrong?"

"I missed you," I said roughly, and took the phone in my hand. Kareena inched over, to be in frame.

Her face softened. "I miss you, too. Did Divya Auntie come by? You don't have to go live with her," she said immediately. "I only wanted you to know you have the option available, if you need it."

I might need it. "I screwed everything up." I poured the story

395

out to her, every last sordid bit, even the parts I hadn't told Kareena, like how much I'd fallen in love with Pooja's hug and Niam's kiss, and how scared I'd been. I even told her my principal wanted to talk to her soon, and why. Though she didn't interrupt me or even move, I was conscious of my sister, silent and stony next to me.

When I finally took a breath, Mama spoke. "My God, Sonia. Are you okay?"

I shook my head. "Yes."

"Lift up your shirt. Let me see your arm." Her face came in close to the camera. I did as she asked, and she had me turn this way and that so the light could fall on my scar. Finally, she breathed a sigh of relief. "It looks okay."

"It's fine. Barely a scratch."

Her lips pressed tight together. "Sonia, next time—pray there is never a next time—if this were to ever happen again, you stay put and wait for help to come."

I stared at her. "What?"

"How could you run off like that? What if your arm had gotten infected? Do you know what kind of bugs are in that water?" She pressed trembling fingers over her mouth. "You could have been so badly injured."

I looked at Kareena, who shrugged. "If I'd waited for the police, then they could have found out about Kareena. And if they didn't, the internet would have."

"Listen to me. It's not your sole job to protect me or your sister. Not at the expense of your life. Do you understand me?" She took a deep breath. "Never again, Sonia."

This conversation hadn't gone the way I'd thought it would. I thought for sure she'd be more worried about Kareena than about this measly scratch on my arm.

"Do you understand me?"

I jumped at the snap in her voice, like she was here in the room. "Yes."

"I agree with her," Kareena murmured.

Mama patted her heart. "You could have died."

"Nah. I had all those swimming lessons under my belt." I tried to smile.

"Thank God I took you to those. You kicked and screamed every Sunday morning, but look how they helped."

I rubbed my nose. "Mama . . . did you hear everything else I said?"

"Yes."

My options were pretty plain when it came to the Coopers: avoid them all forever or explain everything and fall on their mercy and trust they kept quiet. I tried to talk through option one. "I could never see any of the Coopers again. Maybe they'll forget about me." Never get a hug from Pooja or hear a dad joke from George or squabble with James or have another kiss from Niam.

You're mad at him, remember? That was right. I didn't want a kiss.

Mama leaned back against her cracked wall, her face more contemplative than worried. "Are they good people?"

"Yeah," I said reluctantly. "His parents have been nice to me, so far."

"It doesn't matter if they're good," Kareena interjected. "I

397

vote for never talking to them again."

"Other people know about our situation," Mama reminded us. "They haven't hurt us with that information."

Kareena's jaw clenched. "Those other people are like Divya Auntie. She's family."

"She wasn't always. This may be a good start for you to have a community where you live." She smiled when we were silent, but it was a sad smile. "I know. I've scared you both into fearing discovery, but I don't want you to forget that there are still people who will help us. Your friend said his parents are attorneys, yes, Sonia? And they want to help?"

She used to be an attorney. My dad is an attorney. They have connections and can help you. Hell, she's dying to help the person who saved her baby boy.

"They are," I said slowly. My kneejerk anger and fear had made me blow right past those words, but my mom had been able to pick through the emotions to hear them in my retelling.

"The risk is too great."

I gave Kareena a sideways glance. Her shoulders were bowed, like she had the weight of the world on her shoulders.

I thought of the pain in her voice when she'd talked about never seeing Mama again. I swiped my hand over the tip of my nose. As betrayed as I felt by Niam, I couldn't let that keep me from doing what I could for Kareena. Our relationship was turning, and I wasn't about to let her go.

I might be wearing other people's faces, but my voice remains my own.

Everyone has a voice, even if they don't have superpowers, so anyone can be a hero. When we can speak up for ourselves, we can speak up for others.

Makeshift's ending, which I'd found so trite and cheesy a few days ago, now rang in my ears as encouragement. I wasn't a superhero, but I could speak up for Katrina. "I'll go talk to them. That wouldn't be so risky. I can't believe they'll ignore me if I beg them to keep quiet. Not after I helped James." The words were slow as I worked past my immediate terror, but they felt true, deep in my gut. *That hug.* Nobody who hugged me like that would hurt me, I was sure of it.

"I can call them, Sonia."

I had privilege here, and this was my mess. I was not an aggressively passive mouse, I didn't need my mom to handle this for me. "No. I can do it. I'll go in person. Unless Kareena tells me not to. She does have the most at stake here."

We both looked at Kareena. She stared up at the ceiling, then nodded. "Okay. Fine. Hiding doesn't resolve anything, does it?"

A rush of affection ran through me. I grasped her hand. Sometimes hiding was the best option, but we had a chance at something possibly better here. "I'll make this okay, I promise."

Mama scooted closer to the camera. "I love you both. I know it feels like there's thirteen months in this bad year, that there's always a new problem cropping up, but this will pass. I may not be there, but I'll never stop trying to give you the best life I can. I'm always a phone call away. You know that."

"I do." If I was certain of nothing else, I was certain of that.

After she told us to call as soon I got home, we hung up.

Kareena pulled the car keys out of the pocket on her uniform and tossed them to me. "I'm a phone call away, too," she said gruffly. "I won't be sleeping till you get home. And I'm going to track you."

I wondered if any other teen got joy from their guardian tracking their phone. "I know. Thank you for trusting me." Especially when I was only starting to learn to trust myself.

Her smile was shaky. "It's not you I don't trust."

Twenty-Eight

'd hoped Niam was either asleep or out, but he was the one who opened the door to the Cooper house. His eyes widened. "Sonia." He looked over his shoulder furtively and came outside, closing the door behind him. "What are you doing here?"

"I'm not here for you. I need to talk to your parents, please." I kept my tone formal and civil, repeating the words I'd rehearsed in the car. If I didn't, I feared I'd fall apart. It had taken me a while to work up the courage to tackle the walk from my car to the door. I'd spent some time staring at the doorbell, then realized if I wanted to avoid cops, I probably shouldn't loiter in front of houses in nice neighborhoods.

Niam crossed his arms over his chest. I was annoyed to note that his biceps looked huge in that position, emphasized by that soft gray shirt he wore. I wanted to touch those muscles.

No, you do not.

"Why do you want to see them?"

"Why do you think?" Oops. I throttled the sarcasm back and hoisted the tote bag I was holding higher up my arm. "It's between your parents and me."

He rubbed his hands over his arms. It was cold out, and he was wearing no socks and no jacket. "Sonia, I'm sorry. I didn't mean to make a big mess for you. You don't have to do this."

I gave a slight nod. I didn't want to accept his apology, and I was still mad at him, but I wasn't about to raise my blood pressure before this important mercy throwing. "Please, can I come in and see your parents," I repeated.

He lowered his head. Just when I thought he'd deny me entry, he took a step aside and opened the door. I sailed ahead of him, powered by my convictions and the sugar in the few sips of soda I'd had in the car.

He directed me to the living room, where his parents were watching television and cuddling on the couch like a pair of newlyweds. It was so adorable and emotionally healthy I would have barfed a rainbow if I wasn't on a mission.

Pooja looked up and raised her eyebrows when we entered. She straightened away from her husband, like she'd been caught by her parents. "Sonia! I didn't realize you were coming over."

George sat forward as well, and his thin face lit up. "Well, if it isn't our neighborhood Spider-Man."

Oh no.

I didn't have to say anything, because Pooja elbowed her husband. "Don't make her uncomfortable." She got up and walked over to me and grasped my hands. "I would have come to your house myself, but Niam convinced me I should give you some time. I cannot thank you enough for what you did. Niam, is James here? Go get him. Let's have some dessert. Actually, have you eaten dinner, Sonia?"

None of this sounded like someone who was planning to call the authorities on me, but I wasn't ready to let my guard down yet. "I need to talk to you," I blurted out. I dug in my pocket and pulled out a crumpled $5 that had come from the tip jar. I placed it on the coffee table and looked at George. "I'd like to retain you as my attorney."

George raised an eyebrow. "That's . . . not quite how it works. Retaining an attorney like that is akin to yelling the word *bankruptcy* to declare bankruptcy."

"Ah." I looked down at the money. "Television has misled me."

Pooja placed her hand on her husband's elbow. "I understand you want a guarantee of confidentiality?"

"Yes."

Pooja looked over my head. "Niam, can you give us some privacy?"

I didn't look behind me, but I could hear his heavy footsteps moving away.

Pooja lowered her voice. "Is this . . . is it related to what Niam told us? About your mom?"

I swallowed. "Kind of." Those blasted tears started up again, though I managed to keep them from completely tumbling out.

Just the threat of tears was enough for George, though, because pure panic crossed his face. "Never mind. Never mind. Don't cry. Representation's a little tricky with minors. Also,

I do tax law, and I have a feeling you don't need help with a 1099." A deep frown pleated George's forehead. "Pooja—"

"I know." She came forward. "George is limited by the pesky state bar. I am not. Will you talk to me, and trust that I will do my best to help you and not harm you? And guide you to seek legal assistance, once I learn what the problem is?" Her eyes glistened. "You saved my son, and I'm forever in your debt."

Oh my God. This reaction was exactly what I'd hoped for. *Trust your instincts.* I stood on the edge of a precipice, and I took the step. "Okay."

She nodded. "Come with me, dear."

My palms started to sweat as I followed Pooja down the hall to an office. She sat on the comfy couch in there and gestured to the spot next to her. "Have a seat."

I sank down. It was easier than I thought to say the words. "I *am* the one who saved James. At the canal. I jumped in and pulled him out, and then ran away."

"Yes. I know. Can I ask you why you ran away, Sonia? You weren't in trouble."

I wished I'd asked for a glass of water. "No. But . . . my mom was undocumented. She was deported."

Pooja nodded. "Niam suspects you fear the same thing."

"Yes. But not for me. My sister's been taking care of me. She's almost nineteen. She's been doing a great job, too." That was stretching it a little, but I believed Kareena would be doing a great job now that we'd made up.

"Okay. She's a little young, but you're not a child."

"The courts never gave her custody. She's also undocumented."

404

Pooja didn't bat an eye, but Niam had already primed her for this revelation. "Not you, though? You were born here?"

"Yes. My mom came to this country when she was pregnant with me. She didn't intend to give birth here. I was early. It was an accident." I hurried to absolve Mama. "She had to travel for my sister. Kareena was so sick, and they had good medical care in India, but they still couldn't cure her, and there was this medical trial . . ."

Pooja held up her hand. "You don't have to justify your mother's actions, Sonia. I would have done exactly what she did, for far less motivation."

I inhaled and ran through my family history, hitting the high points of my life. When I finished, I linked my fingers together. "Anyway, that's the basic problem. I was scared the internet would figure things out, even if the cops didn't. I'm sorry if I caused you any stress. I truly am."

"I only wanted to find the mysterious Shadow to thank her. And I'm glad I have a chance to somehow repay you. We won't go to the police. I have contacts, and so does George. Neither of us are immigration attorneys, but we can find someone who can help you and your family."

I nearly sagged in relief. "We don't have much money."

"Don't worry about that. We'll find you someone who will do it pro bono."

Pro bono meant free, right? "Do you think they can bring my mom back?"

There was probably too much hope in those words, given Pooja's pitying look. "I'm not sure. But your sister was a child when she came here. There's a possibility we can get her some kind of status."

I shifted. "My mom worried about putting Kareena in the system. I guess there have been registration programs in the past where they deported people who came forward." Other South Asians had warned Mama away from any kind of registry for Kareena. After she'd heard the horror stories, Mama had been too terrified to attempt it.

Pooja grimaced. "I don't know the exact statistics, but that sounds plausible. I'm not surprised so many in our community are wary of volunteering information. I still think it's worth talking to my colleague, though. You and your sister and mom. You can learn about the risks and the benefits and make your decision then."

"The consultation will be confidential?"

"Yes."

I looked down at my feet and nodded. "Okay."

"You have no family in the area, right? It's been you two alone?"

"Yes." I licked my lips. "I know it's not a totally legal guardianship, but we've been doing okay."

"It sounds like you have, but it doesn't hurt to have more support. I'd like to help both of you. And your mother."

I stiffened my spine. "We don't want charity." Actually, I could probably swallow my pride and take charity, but I doubted Kareena would.

"Consider it a reward. For what you did for James."

"I didn't come here for cash."

"I was very lucky that I was given the opportunities I was. I know what it's like to struggle and feel desperate in this country, Sonia. I saw my parents go through it. No one should feel like that. Please take the help. My husband and I can afford it. I'd consider it paying it forward."

I grimaced. I was tempted. "My sister's very proud. Really, the attorney is more than enough reward for us."

"Hmm." Pooja looked up at the ceiling for a moment. "You're already working at the restaurant. How about I find a job for your sister, too. I'll pay her enough that she can afford and have time to take classes, if she wishes."

I did want to cry now. "I can't let you do that. That's too much."

"It's not enough. Trust me." Pooja glanced at the photo of her kids on the wall. It was a large studio portrait of Niam and James as toddlers, their cheeks plump and healthy.

"I'll have to talk to my sister."

"Tell her I'll give her benefits, as well. Health insurance, dental."

I dropped my head in my hands. I'd come in here not ready to hope for anything, and gotten everything. *Maybe you'll start to happen to things.* "Thank you," I said, muffled.

An arm wrapped around my back, and she rubbed my shoulders. "You're good. I'd like to speak with your mom, as well, of course. I can't imagine how much she worries about you."

"She wanted to call you."

"Anytime."

I lifted my head and sniffed. "You're honestly solving all my problems."

"You solved mine, by saving my son's life." She rose to her feet. "Come, I brought some ice cream home from the restaurant today. Ice cream makes everything better, yes?"

It had been a long time since I'd believed that. I would have stayed, but I couldn't really think about sitting across from Niam casually eating ice cream right now. "I need to head home. My sister's waiting for me."

"Understood," Pooja said easily, and walked with me to the door. "Ice cream never lasts long unattended in this house, anyway. The boys have probably demolished all of it."

Twenty-Nine

I did end up having ice cream with Kareena. We polished off a full pint of Chunky Monkey while I told her what had happened with Pooja. "I don't want to take their money," Kareena said predictably. She licked her spoon. She was still in her work clothes, which told me she'd been too distracted while I was gone to change out of the uncomfortable polyester. "But . . . you think she was being serious? About the job for me? With health insurance? And time for classes?"

"Yes. Dead serious. I trust her." I listened, but my usual critical inner voice was silent.

"She could get into trouble."

"I don't think she cares."

Kareena braced herself against the counter and let out a long, shaky sigh. Then she started unbuttoning her hideous pink diner dress. She stripped down to the white T-shirt and bike shorts she wore underneath—more to stop pervs from looking up her skirt than any other reason, I was sure—and grabbed the kitchen shears from the drawer.

"Wait!" I said when I realized what she was going to do. I pointed at the front. "I like the buttons. They're kind of retro. Can I have them?"

She snipped them off for me, and they clinked to the floor. Then she destroyed the thing, until it was nothing but rags.

We stared at the pile of pink on the ground, her name tag the only thing that had stayed intact. *Kayci*, it said. "Good riddance," she muttered, and put the scissors away.

I picked up the buttons carefully and put them in my pocket. "I'm glad you're happy about this."

"I am. I should have trusted you from the start."

"I just learned to trust me a little, so I'm not surprised you didn't."

She pursed her lips. "Did you see Niam while you were there?"

"Only when he let me in." Pooja had walked me straight to my car, and the Cooper men must have been upstairs, because there was no sign of them.

"Are you still mad at him?"

"Extremely."

"It did all work out."

It didn't matter. Whatever, it was fine. I'd forget about him, and that first kiss. I'd fallen out of my crush on his brother; I could do it with him.

What if it had been more than a simple crush, though? "Doesn't matter. He shouldn't have said anything to his parents."

Kareena wobbled her head. "I don't know about that. It sounds like they might have figured it out sooner or later, from what you've said." She gathered up the fabric of her uniform and tossed it into the trash. "We have to call Mom. She's going to be so excited."

Yes, I felt excited, too, but also vaguely guilty? Like, there were so many families in the same position as us. Why had we gotten this break? There was no good answer. I had a hunch I'd be working through these feelings for a while. As much as I wanted to speak to my mom, I also wanted a bit of a mental break. Kareena must have seen something in my face because she nodded. "Go relax. I'll talk to Mom."

Relaxing for me took the form of furiously ripping out the seams of a thrifted dress and robe on the floor of my room like my life depended on it.

I'd spread out Kareena's buttons next to my sewing machine. A row of eight little soldiers, ready to go do duty on another article of clothing.

I wonder what Niam's doing right now.

I shook my head and refocused on my task. I couldn't think about him too deeply or I'd hurt. I wanted to stop hurting for a minute. The silky black brocade I was working with slipped through my fingers as I moved to the other seam. I'd bought the robe and gown a year ago and forgotten I had it.

A suit. A sexy three-piece number, that was what I envisioned for Kareena. It was an ambitious undertaking, given that I'd never put pants together before, but I was confident I could pull it off. I'd use the buttons for the vest.

A rattling sound came from my window and I glanced at it, but there was nothing there. Weird.

I shook my head and went back to work, snipping and pulling. The sound came again. I put my scissors down and went to the window.

Niam stood right below. I wrestled the window open and looked down. "Are you throwing stones against my window?" I hissed.

"No." He shook his hand and pebbles fell to the ground, giving him away.

"How did you even know this was my window?"

"I guessed. It was the only one with lights on. Can you come downstairs?"

"You could have broken it."

"I was trying to get your attention," he said, his voice carrying over the night air.

"Then you call me."

"Yeah, call her," someone shouted from one of the duplexes across the way.

He looked embarrassed, so I took pity on him. "Argh." I slammed the window shut. I briefly considered changing, but if he was going to come to my house at night when I was annoyed with him, he could deal with my loose bunny printed pajama pants and the old school shirt I'd donned.

I stomped downstairs and opened the front door. He wore a jacket, which was fine; I didn't miss his biceps one bit.

He didn't even glance at my tired pajamas but maintained

eye contact with me. "I tried to call you," he said quietly. "You wouldn't answer."

I clenched the door handle. "I needed a break from my phone."

"I figured." He stepped aside. "I know you're mad at me, but will you come with me?"

"Where?"

"To the car. I want to show you something."

I should have said no and slammed the door in his face, but I hesitated. My curiosity was greater than my anger, because I grabbed my jacket. "Fine. But I'm really busy and can't stay long."

I followed him to his sporty SUV, and he opened his back door. I cast him a suspicious look. "What?"

"I know our first date was ruined, so I wanted to try a redo."

My damn curiosity reared its head again. I ducked inside the car. There in the center of the seat was a tray with a proper charcuterie board. I didn't even like salami, but the salami roses he'd made were perfect. There were also finger sandwiches, a tray of little cakes that looked like they'd come from *Alice in Wonderland*, and enough cheese to please even me.

He closed the door behind me and came around to the other side. He was much bigger than me, so he had to struggle to sit facing me. He reached in front of us, to the passenger seat, and came back with a bottle of sparkling grape juice. He offered it to me with a flourish, like it was wine, then unscrewed the cap and poured us each a glass. I picked mine up by the stem.

"Wow" was all I could think to say.

He placed his arm on the back of the seat. "If you want, I can leave, and you can enjoy this alone. No hard feelings. If you want me to stay, that's fine, too."

I took a sip of the sparkling juice. The little bubbles tickled my throat. "You can stay."

"Thank you." He pressed a button, and the sunroof opened up. A tap on his phone, and music filled the tight quarters.

Damn it. This was a main character moment if I'd ever seen one, and I was extremely susceptible to those. "What are you doing here? Why are you doing this?"

"I told you, I wanted to make our first date up to you. And . . . I wanted to see you. You ran out of our house so fast, I didn't get to talk to you."

I cocked my head. "What did that tell you? Maybe that I didn't want to talk to you?"

"You're mad at me."

"No shit."

He put his glass down as well. "Can you explain why? Is it because I told my mom my suspicions?"

I pinched the bridge of my nose. "You assumed you knew better than me, the person who is actually living my life. That's so obnoxious and arrogant. And you *don't* know," I persisted. "You should have asked me or waited for me to tell you. It's like . . . you took my choice away."

He bowed his head. "That makes sense. I'm sorry. For everything."

I wilted. "Well . . . good."

"I don't have any excuses. Except that I like you so much, I wanted to help you. I should have communicated better with you. This could have all been solved."

Don't get sidetracked. But I did. "You like me?"

His eyes lit up. "Of course. How can I help but like a talented, crafty vigilante who has a soft spot for dogs?"

I had no idea where the words came from. Perhaps Hana's and Divya's bluntness was rubbing off on me. "Meanwhile, I like an arrogant chef who thinks he knows it all," I said flatly.

His smile was slow, but it came from his soul. "Do you?"

"Yes."

He offered me a little tea cake, and I opened my mouth. His finger brushed against my lower lip.

The dessert melted on my tongue like butter, a little tart, a lot sweet, filled with silky mousse and moist cake. "You made these?"

He nodded. "I bake when I'm thinking."

I thought of my laid-out fabric upstairs. "Hmm."

"You know, as one of those arrogant chefs who thinks they know it all, I can assure you that some of us are trainable."

I folded my arms over my chest. "I'm not sure I'm convinced of that."

"No? I told my parents days ago that I wanted to go to culinary school."

Oof. I winced. "So I was wrong, too." Yeah, essentially calling him a coward hadn't been the nicest thing I could have said to him. Especially since it turned out I hadn't had the full story either. "And?"

"They said it was fine and it was my life, and I should do whatever made me happy." His smile was small. "Which is exactly what you said they would say."

I tried not to be smug, though I was. "Interesting. I was right."

"I can admit when I was wrong. Another point in my favor." His smile faded. "I am sorry, Sonia."

I twisted my fingers together until he stilled them by putting his hand over mine. "I believe you. Thank you."

He placed his fingers lightly on my thigh and tapped a bunny frolicking over my pants. "These are cute."

The heat of his touch nearly short-circuited my brain. Especially when his thumb made a neat circle over the rabbit. "Got them after Easter a few years ago," I managed.

"We still have more to talk about," he murmured.

"We do."

"But can I kiss you now?"

I nodded, and he lowered his head. Everything I learned days ago from that how to kiss video flew out of my brain when he layered his mouth over mine.

He grasped my chin with his thumb and forefinger. There was a callus on his finger, probably from work, and it rasped over my skin. His lips were soft and full, slightly parted.

He slanted his head, and our kiss deepened. He pressed me back to the seat and followed with his body. I didn't know what to do with my hands. First I rested them on his shoulders, then I satisfied my curiosity and traced his biceps. That annoying jacket was in the way, but I could still feel every dip of his muscle.

Pleasurable shivers raked across my nerves as he dragged his fingertips down my arms, leaving goose bumps in their wake. Damn.

He pulled away, and his breathing was as heavy as mine. Double damn. Thank God the charcuterie board was between us, or we might have really gotten carried away.

"Sonia?"

I gazed up at him. I'm sure I looked goofy happy, because he did. "Yes?"

"Would you like to go out sometime? With just me. No one else in my family will be there, for once."

My smile came from my toes, up my whole body. "Isn't that what this is?"

"I changed my mind. This was a peace offering. We're doing a take three on a real first date."

"I'd like that."

"Good." He kissed me again, small pecks over my cheek, and then hugged me.

"I do like you," I whispered when we broke apart long moments later.

"Me too. It's like . . . you see me." He paused. "It's probably easier when you don't have a mask in the way."

I couldn't help but laugh, the sound wrapping around us.

No masks, no disguises. Just the two of us. There would be no crashing down from this dream, not if I could help it.

No crash, but definitely a knock. We sprang apart and I turned to find my sister's face pressed up against the glass.

Uh-oh.

I lowered the window and gave her a sheepish smile. "Um, hi, Kareena. This is Niam."

"Hi there." Niam waved, but his face was slightly ruddy.

Kareena looked back and forth between us. "Sonia, you understand that you can kiss boys in places that aren't public? So you're not seen by one of our auntie's cousin's sister's nephew's fathers?"

I cleared my throat. "I'm sorry."

"Really sorry," Niam added.

Kareena narrowed her eyes at him, as tough as any older sibling. I should have been annoyed, but signs of conventional sisterly concern and protectiveness were still a thrilling novelty, coming from her. "Niam, right?"

"Yes."

"I think you should go home now. It's pretty late, and I'm sure your parents are wondering where you are."

Kareena might be taking the parental role a little too seriously, actually.

He scratched his jaw. "Okay." He looked at me. "Tomorrow night?"

I nodded shyly. Kareena stepped back so I could open the door, and I got out. "Wait." Niam handed me the cakes through the open door.

Kareena didn't even wait for him to drive off before she snagged one. "He made these? Keep him around for a while. But again: no smooching in back seats in the driveway, please." We started walking to the house, but she paused. "You're sure you know about condoms, right?"

418

I put my head down and marched inside, my ears turning red. "Yes, for crying out loud."

"Okay. . . ." Kareena came inside and shut the door. "Do you know about peeing after sex with a guy? I feel like Coach Adams never went over that in health."

I clutched the cakes close to me. My eyes widened. "You're teasing me."

"No. You really have to go pee after sex."

I rolled my eyes. "For what reason?"

"UTIs," she said succinctly, and I nearly covered my crotch in remembered pain. I'd had a UTI last year, and I never want to have one again.

"It's because of the transfer of bacteria when—"

"Okay, man, I got it!" I waved my free hand, partially to cool my cheeks. "Thank you, noted." Why was this not taught in school? UTI prevention was way more important than binomials.

"Why was he here, anyway?" Kareena went to the kitchen to wash her hands.

I put the cakes in one of Divya Auntie's empty Pyrex containers for later. "He wanted to apologize."

"And did you forgive him?"

I tried to play it cool. "Yeah, I guess."

Kareena offered her fist, and I smiled as I bumped it. "Thanks. Did the call with Mama go okay?"

"Yeah. She's going to call your principal tomorrow. And Pooja, too, after I go into the restaurant and talk to her. She actually said something that reminded me, though . . ." Kareena reached into her back pocket and held out a square of fabric. "I was coming to find you to give that to you."

I unfolded the piece and traced the S. Where was the rest of my infamous rescue outfit, though?

"I took the costume to work and destroyed it. I couldn't bring myself to get rid of the whole thing, so I cut some of it off. You put too much work into it."

"You destroyed it?"

"Yeah. Hiding it was weighing on you, and I thought . . ." She gave an impatient toss of her head. "I wanted to do something for you. Are you mad I took it?"

I should have been, perhaps, but it *had* been weighing on me. She'd eased some of my mental load. "No. My next costume will be even better. And thanks for saving at least this. I can cosplay as myself one day," I tried to joke.

Kareena wiped her hands. "Want to watch some TV with me? You can pick."

I wasn't foolish enough to think that our problems were over. But for the first time in forever, I could see a future where we could have a healthy sisterly relationship that wasn't based in her anger and my anxiety. "Okay. But you can't make fun of what I pick."

Her lip curled up. "No superhero movies."

"No holiday rom-coms, then."

She scoffed, then surprised me by putting her arm around me and pulling me in tight.

It seemed like the most natural thing to hug her back. I thought of that embroidery hoop that hung in the master room.

Love is. I kind of understood it now. "That stitched piece in your room. *Love is.* Do you think it means that love is whatever we want to make it? Open-ended and infinite?" Like a multiverse, each reality spilling over with promise.

Her shoulders shook, and for a second, I wondered if she was crying, but then she pulled back, enough for me to see her laughing face. "Sonia, Mom never finished that thing. It was supposed to say something cheesy, like Love is Kind. She hung it up anyway as a reminder to get it done, and then never had a chance to get back to it."

"Oh." I could see that as a failure but instead, I resolutely chose to focus on the positive. There was optimism in putting that hoop up on the wall. I still liked it, even in its unfinished state. It didn't have to be perfect to be beautiful.

"You goofball." Despite the insult, she didn't move away from our embrace, and I didn't either.

Sometimes it did seem like there were thirteen months in this long dry year, but the kiss of rain was just on the horizon, the clouds heavy with the promise of a monsoon.

And when it did finally fall, we'd be refreshed and new. I squeezed my sister. "I love you, too."

Acknowledgments

D o you have a Jen in your life? Because if not, you need a
Jen.

Jen is one of my oldest friends, my travel buddy, my foodie companion, and my biggest fan. She's also the reason *While You Were Dreaming* exists at all. When I told her six years ago that I had an idea for a young adult novel keeping me up at night, she convinced me to put everything aside and write it. Jen was ready to switch careers and go knock on publishers' doors to sell my manuscript herself. When it did sell, no one was happier than Jen.

Except me, perhaps. There are some stories you write because you want to, and there are some stories you write because you need to, and then there are those rare few that are everything. I'm so grateful for all the people (including Jen) who played a part in bringing *While You Were Dreaming* to a bookshelf near you:

- My agent, Amy Moore-Benson, who was willing and eager to take a risk on a new genre with me;
- My editor, Alexandra Cooper, for showering Sonia with understanding and enthusiasm from the very beginning;
- My *other* editor, Erika Tsang, who has cheered this book on just as she does my adult novels, and helped me manage multiple deadlines (any delays were my own);
- My publisher, and the talented folks in design, publicity, marketing, and sales who have shown this title so much excitement;
- Ash and Pinky, who I promised would one day get a novel that was age appropriate;
- Tai, who helped raise me and carries this family on her eldest immigrant daughter back;
- My mom and late grandmother, who came to America with nothing and did their very best to give us everything;
- My husband of approximately six months(!), who calms my anxiety down on a daily basis, but especially when I'm on deadline, and;
- V, Corey, and J, whose insight, experiences, and generosity were invaluable in shaping some of the most sensitive portions of this novel.

Finally, I'd like to thank you for taking this adventure with Sonia. I wrote the book I wished I could have seen on the shelf when I was younger. I hope that some of you see yourselves in parts of it, too.

If you don't see yourself in it, that's okay. Maybe you'll see

someone else in it, someone who lives in your comm
goes to your school, or works at your coffee shop. Ma,
helps you understand them a little better.

Maybe it refills your well of hope, even a little.

My gratitude knows no bounds. Thank you for making my
dream come true.

Love,
Alisha

someone else in it, someone who lives in your community, or goes to your school, or works at your coffee shop. Maybe it helps you understand them a little better.

Maybe it refills your well of hope, even a little.

My gratitude knows no bounds. Thank you for making my dream come true.

Love,
Alisha